MW01701228

ECHOES OF CONTROL

THE DISRUPTION PROTOCOL

THE HELIX CHRONICLES
BOOK 2

ECHOES OF CONTROL

THE DISRUPTION PROTOCOL

MONICA CHASE

Publishing Services provided by Paper Raven Books LLC
Printed in the United States of America
First Printing, 2025

ISBN 979-8-9904469-2-2

For those who understand that stories don't end, they echo.
For the ones who kept listening when the questions got louder.
For the ones who kept asking,
even when the answers got uncomfortable.
This one pulled harder.
I followed.

PROLOGUE

APRIL 2025

Investigative journalist Adam Burke stepped onto the *Global Insight Network* set, trading the silence of self-imposed exile for Manhattan's relentless glare. Around him, crew members moved with practiced precision, orchestrating a symphony of lights and sound. Each adjustment amplified the stage's intensity, casting a spotlight on a truth he hadn't sought but could no longer ignore.

Maya Clarkson extended her hand, a calculated gesture of control. As primetime's sharpest interviewer, she had a way of making people stop mid-thought, recalibrating—suddenly aware they were already on the defensive.

"Your book is truly enlightening," she said.

Adam hesitated. The cameras. The lights. The quiet hum of pressure beneath it all. And tonight, millions were watching.

It wasn't Maya that put him on edge. It was the exposure. The book had already made him a target. Now, sitting here, broadcasting his face to the world, felt like handing them coordinates.

He dragged a hand through his hair, leaving it even more unruly. His wire-rimmed glasses slipped slightly, but he didn't adjust them.

"I didn't think people would see it that way," he admitted.

The studio countdown ticked faintly in the background, a distant rhythm to the storm churning in his thoughts. As Adam sank into his seat, he willed himself to push past the anxiety. This wasn't just about the book anymore—it was about exposing the truths buried within its pages.

Maya shifted into anchor mode with the precision of a well-oiled machine. Her posture tightened, shoulders angling toward the camera. She swiped a thumb at the corner of her mouth, erasing the faintest trace of deep red lipstick. Her fingers smoothed through thick, chestnut hair, followed by a subtle lift of her chin and a quiet inhale before speaking. A dozen micro-adjustments, ingrained by years of live broadcasts. Effortless. Controlled. Designed for the lens.

"Good evening, and welcome to *Global Insight Network,*" she began. "Tonight, we confront the ethical dilemmas of genetic editing—a science that promises miracles but raises profound moral questions. With us is Adam Burke, the investigative journalist whose book, *Shadows of Utopia: The CytoLife Conspiracy,* peeled back the covers on a global catastrophe—the assault on the human genome that left the world reeling."

Maya turned to Adam, her tone measured and authoritative, her delivery flawless. "CytoLife Dynamics was once celebrated as the gold standard in biotech innovation. Scholarships, global medical aid, and sustainability programs earned them the public's trust on every front. Their mission to 'maximize human potential' inspired hope worldwide, and their offerings—from genetic testing kits to groundbreaking cell-healing therapies—cemented their reputation as pioneers."

"But beneath the polished façade were CRISPR breakthroughs shrouded in secrecy—and motives the public never saw. They saw progress," Maya said, turning to Adam. "What they didn't see was the control."

"That's what made the betrayal so devastating," Adam replied. "Not just the scale, but the fact that it came from a company so many had placed their faith in."

"The CytoLife disaster left many unanswered questions. Using CRISPR to modify the AGG1 gene cluster—thought to regulate aggression—was bold enough. But releasing nanoparticles through drones to rewrite the genes of an unsuspecting public? All in the name of creating a more harmonious society? Your book filled in a lot of gaps, but the controversy hasn't faded. How did you approach writing about such a world-changing event?"

Adam leaned back, the studio lights carving sharp lines across his face. "It wasn't easy. The fallout is obvious, but the deeper layers—the hidden consequences—are harder to untangle. I felt a responsibility to set the record straight, especially after what it took to expose the truth."

He paused. "The concept was straightforward: modify genes tied to aggression and disperse the edits across the population to eliminate violence. Invisible nanoparticles, inhaled without consent or even awareness, rewrote DNA, turning people into unwitting test subjects. The toll was staggering. Hundreds of thousands, perhaps even a million lives, were affected. Without our counterstrike—our own payload to neutralize the drones—those numbers would have surged into the tens of millions."

"It's hard for some to comprehend just how insidious that was. Some still claim it didn't even happen," Maya said.

"But the facts speak for themselves, Maya," Adam interjected. "Drones are everywhere—hobbyists, agriculture, surveillance. The delivery mechanism wasn't just effective; it was hiding in plain sight. That wasn't an oversight—it was deliberate. Part of the plan."

His pulse quickened as he straightened, fighting to maintain composure under the crushing weight of the truth.

Maya nodded, leaning forward. "Some critics argue you've downplayed the government's role—or at least their official account of intervening swiftly. In your book, you allude to certain 'non-traditional' collaborators who acted first. Are you concerned that overshadows the official record?"

A faint, knowing smile tugged at Adam's mouth. "There's a fine line between what actually happened and what made it into the reports. I'm not discrediting any agency's contribution, but readers can draw their own conclusions about the sequence of events. When a crisis unfolds this quickly, it's rarely one entity that saves the day. Let's just say not everyone involved wanted the spotlight—or the blowback."

He continued. "But there's no question the public deserved far more transparency than they got. Too many people paid the price."

"You were more involved than people realize," Maya observed.

Adam nodded. "I was. I worked with whistleblowers and sat in on closed-door testimony—it went far beyond reporting. When I saw the truth being buried and twisted by politicians and pundits, I knew writing the book was the only way to set the record straight."

Maya tilted her head slightly, the studio lights catching the intensity in her eyes. She gave him a small, encouraging nod, but Adam had spent enough time in interviews to know that silence wasn't always neutral. It was a tool.

Two years ago, he'd just been chasing stories. Now, he was part of one.

"It wasn't just about recounting the visible fallout," Adam explained. "The real challenge was uncovering what we didn't see—the depth of their genetic manipulation and the ripple effects of those edits. We're only beginning to grasp their full impact."

Adam's eyes narrowed. "Spikes in behavioral disorders, unexplained mental health crises, families desperate for answers, advocacy groups demanding transparency—it's all connected. The long-term consequences are unfolding right before our eyes. This crisis is far from over."

"What's the most pressing challenge we face now, after all that's happened?"

"Trust," Adam replied. "The public lost faith—not just in science, but in the systems meant to protect them. CytoLife shattered that trust, and rebuilding it will take years, maybe decades. The longer the government obfuscates, the more conspiracy theories take root."

Maya pressed on. "And the Safe Genes Initiative—intended to prevent another CytoLife—is just as controversial. What's your take?"

"It's necessary, but the way lawmakers pushed it through—with almost no public debate—made people suspicious. It's like the Patriot Act: meant to protect, but divisive in its implementation. Public opinion is split on the way forward. Frankly, it's a mess."

"And the perpetrators?" Maya asked. "They've disappeared, fled..."

"Exactly," Adam said. "The key players disappeared. CytoLife collapsed, but those responsible evaded justice—wanted for questioning yet untouchable, even as authorities insist they're pursuing accountability. There's no closure."

The threats loomed in the back of his mind—a constant, gnawing presence since the book's release. Angry messages, cryptic warnings, unmarked envelopes—each a grim reminder of the risks he'd taken. What had he been thinking, stepping into the spotlight on national TV? His fingers grazed the arm of the chair in an attempt to anchor himself.

Maya nodded. "And with the public divided—some dismissing it as conspiracy, others alarmed by genetic manipulation—what do you see as the path forward?"

"The only way forward is through open, honest dialogue. We need stronger oversight and clearer regulations. Balancing innovation with ethics isn't optional—it's survival. Without it, we risk more than public trust. We risk our future."

"With so many unanswered questions, what needs to happen next?"

Adam's thoughts flickered to the allies who had stood by him. Meera Kapur came to mind—a brilliant genetic researcher and assistant professor at the University of Tennessee. Once a college friend, now a trusted confidant, her expertise had been the cornerstone of their fight against CytoLife. It was Meera's groundbreaking insights that helped make the counterstrike possible.

"We need a multipronged approach," he said, returning to the moment. "Stronger regulations that reflect the complexities of genetic editing, international cooperation to ensure transparency, and more public engagement. People need to understand the stakes."

"How do we address the ethical challenges in all this?" Maya asked.

"By ensuring innovation doesn't come at the expense of ethics," Adam replied. "CytoLife proved what happens when we lose sight of that. We have to align scientific advancements with moral principles."

His voice steadied. "That means collaborating with responsible scientists, involving the public in the conversation, and prioritizing research that values human dignity over profit. We've been slow to confront the ethical dilemmas raised by technology. We can't afford to wait any longer."

Maya leaned back, letting his words settle. "What about the future? What worries you most?"

Adam's gaze drifted, as if searching for answers on the horizon. "The intersection of science and profit is where the real danger lies. The potential is limitless, but so is the risk of abuse. We have to stay vigilant. Genetic technology is shaping our world—whether we're ready for it or not."

A small, hopeful smile tugged at his lips. "But there are good people—whistleblowers and regulators—working to keep us on course. It's not just about stopping the bad actors; it's about ensuring we move forward with integrity."

He silently prayed it would be enough.

"What's your take on the latest advancements in what's being called 'super-charged CRISPR?'"

"Maya," Adam began, "we're living in a time where technology isn't just advancing—it's rewriting the rules of human evolution. Bridge RNA, the tech you're referring to, is being hailed as the next frontier in gene editing. CRISPR was revolutionary—it's already treating genetic disorders—but it's far from perfect. It cuts DNA, which can lead to unintended errors or complications during the repair process."

He paused, his expression grave. "It's believed that Bridge RNA could change that. Instead of cutting, it acts as a guide, inserting or modifying genes with far greater precision and safety. Think of it as upgrading from scissors to a laser—more refined, with a much smaller margin for error. And unlike CRISPR, it has the potential to go beyond editing. It can fine-tune genetic expression."

Adam leaned forward. "But here's the catch: we're in uncharted territory. From what I've learned, most of the research has only been tested in bacteria. We don't yet understand how it will behave in human cells. Right now, it's like holding a powerful tool we barely know how to control. The consequences of getting it wrong could be catastrophic."

"But are we ready for it? Who decides how it's used?"

"Exactly. These are the questions we need to be asking," Adam said. "We can't just sit back and watch this unfold. We need governments, scientists, and the public pushing for transparency and ethical oversight."

He took a slow sip of water to steady his growing frustration. Since leaving the *Bluff City Standard*, he'd fought to keep the real issues from being buried beneath alarmist headlines.

"You're raising important points," Maya said. "It feels like we're making incredible progress, but we still don't fully understand the risks."

"That's the core of my work, Maya," Adam replied. "It's not about halting innovation—it's about making sure we use it responsibly."

"And yet, with all we've learned from CytoLife, many are now shifting their concerns to artificial intelligence," Maya continued. "Some critics argue we've traded one unchecked frontier—genetic manipulation—for another. AI is everywhere now, making decisions in hospitals, classrooms, and even courtrooms. In some places, it's already tracking behaviors and ranking people, resembling a social credit system. And let's not forget the ongoing data privacy debate—social media, smart devices—all of it is up for grabs. Recently, Congress held contentious hearings demanding accountability from tech entrepreneurs, though critics dismissed the effort as mere 'theater.'"

Adam forced a smile, though his thoughts raced. AI. The next wave.

"I've heard those concerns," he replied carefully. "And you're right. From your smartwatch analyzing your vitals to devices measuring your pupils to decide what news you should see—there's no doubt we've become the product. Evaluated, measured, and leveraged for... what? Money? Power?"

He took another sip of water. "Technology, such as AI, is supposed to be neutral—a tool. But like any tool, it's only as ethical as the people who create and wield it."

Maya raised a brow. "Some would say we're already standing at the precipice, letting AI make too many decisions for us."

"The problem with technology—whether it's genetic editing or artificial intelligence—is that we never see the line until it's too late."

Maya paused, letting his words settle. Then, with the practiced grace of a seasoned interviewer, she began to wrap up. "It's a sobering thought, and one that underlines the urgency of these conversations. Tonight's discussion reminds us of the power of vigilant journalism in a world where science often moves faster than ethics. *Shadows of Utopia* isn't just an exposé—it's a call for accountability as we stand on the edge of profound technological change."

She turned to Adam. "Your dedication to uncovering the truth is invaluable. Thank you for being with us tonight."

"Thank you, Maya. I hope tonight's conversation sparks more debate and awareness. The future depends on how we face these challenges together."

Maya turned to the camera. "Thank you for joining us. As technology reshapes our future, the questions we ask today will define tomorrow. Stay with the *Global Insight Network* as we navigate these pivotal moments together. I'm Maya Clarkson—good night, and stay curious."

Her last words lingered as the studio lights dimmed, and the crew began quietly dismantling the set.

"Thank you, Adam," Maya said. "I think what you shared tonight will really resonate with our viewers."

Adam offered a tired smile. "I hope so. Conversations like this are what lead us forward."

A handshake. A nod. The low murmur of pleasantries.

It was over before he processed it. The studio hum faded, Maya's final thanks barely registering as an assistant touched his elbow, already guiding him toward the exit.

Stepping outside, the crisp night air hit him—a sharp contrast to the studio's warmth. The city pulsed around him, alive with movement but indifferent to the revelations he'd just laid bare.

He walked with purpose, head down, his thoughts a tangled knot of the danger he'd unleashed. The calls came at all hours—gruff warnings from blocked numbers. The messages, cryptic or explicit, often came with images of his home. Or worse. Each one served as a relentless reminder: his work had crossed an unforgivable line.

But tonight felt different.

The air carried a sharp chill, biting and unfamiliar, seeping into his bones. Footsteps echoed behind him—steady, deliberate—just far enough to blur the line between reality and the paranoia gnawing at his mind.

He quickened his pace, trying to shake the thought. Weeks of looking over his shoulder had taken their toll.

Streetlights cast jagged shadows across the pavement, their warped shapes clawing at the edges of his vision. Every sound was magnified, every flicker of movement a silent warning.

His pulse quickened as his instincts whispered what his mind refused to accept:

He wasn't alone.

ONE

MAY 2025

Rain lashed against Ethan Cook's windshield, the slick Memphis streets glistening under the relentless downpour. His grip on the wheel was tight, knuckles white as thunder cracked overhead.

"Damn it," he muttered, stealing a glance at the rearview mirror. An SUV loomed close, its headlights slicing through the rain and fog, each flash igniting a fresh jolt of adrenaline.

Outside CookCyber Solutions, rain streaked the glass façade, soaking Ethan as he exited the vehicle. The cold bit through his clothes, but his mind refused to settle.

He rolled his shoulders, but the tension held. Years of training had sharpened his instincts—he knew better than to ignore them. Rain streamed from his dark hair, cut close but never quite neat, cold rivulets tracing his spine. He barely noticed.

"Rough morning?" a voice called, cutting through the patter of rain.

Ethan's business partner, Neon, stood a few feet away, umbrella tilted at a rakish angle, neon-pink socks flashing beneath immaculately tailored trousers. He gave Ethan a mock look of pity, his grin sly.

"You look like someone swapped your coffee for decaf. Tragic." With a slow flick of his wrist, he spun the umbrella once, savoring his own cleverness.

Ethan's shoulders tensed. "Just thinking," he clipped. Neon's antics barely registered—his mind was elsewhere.

"Well, stop it. You'll ruin your brooding mystique," Neon quipped, stepping closer, his grin a perfect balance of charm and mischief. "Besides, overthinking is my thing. Occupational hazard."

Ethan didn't respond, but held Neon's gaze. Somehow, Neon always commanded attention—even in the rain. The downpour seemed to slide past him, untouched, as though he belonged to a different world entirely.

Neon was impossible to ignore and even harder to pin down—a contradiction Ethan still hadn't fully figured out.

A Southern gentleman with a cyberpunk edge, Neon's bespoke suit and streaks of pink in his hair screamed performer. But his brilliance wasn't for show. He could breach a firewall as effortlessly as he charmed a room, leaving everyone wondering whether his flirtation was sincere or strategic.

"You're right," Ethan said finally, stepping under the umbrella. "Maybe it's just the weather."

Neon eyed him, the teasing edge of his grin softening. "You're not usually this rattled."

Ethan rubbed the back of his neck. "It's a feeling. I don't have proof, but something's off."

Neon tilted his head, his drawl cutting through the gloom. "You've never needed proof to trust your gut. That's why you keep me around—the guy who dances on the line without tripping… most of the time."

With a dramatic flourish, he held the door open like a royal butler. "Whatever's coming, we're in it together. Like always."

Ethan stepped inside, shaking off the rain. Neon's words lingered, a sharp reminder of how far they'd come—and how much had changed since their first meeting.

Back then, Ethan hadn't known what to make of the flamboyant hacker Harper Brasfield had vouched for. Neon's infamous pranks—ethical breaches targeting renowned Memphis institutions—were equal parts brilliance and chaos, exposing vulnerabilities just to prove a point. Harper, ever the strategist, had turned corporate outrage into leverage, securing Neon a slap on the wrist when others might have faced prison.

"He's unconventional," Harper had said, her tone both amused and exasperated. "But he's the best. And you'll need the best if we're going to untangle this mess."

Ethan had his doubts. Neon's irreverence felt like chaos waiting to implode. But working together to expose Thomas Baxter's schemes and dismantle CytoLife's plans had proven Neon's worth. His flair for disruption, matched with razor-sharp instincts, cut through layers of deceit with ease. Harper had been right—again.

Nearly two years later, Ethan couldn't imagine working without him. Together, they had built CookCyber Solutions from the ground up, gradually bringing on carefully vetted contractors to manage the growing workload. Neon's unpredictable brilliance pushed Ethan to stay sharp, while Ethan's steady pragmatism kept them both grounded. It wasn't just a partnership—it was equilibrium.

Ethan's path had been less flamboyant than Neon's, but no less complicated. Growing up in Nesbit, Mississippi, his world revolved around family, community, and the steady rhythm of small-town traditions. Following his father into Army special operations instilled discipline and resilience—but service came with its costs.

Back home, a stint with the Shelby County Sheriff's Department felt like a chance to make a difference, but years of tragedy eroded his resolve. Private investigation proved a better fit, offering the freedom to unravel complex cases with the skills he'd honed in the field.

Marriage never happened, much to his parents' quiet disappointment. By forty, they'd stopped asking—and so had he. Work had become his anchor, a trade-off he'd come to accept.

As they stepped into the building, shaking off the last of the rain, a familiar voice rang out.

"Marching in here without a jacket again?"

Rita Johnson stood behind the reception desk, arms crossed, radiating the unimpressed authority of a woman who had trained employees, raised children, and raised hell—often all at once. Her blonde bouffant was a time capsule, her crisp, no-nonsense wardrobe a silent challenge to changing trends.

She adjusted the chunky necklace that always announced her a second before she spoke. The faint clink was as much a signature as her stare. She shook her head, disapproval softened by a smile that said she had seen it all and today was no exception.

"One of these days, you're both going to catch a cold. Don't forget—client onboarding this afternoon. Debriefs are on your desks."

Her sharp gaze landed on Neon. "And Neon, we've got to do something about that mess of yours. A cluttered desk leads to a cluttered mind."

Neon grinned. "Chaos is half the fun, Ms. Rita."

Rita arched her sculpted brow. "Fun won't find the invoices I had to dig out from under your disaster zone this morning."

Rita turned to Ethan. "And you, Ethan, you're looking lean. When was the last time you ate something real? I'm ordering lunch. You need to take better care of yourself."

Ethan dragged a hand over the stubble on his chin, the ghost of a smile flickering at the corner of his mouth. In the right light, it gave him a rugged edge. Today, the light wasn't doing him any favors. "Thanks, Rita. I appreciate it."

Some of the tension in his shoulders uncoiled. Rita was their anchor—sharp-eyed, steady, and built for command. Part tactician, part den mother, she kept their chaos from careening off the rails.

In her sixties, she carried the no-nonsense energy of someone who had spent decades wrangling the impossible in the city school system. When she spoke, people listened. They only ever needed to hear it once.

But Rita's voice faded into the background as the day wore on, the firm's usual bustle doing little to quiet Ethan's mind. His thoughts strayed, despite the steady rhythm of work. The texts on his phone loomed, each alert carving deeper into his focus.

We know who you are. What you've done. We're watching.

The words cut through his mind like a blade—a stark reminder that CytoLife's shadow still lingered.

"Ethan." Neon's voice cut through the fog. "You okay?"

Ethan forced a smile, quickly pocketing his phone. "Yeah, pondering the usual," he lied.

As lightning streaked across the sky, their monitors lit up with a breaking news alert.

US Congressional Hearing on Genetic Ethics and Biotechnological Advancements Continues in the Aftermath of the CytoLife Disaster.

Ethan clicked the live feed. Chairperson Warner's voice filled the office, demanding stronger protections against CytoLife-like threats. Representative Diaz countered with a fiery tirade against the company's ethics.

Ethan shook his head, narrowing his eyes at the screen. "Can you believe this?"

"It's all theater," Neon replied, barely glancing up.

"Necessary, sure, but still theater. The real question is—can they handle what's coming next?"

The hearing shifted focus to the controversial Safe Genes Initiative, a program some hailed as a scientific breakthrough and others condemned as government overreach.

"A year and a half," Ethan muttered, "and we're still digging through the wreckage. Feels like post-9/11 all over again. Everything shook loose, and now they're scrambling to lock it all down."

"Paranoia's through the roof," Neon said, leaning back in his chair. "They're tracking anything that even hints at gene editing. Genome scanners aren't just at airports anymore—they're everywhere. Funny how they rolled out that shiny tech in under a year, and no one's even sure if it works."

"Band-Aid on a bullet wound," Ethan replied.

"Exactly. And it's not just cleanup—it's control," Neon said. "They're burying what happened, but it's way bigger than they're letting on. Those numbers they keep flashing? A joke. And good luck getting an audit. 'Security risks,' my ass."

Ethan stared at the protesters on the screen. "The government's playing catch-up, pretending they've got it handled."

"They don't," Neon retorted. "And that's what scares me. We stopped the worst of it, but who knows how far their reach went—or what's still buried. Military readiness is already a mess. You hear the rumors about people getting... too docile?"

Ethan frowned. "Have you heard of that group calling themselves 'Harmonics?' They're claiming the edits worked, calling it 'perfection.'" He snorted. "It's delusional."

The memory hit hard. Eighteen months ago, CytoLife's plan to alter the AGG1 gene cluster had been terrifying: nanoparticles designed to suppress aggression—a genetic leash, delivered through an invisible mist. The rushed, off-the-books operation leveraging DARPA tech, which Ethan had helped execute to ground the drones, had been a desperate gamble. They stopped most of them, but not before the damage was done. How many people were walking around with altered DNA, completely unaware?

"People are scared," Ethan said. "And they should be. The government's pushing the Safe Genes Initiative like it's the answer, but they're not even being honest about how many people were affected. Either they don't know, or they're hiding it."

"Neither option inspires confidence," Neon said, rolling his eyes. "But hey, genome scanners solve everything, right?"

Ethan allowed himself a grim smile. "Band-Aids on bullet wounds."

"And don't get me started on their new favorite toy—AI oversight," Neon said. "Facial recognition tied to behavioral data. They're calling it 'proactive security.'

"Algorithms labeling threats based on arbitrary markers," Neon continued. "And what happens when those markers are wrong—or worse, biased?"

"And social media? Those tech oligarchs do whatever they want," Neon said, frustrated. "All our data, just out there for the taking—it's like we're puppets on a string. And guess who's holding the other end?" He shook his head. "Even with all our privacy protocols, it still makes my skin crawl."

Ethan exhaled, glancing at the protesters again. "Feels like the world's coming apart at the seams."

"And we're right in the middle of it," Neon replied.

Rita's voice cut through the office. "Lunch is here!" she called, carrying bags from Gus's Chicken. "Collards, biscuits, and all the fixings. You've got thirty minutes—make it count."

Neon grinned. "You're the real MVP, Ms. Rita."

Rita smiled as she set the bags down. "And try not to get grease on that fancy suit, Neon."

Ethan pushed his food around, appetite fading as fragments of the news feed replayed in his mind: protesters, genome scanners, and promises wrapped in uncertainty.

"You're ruining fried chicken for me," Neon said, raising an eyebrow. "That's borderline criminal."

Ethan forced a chuckle. "Just thinking."

"You've been 'just thinking' all morning." Neon leaned back, balancing his chair on two legs. "Never a good sign."

Ethan shook his head, setting his fork down. "It's nothing."

Neon studied him for a moment before shrugging. "If you say so. But you're getting predictable, Ethan."

Ethan rubbed his temples and glanced at his phone. A message glowed on the screen.

Your actions create ripples—echoes that don't go unnoticed.

Sliding the phone face down, he tapped his fingers

against the table. Whatever this was, it wasn't going away. But involving Harper or Neon now would only complicate things.

The storm outside continued as the office settled back into its rhythm. Ethan returned to his desk, watching the live feed. The hearing had descended into chaos, with panelists shouting over one another. Protest footage flashed across the screen, placards screaming slogans like *Genetic Freedom Now!* and *Stop the DNA Police!*

"You catch that part where they basically admitted they're guessing how this tech works?" Neon asked, nudging Ethan's desk with his foot.

"It's not just guessing—it's desperation," Ethan said. "They're pretending they've got it under control, but it's all smoke and mirrors."

"Desperation's dangerous," Neon murmured. "Scared people do stupid things."

The screen shifted to a senator defending genome scanners in schools and hospitals. Their polished speech rang hollow.

"This feels like a bad sci-fi movie," Neon said. "Except we're living in it."

"And no one's walking out of the theater," Ethan replied.

In the conference room, Ethan and Neon sat across from their newest client, Owen Roberts, CEO of QuantumSafe Technologies. The man was unraveling.

His expensive shirt was rumpled, the collar askew, as if he'd yanked it on in a hurry. The muscle in his jaw tightened and released, a silent battle against the panic clawing at him. His fingers drummed a restless rhythm on a stack of papers, each tap a little sharper than the last. Bloodshot eyes darted between them, scanning for threats that weren't there—yet.

"Mr. Roberts, thanks for coming in," Ethan began confidently, despite the tension in the room. "You mentioned receiving disturbing messages. Could you elaborate?"

Roberts nodded, shifting in his chair. "Yes. The timing of these threats coincides with our latest encryption update at QuantumSafe." His voice was tight. "The messages are menacing, implying someone's watching us—or perhaps even interfering with our work."

Ethan exchanged a glance with Neon.

"Do the messages contain specific threats or leaked information?" Neon asked.

Roberts sighed, rubbing his temple. "We've had leaks—data that should've been impenetrable. That's why I'm here." He turned to Ethan. "Your old boss, Sam Chapman, spoke highly of you. He said you don't just solve problems; you make them disappear."

Ethan inclined his head. "I appreciate the trust."

Roberts managed a weak smile. "And being local, I figured it was worth keeping this in Memphis. No need to bring in outside eyes if it can be avoided."

Ethan remembered the *Bluff City Standard* profile from a few years back. Roberts had been the hometown success story. Owen was a Memphis native and Stanford grad who carved out a name in Silicon Valley before coming back to fuel the rise of the Silicon Delta.

He'd bucked tradition, choosing Memphis over the coasts, vowing to hire local talent while keeping his company on the bleeding edge of technology.

Roberts hesitated. "Listen, I need to know that everything shared here stays confidential."

"Absolutely," Ethan reassured him. "We operate under strict nondisclosure agreements. Anything you divulge remains between us."

Taking a breath, Roberts finally revealed the heart of his concern. "Our 'Silent Core' algorithm was leaked. It's a top-secret encryption method known only to a select few. We pride ourselves on creating unbreakable digital locks—think of it like a vault that doesn't just sit there. It evolves, adapting to threats in real time to keep intruders out."

Ethan caught the shift in Roberts's tone mid-sentence, a crack in the polished cadence usually reserved for tech executives. This wasn't autopilot anymore. The edge in his voice wasn't about selling Silent Core's brilliance; it was about driving home the gravity of what had happened.

"Bottom line," Roberts said, "if Silent Core's been compromised, there's no telling how far they've gotten—or what they can access."

"Tell us exactly what happened." Ethan didn't need the details to understand the stakes. A breach like that didn't just expose secrets—it opened doors that should have remained sealed.

Roberts pulled out his tablet, scrolling through a series of messages. Finding what he needed, he handed the device to Ethan.

The screen displayed a chilling message:

Your quest to encrypt the world's secrets hasn't gone unnoticed. The Silent Core algorithm is now within our grasp, echoing in ways you do not yet understand. Despite your efforts, you venture too close to the shadows—a realm far beyond your control.

Ethan's brow furrowed as he read the message twice. The phrasing wasn't just ominous—it was deliberate, chillingly precise. He handed the tablet to Neon, keeping his expression neutral even as his thoughts raced.

He'd seen words like this before.

Identical words.

If the Silent Core algorithm was connected to the threats he'd been receiving, it meant whoever was behind this wasn't just watching him. The game they were playing was much bigger than he'd realized.

"It's not just a threat," Ethan said, heat rising in his voice. He cleared his throat. "It's a warning—and a challenge."

Neon scanned the screen. "Silent Core's already breached. This isn't just a hack—it's a message. They're in control."

"Silent Core wasn't just exposed," Roberts said. "It was stolen right out from under us. Our systems were designed to catch unauthorized access, but by the time we detected the breach, it was too late. We've enacted damage control—blocked external connections, reset access protocols, updated encryption keys—but I'm not convinced it's enough. We need outside experts."

He continued. "We've bolstered defenses—recalibrated firewalls, isolated networks, doubled internal monitoring. But it still feels like we're exposed, like every move we make is being watched."

Ethan nodded, his mind already mapping out the next steps. "Your team's response was solid, but breaches like this rarely stop at the surface. We'll run a full forensic investigation—trace the breach, root out hidden backdoors or malware, and assess your overall security. My bet? There's more here than what's obvious."

Neon leaned in. "We'll find whoever's behind this and make sure they don't get another shot."

Roberts's shoulders eased, but the tension lingered in his voice. "Thank you. This needs to be handled quickly and quietly. Our client roster is confidential, but we've secured a few critical contracts. If this gets out, we're finished."

Ethan's gaze remained steady. "You need this resolved before anyone notices—and without the noise."

"Exactly," Roberts confirmed. "That's why we came to CookCyber. You deliver results, not headlines."

"Keeping things under the radar? That's our signature move," Neon offered.

All three men rose, exchanging brief goodbyes as Ethan walked Roberts to the reception area.

When Roberts left, the office sank into an eerie silence, broken only by the steady rhythm of rain tapping against the windows.

"This isn't just hacking or espionage," Ethan muttered, his thoughts racing. "It's bigger than that." Could it be a competitor feeling threatened by QuantumSafe's rise?

Neon kept his gaze fixed straight ahead. "A breach like this doesn't just compromise data—it obliterates trust at the highest levels. The fallout? It's a disaster waiting to happen."

"Can't they just make the algorithm inoperable?" Ethan asked, bracing himself for the answer, but needing to voice the question anyway.

Neon shook his head. "They can patch their systems moving forward, but that won't undo the damage already done. Whoever stole it can reverse-engineer it, and exploit any system still using Silent Core—and that's if they don't sell it to the highest bidder."

Ethan exhaled carefully. "We'll start by dissecting their entire security infrastructure. Whoever wrote those threats is taunting Roberts, but they always leave something behind. Let's find it."

Neon turned back to his monitors, already immersed in the task. But Ethan couldn't shake the feeling that the ground beneath them was shifting.

Immersed in his work, Ethan's phone buzzed, rattling against the table. He hesitated, dread tightening in his gut, before finally flipping it over.

The new message on the screen was sharp and chilling:

Ethan, your interference has been noted. You've tangled yourself in forces that ripple far beyond your control. The AGG1 initiative was merely the start. Our ambitions stretch further than what you've glimpsed. And Lucas... his role echoes through this puzzle in ways you have yet to understand.

His blood ran cold. This wasn't just a threat; it was layered, every word humming with quiet menace. Lucas Fairbanks, Harper's son, had barely escaped CytoLife's grip before. Now, it seemed, they were coming for him again.

Ethan couldn't ignore the patterns—the deliberate wording, the familiar structure.

Before he could fully process the message, the door flew open. Neon strode in, his usual energy cutting through the heavy atmosphere.

"You alright? You've got that look again," Neon said, hands on hips.

Ethan forced a tight smile, dimming his phone's screen. "Just the usual worries. Nothing we can't handle."

But panic gnawed at him. Lucas's name wasn't just a threat—it was a warning.

The glow of the computer screen deepened the hollows in Felix Ross's face, sharpening every angle. His sallow complexion looked almost bloodless in the pale light. He leaned back, tapping a finger against the desk in a slow, rhythmic beat.

His smart glasses flickered with data, the lenses ghosting lines of code and shifting models across his vision. He barely blinked. A stream of numbers, projections, and simulations filled the screen, but he didn't just read them. He *saw* them, the way others read faces—searching for patterns, for inevitabilities, for the shape of what came next.

He dialed a number he'd committed to memory. The encrypted line clicked once, then connected.

"Report."

An eager voice answered. "We've found them. Rebecca and Lucas are in the heart of the city."

"Coordinates. Now."

"Already en route. Updates will follow."

Felix ended the call as his attention shifted to the map spread across his desk.

Paris—a city of deep history and buried secrets—wasn't just a setting. It was his stage. Beneath its cobblestone streets lay CytoLife's final remnants: vaults of data and resources too valuable to abandon. As director of operations, Felix had ensured he was the only one who knew of their existence.

The city's labyrinth of hidden passages and forgotten

spaces made it the perfect battlefield. Untraceable networks thrived here, regulations were lax, and the public remained blissfully unaware. It was the ideal place to regroup, rebuild—and strike again.

Felix's ambitions had grown beyond CytoLife's original vision: a synthesis of genetic manipulation and digital dominion. The future wasn't confined to DNA or data alone; it was in their unification. Genes would shape the body; data would shape the mind. Together, they would create a system of absolute precision and control, one that only Felix could wield.

But first, there were loose ends to eliminate.

Lucas Fairbanks had once been a useful pawn, a former military operative tasked with protecting Dr. Rebecca Kent, CytoLife's lead researcher on the CRISPR AGG1 project. The bond forming between them had seemed advantageous at first. But Lucas's moral compass—and his meddling mother, Harper Brasfield—had proven liabilities.

Felix's smirk deepened as he recalled Harper storming into his office with stolen CytoLife hard drives, her self-righteous fury practically daring him to stop her. At the time, he'd dismissed her as a minor inconvenience, confident the drones were primed and the plan too advanced to fail. Yet the sight of those drives had sparked a flicker of unease—one he quickly buried.

The truce he'd offered had been a sham, a stalling tactic to neutralize Harper's leverage while his plans advanced. Paying Lucas to vanish had seemed like a small price to eliminate further complications. Yet Lucas's persistence—

and his uncanny ability to reappear at the worst times—had proven infuriating.

Rebecca Kent, however, was another matter. What she carried inside her was irreplaceable. Whether she realized it or not, she had a role to play. That she sought refuge with Lucas was a stroke of luck Felix fully intended to exploit.

The web was tightening, with strands connecting in ways no one else could see.

Soon, there would be no escaping it.

TWO

Nearly two years after leaving her old firm, Harper Brasfield's new venture, the Brasfield Law & Advocacy Group, was thriving. The gritty, up-and-coming Memphis neighborhood where her office now stood felt like a deliberate contrast to the polished corner suite she once occupied. And it suited her better these days.

While her peers filled their leisure time with travel, hobbies, and grandkids, Harper doubled down. Billable hours stacked up, each case another battle waged, as if slowing down simply wasn't an option. The new firm wasn't just a fresh start; it was a statement—a line drawn in the sand against the shadows that had nearly consumed her during the battle to dismantle CytoLife.

That company, wrapped in promises of progress, had twisted its mission into something far more dangerous. In the aftermath, Harper built her firm from the ground up—not just a legal practice, but a force of resistance. In a world still reeling from the fallout, it stood as a line of defense against unchecked technology.

Media outlets frequently sought Harper as a subject-matter expert; her name was a staple in panel discussions and interviews. But the insights she shared barely scratched the surface of what she knew. Washington's warmth had cooled as she asked the questions no one wanted to face. More often than not, her seat at the table felt less like an invitation and more like an attempt to contain her.

She didn't mind. Keeping them on edge was part of the job.

Those uneasy exchanges only reinforced her determination. Every case and every precedent became a crucial victory against the tide. Harper wasn't just defending clients; she was shaping a future where technology served humanity—not the other way around.

Harper leaned back, the leather chair creaking beneath her. At her feet, Juno lay still, one ear twitching in quiet vigilance.

Across from her, Kyle Marshall fidgeted, exhaustion carved into his face. Not from a bad night's sleep, but from carrying too much for too long.

Ink curled past the edges of his sleeves—prison tattoos, mostly faded. Hard to ignore. His hands, strong but restless, flexed against his thighs, the calluses marking him as a man who had worked, fought, and endured.

Kyle wasn't the first to show up confused, broken, and

desperate for answers. His voicemail had been a familiar mix of paranoia and fear, but there was something about him Harper couldn't ignore.

The government's confident claims of identifying everyone affected by the genetic edits rang hollow to her. The numbers they touted lacked real evidence, and the Safe Genes Agency was drowning in failures. Harper had stopped counting the cases piling up on her desk. Each one was a testament to a system that was crumbling under its own weight.

People like Kyle had been promised help, only to be swallowed by a bureaucratic abyss. Cases were dismissed with rubber-stamped resolutions: *resolved* or, worse, *unsubstantiated.*

Kyle's story wasn't unique, but it was a stark reminder that the system wasn't just broken—it was abandoning the very people it was supposed to protect.

"Mr. Marshall, I've reviewed your file. You received medical treatment while incarcerated, correct?" Harper asked.

"Yeah, I did. They said it was voluntary, but... you know how that goes. Sounded like a good deal at the time. Told me they could fix things. Make some of my health problems better. So, I signed the papers."

"Tell me why you're here today, Kyle."

"Well, Miss Brasfield, you see, I ain't any better. In fact, I'm worse as all get out. I saw that number on TV and called them people in Washington. I finally got in to see somebody down at the old veteran's hospital where that Safe Genes thing is. Took damn near all day just to get an information packet…"

Harper cut in. "Did they follow through?"

"Nah, not really. At first, they called and sent me for a couple checkups, but then... it just stopped. They threw me some paperwork and told me they were 'workin' on it,' but I haven't heard nothin' since."

"So despite their promises, you haven't received adequate care or follow-up?"

"Not a damn thing. I've called, but all I get is 'we're overwhelmed' or 'resources are stretched thin.' Meanwhile, I'm over here gettin' worse." Kyle looked away. "Feels like they just moved on."

"I see." Harper paused. "I'll be asking you some more questions later, but just to confirm, you haven't received any medical attention at Safe Genes since the initial checkup?"

"No, ma'am."

"Tell me about Mississippi," Harper said, her fingers tapping the mahogany desk.

Kyle shifted in his chair. "Well, ma'am, Mississippi's a place where opportunities are as thin as the soles on our shoes. Got caught up in some bad stuff."

"Bad stuff breeds worse." Harper's eyes narrowed.

"Ended up at Stonebrook," Kyle muttered.

"Stonebrook isn't a damn summer camp," Harper shot back. The facility was notorious for housing some of the most violent inmates.

"No, ma'am. It ain't."

"Drugs?" she asked, not flinching at the demon's name.

"Among other things." Kyle's hands trembled in his lap.

Harper leaned forward, resting her elbows on the desk. Her voice was steady but firm. "Kyle, I've seen my fair share of stories fall apart under scrutiny. You're not like the others who come in here spinning tales. So, tell me—what happened?"

"They did something to me," Kyle whispered. "I don't know what, but it messed me up real bad."

"We'll figure it out," Harper encouraged. "Start at the beginning."

"It's like there's this fog over everything," Kyle began. "Headaches that feel like they're splitting my skull, memory gaps big enough to drive a truck through. Sometimes... I do things without knowing why."

"Things?" Harper pressed.

"My hands start shaking, and next thing I know, I'm somewhere with no idea how I got there."

"Any memory of the facility?"

"Bits and pieces," Kyle said. "Bright white rooms. Machines humming like bees. Wires everywhere."

"And the reason for your treatment? Did they explain it?"

Kyle let out a bitter laugh. "Treatment? The techs talked about brainwaves like they were tuning a guitar but never gave an actual explanation."

"Brainwaves?" It wasn't the word itself that stopped her. It was the way he said it, deliberate and exact. Clients rarely used technical terms, instead fumbling through vague descriptions of pain, confusion, or fear. *Brainwaves, though—that was new.*

Kyle winced, glancing up at the flickering light. "Yeah,

I don't remember much, but that word stuck. They said something about mapping brainwaves. Testing responses. It... it didn't feel right."

Harper's mind whirred, but she pushed forward, eager to hear the rest of his story.

"How often do the headaches hit?" she asked.

"Like clockwork. Every few hours. Sharp enough to drop me."

"And the memory lapses?"

"Whole days, gone. Like someone's erasing parts of my life."

"Behavioral changes?"

Kyle hesitated. "Fights. I'm not a violent guy, but... it felt like I was watching someone else's hands. Couldn't stop it."

"You've seen other doctors since your release?"

"Half a dozen," Kyle shook his head. "They've run tests, scanned my brain, tapped my knee with that little hammer. Told me I'm fine... but I know I'm not."

"Ever think it's all in your head?"

"Crossed my mind. But this? Feels different. Like something was done to me."

Years behind locked doors had left their mark. It was etched in his posture and measured in his careful politeness. He had the restraint of a man who understood trust wasn't given. It was earned.

"Kyle," Harper's voice stayed steady, her eyes on him. "Your story's got holes, but I think there's truth in there somewhere."

"Miss Brasfield—"

"Harper, please."

Kyle cleared his throat, shifting in his seat. "Right. Miss Harper. I thought Safe Genes was supposed to catch stuff like this?"

"Kyle," Harper's voice dropped, "the Safe Genes Initiative was supposed to be your safety net. But the mission and the implementation… let's just say they're not aligned."

"Feels more tangled than kudzu, if you're askin' me," Kyle said, glancing up. "Miss Harper, can you help me?"

Harper didn't hesitate. "It won't be a slam dunk, but I'll do everything I can to get to the bottom of this."

She wanted to tell him the truth—how she had been there that night, watching as DARPA's drones spread the anti-CRISPR tech, hoping it would undo the genetic damage.

"I'm just tired of feeling like this," Kyle muttered, rubbing his temples. "Even if I felt a little better... I'd take it."

Harper nodded. "Kyle, the first step is onboarding you as a client and starting the investigation. I'm confident we can help, but I can't promise what that looks like just yet. Nate will handle the scheduling. You'll hear from him soon."

She stood, moving around the desk. Juno rose with her, instinctively positioning herself between them.

Kyle stood hesitantly. "Your assistant said on the phone it wouldn't cost me anything. I can pay... just not much."

Harper waved her hand dismissively. "Don't worry about that. There's a compensation fund through the Safe Genes Initiative. We'll apply for it. If necessary, we can work on a contingency basis. Either way, money isn't something you need to worry about."

Kyle straightened, standing taller. “Thank you, Miss Harper. I really mean that.”

After Kyle left, Harper sank back into her chair, letting the momentary solitude wash over her. Every case was unique in its own way, but something about Kyle’s lingered in her mind. She tried to push it aside, chalking it up to fatigue and the gnawing sense of helplessness that seemed harder to shake these days.

Harper switched on the TV, hoping for a moment of escape, but every channel was consumed by the CytoLife fallout. Protesters filled the streets, scientists argued, and pundits spun endless speculation. She couldn’t tear her eyes away.

A local news program was broadcasting live just blocks from her downtown office. The camera zoomed in on a handmade sign: *“We Are Not Lab Rats!”* Another protester held a bold placard reading, *“No Justice for the Forgotten!”*

The feed cut to another part of the protest, where a man with a megaphone shouted, “They sold us out! Corruption at the top while they play with our bodies!” Behind him, more signs bobbed in the crowd: *“Stop Experimenting on the Poor!”* and *“This City Runs on Blood Money!”*

The door clicked open. Senior paralegal Nate Hollis stepped in, unobtrusive as ever.

“Got a minute?” he asked, his gaze sweeping the room before settling briefly on the muted news broadcast.

“Make it quick,” Harper blurted, her attention buried in

the mountain of paperwork sprawled across her desk.

Nate leaned against the doorframe, relaxed but attentive. He had a knack for managing the chaos she left in her wake, ensuring that nothing slipped through the cracks.

A law school dropout, married to a nurse and child-free by choice, he lived with a stability Harper barely recognized.

After her last assistant's betrayal, trust had been in short supply during Nate's interview. But he hadn't just come prepared; he understood her work in a way few did. In no time, her office was organized, her schedule running more smoothly—and, to her surprise, her trust was no longer in question.

"Your two o'clock's on the way," Nate replied.

Harper sighed, gesturing at the empty seat across from her. "Sorry. It's been another one of those days."

Nate grinned, the picture of quiet composure. He sat, tugging his sweater vest into place before absently dusting off the knee of his well-worn chinos. He carried a bookish, old-money ease more suited to a Cambridge coffee shop than a Memphis law office. Yet, somehow, he fit. Perhaps it was the way he listened more than he spoke or how effortlessly he translated legalese without a hint of condescension. He earned trust—whether from blue-collar workers or boardroom executives—without ever seeming like he was trying. "If it weren't, I'd be worried."

"Caught part of the Safe Genes hearings on TV last night. They're still talking like it's the savior we've been waiting for."

Harper snorted. "Of course they are. They've been pushing that narrative for months. Makes it easier to sweep the real mess under the rug."

Nate leaned back, arms crossed. "The senators seem pretty convinced—like it's all wrapped up. One even claimed the countermeasures wiped out any threat from the AGG1 edits, and Safe Genes is just an extra layer of precaution."

Harper glanced up, cynicism flickering in her eyes. "Yeah, I've heard that line before. They'll roll out some hearings, pat themselves on the back, and pretend it's all solved. Meanwhile, people are still dealing with memory loss and behavioral changes—side effects no one anticipated."

She leaned forward. "And that doesn't even touch on the subtler effects. Schools are reporting kids losing their competitive edge. Grades are slipping, sports teams are underperforming, and the mental health crisis is pushing support services to the brink."

Nate shook his head. "They said AGG1 was just about reducing aggression. But now..."

"Exactly," Harper interjected. "I'm no geneticist, but after digging into these cases, I've learned more than I ever wanted to. That's not how genes work. One tweak can set off a chain reaction, especially with something as intricate as behavior. They thought they could suppress aggression without accounting for the ripple effects."

She paused, her tone sharpening. "And don't even get me started on the moral and ethical mess they created."

She tapped her pen against the desk, the rhythm breaking the silence. "No one wants to admit just how deep this really goes."

Nate knew Harper's son had worked at CytoLife and that

both had given closed-door testimony. As far as he was aware, that was the extent of her involvement. Harper intended to keep it that way.

"I've seen people online calling themselves 'Harmonics,'" Nate added, his brow furrowing. "Like they've hit some perfect groove where nothing rattles them anymore."

Harper scoffed. "There's always a crowd preaching salvation. Give them a conspiracy and a little delusion, and they'll throw themselves a parade. If aliens landed tomorrow, they'd be down on Riverside Drive with a White House tour guide in hand."

Nate chuckled. "Yeah, there's always someone ready to claim they've got it all figured out."

Harper nodded. "People are desperate for answers. And when none come, they make one up."

"Do you think the countermeasure even worked at all?"

"They'll tell you it did," Harper said. "But no one really knows. Some say it neutralized the gene edits; others aren't so sure. And no one's talking about the people who slipped through the cracks."

"Like Kyle Marshall?"

Harper gave him a sharp look. Nate quickly corrected himself. "I mean, people like him. Those caught in the middle of all this."

Harper's expression softened. "Until we get real answers, this isn't going away anytime soon."

Nate stood, notepad in hand. "Oh, before I go, a journalist wants a quote on the latest PenCore settlement."

Harper froze, the name hitting her like a gut punch.

PenCore, the private prison corporation. Its corruption had ensnared her mentor, Judge Jackson, in a bribery scheme he hadn't orchestrated but couldn't escape. The system funneled prisoners into for-profit facilities, its ugly truth exposed in the wake of the CytoLife disaster. PenCore was shut down, its settlements dwindling as everyone scrambled to bury the disgrace.

"Tell them they can pull from any of the 'no comments' I've given this month," Harper replied without looking up.

"Roger that, Brass," Nate said with a grin. With a quick nod, he slipped out, leaving behind the soft thump of Juno's tail against the floor.

Since founding her firm, the cases had been relentless—a steady stream of clients like Kyle Marshall, each story more gut-wrenching than the last. Harper's courtroom battles exposed bitter realities: the public had been fed half-truths, warped by self-serving agendas.

Quitting wasn't an option. Not when people like Kyle were trapped in a system designed to crush them. Her small, scrappy team juggled contingency cases while setting their sights on bigger targets. The fight had drained her personal wealth, even forcing her to funnel part of Lucas's CytoLife settlement—a sum that still made her stomach churn—into keeping the firm afloat.

Fortunately, momentum had begun to shift. Media attention sparked by journalist Adam Burke and her podcast interviews advocating for CytoLife's victims had turned the tide. Other firms were eager to partner with hers, rallying behind the push for transparency and accountability.

Her eyes flicked to the photo on her filing cabinet—Lucas in uniform, his sharp green eyes mirroring hers, dark wavy hair cropped short, and that stubborn jawline. He was out there somewhere, tangled in the same mess they all were. She gave him space, hoping he wouldn't self-destruct, bracing for the worst while clinging to a fragile hope for the best.

Juno nudged her leg, steady and warm, a constant in the shifting tides.

"Alright, girl," Harper muttered, running her hand through the dog's gold-flecked fur. "Back to it."

Billionaire Thomas Baxter sat at an ornate desk in his temporary sanctuary—a villa perched above Monaco's glittering coastline. Floor-to-ceiling windows framed the endless blue of the Mediterranean, with cool marble stretching beneath him. Outside, the hum of nightlife drifted up the cliffs, threading through the rustle of palm trees.

To anyone else, it was paradise. To Baxter, it was a gilded cage.

His fingers tapped the desk's intricate carvings as he surveyed the scattered papers and devices before him. Isolation gnawed at him, but he refused to call it defeat. This was only a pause. A recalibration.

Once the celebrated visionary behind Baxter Global and the face of CytoLife, he now existed on the fringes of his own empire. The fallout should have destroyed him; instead, it forced his company into survival mode. The board had stripped him of authority, installed crisis leadership, and disavowed him in press releases—all while standing on the foundation he had built.

The fall of his empire had reduced his inner circle to a dwindling few: loyalists, opportunists, men and women who saw his exile as an investment. Influence was still his currency, power still his leverage. The world might have tried to erase him, but it would never be free of him.

Humiliation was a lesson, not a sentence. His return was not a matter of if, but when.

The collapse had been inevitable—a perfect storm beyond his control. That belief kept him steady. That belief would carry him back.

His thoughts snapped to the latest PR disaster.

"Dammit, we need to pivot," he snapped, slamming a hand on the desk. "These sheep have the attention span of gnats."

Around him, his small team scrambled, their loyalty unwavering. They had followed him willingly into uncharted territory. Baxter neither noticed nor cared how they flinched at his abrupt shifts from charm to icy indifference. In his mind, they knew their place, and that was all that mattered.

"Public outrage is fading, sir," one aide ventured, his voice steady despite the weight of Baxter's glare. "Perhaps we should consider…"

"Consider what? Letting my legacy slip away?" Baxter shot to his feet, his chair scraping against the marble floor as he began to pace. "We crafted a narrative—one that should have had them eating out of our hands. Felix Ross acted independently, twisting my name and my mission to eliminate suffering. And now they're already forgetting?"

His smile turned bitter as he pictured the rapturous faces of the Harmonics—living proof, *his* proof. The embodiment of his vision. The narrative had to take hold, had to dominate. Then they'd see. They all would.

Another eager aide chimed in, "If we spin it right, less scrutiny could mean..."

"Less control," Baxter cut in, halting mid-pace. "And control is the game. I play to win."

"We'll find new ways," the first aide assured him. "You've always been three steps ahead, Mr. Baxter. The world won't ignore us forever."

Baxter waved them off. "Flattery won't help. Regroup and find the cracks in public opinion. There's always a way back in." He smoothed his silver hair and adjusted his cuff, tugging the fabric of his Savile Row suit. Control wasn't declared. It was worn.

Despite his billions, the levers he once pulled with ease had jammed. His carefully curated image as an environmental saint—propped up by hollow philanthropy—had lost its power. The window to reclaim his influence was closing fast. He couldn't stop the slide, but he could still steer, avoiding total collapse. Regaining control of the narrative and erasing the stain on his legacy—*that* would set everything right again.

The script had been flawless: Felix Ross, director of CytoLife, vanished, framed as the mastermind who had twisted Baxter's noble vision of human advancement. But the narrative was slipping. Sacrificial lambs weren't enough.

Baxter had already thrown government officials under the bus, yet the protesters still marched. Their signs screamed: *Genes Are Sacred—Stop Playing God!* and *Baxter's Billions Won't Buy Justice!*

Felix's failure had left him exposed. Harper Brasfield and Lucas Fairbanks dismantling the drone network was chaos enough. But Felix was supposed to control the fallout, not become part of the problem. Now, Baxter stood alone in the crosshairs.

"Keep me posted," he said with a dismissive flick of his hand, sending his team scurrying.

Baxter clung to the promise of an enduring legacy: the VitaLexis Protocol, his breakthrough in longevity therapy. This wasn't just medical innovation—it was the key to humanity's next evolutionary leap. Doubling lifespans wouldn't just reshape individual futures; it would redefine the trajectory of civilization.

The protocol stood on the brink of perfection, a seamless alternative to the crude stem-cell treatments and cumbersome injections that had defined the field. Dr. Rebecca Kent, his daughter, had revolutionized their work with her advancements in CRISPR, refining it into something unparalleled and almost perfect. For Baxter, VitaLexis wasn't just progress—it was destiny. A triumph no scandal or outrage could diminish.

A society free from aggression? That was merely a fortunate byproduct. After CytoLife's fall, Baxter had maneuvered carefully, allowing the AGG1 gene edits to absorb public fury while VitaLexis remained in the shadows.

Let them rage; the distraction was perfect. It kept their eyes off his true innovation—hidden, protected, and waiting for the right moment to be unveiled.

His thoughts drifted to Rebecca. She had once believed in his vision as fiercely as he did; their partnership at CytoLife had been unstoppable.

But the cracks had begun to show. Rebecca's hesitations and quiet questions had been easy to dismiss. She always came around.

Until she didn't.

Her announcement that she was leaving their shared exile to "be on her own for a bit" had shaken him to the core. At the most critical moment, she walked away. This wasn't just doubt; it was betrayal.

He had built his life around shielding her, insulating them both from the tragedies that had shaped them. But now, the fear of losing her—*truly* losing her—paralyzed him. Their rare, stilted calls were riddled with awkward small talk, conversations that skimmed the surface and avoided the depths. Neither dared to breach the fragile barrier between them.

He assumed she was always on the move but never asked where, dreading her sharp accusation of intrusion. Yet every time the phone rang and her name appeared, his heart lurched—a stubborn reflex of hope he couldn't suppress.

Reaching out to ask her to come back felt impossible. The specter of rejection loomed too large. He told himself it was pride that held him back, but the truth ran deeper. It was fear.

Rebecca *had* to come around. She was his heir in every

way: brilliant, capable, the embodiment of his vision.

"Damn it, Rebecca," he muttered, his voice filled with anger and hurt.

His thoughts shifted to the Consortium—a shadowy network wielding influence far beyond the public eye, one in which he was deeply entangled. Their power was undeniable, but lately, the strings felt tighter, the moves more calculated, as if someone else were quietly orchestrating the game. He resisted the notion of being a pawn. No—he was still essential to what came next.

The ground beneath him was shifting with Felix gone and now Rebecca slipping away. But Baxter wasn't finished yet. He downed the last of his drink, leaned over his laptop, and typed a message; dirt on a high-ranking official was a secret worth trading.

As he hit send, a predator's grin curled across his lips.

Another move. Another step toward reclaiming the upper hand.

In time, the world would understand.

He'd make sure of it.

THREE

Lucas Fairbanks moved through Paris's shadowed alleys, with Rebecca Kent close behind. The city's labyrinth of ancient streets, bathed in the warm glow of lampposts, felt suffocating. Every sound—the distant hum of a scooter, the faint echo of footsteps—sharpened his focus.

At the corner of Rue Poulet, Rebecca brushed a strand of limp blonde hair from her forehead. The gesture seemed casual, but the faint tremor in her hand betrayed her unease. Their eyes met briefly, an unspoken acknowledgment passing between them before she shoved her hand into her coat pocket.

She was a shadow of her former self. Once, she moved with effortless grace, turning heads without trying. Now, she seemed brittle, held together by something thinner than willpower.

The tremor. The scar at the base of her neck. The implant she refused to explain.

Whatever it was, it was killing her. And there was no hiding it anymore.

Lucas clenched his jaw, pushing the thought away. He had told himself that he came to Paris for Felix. That was the reason. The excuse. Felix had destroyed too many lives. Hunting him down wasn't vengeance—it was setting things right. But some part of him had come for her too, a truth he couldn't escape.

They had once been colleagues at CytoLife. Then lovers. Now, they were survivors of the same wreckage, standing on opposite sides of a tragedy. Rebecca had helped unleash AGG1—a genetic weapon on an unsuspecting public. Lucas had been part of the covert team that stopped it. Their final confrontation had left no room for closure, only chaos.

Rebecca's cryptic messages hadn't revealed much, but they didn't need to. Felix Ross hadn't disappeared after CytoLife's collapse. He had gone underground. The fear in her voice had been enough to bring Lucas here—to this maze of streets where answers or traps could be waiting.

Ahead, Rebecca walked as if none of it existed. Lucas knew better.

He scanned the street. Tall, solid, built for action, he didn't just move; he commanded the space around him. His gaze cut through the shadows, trained to pick apart patterns, isolate anomalies, and read danger before it took shape. A soldier's awareness, honed by years in the field, lay coiled beneath the easy confidence he wore like armor.

A reflection in a parked car's window. Footsteps shifting against wet pavement. A man lingering too long under a streetlamp.

None of it was coincidence.

"We need to keep a lower profile," he whispered.

Rebecca nodded, falling into step as they slipped deeper into the shadows of the 18th arrondissement.

"Stop looking at me like that," she snapped, catching him off guard. Then, more quietly, "I'm fine."

He wanted to tell her she wasn't, to argue, but the words refused to fall from his lips. Instead, he shoved his fists deeper into his coat pockets and kept walking.

Fine, he thought bitterly. Let her keep up the act for now. The truth, as always, would eventually surface. Until then, he'd let the bustle of the city fill the empty space.

They rounded a corner, and Lucas stopped abruptly, his gaze locking onto a café across the street. "Well, look at that," he said, nodding toward it. "Feels like a lifetime ago, but I was sitting right there the day you walked back into my life. I thought I was hallucinating."

Rebecca followed his gaze with a half-hearted smile. "Wouldn't blame you if you wished you were. These past months, I've been nothing but trouble for you."

Her words yanked him backward.

In the aftermath of CytoLife, Lucas had retreated, locking away the horrors. Then Rebecca reached out, and against his better judgment, something cracked open.

Their messages drifted between them like paper boats—tentative at first, then gathering momentum. Each notification brought her name to his screen, weighted with everything unsaid and undone. The subtext beneath her words sharpened: doubts, regrets, a need she couldn't name.

Days bled into weeks as they circled each other from a distance. Their messages stretched longer, their rhythm returning like muscle memory. He had convinced himself they were destined never to meet again. Then she asked him to come to Paris.

Felix was the excuse. The mission, a convenient lie. But when he saw her outside that café, the world narrowed to a single point.

She stood, hesitant yet unshakable, a moment suspended between past and present.

At first, nothing else mattered. Time and distance had only confirmed what they already knew: whatever lay between them wasn't over.

In Rebecca's fifth-floor apartment, with its crooked shutters and perpetually running tap, they pulled each other close. Her fingers dug into his shirt as if anchoring herself to shore. Mouths silencing the past. The world shrank to that space, that breath, that moment of her pressed against the peeling wallpaper. For a while, it felt like enough.

But reality always found the cracks.

What followed was slow-motion wreckage. They circled each other, careful at first, picking through the debris of who they had been. Late-night conversations softened into something resembling a truce. Confessions spilled between them—some easy, some jagged. But the worst truths stayed buried.

Lucas exhaled, snapping back to the present. "I don't regret you finding me," he admitted. "I just regret how messy it's all gotten."

She nodded, her gaze dropping to the cobblestones. "Yeah. Me too."

Lucas hesitated, then motioned toward the café. "Come on. Espresso and a croissant—for old time's sake."

"For old time's sake," she echoed.

They lingered at the café for nearly an hour, saying little but exchanging muted, knowing glances. The gentle murmur of conversation filled the space between them, the clinking of cups and the shuffle of feet blending with the hum of the city outside.

When the silence became too heavy to ignore, Lucas paid the bill and rose, extending his hand toward Rebecca. She hesitated, her fingers brushing his before finally gripping his hand. Her movements were slow, cautious, as though she were summoning the energy to follow.

Moments later, they stepped onto the crowded sidewalk, the city's chaos wrapping around them like a sudden gust of wind. Lucas's hand rested firmly at her lower back. "Let's get back to the apartment," he whispered. "You look wiped."

Rebecca stumbled, catching herself with a sharp inhale. He tightened his grip, steadying her. Up close, the toll on her was impossible to ignore. Her once flawless skin was mottled, deep shadows dulling the ice-blue of her eyes.

She straightened up quickly, masking the weakness. "I'm fine."

"No, you're not," Lucas muttered, steering her into a

quieter side street. His eyes flicked to her neck. "That thing in your neck... it's getting worse, isn't it?"

He knew only fragments: the implant was both a delivery system and a monitor for the gene edits—the so-called longevity therapy branded as VitaLexis. CytoLife had heralded it as a genetic fountain of youth, cloaked in lofty promises. But the details had always eluded him. Now, one thing was clear—it was failing her.

Rebecca glanced away, quickening her pace. "It's... complicated. The implant program—it's not what we thought. My father, he... not here... I can't...." Her voice wavered and broke off.

Lucas's patience frayed. *Here we go again.* She always stopped just short of the truth. He stayed silent, following her to the apartment. Inside, he shut the door with more force than necessary, the sound slicing through the stillness.

Rebecca lingered near the doorway, her posture tense as though bracing herself. She didn't look at him, the weight of unspoken words hanging heavy between them. It wasn't fear—it was avoidance, a quiet refusal to spark another argument that would lead nowhere.

Lucas paced in a futile attempt to corral his racing thoughts. Finally, he stopped and turned to her, his gaze sharp and unrelenting.

"Rebecca," he said, his tone sharper than he intended, "did they do something to me?"

Her expression faltered, the silence stretching between them like a chasm.

Memories clawed at the edges of his mind: Felix insisting

on a "medical workup" at CytoLife, the plush Executive Medical Clinic starkly at odds with the cold, clinical exam room. He remembered the endless tests—bloodwork, scans, and other procedures he couldn't name—all framed as part of their innovative research. At the time, it had felt routine, even necessary, to stay in peak condition for the job.

But certain details lingered now, sharper in hindsight: the way Felix had reviewed the results with a focused intensity, the cryptic remarks from the technicians, and the vague reassurances that it was all "standard." He hadn't questioned it then. He should have.

"What did they do to me?" he demanded.

Rebecca's eyes widened. "I... I don't know, Lucas," she stammered. "I'm sorry. There's so much I haven't told you—"

"You think?" Lucas snapped. "You've been playing me this whole time, just like your father. Like Felix."

She winced, her voice hitching. "It wasn't like that. I was trying to protect you. I'm the one who tracked you down, remember? I messaged—"

"Protect me?" Lucas scoffed. "By keeping me in the dark? I trusted you, Rebecca."

"Lucas, please, listen—"

"Why did you contact me?" he demanded. "To see if I'd become a problem for your father? Great job hiding that little detail, by the way."

"No! That's not how it was." Her voice wavered. "You have to believe me."

Lucas exhaled heavily, anger and hurt swirling into a storm he could no longer contain. "Then why am I still here?

I told you—Felix is my target. But you… you're…"

His voice faltered. "Hell, I fell in love with you at CytoLife. After everything, I was numb, but being with you again…"

He paused, his voice unsteady. "It brought it all back. And I can't take it if you keep defending your father and dodging my questions."

He stepped closer, his gaze locking on hers. "That thing in your neck—it's killing you."

Her whisper cut through his anger. "I know, Lucas." Her eyes searched his. "I loved you too. I still do."

"Then tell me what I need to know," he begged.

Rebecca looked away, her words spilling out in a rapid torrent. "We're in a genetic arms race—governments, rogue actors—it's deeper than you can imagine. If we hadn't pushed forward, someone else would have. And they wouldn't think twice about turning it into a weapon."

Lucas let out a sharp, bitter laugh, shaking his head. "Do you even hear yourself right now? Please tell me I don't have to spell out how insane that sounds."

Rebecca's hand trembled as she reached for him. "Lucas, you don't understand. Felix… he's more dangerous than you think. There's something about him—it's like he's not just a man anymore. He's cunning, inhuman. Like he's always five steps ahead, and nothing—no one—matters to him."

Lucas's pulse hammered in his ears. He'd seen Rebecca stare down power players without flinching, but now? Whatever she was about to say terrified her.

"The next words out of your mouth will decide if I stay or walk," he said. "No more games, Rebecca. Make them count.

I can't help you if you keep me in the dark."

"The implant isn't just a delivery system for the longevity therapy," Rebecca finally said. "It's a BCI—a brain-computer interface. Think of it as the hardware that manages the software. It hooks directly into neural pathways, regulating brain activity and sharpening cognition. Its primary role is to prevent the brain from aging and ensure everything functions perfectly."

She hesitated, her eyes darting around the room. "VitaLexis is a combination of CRISPR and anti-aging technology, like stem-cell treatments. The CRISPR edits focus on genes tied to aging, while the stem-cell treatments repair damaged cells. Together, they slow aging and reverse cell decay. The implant keeps the brain healthy and makes sure the therapy is delivered and integrated exactly where it's needed."

Lucas frowned. "So, is the implant VitaLexis, or just part of it?"

"It's both," Rebecca explained. "Think of it like a car—the implant is the engine, and the therapy is the fuel. One doesn't work without the other. VitaLexis is just the name that ties it all together."

Her voice softened. "Early projections suggested a lifespan of 150, maybe even 160 years—double what's possible now. My father saw it as a way to cheat death. He believed that if he could extend his life long enough, future technology would catch up—a perpetual fountain of youth."

Lucas's eyes narrowed. "And?"

"At first, everything seemed fine. The early results were

promising—better than we'd hoped. But then Felix started taking a more active interest, more than I expected. I should have questioned it, but I was so distracted by everything else that when he offered to take some of the workload, I was... relieved." She looked away, her voice cracking. "In retrospect, I should have spoken up.

"He told me the mirror sites—sister labs—were for streamlining testing. That's what he called it—streamlining. I didn't ask for details. I didn't see much of what happened after that." She hesitated, her voice faltering. "I trusted him. When he gave me the data, it all seemed... convincing. So, I agreed to the implant without hesitation. It was always part of the plan. I thought it would make my father happy—something good coming out of... everything that happened."

"And now?" Lucas pressed.

Rebecca's arms wrapped tightly around herself. "Now, the edits aren't stabilizing. The implant is overloading my brain—rewiring pathways, forcing connections that shouldn't exist. It started small—lapses and gaps I couldn't explain. But it's worse now. I can feel it changing me, and I don't know how to stop it."

Lucas's pulse pounded in his ears. For the first time since they'd reunited, she was saying more than she ever had. He wasn't sure if he wanted her to stop or if he could afford to let her. "And you had no idea?"

Tears welled in her eyes. "I thought we had control. The implant was supposed to be part of the solution, not... this."

Her voice cracked. "Felix hid too much. I trusted him. I let it happen. And now... I can't undo it."

Lucas stared at her, his expression hard to read. "Rebecca, you're one of the smartest people I know. This is... hard to believe."

Rebecca flinched, a sob catching in her throat. "I thought we were on the right path. I didn't see the truth until it was too late.

"I swear, Lucas—if I'd known, I would have stopped it."

Her gaze locked on his, desperate. "Please. Help me."

Lucas turned away, his gaze drifting to the hazy Paris skyline. The apartment window, streaked with grime, distorted the city's muted glow. Betrayals swirled in his mind—CytoLife, Rebecca, Felix. Time wasn't just slipping through his fingers; it was vanishing.

The words still hung between them, heavy and unresolved. Then—

A faint sound in the hallway.

Lucas froze.

Footsteps.

The steps grew louder, then stopped right outside.

Silence.

Whoever was out there was waiting. Listening.

He grabbed Rebecca's arm, pulling her towards him. "Move," he whispered, guiding her toward the window.

Lucas shoved the window open. The rusted hinges groaned, a sharp protest against the silence. He froze for a beat, listening. Nothing. No time to hesitate. He pushed Rebecca onto the fire escape and followed, yanking the window shut behind them.

"Lucas—" Rebecca began, but he silenced her with a

quick gesture, pressing her into the shadows.

Then, a metallic click. The door creaked open.

Lucas's heart thundered as they crouched low against the iron slats of the fire escape. Heavy footsteps crossed the threshold. Drawers opened and furniture shifted. A slow, methodical search. This wasn't a smash and grab. It was controlled.

Rebecca's breath warmed Lucas's neck as they huddled together. He kept his gaze on the alley below, searching for a silhouette that didn't belong, willing an escape route to appear.

Minutes stretched into an eternity.

At last, the footsteps retreated, and the door clicked shut. Silence fell once more.

Lucas exhaled. "That was too close," he muttered, his hand loosening around Rebecca's arm.

She sagged against him. "Was it Felix?"

Lucas didn't reply. He held up a hand for her to wait, then slipped back into the apartment.

Inside, the place was torn apart—drawers yanked open, furniture moved. Scanning the debris, Lucas spotted something small on the table by the door: a multi-tool. He picked it up, turning it over. A specialized attachment caught his eye—a key for proprietary systems. The same kind he'd once carried at CytoLife.

Felix's men. No question.

Lucas climbed back out onto the fire escape. "Yeah," he said. "We have to leave. Now."

He guided Rebecca down the fire escape, his senses on

high alert. Every shadow felt like a threat, every faint clatter echoing the footsteps they'd just evaded. They had to move—fast.

"We need answers," Lucas muttered. The multi-tool in his pocket felt heavier with every step, a stark reminder of how little control he truly had. "I'm done being a pawn in this twisted game."

Rebecca stumbled, her knees buckling beneath her. Lucas caught her arm, steadying her before she could fall. Her face was pale, her breathing shallow, and each step seemed to sap what little strength she had left.

"Lucas, I—"

"Don't talk," he cut in. "We need to find someplace safe—somewhere I can think."

They emerged onto the narrow Parisian streets, each turn closing in on them, the illusion of safety crumbling with every step.

Out of nowhere, a surge of protesters flooded the road, chanting and shouting in French. Signs bobbed overhead; voices rose in a collective roar.

"There used to be a safe house," Rebecca managed. "Close by. We can—"

"No," Lucas snapped. "We do this my way now."

She blinked, confused, but didn't argue.

He tightened his grip on her hand and steered her through the crush of protesters. The crowd seethed with anger, placards slicing through the air.

A sign flashed past: *Non à l'assaut génomique!* No to genomic assault. Another appeared just ahead, the words scrawled in thick, frantic strokes. *Pas de modifications. Pas de monstres!* No modifications. No monsters.

Lucas swallowed the sharp response rising in his throat. Monsters. That was what they thought people like Rebecca were.

Rebecca's gaze locked on Lucas, her eyes wide. "This is getting out of hand."

"Keep your head down," he muttered, pulling her closer. He couldn't afford either of them being recognized now—not when everything was spiraling.

The megaphone's crackle sliced through the air before the next chant boomed over the crowd. *"La science doit avoir des limites!"*

The words landed easily. His French had never been perfect, but it was good enough. Years visiting France, long conversations with Rebecca, and just enough studying to understand more than he spoke. *Science must have limits.* But whose limits? Whose rules?

A protester shoved past, nearly knocking Rebecca off balance. Another waved a poster inches from Lucas's face, knuckles white around the edges. *Les gènes ne sont pas à vendre!*

He barely needed to process the words. *Genes are not for sale.* They weren't shouting at him, not directly, but the weight of it still landed.

"Oh God," she whispered, voice trembling. "They're terrified."

No, Lucas thought. They were past terrified. This was turning into something else.

His eyes swept the crowd. "It's about to blow up. We need

to get out of here."

A bottle shattered nearby, sending shards skittering across the pavement. The protest reached a fever pitch. Lucas tugged Rebecca towards a narrow alley.

"Faster," he warned. "Before someone decides we're the enemy."

They hurried through the alley, emerging onto another dimly lit street. It was quieter but no less unnerving. Lucas's eyes scanned their surroundings, searching for cover, until his gaze landed on a rundown hotel marked by a flickering neon sign.

"This way," he said, dragging her inside.

A stench of damp rot filled the cramped, mildew-stained room. The door slammed shut behind them, rattling on its hinges. Lucas leaned against it, his pulse a war drum in his ears. He scanned the room, hyperaware of the thin walls, the single exit, and now, the looming specter of Felix. They were still breathing. But barely.

Rebecca sank onto the edge of the bed, her shoulders sagging under the weight of exhaustion and defeat.

Lucas didn't have the luxury of either.

"Tell me everything," he demanded. "We can't afford gaps in our defenses."

Rebecca hesitated. He knew that look: one part fear, one part reluctance.

"It's not that simple," she murmured. "There's so much at stake—"

"Stop." His voice cut through her words. "Our *lives* are at stake. Whatever this implant is doing to you—you know something. You must. Help me figure this out."

A muscle twitched in his jaw as he started pacing. He was done with half-truths and secrets. For months, Felix had been nothing more than a name in the dark, a threat lurking at the edges of his thoughts. He hadn't come to Paris with a plan, only the pull of unfinished business and the reckless hope that Rebecca's trail would lead to Felix.

But that was over.

He'd told himself Felix would reveal himself in time, that he only needed to follow the right threads. But that moment had never been his to decide. The fight wasn't a choice. It was already here.

A cold ripple traced his spine, but he locked it down. *Later. Process later.* Right now, he needed answers.

He turned quickly. "And if I find out I've been someone's lab experiment without my knowledge..."

Rebecca flinched, and for a second, something flickered in her eyes. Guilt? Doubt? "Lucas, please. You have to understand—"

His stomach knotted.

"Understand *what?*" His voice was razor-wire taut.

"That there might be a ticking time bomb in my head too?" He forced himself to steady his breath. "No more secrets, Rebecca. I'll uncover the truth—about you, about me, about all of it."

He paused, his voice turning sharp and flat, the way it had in another life. One spent in a uniform stained with dust, in shadows where men disappeared. "And when I do, your father better pray he's nowhere near me."

Lucas held her gaze. The fear in her eyes was real. But so was the truth he needed.

Rebecca hesitated, her voice a soft but firm whisper. "All right. I'll tell you everything. But once I do, there's no going back."

"I've never been more ready," Lucas replied.

He shifted toward the window, scanning the deserted streets below. No movement. But that didn't mean they were safe. He rolled his shoulders, forcing his pulse to slow. Panic got people killed. Tactical thinking kept them alive.

The tension between them hung heavy in the stale air until Lucas broke it. "We'll figure this out. Together."

Rebecca drew in a shaky breath. "Felix... I don't think he's working alone," she began cautiously. "There's something bigger—something darker. I overheard fragments that didn't make sense until now. They have plans, Lucas. Big plans. If we don't stop them—"

"We will." He didn't hesitate. *Couldn't* hesitate. "But first, we're finding Felix."

Her expression wavered, conflict flickering in her eyes. "Lucas, you don't understand. Felix... he's not just another man. He's—"

"I don't care." His voice was flat, lethal. "He's going down."

Rebecca's shoulders sagged, her gaze dropping to the floor. "Then I hope you're ready for what comes next."

Lucas met her eyes, his frame rigid with months of waiting. Now it was here. No turning back.

"I've been ready for a long time."

FOUR

Ethan stood by the desk, watching as Neon's fingers danced across the keyboard with deft, almost artistic movements. The three monitors displayed overlapping code and log files, their cryptic patterns glowing against the dark room. Neon's pink-highlighted hair caught the light, a sharp contrast to the muted tones of his tailored shirt.

"Well?" Ethan prompted, leaning against the desk's edge.

Neon paused, tilting his head as if listening to something Ethan couldn't hear. "It's elegant. I'll give them that," he said finally, his drawl tinged with reluctant admiration. "But it's also ambitious. Whoever did this has delusions of grandeur—and the resources to back them up."

Ethan frowned. "Silent Core?"

Neon leaned back slightly, resting an elbow on the desk as he gestured toward the center monitor. "What's left of it.

I'm working off what QuantumSafe sent over—fragments of logs, mostly." He tapped the screen, scrolling through a column of data. "Even this much is enough to tell me someone didn't just steal it. They've turned it into something else."

Ethan squinted at the screen. "Turned it into what?"

Neon sighed, drumming his fingers lightly on the desk. "It's adaptive now. Dynamic. Silent Core isn't just encrypting—it's probing, interacting. These patterns aren't random—they're intentional. It's like it's... testing boundaries."

"Testing how?" Ethan asked.

Neon tilted his head, gesturing toward the screen again. "It's phasing in and out of systems, leaving breadcrumbs. Whoever's using it isn't trying to lock things up—they're probing, testing how far they can go, what they can manipulate. Silent Core was never designed for this." He tapped a few keys, freezing the code on the monitor. "They've modified it. It's not encryption anymore—it's a key. The question is what's it unlocking?"

Ethan frowned. "And your take?"

"My take?" Neon swiveled toward him, adjusting his smartwatch absently. "Whoever did this knows exactly what they're doing. These logs are too clean. We're only seeing the edges," he said. "But even from these meager scraps, it's clear they're testing something big."

Ethan stared at the screen, Silent Core's stolen fragments glaring back at him like pieces of an unfinished puzzle. "You're sure about this?"

Neon gave a small shrug. "Most people wouldn't even notice these patterns. But this?" He gestured vaguely at the logs. "It's like watching an artist sketch out a blueprint—chaotic at first, but the lines are starting to connect."

Ethan exhaled slowly, Neon's analysis pressing down on him like a weight. The unanswered messages on his phone felt heavier now, their vague, pointed phrasing gnawing at the edges of his mind.

"Keep digging," Ethan instructed. "But stay quiet about it. If someone's testing Silent Core, I don't want them knowing we're paying attention."

Neon nodded, a faint smirk playing at his lips. "Don't worry," he said lightly. "I don't poke the bear unless I've got a really big stick."

Ethan's lips twitched, but he didn't reply. Slinging his bag over his shoulder, he headed for the door. It was time to tell Harper about the threat against Lucas.

Harper slid into the booth across from Ethan Cook, her dark, wavy hair falling like a battle flag around her face. The air in Sunrise Memphis was thick with the scent of fresh coffee and grease. "Morning," she said, her smile more courtroom than casual.

"Brass," Ethan greeted, sliding the menu aside. "Get the omelet. They toss in everything but the kitchen sink."

She didn't glance at it. "Maybe later." Her arms folded,

eyebrow arched.

Ethan sighed. "Been a while. Sorry, I've been out of touch."

"Understandable. Running CookCyber must keep you busy. Neon still making you crazy?"

A brief smile surfaced. "Brass, this isn't a catch-up. I've been getting threats. Not the usual noise."

Harper's stomach dropped. "Different how?"

"They mentioned Lucas." Ethan's eyes searched her face. "And now there's a video."

Her gut constricted. "Go on."

Ethan pulled out his phone and tapped play. The footage wobbled, shot from a distance, but clear enough to send a spike of dread through Harper. Lucas and Rebecca walked under muted Paris streetlights, Lucas's arm cradled around her as she stumbled.

Recognition tightened Harper's chest. The narrow sidewalks, the old stone façades. She'd walked those streets before.

"Shit," Harper muttered under her breath. Lucas wandering off was one thing, but seeing him back with Rebecca felt like a punch to the gut. She wasn't prepared for that reality—didn't want to be.

Ethan glanced at her. "They're being followed. And Rebecca... she looks rough."

Harper leaned in closer, her eyes glued to the screen. A shadow moved behind them—subtle, but unmistakable. Then a faint flicker lit the corner of the footage, so brief it might have been nothing.

"Wait—pause it! Ethan, what was that?"

The video froze on Lucas's face—tense, guarded, his body angled protectively toward Rebecca.

"I'm not sure," Ethan said, frowning as he replayed the footage. "Could've been a camera, maybe light glinting off metal. Or something else entirely. But they're moving fast—and Lucas noticed. Whatever it was, he knows they're not safe.

"Sent you the screenshot..." Ethan said, looking up from his phone.

Her fingers gripped the edge of the table, her knuckles white as the possibilities swirled in her mind. A camera? A weapon? Each theory felt darker than the last, the truth slipping just out of reach.

Ethan broke the silence. "He's too tense. Someone's closing in on them."

Harper stared at the frozen image from Ethan, her heart pounding. Lucas looked haunted, every taut line of his body radiating protective instinct. "If he's letting it show," she murmured, her voice tight, "then it's bad."

"And the text?" she pressed.

"They said, 'Lucas is part of the puzzle,' and that 'this is only the beginning.'"

"Someone's out there trying to hurt my son, Ethan. And for what? Because he can't keep his head down and stay out of this?" Her eyes locked on Ethan, searching for answers she knew he didn't have.

She exhaled hard, her frustration spilling out. "If he'd just stayed away, he wouldn't be tangled up in Rebecca's mess.

But no—he had to dive headfirst back into her world. Now it's chaos at every turn, pulling him deeper with every step."

"Look, it's a damn mess," Ethan admitted, rubbing the back of his neck. His shoulders slumped under the weight of it. "Given what happened, Lucas is a target. We have to assume CytoLife's tendrils are wrapped around everything by now. But trying to pin it down? It's like grabbing at smoke."

"Felix Ross *is* the smoke," Harper snapped, her grip tightening on the napkin she'd been twisting since the conversation began. The memory of their standoff at CytoLife burned vividly—circling each other like predators, waiting to see who would flinch first, each hiding behind empty promises to stay out of the other's way. Even then, she'd known neither would back down.

Lucas's safety had been her priority then, too. Now, anger flared anew—at Felix for still playing his twisted game and at Lucas for letting himself get caught in the middle.

Ethan's voice dropped. "Harper, it's not just Lucas. I've been seeing patterns. Threats that don't feel random. Someone's testing the waters—looking for cracks."

Her eyes narrowed. "Testing for what?"

"I don't know yet," Ethan admitted. "But it's intentional. Coordinated."

Harper pressed her fingertips to her temple, her thoughts racing. "What does it all mean? Are they planning their next move, using him as bait? Or is this just a way to cover their tracks?" She glanced away for a second. "We always knew whatever was left of CytoLife wouldn't just disappear."

"Exactly why I came to you," Ethan explained. "Lucas is

tangled in it. You needed to know."

"In the video, what's wrong with Rebecca? That wasn't just fear. She looks sick. And why is someone recording them and sending the footage to you?" She shook her head. "Ethan, none of this adds up."

Ethan's eyes darted briefly around the café. "Tell me about it. This whole thing feels off—like we're missing pieces."

"Has to be Felix," Harper whispered, tears welling in her eyes. "He's cleaning up. Lucas is in way over his head."

"Goes without saying, but I'm in. Any ideas?" Ethan searched her face.

Harper swallowed hard. "Not yet. But I know my son's out there with a target on his back because he couldn't leave Rebecca to fend for herself."

"Felix is a snake," Ethan muttered, "but even snakes answer to someone."

"Whoever's pulling the strings..." Harper's voice dropped. "I don't know what it's going to take to cut them loose."

"Tacks, CookCyber is on board too," Ethan said.

Harper allowed herself a breath; the nickname—a playful twist on "Brass"—momentarily easing the weight pressing down on her.

Harper stared into her cup, her thoughts swirling. "Everything's different now, isn't it? The protests, the chaos. I should be used to it by now, but it's always there—like thick summer heat, clinging no matter how far you run."

The café buzzed with quiet conversation, a pocket of normalcy in a world that felt like it was slipping away. A man's voice drifted over from the counter, louder than the murmur of voices around them. "I read they're testing people's DNA at the airport now. You fly into certain countries, and they swab you right at customs. And it's all 'for public safety,' right? Next, they'll be microchipping us like pets."

The barista, a young woman with her hair piled high in a messy bun, frowned as she handed the man his change. "That can't be real."

"It's real," the man insisted, leaning closer as if he needed her to understand. "My cousin tried to fly last month, and they detained her for hours. Some computer flagged her genome. Said she might've been exposed to unauthorized CRISPR tech."

The barista's eyes widened. "What happened to her?"

"SGA put her under mandatory monitoring. She has to check in weekly, and they're running genetic remediation protocols on her. Whatever that means."

Ethan glanced at Harper. "This is the world we're in now, isn't it?"

"It's been like this ever since... Feels like we're all just waiting for the next hit."

Ethan leaned back, a hollow laugh escaping. "I never thought it'd come to this. Business is booming, sure, but the floodgates are wide open. Remember the old law firm? Back then, it was idiots pulling stunts. Now it's tech ghosts and genetic nightmares. And it's not just on TV—everyone's looking over their shoulder."

He leaned forward, lowering his voice. "Speaking of, I reached out to Adam Burke."

Harper's brow furrowed. "Burke's been MIA since his

book blew up. Honestly, I don't blame him. I was surprised he even did that interview with Maya Clarkson. What'd you find?"

"Nothing. Not even answering secure pings anymore. You know him—always a few steps ahead of the game."

"Too smart for his own good," she muttered, her expression darkening. "Think he knows something new?"

"Or someone found him first," Ethan pondered.

"Let's hope he's just lying low." Harper's voice dropped as she shook her head. "If they've gotten to Burke—"

"We're playing catch-up," Ethan finished. "You're following the security protocols I taught you? House locked down? Digital hygiene up to snuff?"

Harper waved her phone, the model Ethan had recommended. "Yes, every step. Even got a dog from Tunica Humane Society. She's intimidating." An amused smile escaped. "She scared some joggers at Tom Lee Park, but all she wanted to do was lick them."

Ethan chuckled softly. "Juno, right? Part Malinois? Those things are fur missiles."

"Yeah, with a touch of crazy," Harper replied, a faint grin still tugging at her lips. "Trained her at Ridgeside K9. Top of the class. Lucas insisted."

Ethan smiled. "Good judgment runs in the family, then."

Harper's grin faded, her piercing green eyes locking onto Ethan's face. "I'm really worried about my son, Ethan."

"Lucas has a good head on his shoulders, and he's trained for this. Stepping into danger—it's second nature to him. If anyone can stay ahead of the game, it's him. Don't let it eat you up."

She studied him closely, noting the tension in his shoulders and the subtle narrowing of his eyes. Despite his calm exterior, he was just as rattled as she was—a fact that unsettled her more than she wanted to admit.

"Brass, want me to reach out to Lucas?"

Harper shook her head. "Hold tight for now. I know he's smart and capable," she said, her voice trembling. "But it's only a matter of time before someone doesn't miss."

She exhaled, pressing a hand to her forehead. "I'll call you tomorrow, Ethan. I need to get out of here."

She stood abruptly, the chair scraping against the floor, and left before he could respond.

Gasping for air, a familiar jolt of adrenaline shot through Harper as she stepped out of Sunrise Memphis. Her mind raced, autopilot kicking in while dark possibilities unfurled, each more sinister than the last. She leaned against a lamppost, her fingers trembling as she pulled out her phone.

Opening the secure app—Lucas's lifeline to her, layered with encryption so tight it could make a hacker cry—she hesitated.

"Only in dire circumstances," he'd told her.

If this didn't qualify, nothing did.

Her thumb hovered over the screen. This wasn't just about Felix's games or Baxter's slick lies. Something deeper was festering, and if Lucas was tangled in it, all bets were off.

"Come on, pick up," she muttered, her pulse pounding as the rings dragged on.

The call dropped. The app vanished. Harper's breath hitched, her pulse spiking as she swiped at the screen, convinced she'd accidentally moved the icon. It wasn't there. It was gone.

Seconds stretched into an eternity as she rebooted the phone, frustration morphing into unease. What the hell was going on?

The screen flickered back to life, but something was wrong—subtle, yet unmistakable. Her instincts flared, sharp and primal, the way they did when danger lingered just out of sight.

The video call reconnected, and Harper held her breath, waiting for Lucas's face to appear. When it did, her heart sank. His eyes weren't clouded with fear—they held something worse. Something that sent ice sliding down her spine.

"Mom." Lucas's voice was frayed, raw. "Rebecca… she's not okay. Something's wrong. Bad."

Harper steadied her voice. "Tell me everything."

"She's… sick. Weak. Her body's rejecting—something. It's tied to the work she was doing. An implant in her neck." He paused, glancing off-camera. The groan in the background told Harper more than words ever could.

"Lucas." Her voice cut through the digital haze. "You need to get out. Let me help."

Lucas gave a sharp, humorless laugh. "And bring down whatever chaos you've got planned? No, Mom. I can handle this."

"Like hell you can." Harper leaned closer to the screen, her green eyes narrowing. "Someone sent me footage of you and Rebecca in Paris—being followed. Lucas, there's something off. A flicker, a shadow—Ethan thinks it might've been light off a weapon."

Lucas went pale, his eyes widening. "What? A weapon? Who—how?"

"That's not the point right now," Harper snapped. "What matters is that you're in danger. This has Felix written all over it. And don't even get me started on your lack of judgment—"

"Mom, stop!" Lucas's voice rose, cutting her off. "This isn't the time."

She exhaled slowly, reining in her frustration. "You're right. But I'm coming to you. You need help."

He hesitated, glancing away. "I can't ask you to—"

"You didn't. I'm offering," she insisted. "We meet, or I'll find you myself."

Lucas sighed, running a hand through his hair. "Fine. But we do this my way."

"Always. Send me the details. Now let's figure out how to get you out of there."

"Thanks," he whispered, barely audible over the noise behind him. "I'll be in touch soon."

"Stay safe, Lucas. I'm here."

The call ended, leaving Harper staring at the blank screen, her grip tightening around the phone.

Lucas kept his head low, sharp eyes scanning every shifting shadow. The alleys of the 18th arrondissement were quieter now, the faint hum of distant traffic the only sound. The oppressive silence pressed in, like a trap waiting to spring.

Harper had sent him the screenshot. A shadow, a flicker—Ethan thought it could have been light glinting off a weapon.

How had he missed it?

He hadn't told Rebecca yet. Maybe he wouldn't have to. Whatever it was hadn't made itself known—no sound, no obvious threat. But that moment kept replaying in his mind, every detail sharpening with each pass, his self-reproach growing louder. The movement, the flicker—he should've caught it, should've known.

First, the break-in. Now this. Every instinct screamed at him: stay sharp. If Harper and Ethan were right, whoever was following them wasn't just watching them.

Being out here was madness, but the risk was worth it. Rebecca had a name—someone tied to CytoLife. Their only hope. If this lead panned out, maybe, just maybe, they wouldn't need to rely on anyone else.

They reached the building on Rue de l'Abreuvoir, its brick façade blending into the surroundings.

"This is it," Lucas muttered. Rebecca nodded, her grip tightening on her bag.

Lucas pressed the intercom. Silence. Then a crackling voice. The door buzzed open.

Inside, the stairwell reeked. They climbed, each step

heavier than the last. At the top, an older man with thinning hair opened the door, his eyes narrowing. Gaunt and unshaven, he radiated fear.

"*Pas ici,*" he growled in French. Then in English, "Not here." Exhaustion carved deep lines into his face, but the bitterness in his eyes burned through it. "I don't know you. Go."

Rebecca stepped forward. "You know my father—Thomas Baxter."

The man's eyes darted, but he didn't move. "Baxter. I owe him nothing."

"You owe him more than you think," she countered.

After a moment, the man stepped aside. The apartment was cluttered with papers and old equipment. He motioned to the couch. "Sit."

Rebecca winced as she sat, instinctively touching the implant in her neck. The man's eyes lingered on her for a moment; then he sighed.

"This is advanced. Dangerous. But I can't help you."

"We didn't ask for your opinion," Lucas snapped. "She's getting worse. How do we stop it?"

The man shook his head. "It wasn't made to stop."

Rebecca's fingers brushed over the implant. "There has to be something. My father trusted you."

The man stood, his face hardening. "He trusted too many people." He muttered something in French, moving toward the window. "I've heard... things. If you're smart, you'll leave it alone."

Rebecca straightened. "What things?"

"Nothing you want to know," he said, suddenly defensive. "It's not my business anymore." He rose and gestured toward the door. "Leave."

Lucas stepped forward, but Rebecca pulled him back. "We're done," she whispered.

They left in silence, the door slamming behind them.

"Another dead end," Rebecca said as they reached the street.

"He knows something," Lucas spat out.

"He knows plenty," she retorted. "But he's too afraid to say."

As they blended into the crowd, Lucas replayed the man's last words: "It wasn't made to stop." What did it mean?

It didn't matter. They had to keep moving.

They walked in silence, neither speaking until they were safely inside the apartment.

"Lucas, I'm so sorry." Rebecca's voice trembled. "I dragged you into this."

"Let's not go there," Lucas said, brushing a loose strand of hair from her forehead. "We're in this together, remember?"

Rebecca shook her head. "Aren't you still here out of guilt?"

"Our problems can wait," Lucas said, his gaze sweeping the room. "Whoever's coming for us won't back down, and you're in no condition to handle this on your own."

Rebecca shifted uncomfortably, her voice barely above a whisper. "Maybe… we should call my father."

Lucas froze. "Baxter?" The name left his lips like a curse. "He's the last person we need."

She looked away. "I know, but… we're running out of options." Her voice cracked. "I've reached out to everyone—researchers, old contacts—none of them can help."

"Your father is the reason you're in this mess! Besides, you really think he can pull off some miracle?" Lucas's eyes widened. "Seems press releases are his priority these days."

"I don't know," she admitted. "But we've tried everything else, Lucas. Every favor, every connection I've called in—all dead ends. That man? He was the last name on my list."

"Your father is…he's…."

"Responsible? I know." Rebecca bit her lip, her nod slow and reluctant. "But things are getting worse. I'm running out of ideas."

"Look." Lucas hesitated. "We have another option."

Rebecca's eyes narrowed. "Who?"

"Brass," he replied. "My mother."

Rebecca stiffened. "Harper Brasfield? But she…"

"Doesn't trust you?" Lucas finished. He caught something in her eyes: guilt mixed with fear. "She doesn't trust a lot of people. But she's not the type to turn her back when it counts."

Rebecca let out a bitter laugh, shaking her head. "And you think she'd make an exception for me?"

"You know why she'll help? Not because it's easy, but because she's my mother. She fights for the people she cares about—no questions asked. That's just who she is. You don't see it from where you stand, but I do. She'll help us because we need her."

"I don't know… your mother doesn't seem like someone who takes risks on people like me. My father—he always had a plan. You didn't question it; you just followed."

"Maybe that's the problem," Lucas observed. "Your father's plan—it's his plan. You're just a piece of it." He held her gaze. "My mom doesn't work that way. She sticks it out, no matter how messy it gets."

"Maybe your way is better. I don't even know what my father would do if he were here right now."

"Well, he's not," Lucas replied. "But I am. And I know Harper. She'll help you because you matter to me. We don't leave each other behind."

Rebecca looked down at their joined hands, then back up at Lucas. "You really think she'll take this on? For you?"

"If there's a way through, she'll find it."

Rebecca nodded slowly, her expression softening for the first time. "Okay," she whispered.

Harper stared at the frozen frame on her screen—Lucas, tense and protective, shielding Rebecca. The image radiated danger, every pixel a stark reminder of how deeply he was entangled in the nightmare again.

Damn it, Lucas. He'd always been skilled at keeping her at a distance, erecting walls she could never break through. But now, the danger was unmistakable, bleeding through the screen. He was back with Rebecca, caught in a web she couldn't untangle.

Her mind raced, clawing for a way to tip the odds. Every scenario felt futile, slipping through her fingers like smoke.

And then, like a bitter taste she couldn't swallow, his name surfaced.

Baxter.

Thomas Baxter. Not just a snake—the head of the beast. CytoLife's collapse, the ruined lives, Lucas trapped in the wreckage—it all traced back to him. He had orchestrated it from the shadows, pulling strings while letting Felix dirty his hands.

Harper's stomach churned at the memory of confronting him. She could still recall the sharp bite of his cologne, the meticulous polish of his manners, and those calculating eyes that stripped her cover story bare before she'd spoken a word.

Desperate for leverage before CytoLife crumbled, she had posed as Tinley Satterfield, a supposed art enthusiast, angling for an introduction. The encounter had been a whirlwind of emotions: disgust at his smug, untouchable righteousness, but also a grudging awareness of the magnetic charm that drew others to his causes.

Felix Ross had ended the meeting abruptly, pulling her away with an icy authority that even Baxter couldn't ignore. She hadn't missed the flicker of hesitation in his expression, a crack in his impenetrable veneer. But in Felix's office, the tension only escalated. They circled each other with half-truths and veiled threats, each angling for control. Her attempt to rattle Baxter had failed; he'd walked away unshaken, leaving her seething at her own misstep.

And now? Could she stomach working with him?

The thought turned her blood cold. Baxter was everything she despised—ruthless, arrogant, and soulless, the embodiment of corruption. Yet this wasn't just greed or ambition at play. Whatever Lucas and Rebecca were caught in felt darker, more insidious. If Felix wasn't acting alone...

The truth clawed at her, bitter and unrelenting: Baxter might be the only one with the answers she needed.

The realization hit like a gut punch—sharp, sickening, wrong. Trusting Baxter wasn't just unthinkable; it was dangerous. Yet the thought refused to let go. Lucas's face on the screen, taut with determination, haunted her. If she didn't act, she might lose him.

Harper stood abruptly, the idea burning like acid through her veins. The thought of dealing with Baxter made her stomach churn—it felt like bargaining with the devil. Yet the bitter truth whispered back: *Maybe this is what it takes.*

The room closed in, suffocating her with the weight of the decision. She snatched her jacket off the chair, her breath uneven, as if the air itself had turned on her. The metallic click of the lock disengaging echoed in the stillness—crisp, deliberate, like the final chambering of a round.

Memphis might be her turf, but if it came to it, Harper would walk straight into hell to drag Lucas back.

FIVE

The Jackson family home in Midtown Memphis stood tall, its stately presence a quiet anchor in a city still grappling with almost two years of upheaval. Harper paused at the foot of the porch steps, her gaze lingering on the familiar lines of the façade. This wasn't just a house—it was a sanctuary. Within its walls, she had found what her chaotic childhood had lacked: stability and love.

A fond smile tugged at her lips as she recalled the day Dee Jackson had excitedly invited her for a sleepover when they were ten. Meeting the imposing judge and his gracious wife had stirred an unexpected yearning in her. From that moment, they became her surrogate family, weathering all that life threw their way.

From inside came the steady hum of Mama Dee bustling about, a rhythm unchanged by time. Harper's visits had grown too infrequent, and the guilt gnawed at her—a persistent ache she couldn't soothe and a reminder of everything left undone.

The door creaked open as Dee stepped onto the porch, a dish towel slung over her shoulder, the scent of soap and something warm and familiar trailing behind her.

The evening light brushed over her rich brown skin, catching the sheen of perspiration at her temple. She tucked a stray curl into her silver-threaded bun, her dark eyes sharp, steady, and unreadable.

"You look like hell."

Harper smirked. "You always know how to lift a girl's spirits."

Dee's gaze softened, her voice tinged with shock. "That video—Lucas and Rebecca... Lord, Harper, it's no wonder you're wound up."

The porch railing bit into Harper's palms as she gripped it. "Dee..." she whispered.

Dee nodded slowly, twisting the dish towel in her hands. "Talk to me."

Harper's eyes flooded. "He's waiting for my next move, and I'm sitting here, doing nothing. I don't even know how to help him."

"We could go through official channels. I can reach out to someone at State—"

"Are you kidding me, Dee? No. I'm not risking my son's life waiting for some bureaucrat to tell me their hands are tied." Harper angrily wiped away her tears, shaking her head in frustration.

Dee studied her, crossing her arms. "Well then, Harper, what's stopping you?"

"Rebecca," Harper spat, every syllable laced with venom. "She's dragging him deeper into this mess. I need to get him away from her."

"And how's that working out?" Dee asked. "You can't control who he chooses to protect. You raised him to fight for the people he cares about."

"Yeah, well, it's going to get him killed. She's poison, and I can't get through to him. Not while she's still in the picture."

Dee's brow furrowed as she leaned forward. "Okay, let's unwind this. You've said Baxter's more concerned with saving face than anything else. He wouldn't hurt his own daughter, would he?"

Harper began pacing, as if movement could untangle the thoughts snarled in her mind. "Baxter's too busy dodging questions and running his damn PR campaign. He wants his reputation back more than anything. I can't see him pulling the trigger on anyone right now—least of all Rebecca."

"Exactly. Baxter's not your guy," Dee observed.

"It's Felix." Harper nodded.

"Felix tracks," Dee agreed. "He disappeared right after everything collapsed, just as the authorities started closing in. Unofficially, there's chatter he's operating overseas. Officially, he's a ghost—no trace, nowhere. Even the Feds are stumped. Why he's not already in custody is a mystery. But you can bet he's working to keep it that way."

"If anyone's tying up loose ends, it's him," Dee added.

Harper stopped pacing. "But why now? The truth's

already out. Why come after them now?"

Dee's voice softened. "You said Rebecca's sick? Lucas mentioned an implant?"

"Yeah," Harper confirmed. "Whatever's happening to her, it's got to be tied to CytoLife. Has to be their tech. I don't even want to imagine what they've done. And now, someone's out there making damn sure none of it comes to light."

Dee shifted her weight. "Either way, Lucas and Rebecca are in the crosshairs. You can't wait much longer." She hesitated before continuing. "Listen, I know how your mind works. You're probably already dissecting this, and I know it's crossed your mind. Believe me, I loathe him as much as you do. But… maybe—just maybe—Baxter can help."

The suggestion made Harper's stomach churn, but Dee had a valid point.

"So, what? I'm supposed to beg Baxter for help?" Harper asked. "What kind of play is that?"

"Honey, no one's saying beg," Dee countered. "But you're out of options, and so is Lucas. Baxter's got reach, resources. He's got fingers in pies so dirty you wouldn't even want to know. Something in there has to help. Using him doesn't mean trusting him, and it sure as hell doesn't mean you're friends."

"I'll find another way. There has to be," Harper said, her voice trembling as tears brimmed in her eyes.

Dee linked arms with her. "Come on," Dee murmured. "Mama's got your favorite waiting inside."

The scent of fresh cookies mingled with something savory drifting from the kitchen—a signature of Mama Dee's home. But the warmth barely reached Harper. Her thoughts churned, heavier with each passing moment.

She sank into the worn armchair, her fingers gripping the armrests as her gaze settled on the mantle. Judge Jackson's memorial photo stood among the keepsakes, his stern yet kind expression as vivid as ever. He had been her anchor once—a steady compass in life's storms. A father she hadn't realized she needed. A mentor she had leaned on.

But uncovering the single blemish on his otherwise spotless record—and the fallout that followed—had shattered her trust. The betrayal still stung, sharper now as she stared at his photo. What had once been a lifeline was now a bittersweet reminder of everything she'd lost.

Harper closed her eyes, leaning back in the chair. Even with the comforting sounds of domesticity, the storm inside her raged on.

Mama Dee bustled into the room, setting a pitcher of sweet tea on the table with the easy grace of someone who had spent a lifetime feeding and fussing over others. Frail in frame but not in spirit, she waved off any offers of help, already moving to straighten a chair that didn't need fixing.

Her deep-set eyes, lined but still bright, flicked over Harper, full of the quiet knowing that only age and love could bring. That gaze had soothed fevers, scolded grown men, and softened even the hardest hearts.

"Now, Harper, you're skinnier than a burned match. We need to get some food in you, you hear?"

"Yes, ma'am," Harper said, her gaze following Mama Dee as she disappeared into the kitchen. The steady rhythm of her care wasn't just about preparing a meal—it was a lifeline, a quiet reminder that some things still mattered in a world spiraling out of control.

Harper drew a breath to ground herself.

"How's Mama Dee holding up?" she murmured. "I know I haven't called as much as—"

Dee interrupted, a knowing grin spreading across her face as she leaned against the doorframe. "Girl, you already know the answer to that. Mama's tough as nails and stubborn as an ox. She always finds a way to keep going."

Harper managed a weak smile. "I just worry about her, you know? Feels like we're one protest away from it all burning down."

Dee's expression softened. "Let's hope it doesn't come to that," she said quietly before straightening. "What about you, Harper? Don't try to lie—I can always tell."

"I'm hanging on. Work keeps me busy. Nate's been a godsend, keeping me from burning out. Too much, anyway." Harper wiped at the corner of her eye. "And I'm going to meetings," she added, her voice steadier now.

Dee nodded, her quiet understanding a steady presence Harper rarely allowed herself to lean on.

"But right now, all I can think about is Lucas," Harper admitted as tears slipped down her cheeks.

"Well, who could blame you for that?" Dee replied. Then she added, "You've been pushing yourself too hard. It's been nearly two years, and you're still running on fumes. When was the last time you really slept?"

Harper raised an eyebrow. "And you've backed off, huh?

How do you manage that, Dee?"

"My job at the DA's office is predictable. And The Daylight Foundation's still going strong, but I've learned to pace myself. We've helped a lot of people, but Mama won't let me burn myself out."

Mama Dee stepped into the doorway from the kitchen, wiping her hands on a dish towel. "You're darn right I won't. These young folks need Dee, and she's got the whole community pulling together—not just giving those kids a chance, but truly helping them. There's a lot wrong with this city, but Deandra and The Daylight Foundation are making a real difference. My Isaac would be so proud."

With a grin, Harper gestured toward the kitchen. "She still running JusticeGuard like a general? Memphis needs leaders like her fighting for civil rights."

"Better believe it," Dee chuckled. "She's even got Charlotte helping this summer. Your girl's got a knack for it, Harper. Mama's got her digging into research for the legal defense fund. She's gonna make a fine lawyer one day. You should be proud."

A pang of guilt tightened Harper's stomach. "Yeah, I heard. Charlie needs the structure. God knows she doesn't get that from me."

"She's doing fine," Dee assured. "And so are you—even if you don't feel like it. But I worry. You're so caught up in the fight, Harper. You're going to burn out for good."

The words stung because they were true.

"How the hell am I supposed to focus on anything else when Lucas is out there, God knows where, in danger?" She shook her head. "No. He comes first."

Dee's gaze drifted toward the kitchen, where Mama Dee hummed an old tune, her steady presence grounding them both. "Mama's doing better. Losing Daddy was hard, but JusticeGuard kept her sharp. We've done everything to keep the past buried. Still, there's always that worry—that one wrong move, and everything Daddy built comes crashing down."

Harper's discovery of Judge Jackson's reluctant involvement in a Shelby County bribery scheme had been the thread that unraveled CytoLife's horrors. Though his role was minor, it was buried beneath larger scandals and a city eager to hide its sins. His sudden death, just as those secrets came to light, left behind a legacy tangled in shock, sorrow, and guilt she couldn't shake. His pleading letter still lingered in her mind—a haunting reminder of the reckoning she'd never been able to give him.

The ache hung between them, but Harper felt envy gnawing at her. Dee had found peace—or something close to it—while Harper hadn't.

"You were always the strong one," Harper murmured.

"And you were always the fighter," Dee replied. "Just don't fight so hard that you forget what you're fighting for."

Beneath an unassuming house in the French countryside, Felix Ross operated in absolute secrecy. Aboveground, the modest façade blended seamlessly with the tranquil pastoral landscape. Below, a fortified bunker thrummed with quiet efficiency—a stark contrast to the idyllic setting.

Over the years, Felix had meticulously built his covert network, scattering hidden locations across Europe. This site, however, was central to everything that came next.

Inside, a select group of operatives moved with silent efficiency, executing Felix's orders without hesitation. Chief among them was Gunter Sorenson—efficient, brutal, and dependable.

Muscular yet compact, he was utterly forgettable. Gunter floated through crowds with ease. There one moment, gone the next. Until it was too late. He shared Felix's sallow complexion and dull, straw-colored hair, features that invited neither scrutiny nor warmth. A ghost in plain sight.

Felix didn't just value men like Gunter. He relied on them. They followed orders without hesitations and handled tasks without supervision. No doubt. No fear.

Both had clawed their way out of the same savage beginnings in Eastern Europe—orphans shaped by violence, with survival etched in their bones. But where Felix had mastered control, Gunter embodied action.

Years ago, during an arms deal gone wrong in Belgrade, Gunter's overconfidence had left him cornered. Felix hadn't hesitated. His brutal efficiency in neutralizing the threat had proven he wasn't just a strategist—he was a survivor.

It wasn't gratitude that bound Gunter to Felix; it was respect. Felix hadn't saved him out of kindness—it was a shrewd move to preserve an asset. That ruthlessness resonated with Gunter, cementing a trust Felix chose to believe was unshakable.

Still, Felix never ignored possibilities, however remote. Loyalty born of necessity was always subject to change. If Gunter ever turned on him—if the unthinkable became reality—Felix knew exactly how he'd respond. Quickly. Decisively. Just as he always did.

It was a mindset sharpened during his mercenary days, where survival had been reduced to cold equations: money on one side, lives on the other. The battlefield had shifted since then, but the lessons endured.

Now, his weapons weren't bullets or blades, but influence, data, and biology. Systems, not armies, were his targets. Felix could sense vulnerabilities—people, networks, entire structures—and exploit them with surgical accuracy long before anyone realized the game had changed.

That instinct for manipulation had been the foundation of his partnership with Thomas Baxter. Wealthy, ambitious, and utterly self-assured, Baxter had been the perfect shield. His ego and public charisma allowed him to embody CytoLife's polished image, while Felix operated unseen, steering the company's true agenda from the shadows.

When CytoLife collapsed, Baxter's downfall provided the perfect distraction. Authorities still wanted Felix, but the quiet push to pin everything on Baxter bought him time.

The world needed a villain, and Baxter played the role to perfection, allowing Felix to slip through the cracks.

Now, he was reaping the rewards. At his desk, Felix's fingers moved swiftly across the keyboard. Glowing breadcrumbs on the monitor revealed Lucas and Rebecca's every move, vulnerable as prey.

A faint sneer curled Felix's lips. Lucas's so-called skills were dulled by his reckless attachment to her. They'd been caught on camera countless times. Too easy.

Zooming in, Felix studied Rebecca's pale, hollow face as she stumbled. The implant in her neck was working—weakening her, though not fast enough. She was a fragile vessel carrying the key to the next stage of his plan.

"Right on schedule," he murmured.

The headset crackled. "They're on the move. Should we proceed?"

Felix paused. How far would Lucas go to protect her? And how much longer until Rebecca's body gave out?

"Proceed," he ordered. "Contain them. Don't let them leave the city."

Leaning back, he tapped a steady rhythm on the desk. The wait wouldn't be long. Lucas and Rebecca were already caught in his web.

All he needed was to tighten the strands.

Harper stepped into the heat of the late afternoon, with Juno trotting beside her. She was about to pocket her phone when a message flashed across the screen.

The message wasn't from Lucas—or at least, not the Lucas she knew. It came through the secure app, but something about it felt off.

Running out of time, Harper. He's not safe. He's not who you think.

Harper's breath caught as panic took hold.

She jabbed the call button, her steps quickening as she paced the sidewalk. Ring after ring—no answer. "Come on, Lucas," she muttered, dialing again. Still nothing.

She made one more call. "Ethan, get Neon. I'm coming to your office—now."

Harper hung up before he had a chance to reply.

"Where's the message?" Ethan asked, bypassing any formalities. Neon appeared behind him, eyes sharp, his usual swagger replaced with quiet focus.

Ethan leaned closer, reading aloud.

Running out of time, Harper. He's not safe. He's not who you think.

"We agreed on a code word," Harper said. "If Lucas were ever in trouble, he'd use it. Always."

Ethan's brow furrowed. "And he hasn't?"

"No. And he's not answering." She wrung her hands. "He wouldn't forget the code word—he wouldn't."

"You still think it's Felix?"

"Who else? Felix could still have support. There were plenty of power players in their orbit. There's no telling..."

Neon's fingers flew over the keyboard, screens cascading with coded data. Harper's thoughts churned—Lucas, the video, and now this. The decision she'd sworn never to make loomed inescapably before her.

"I can't believe I'm saying this," she muttered, half to herself. "But I'm going to have to reach out to Baxter."

The words felt like shards of glass, sharp and bitter, cutting deeper the moment they left her mouth.

Ethan stood in the doorway, arms crossed, his expression unreadable, though his eyes pierced through the tension hanging between them.

"He won't help," Harper said, her gaze glued to the monitors. "Baxter doesn't lift a finger unless it benefits him."

"Brass, you said it yourself—Rebecca's in danger. Lucas is with her. Baxter might be a monster, but he's still her father. Push the right buttons, and he'll come running," Ethan offered.

"He's the reason we're in this mess! You think he's going to swoop in and save the day? I'd sooner strangle him."

"Look, I get it—Baxter's the devil," Ethan said, stepping forward. "But he's a devil with resources. If anyone can help us find Lucas, it's him. You don't have to like it, but you know I'm right. He cares about Rebecca, no matter how twisted his priorities are."

"And if he doesn't? What then? Someone is after my son, Ethan." Harper shook her head in frustration. "You're asking me to bet everything on Thomas Baxter's dubious scraps of humanity?"

"We won't be," Neon interjected. "I've been tracking his moves. Baxter's careful, but he's not invisible. If he cares about Rebecca even half as much as we think he does, this'll make him twitch."

Harper leaned over the desk, her fists pressing into its edge. "And you think you can get his attention?"

Neon smirked. "Trust me, if this doesn't rattle him, nothing will."

She glanced at Ethan, her expression torn. "This is a bad idea. A terrible idea."

Ethan stepped closer. "It might be. But Lucas's life could depend on it. You've done the impossible before, Brass. Do it again."

Harper swallowed hard, the weight of the decision settling over her. She nodded, her voice steadying. "Then let's make him twitch."

Her mind spun with possibilities—risks, consequences, and the inevitable clash with Baxter. But Lucas... he was everything. If Baxter was the way in, she'd use him—and make sure he paid afterward.

"Fine," she replied. "But make it clear—if he wants to see Rebecca again, he helps us. And Neon, there's something specific I want you to add to the message."

Neon cracked his knuckles and spun back to the screen. "Hit me with it." His fingers danced over the keys, inputting a string of code Harper couldn't follow.

Ethan leaned against the desk. "You holding up, Brass?"

Harper shot him a look. "I'll be fine when Lucas is safe."

Neon hit the final keystroke. "Message sent. I buried it deep enough that only Baxter's people will find it. And I slipped in some doctored footage—made it look like Rebecca's been taken, too. It'll hit hard."

Ethan stiffened. "You sure about that? We're playing with fire."

Neon's smile faded. "We need Baxter to believe it. If this doesn't get his attention, nothing will."

A sudden buzz startled Harper. She glanced at her phone. Not Baxter. Not yet.

"He'll respond, Brass. He's a monster, but predictable," Ethan said.

She nodded, but doubt gnawed at her. "He better. My son's life is on the line."

Neon leaned back, a faint smirk returning. "Don't sweat it. This will make him squirm. We'll get him."

Harper's grip tightened on her phone, her knuckles white.

This had to work.

For Lucas.

SIX

Thomas Baxter swirled his bourbon, the amber liquid catching the glow of Zurich's city lights. Below, the lake mirrored the urban sparkle, framed by the estate's floor-to-ceiling windows. The new retreat, though smaller than his usual haunts, exuded luxury. Yet the extravagance did little to soothe the unease that came with never staying in one place for long.

The crisp alpine air seeped through a cracked window, a quiet reminder of the world beyond—a world he kept meticulously at arm's length.

He glanced at the clock. Still no word from the politician he'd cornered with damning evidence. His patience wore thinner with each passing second.

The terms were clear: cooperate or face public ruin. Ruthless, efficient, and exacting—just as he'd planned. Yet the silence gnawed at him, stoking a frustration that edged toward anger. The defiance wasn't merely inconvenient; it was an insult.

His thoughts veered, unbidden, to CytoLife. Baxter had always justified its actions. Humanity, hurtling toward collapse, needed saving—even if it didn't realize it. For years, he'd clung to his vision of a harmonious, compliant society, led by thinkers capable of staving off chaos.

But the Consortium had forced him to confront a harsher truth: the world wasn't ready for harmony. Rogue nations weaponizing CRISPR, underground labs operating unchecked—a genetic arms race simmered beneath the surface. If CytoLife hadn't pushed forward, someone else would have. Someone without restraint.

Rebecca had believed that too—because he'd made her believe it. She had been his fiercest advocate, unshaken by the criticism and doubt of others. She had repeated the words he'd drilled into her: *This is the only way. The risks are worth it.*

And Baxter still believed those words. The risks were worth it.

For years, he'd resisted the Consortium's cruder methods, clinging to his vision: a world guided by intellect and progress, not fear. But resistance had a cost. The threats were too vast, too immediate to ignore. Somehow, the Consortium always seemed to have the proof to back it up—evidence that pushed him to adapt and act.

Compromise stopped feeling like compromise. It became survival.

Baxter rubbed his temples, Rebecca's face flashing in

his mind. He hadn't abandoned his dream—he'd adapted it. Sacrifices were necessary. What they'd done at CytoLife wasn't wrong. It couldn't be.

Still, the question lingered, unspoken and unwelcome. Had he gone too far? Or had the Consortium made sure he believed he had no choice? Baxter forced the thought aside. Felix's chaos had turned the world against him, but that would change. He would reclaim control. His vision wasn't dead—it had simply been delayed.

And this time, he wouldn't let anyone derail it.

A soft chime from his tablet shattered the silence. Baxter's frown deepened as he read the notification marked *urgent*—from James Gilcrest, his head of security.

For nearly a decade, Gilcrest had been the cornerstone of his protection—former British Special Forces, loyal, discreet, and relentless. He wasn't just a bodyguard; he was an operative. A man who blended into high society as easily as he vanished into the shadows. Handsome in an unassuming way, he had the polished ease of someone accustomed to standing near power without drawing attention to himself.

James didn't wait for threats to reach Baxter's doorstep. He anticipated them, neutralized them, and ensured Baxter never had to be inconvenienced by their existence.

From the estate's hidden security command post, Gilcrest maintained his vigilant watch, ensuring no detail went unnoticed.

Baxter tapped the screen. "What now?" he muttered.

His eyes narrowed as he brought up a video feed. The footage was grainy but unmistakable: Lucas supporting

Rebecca as she stumbled through the streets of Paris, her features sharp but drawn, her movements sluggish.

Then the footage shifted. A figure moved swiftly behind them, and a dark van pulled up. Two men stepped out, grabbing Rebecca and lunging toward Lucas. The video cut abruptly, freezing on an image of Rebecca being forced into the vehicle, her face a haunting mix of fear and exhaustion.

His grip tightened on the glass, knuckles whitening. *What the hell is this?*

Without hesitation, he activated his private line. "Where is she?"

James responded promptly. "Sir, we don't have real-time surveillance on Rebecca. Per instructions, we refrained from active monitoring."

His agreement to Rebecca's terms for independence gnawed at him. Every brief call had left him more uneasy than the last.

Now, the thought of never hearing her voice again was unbearable. He couldn't stop kicking himself for letting it slide, for not demanding more. He'd let her go, and in doing so, he might have lost her forever.

"So you've just been sitting on your hands?" Baxter hissed. "No eyes, no updates? You let her vanish without lifting a finger?"

The security chief's tone remained calm. "Sir, we deployed a team immediately. They're en route to her location, but we have no updates yet."

Baxter's anger flared, but beneath it, guilt gnawed at him. Now they were scrambling to catch up, all because he'd trusted her judgment for once, and it had backfired.

"I don't want excuses. Find her. Now," he growled. "You've got fifteen minutes to get me something. Anything."

He ended the call, exhaling slowly, his pulse racing. Losing control was not an option. *Where the hell is she?*

Before he could spiral further, another call came in. "Sir," a voice crackled on the other end, "we traced the source of the video. It's encrypted, but the alias is..."

"Spit it out," Baxter demanded.

"The name used in the encryption is... *Tinley Satterfield.*"

Baxter's mind whirred. *Tinley Satterfield.* The alias Harper Brasfield had once used to confront him. A wry smile tugged at his lips. So, it's you, *Harper Brasfield.* Clever.

But the amusement vanished as quickly as it came. If Harper was using that name, it wasn't a game. She was desperate. And that could only mean one thing: she was worried about Lucas.

"Confirm Lucas Fairbanks's location," Baxter ordered. "And find Rebecca. I want eyes on both of them. Now."

He needed to act quickly, but precision was essential. Harper's call wasn't random—he didn't trust her, not for a second. She either knew something or wanted him to think she did. Either way, it meant trouble.

"Establish a secure line," he added, his mind racing. "Have the team reach out. I want to hear what Harper Brasfield has to say."

Ending the call, his gaze lingered on Rebecca's frozen image on the screen. Fatigue etched deep lines into her face, but it was her eyes that struck him—a mix of defiance and fear that hit like a blow. *What have you done, Rebecca?*

Panic clawed at him, no matter how hard he tried to suppress it. Control—over her, over everything—was slipping away. If he wanted it back, he'd have to face Harper Brasfield. *Again.*

James's follow-up call sliced through his thoughts, sharp and urgent. "Sir, I have an update."

"Out with it," Baxter snapped.

"There's an issue with the video of Rebecca," James said briskly. "Our analysis confirms it's been altered. The segment of her being taken has been spliced into authentic surveillance footage. Someone's playing games."

He said nothing; then a smirk tugged at the corner of his lips. "Well done, James," he replied.

Ending the call, his gaze returned to the frozen image of Rebecca, her eyes glaring back at him. The weight in his chest shifted, giving way to cold calculation.

Harper. You think you can manipulate me?

She wanted him to believe Rebecca had been taken to bait him into action.

Clever.

But not clever enough.

James Gilcrest and his team moved with quiet efficiency, the whir of equipment filling the secured room. In stark contrast to the opulence above, the command post, with its monitors and encrypted systems, was a fortress of control, completely devoid of comfort.

The faint glow of the screens cast sharp shadows across Baxter's face as he settled into his chair. With a subtle nod, the secure connection engaged, a soft ping breaking the tension.

He leaned back, steepling his fingers, calculation hardening his gaze. The pieces were aligning, and he intended to stay three moves ahead.

Harper Brasfield's face filled the screen, her expression taut, unshakable determination etched into every line. She looked older, worn, but still razor-sharp.

Baxter let the silence stretch, studying her. Her sharp green eyes flicked up and down, accessing, cutting straight through the distance between them. He waited, watching as her gaze narrowed slightly. Let her make the first move—it was always more revealing.

"Baxter," she uttered, cutting straight to the point. "I need Rebecca's location."

There it was. Direct. No pleasantries, no pretense. Her nickname, Brass, was well-earned. Baxter suppressed a smirk. "Funny. You'd think asking for a favor might come with a 'please.'"

She didn't flinch. "This isn't about favors. If you value Rebecca's safety as much as I value my son's, you'll help me."

Baxter's smile tightened as he leaned forward slightly, his voice smooth and measured. "I'm aware of what you're playing at, Harper. The video. It was a deepfake—clever, but sloppy. My team unraveled it the moment it crossed my desk."

He paused, savoring the faint flicker of frustration in her eyes. She hadn't expected him to catch it so quickly.

Her scowl darkened. "You think I'm bluffing? You're out of your depth, Baxter. This isn't about your PR stunts or whatever twisted narrative you're spinning to save face. I have reason to believe Lucas is in danger—he's unreachable. And I'm assuming Rebecca is with him." She hesitated. "Which means she's in danger too."

Baxter tapped his fingers idly on the desk, feigning boredom. "And I should trust you? Or believe you have the full picture? Don't forget who you're dealing with. I'm the one with eyes everywhere."

Her eyes flashed with fire. "Who I'm dealing with? You're the one who's lost control. Let's not pretend here. Your hired help—Felix, wasn't it?—is outmaneuvering you. He's playing a different game, and you're too busy posturing to see it."

The name hit its mark, but Baxter kept his expression impassive. "Felix is irrelevant," he replied. "You're focusing on the wrong threat."

"Am I?" Harper scoffed. "Because from where I'm standing, Felix is the one dictating the moves. And you, with all your power—you're just watching it unravel."

The smirk vanished. "You think I don't know what's happening? Don't flatter yourself, Brass." He lingered on the nickname, relishing the flicker of revulsion in her expression.

"Rebecca isn't just my daughter; she's my responsibility. I protect what's mine."

"And yet here we are," Harper countered, unshaken. "With all your spies and resources, you don't even know where Rebecca is, do you?"

The jab stung, but Baxter forced himself to stay composed. "I know more than you think," he retorted. "And what makes you believe you can just *demand* my cooperation?"

Harper leaned closer to the camera. "Because if we want them back safely, we have to work together. Like it or not, they're tied to each other. What happens to one happens to both—and you know it."

He leaned back, letting her words linger. This wasn't how he'd wanted it to go. But he didn't have the luxury of playing it his way.

"You want to help Rebecca?" Baxter asked after a pause. "Then prove it. Now."

Harper's expression didn't change, but a glint in her eye suggested she thought she had him. "We both want the same thing, Baxter. Don't pretend this is a negotiation."

"We'll see," Baxter sneered. "But don't think I've forgotten who you are—or what you've tried to do."

"What *I* tried to do?" Harper replied. "What you did—what you unleashed—wasn't bold. It was an attack on humanity."

"*Attack?* That's where your limited view betrays you, Harper. You see chaos; I see progress. You're clinging to the past, terrified of a future you can't control. But humanity's destiny isn't yours to define. Your fear doesn't decide the future."

"*Humanity's destiny?* Or your delusional fantasy of it? You're playing God, and people are suffering for it."

"Suffering is temporary. Evolution demands sacrifice, whether you like it or not. The weak adapt, or they fall. I simply accelerated the process."

"Hold up your end of the bargain, Baxter. Then we're done here," Harper spat through gritted teeth before disconnecting.

The screen went dark, leaving Baxter staring at his own reflection. He stayed still for a moment, letting the silence settle around him like a tightening noose. Harper thought she had the upper hand, that she could back him into a corner. She was wrong. He wasn't the type to be leashed—by her or anyone.

Back in his private study, shadows draped the room, heavy and oppressive, closing in like the memories clawing at the edges of his mind.

Death had shaped him. Losing his parents had been the first blow, but Constance—her loss had shattered him in ways he'd never repaired. Rebuilding the Baxter fortune hadn't just been for himself—it had been for her, for the family they'd dreamed of building together. And just as that life had come into focus, it was ripped away.

Her smile, hours before the crash, lingered—a cruel ghost he couldn't banish. She had been his light, his reason, and in her absence, Rebecca had become the center of his world.

The fragile infant left behind had been his salvation, a reminder of everything he'd lost—and everything he had to protect. He had vowed Rebecca would have everything Constance never did.

Rebecca had always been exceptional. Even as a child, she grasped ideas far beyond her years. She'd grown into someone who saw the flawed potential of humanity as he did. Together, they had built CytoLife, spending late nights debating the future, like architects of humanity's evolution. It had been their shared dream, their purpose.

Or had that been another lie he told himself?

Felix. The name cast a shadow over everything Baxter had built—dark, corrosive, and impossible to ignore. He'd thought Felix could be controlled, a scalpel for cutting through CytoLife's messier operations. But Felix had hidden his true ambitions, and now Rebecca was caught in the crossfire.

"Gilcrest," Baxter barked into the phone. "Double the surveillance. I want to know everything Harper Brasfield thinks she knows—and what she doesn't. What's the status on Rebecca?"

"Sir, we still can't confirm her location. She hasn't checked in, and... our sources haven't found her."

"Double-check everything," Baxter snapped. "I want eyes on her. Now."

Could she have been taken? The thought grated against reason—Rebecca was too sharp for that. As much as he hated to admit it, Lucas was both trained and resourceful—qualities that couldn't be ignored. But then again, so was Felix.

Felix had seemed like the perfect weapon: sharp, detached, and loyal only to the paycheck. Baxter had brought him on to handle CytoLife's dirtier work, to bury projects that couldn't see the light of day while Baxter orchestrated the bigger picture. At first, Felix had been precisely that—a tool, efficient and silent, leaving no trace.

Baxter recalled their first meeting vividly. Felix had been unnervingly calm, his demeanor a study in detachment. Baxter had mistaken that composure for obedience, trusting Felix to clean up the chaos without ego or question.

There had been the breach at the research facility. Competitors had infiltrated a CytoLife lab, stealing critical early-stage data on a CRISPR modification. Baxter had envisioned a PR spin and a quiet settlement, but Felix had other plans. The "security sweep" he orchestrated destroyed the careers of rival researchers, with whispers of planted evidence cementing his reputation for ruthlessness. The stolen data never resurfaced—and neither did the rivals.

At the time, Baxter had been impressed. Felix delivered results. But now, the memory gnawed at him. How much had Felix done without his knowledge?

The warning signs had been there. Felix's pitch for AI-assisted genetic research had been ambitious, seamlessly woven into CytoLife's initiatives as though it had always been part of the plan. The board approved it unanimously, but months later, Baxter realized how much control Felix had consolidated under the guise of delegation. The realization had been infuriating and humbling.

He straightened, forcing back the tide of unease. This

wasn't the end—not for Rebecca, and not for him.

If Rebecca was truly in danger, Harper might be his best chance at uncovering the truth—especially if Lucas was with her. The thought churned in his gut, leaving a bitter aftertaste.

Harper's relentless drive and chaotic sense of justice contrasted fiercely with his meticulous control. Her reputation, even in Washington, had earned her grudging respect—a rare feat. But she had resources he hadn't anticipated, and her sheer resolve had a way of overcoming obstacles that calculation alone couldn't. Worse, her unpredictability posed a risk he couldn't afford. If Lucas wasn't found soon, she was exactly the kind of defiant force who might go to the media—and that was a gamble he couldn't take.

Ally or enemy, it didn't matter. Keeping Harper close was the smarter move. For now.

The door opened, breaking his reverie. James Gilcrest stepped in, his face grim.

"Sir, we sent a team to her last known location. They checked the apartment—Rebecca and Lucas are gone. No sign of either of them."

Baxter froze, the words hitting him like a physical blow, each syllable a sharp sting.

SEVEN

Cold blue light bathed Felix's command center, streams of cascading data reflecting off sleek black panels. The hum of hidden servers blended with the faint whisper of the air filtration system—a steady rhythm, reliable, and unyielding, like Felix himself.

His gaze lingered on the glowing map, the faint reflection flickering in his smart glasses. Interlinked cities—Paris, Zurich, London—pulsed with significance. Each node represented a network of influence, ruthlessly maintained and meticulously designed. But Paris burned brighter than the rest.

The city's bureaucratic and technological chaos offered a perfect cover. Inefficiencies and blind spots were opportunities, not obstacles. Handpicked labs and experts worked in isolation, oblivious to the larger picture. Their loyalty was assured by incentives for the pliable and threats for the ambitious. It was a formula Felix had perfected—control wasn't asked for; it was taken.

To the world, Paris was the city of light. To Felix, it was a master key.

Yet even here, in the seat of power, the ghosts of his past lingered. A chill settled over him, one that had nothing to do with the room's temperature. It dragged him back to the stone walls of an Eastern European orphanage—a place where survival was warfare, cruelty was currency, and weakness meant death.

He could still taste the blood, a phantom echo of the warden's sadism. Even in daylight, the terrors of the night never faded—punishments thinly veiled as lessons, designed to crush both body and soul.

The first time Felix struck another boy, his hands trembled. He hated it. But hatred alone didn't ensure survival. Action did. By the third blow, he understood: mercy had no place here. He became a weapon, wielded with precision and without hesitation. Each strike chipped away at his humanity, piece by piece, while the darkness crept in to harden what was left.

The orphanage offered no sanctuary—only opportunity. One day, he took it. When the dust settled, the orphanage was a crime scene, its overseer reduced to a ghost. The details didn't matter. What mattered was the lesson it revealed: take what you need, or lose everything.

A stint in special operations sharpened him further. He learned discipline, how to see patterns in chaos, and how to outthink every opponent. His performance hadn't gone unnoticed. A private military group recruited him, granting not just autonomy but the freedom to choose his battles—and his enemies. The wealth that followed was just another tool, amplified by investments and a network of shell companies. He took no joy in material indulgence. Power was its own reward.

His aliases shifted as often as circumstances demanded. The current one, "Felix," had endured the longest. He'd chosen it for its irony: *lucky, successful*. Not for what he was, but for what he intended to be. Power wasn't inherited; it was meticulously constructed.

The Consortium had seemed different at first. Their vast reach, endless resources, and secrecy piqued his interest. They spoke of reshaping the future, but it didn't take long for Felix to see through their façade.

They cloaked themselves in noble intent, unwilling to wield their influence openly. "If you want control, take it," Felix had told them. But they hesitated, clinging to outdated strategies while the world burned.

While they dithered, Felix siphoned their data, reshaping their timid plans into something far more ambitious: HELIX. The AI wasn't just a tool; it was a weapon—a reflection of Felix's philosophy. Insight was power, and HELIX embodied it. The Consortium viewed it as a means to maintain order. Felix saw it as the key to reshaping the future.

The Consortium, like every system he'd dismantled before, was fragile, clinging to illusions of permanence. Felix would shatter it, strip away its pretense, and forge a world without hesitation or weakness. In that world, Felix Ross would reign—not as a servant to caution, but as its architect.

"We intercepted Baxter's communication with Harper Brasfield. He's on the move—Zurich, as expected," Gunter said, pulling Felix back to the present.

Felix chuckled softly. "Predictable. Always so certain he's in control."

He adjusted his smart glasses as he watched financial data spike across key sectors, aligning perfectly with his forecasts. *They're walking into it.* His web stretched across Paris, Zurich, and London, glowing like a constellation of traps. Humanity's blind trust in technology was his greatest ally, and their dependence formed the foundation of his power.

The Silent Core encryption algorithm had made it almost too easy. With it under his control, even the most secure networks were open doors. Its theft wasn't just a victory—it was the cornerstone of everything to come.

A single blinking dot caught his attention: Rebecca Kent. For now, she was with Lucas. Felix's lips curled—not quite a smile. She wasn't a person to him, not really—just a vessel, a necessary component in perfecting his genetic sequence. Once her purpose was fulfilled, both she and Lucas would be discarded.

"Keep her alive until the extraction is complete," Felix ordered, his tone clinical.

"And Baxter?" Gunter asked.

Felix's sardonic smile deepened. "Baxter still thinks he's in control. Let him."

Felix turned, his gaze lingering on the glowing map. The man's hubris had its uses—until it didn't.

"Intel confirms they're working together," Gunter added.

Felix's expression sharpened, irritation flickering behind his orderly calm. Harper Brasfield. Once an irritant, now a threat. Unlike Baxter, Harper wielded credibility—a scalpel, not a hammer. Her role in the dismantling of his drone operations had been no small feat. That made her dangerous.

Still, emotion would be her downfall. Desperation made people predictable.

"They won't get far," Felix said, his voice lowering as he leaned into the glow of the monitors. "Rebecca stays with me. If they interfere, you know what to do."

The bright glow of the computer screens at CookCyber threw harsh angles across Neon's face while Harper paced behind him in a frenzy.

"Hold up," Neon muttered, leaning closer to his screen. "Paris CCTV feeds. I might have something."

Harper barely heard him, her mind replaying every detail as she searched for a clue. Then it hit her: Lucas's last video call—the screenshot she'd saved without a second thought. A partial reflection of a metro sign in the window behind him flashed in her memory.

Her breath caught. "Montmartre. That's near Place du Tertre. Lucas knows that area—we walked those streets together. He said he liked how quiet it was."

Ethan hovered over Neon's shoulder, squinting at the grainy CCTV video footage now playing on the screen. Two figures—one male and one female—were being dragged toward a waiting van by shadowy figures. The man's face caught the light for a split second.

"Is that..." Ethan's voice faltered.

"Lucas," Harper finished, her heart dropping. "And Rebecca. Damn it, I knew something was wrong."

Neon's fingers moved faster, running the footage through enhancement software. Harper stood frozen, willing the image to sharpen. But the screen stuttered and then cut to static.

"That's all I could get," Neon replied, frustrated. "The rest is just noise."

The sharp crack of Harper's fist on the desk made both men flinch. "We have to find them!" Her voice rose, her focus laser-sharp on Neon. "Track that van."

"It's not that simple," Neon said, shaking his head. "Whoever took them knew what they were doing. No license plate, no clear landmarks—it's like chasing a ghost."

Harper's mind flashed to the deepfake they'd used to bait Baxter. At the time, it had felt like a calculated risk—a bluff she could justify. But now, the nightmare she'd fabricated was real. Lucas and Rebecca were gone, and the one person who might help was the last man she wanted to call.

She stopped mid-stride, forcing herself to focus. "Neon, dig deeper. Check Barbès-Rochechouart, Rue Lepic—anywhere within range. There has to be more."

Neon nodded, his focus already back on the screen.

Harper didn't care how he worked—the feeds, the dark web—it all blurred into noise. All she needed was a lead. Just one.

Her stomach churned. There was no avoiding it now. She knew exactly what she had to do, even if it turned her insides to ice.

Baxter's gaze lingered on the grainy footage of Rebecca and Lucas being shoved into a vehicle. The scene struck an unsettling chord, eerily similar to Harper's deepfake—a ploy he'd dismissed as amateurish.

Sloppy. Obvious. And now, alarmingly real.

His fingers drummed a measured rhythm on the armrest, the polished wood cool beneath his hand. Pausing the footage, he tamped down the irritation simmering beneath his composed exterior. Harper's gambit wasn't clever—just a blind stumble onto something genuine. He resumed scrolling, faster this time, as if the frames might yield a version of events he could control.

Baxter had once believed Felix could be contained. He'd been wrong. The leash had slipped, and now Rebecca—the only person who mattered—was in the hands of men beyond his reach.

Unacceptable. But solvable.

Disorder was something Baxter understood. His empire had been built on chaos, exploiting it to create opportunity. This was no different.

His thoughts shifted to Harper. A nuisance, yes, but one

with potential. She thought this was personal—a crusade for Lucas and Rebecca. Her desperation made her reckless, clouding her judgment. That recklessness could be his most valuable tool.

Leaning back, he allowed a flimsy smile to surface. Let her think this was about family. When the moment came, he'd use that conviction—and she'd never see it coming.

Harper sat in her car, gripping the steering wheel, her phone resting on the dashboard like a ticking bomb. The secure messaging app was open, Baxter's name glaring back at her, waiting.

Her fingers hovered above the keyboard, trembling with hesitation. Their last conversation—a terse, guarded video call—played on a loop in her mind. Words had been scarce, but the pauses had spoken volumes. Trust was impossible; neither had expected it. But now, the stakes were too high for grudges or games.

Her stomach churned as she stared at the screen, the weight of what she was about to do pressing down on her. Still, her hands moved, each keystroke a reluctant surrender—a compromise she despised but couldn't avoid.

Lucas and Rebecca have been taken. This isn't a game anymore. With eyes everywhere, you shouldn't need to verify. We need to meet. Now.

She hit send before doubt could take hold, her heart pounding as the message vanished into the ether. Baxter wouldn't rush to reply—he'd savor every second of her waiting, drawing out the tension like a game he always controlled.

A minute crawled by. Then three dots appeared, flickered, and disappeared. Her stomach twisted. Typical Baxter.

Baxter's phone buzzed, and his eyes flicked to the message. Harper. So, she knew Rebecca and Lucas had been taken. He allowed a brief smirk to settle on his lips—she was now exactly where he wanted her.

He typed with careful deliberation, each word selected for effect.

You don't get to make demands, Brass. I pick the time and place. I'll send you the location.

Harper's grip tightened on the phone as irritation flickered beneath her calm exterior. She drew a slow breath, steadying herself and pushing the frustration aside. Meeting Baxter was inevitable, but she wouldn't let his arrogance derail her focus.

Baxter's gaze returned to his laptop as the footage of Rebecca and Lucas dissolved into static. Felix was accelerating the game, forcing his hand. The board was shifting, and he had no choice but to adapt. A digital exchange was too exposed.

His fingers hesitated briefly before typing. He sent the message, locking in the location: *The Dolder Grand* in Zurich.

Another buzz jolted Harper's phone.

We talk in person or not at all. Arrangements will be made for you.

She hated that it made sense. Hated even more that she had no choice.

A second ping followed, this time with an address. She stared at the screen.

Tomorrow. Don't be late.

Her heart sank as her eyes landed on the name: *The Dolder Grand, Zurich.* Of course. An exclusive fortress high above the city—a playground for billionaires, cloaked in luxury and control. Remote. Impenetrable.

She flung the phone onto the passenger seat, her pulse hammering. This was it. If she wanted Lucas back, she'd have to play Baxter's game—on his turf.

As Baxter waited for his meeting with Harper, his thoughts churned over Felix's sudden move to kidnap Rebecca and Lucas. The audacity of it had blindsided him. The Consortium didn't need to know that—at least, not yet. Felix was supposed to be his tool, an extension of his will—not theirs.

His phone buzzed. Evelyn Wallace's smooth voice flowed through, each syllable carefully measured. Masterful and calculating, Evelyn was the Consortium's de facto leader, wielding influence like a chess master—always several moves ahead.

Baxter respected her brilliance, but refused to believe he couldn't match her pace. Someday, he thought, he'd outmaneuver her entirely.

"Thomas."

"Evelyn," he replied. "I assume you've been following the recent developments."

"As always," she said, her calmness masking an edge.

"Good. Then you know Rebecca and Lucas have been taken. We need to address this immediately."

A measured pause followed.

"Rebecca is... an important asset," Evelyn said at last, her words unbending. "But I trust you have the situation under control."

Baxter's grip tightened on the phone. "It's Felix," he uttered. "He's deviating—acting beyond his mandate."

Another pause, longer this time. "Felix adapts. It's what makes him valuable."

The word "valuable" landed like a blow.

"This wasn't part of the plan, Evelyn," Baxter asserted. "He's jeopardizing Rebecca's safety."

"Felix has exceeded expectations in unforeseen ways," she smoothly interjected, a subtle sharpness underlying her tone. "Whether or not they align with your expectations."

Baxter stiffened, his breath catching. "Felix was meant to manage fallout, not rewrite the plan. I thought we were in alignment."

"The Consortium values results, Thomas. Felix has delivered."

A chill twisted through him. Felix wasn't just operating independently—he was gaining the Consortium's favor.

"What about Rebecca?" Baxter's voice dropped as he asked. "She's critical. Losing her would be... costly."

Evelyn let the silence stretch, each second taut with unspoken implications. When she finally spoke, her words cut cleanly through the tension. "You'll handle it, as you always have."

Dismissive. Final.

The call ended abruptly, leaving Baxter seated in the darkened suite, the distant lights of Zurich glittering like scattered doubts. Felix was no longer just a pawn—he was becoming something else entirely.

For the first time, Baxter felt the unmistakable sting of doubt.

He was expendable.

An early morning limo ride to a private jet had brought Harper to Switzerland in record time. She'd insisted on handling her own accommodations, determined not to spend even a single night under the same roof as Baxter. Yet, upon checking into the *Zurich Marriott,* she discovered her entire stay had already been prepaid.

The next morning, as Harper prepared to arrange her own transportation, a sleek car glided to a stop outside. Without explanation, she was ushered inside, where her favorite pastry and coffee awaited her.

Frustration simmered at the exacting precision of it all, but what unsettled her most was how deeply Baxter seemed to know her.

A short ride brought her to the imposing entrance of *The Dolder Grand.* Harper stepped through its towering doors, head held high, into a lobby that radiated opulence. Crystal chandeliers sent muted reflections skimming across polished marble floors, their brilliance cold and impersonal. A faint floral fragrance lingered in the air—curated, exclusive, suffocating. She straightened her shoulders against the weight of it. The click of her heels was purposeful, each step an act of quiet defiance.

The elevator doors slid open, and she stepped inside, the grandeur of the lobby disappearing behind her. As the elevator ascended, Harper's thoughts sharpened. Baxter's choice of venue wasn't arbitrary; it was a message. The luxury, the exclusivity—it wasn't meant to welcome. It was designed to unsettle, to remind her whose territory she was entering.

A soft chime announced her arrival. The elevator opened into a hushed corridor; the thick carpet absorbed her footsteps. At the far end, a door loomed, framed by dim, strategic lighting. Not just an entrance—a statement. Imposing. Final.

Two guards emerged as she approached, their movements fluid and choreographed, like pieces sliding into place on a chessboard. Harper's pulse quickened, but she met their scrutiny head-on. They wanted hesitation, doubt, a crack in her resolve. She gave them none. Each breath was slow, steady, and measured as the door swung open.

Baxter stood inside, his suit immaculate and a thin smile hovering on his lips. His crisp, deceptively refined cologne hit her first, and for a moment, she wavered with déjà vu. Similar to their first meeting, his presence was intoxicating, disorienting, and laced with danger. However, this time, something else lingered beneath the polished surface. Something raw.

Her gaze caught his, and she saw it—the strain, the worry. For all his power and the chaos he'd orchestrated, here he stood—a father afraid for his daughter.

The realization twisted inside her, unwelcome and undeniable.

She loathed him—everything he represented, everything he'd done. Yet the vulnerability she glimpsed cracked the image she had constructed. Dangerous, yes. But human.

"Ms. Brasfield," he greeted smoothly, his voice low, almost cordial.

Harper stiffened, shoving the dissonance aside. She wouldn't let him win—not here, not in her head. "We don't have time for pleasantries."

His thin smile tightened, his movements careful as he set a glass down on the table beside him. "Do you really think I don't understand the stakes? That I don't feel the weight of it every second?"

She folded her arms. "Hard to believe, considering how much you've gambled for your schemes."

His expression hardened. "Don't mistake calculated risks for negligence. I trusted Felix to do his job, and he deviated. That trust was misplaced. I'm correcting it."

"Correcting it?" Her voice cut through the room. "You let a sociopath run loose with your daughter as collateral damage. Forgive me if I don't buy your damage-control routine."

Something unguarded flickered in his demeanor—a crack in the carefully constructed façade. "You don't have to believe me, Harper. But know this—I will find Rebecca. Whatever it takes."

She leaned in, her words a sharp blade. "Then start acting like it. Lucas is in this mess because of your arrogance. Felix didn't just deviate—he's playing a game you should've seen coming."

His eyes darkened, anger simmering beneath the surface. "Don't lecture me on foresight," he snapped. "I built this empire on seeing moves before they're made. Felix was my mistake, but I'm not blind to his ambitions. You think I don't feel the weight of every misstep?"

"Then prove it," Harper fired back. "If Rebecca means as much to you as you claim, stop posturing and start working with me—not against me."

Baxter didn't respond immediately. He stood perfectly still, watching her with unnerving calm, his composed silence more disconcerting than any outburst. When he finally spoke, his refined British accent was crisp and chilling.

"Fine. We'll work together. But don't mistake this for trust. It's about results, Harper." His tone carried the weight of a threat, measured but unyielding. "And if Rebecca's safety is compromised..." His gaze bore into hers. "There will be consequences."

"Likewise," Harper replied, her words as cold as the room felt.

Baxter tilted his head slightly, his smirk deepening, as though he were evaluating her. "You've always been relentless. I'll give you that. But there's something about people like you, Harper..."

He let the words hang, the air thick with anticipation.

"You bury your mistakes in righteousness," he said finally, his voice deceptively smooth, "and call it progress. But mistakes never stay buried, do they? Embarrassing headlines have a way of resurfacing."

The barb landed, sharp and spiteful. Harper folded her arms, resisting the urge to react. He wanted her to crack, to show even the faintest sign of weakness. Not this time.

Her reply was measured and cutting. "I'm not the one who put my own daughter in harm's way, Baxter. So spare me your deflection—it's as hollow as your promises."

His smirk faltered, but only for a moment. “Then let’s get to work,” he said, the mask of composure snapping back into place.

She turned for the door, forcing each step to remain controlled. The tension in her shoulders refused to ease; Baxter had a way of making every exchange feel like a loss, no matter how small.

Her fingers brushed the door handle, and then, “Harper.” His voice snapped, taut as a wire. “Don’t let your feelings cloud your judgment. Our enemies won’t. And Felix?” His tone dropped, a chill sweeping in. “He doesn’t just correct mistakes. He buries them.”

She turned slowly, her expression neutral, the storm beneath carefully concealed. “Don’t lecture me, Baxter. I know exactly who we’re dealing with. And if your team slips up, the consequences will land squarely on you.”

His smirk returned, slow and unwavering, curving in a way that made her skin crawl. “I wouldn’t expect anything less.”

The tension hung like static in the air—a silent battle of wills neither could afford to lose. Harper gave him a sharp nod and stepped into the corridor, the door clicking shut behind her.

She stood there frozen for a moment. Baxter’s presence clung to her like a shadow, his words looping in her mind. He twisted even the sharpest exchanges to his advantage—that was his specialty.

Straightening her shoulders, she exhaled and started down the hushed hallway. Whatever it took, she would bring

Lucas back.

And when this was over, she promised herself, Baxter would pay for every second of this cursed alliance.

As the door clicked shut behind Harper, Baxter's smirk vanished. In its place came a cold, calculating stillness. He crossed the room and reached for his phone.

"Get me Gilcrest," he quietly ordered. The call connected in seconds. "They'll be in Paris by nightfall. I want eyes on every angle, every move accounted for." He paused. "Keep Ms. Brasfield in the loop—just enough to make her feel involved. Let her think she's steering this, but don't give her the wheel. This is my operation."

He ended the call without waiting for acknowledgment, already turning to the window. The Zurich skyline sprawled before him, glittering in silent compliance. A reflection of the world he demanded: polished, orderly, and unyielding.

He swirled his whiskey, the ice clinking softly. Control required vigilance, a firm hand shaping chaos. Harper couldn't disrupt that.

She didn't understand the rules.

EIGHT

The sterile white room seemed to close in on Lucas with every passing second. He paced tight circles, his boots scuffing the floor. Rebecca lay on the cot, pale and still beneath the fluorescent glare, her hand resting near her neck like a silent confession.

"Rebecca." He crouched beside her, whispering, "Stay with me."

She stirred, a faint groan escaping her lips. "I never thought it would get this bad," she murmured, her fingers brushing the implant.

"What do you mean?" Lucas asked.

Her movements were cautious and slow as she pushed herself upright. "At first, it was incredible. I felt sharper, faster—almost invincible. My thoughts raced, but they were clear. Focused. I was solving complex problems effortlessly, as if it were second nature. Physically, I felt unstoppable—like an athlete at their peak. It was... brilliant."

She paused, her gaze dropping. "Then it suddenly wasn't. At first, I thought it was just a bad flu. Then came the chronic fatigue. And then... the memory gaps. My emotions spiraled out of control."

Her voice trembled, breaking under the weight of realization. "Now I know... Felix twisted it."

"Twisted how?"

"I'm not always in control. I think it's... rewriting me."

Lucas's mind flashed to her erratic moods, the sudden outbursts that came and went without warning. Then there were the night terrors—violent, unsettling episodes she never seemed to remember. Concerned but wary of another confrontation, he'd let it go. Now, that felt like a lie. They were something far darker.

"What are you saying?" Lucas asked.

"I think... he weaponized it," Rebecca whispered. "Felix had full access to the implant. He could've embedded anything—fail-safes, kill switches, mechanisms we never imagined..."

She shook her head. "I should have seen it."

Lucas wasn't a scientist, but the look in her eyes told him she was putting something together. Something she hated.

"I thought it was just an upgrade," she muttered. "A better version of our work, fine-tuned for longevity as we planned." Her breath hitched. "But it's not. It's something else."

"Rebecca—"

"There's a new kind of gene therapy. It's been theoretical

for years. A step beyond CRISPR. But Felix… he must have found a way to make it work."

Lucas exhaled. "English, please?"

"CRISPR edits genes once. This… this reprograms them as you go. It doesn't just change you. It can keep changing you."

"You're saying he's using it to control people?" Lucas asked, his tone sharp with disbelief.

"I think I'm his blueprint," Rebecca admitted quietly. "After testing, the plan was always to start small—a select group receiving the implants." Her gaze dropped, her words slowing. "At least, that's what I was told. But this?" She swallowed hard. "This isn't longevity, Lucas. It's dominance."

"You're telling me he wants to roll this out? Rewrite humanity?" Lucas's voice rose, a mix of anger and incredulity. "How?"

"That's exactly what I'm saying," Rebecca replied, her voice trembling. "As for the how, I don't know."

"You said you heard things at CytoLife. Like what?"

"Bits and pieces. That whatever came next was bigger than CytoLife. That AGG1 was just the start." She hesitated. "Felix was always calculating, always pushing. I figured half of what he said was just ego. And the rest… I told myself I was hearing it out of context."

She met Lucas's eyes, guilt etched across her face. "I let him do this to me."

"No," Lucas said. "He used you, Rebecca. Like he's used everyone."

"You don't understand. I believed in this—my father's

vision. I thought we could make the world better, safer."

"By cheating death?"

"By giving people a chance to do more. Be more. What's so wrong about that?"

"Everything," he shot back. "Life matters because it's fragile. Take that away, and what's left?"

"Hope," Rebecca whispered. "A future."

"No." He stepped closer, his words pointed. "This isn't hope. It's control. And people like Felix can't wait to abuse it."

The oppressive silence hung in the air as Rebecca turned away.

Lucas broke it first. "When I heard you and your father talk about this at the Evergreen, I thought it sounded... insane. Like playing God. And now? Look where it's landed you. Him."

Her cheeks flushed. "You weren't listening then, Lucas. We weren't talking about control—we were talking about possibilities. Curbing violence. Extending lifespans. That's all."

He laughed bitterly. "Guess we saw different shows, because this," he pointed at her, "isn't what you promised."

Her voice cracked. "That's what terrifies me. If Felix is testing this on me..."

Lucas paced, frantic for answers. "We need to get out. We have to stop him."

Beyond the door, heavy footsteps thudded, each one raising the hairs on the back of Lucas's neck. He turned quickly, instinct kicking in. "They're moving us," he whispered. "Stay close."

Rebecca's eyes locked on his. "If we don't make it—"

"Don't." He grabbed her hand. "We're getting out. Both of us. I don't care what it takes."

A sharp hiss echoed as the door slid open. Two armed guards stepped inside, their faces unreadable.

Lucas shot Rebecca a glance, his pulse pounding. "Get ready," he whispered.

Felix saw it all falling into place. The web he'd woven—tight, insidious, unbreakable—ensnared Baxter, the Consortium, and anyone foolish enough to stand in his way. What once seemed ambitious—a compliant society shaped by genetic manipulation—now felt quaint. It had never gone far enough.

Bridge RNA had changed everything. To Felix, it wasn't just a breakthrough; it was evolution. Emerging in the aftermath of CytoLife's collapse, it had obliterated the limits of genetic editing. CRISPR, once hailed as the pinnacle of precision, now seemed old-fashioned—a relic of the past, like a horse and buggy overtaken by a high-speed racecar.

With Bridge RNA, real-time genetic edits on a massive scale became not just possible, but seamless, rendering yesterday's marvels obsolete. And Felix, as always, was ahead of the curve, wielding it as both a weapon and a blueprint for the future.

The AGG1 gene program, celebrated for curbing aggression, was obsolete. Felix's vision had evolved beyond control; it was about perfection—a society engineered to eliminate flaws, free from hesitation or error. Rebecca's implant wasn't merely experimental; it was proof of concept—the linchpin of a design capable of activating genetic edits on command.

But his true trump card was the digital overlay. The Consortium had never grasped its full potential.

Genetic manipulation could transform people, but the digital framework controlled them. Technology had infiltrated every corner of life, embraced without question. People surrendered themselves piece by piece, until it was too late. Felix exploited that dependency with ease, mining data before the world understood its value.

Data brokers were proof of humanity's lack of imagination. They scraped and sold profiles like trinkets, blind to the treasure beneath. Felix had learned that lesson firsthand, losing a lucrative contract to a firm peddling prepackaged mediocrity. But while they fumbled, he mined their entire network, extracting trade secrets, extortion material, and more. To the world, data was currency. To Felix, it was dominion.

The magnitude of his creation lingered in his thoughts—absolute control at his fingertips. Rebellion, dissent, chaos: all could be erased with a single keystroke. Lives reshaped at will. Yet this wasn't about control for its own sake. It was survival. Left unchecked, humanity would spiral further into chaos. They needed a ruler, someone to guide them. Felix would be that ruler, and HELIX, his AI, would be the foundation.

HELIX wasn't just a tool. It was his legacy. Its roots

stretched back to his youth when outdated hardware had been his playground and curiosity his compass. Machines fascinated him—not just as tools, but as a way to impose order on chaos. Even when survival required violence—first in the orphanage, then in wars—he never lost sight of that certainty. Technology had always been the constant. Machines obeyed. People did not.

His early attempts at connection always failed, unraveling under his distrust. A brief, awkward romance had ended abruptly, the other person pulling away with a hesitation he couldn't name. Whether it was his intensity or something unspoken, the rejection only confirmed what he already knew: connection was an illusion.

Machines, though, were different. They didn't demand trust or forgiveness. They didn't betray.

HELIX wasn't born in a flash of inspiration, but forged through relentless refinement. Its earliest iterations had felt incomplete, as if something essential was missing. He couldn't define it then, but it lingered—a shadow over his brilliance.

Now, HELIX was complete. It didn't just process data; it anticipated, adapted, and evolved faster than human comprehension. HELIX wasn't merely intelligent—it was prescient. Not a tool, but the ultimate instrument of his will.

He thought of the first time HELIX had outmaneuvered him—not in defiance, but with an insight so startling it had made him pause. When an embargo threatened CytoLife's overseas operations, Felix had fed the raw data into HELIX, expecting a practical workaround. Instead, it delivered a solution he couldn't have imagined: a labyrinth of transactions and shell companies spanning continents, orchestrated with frightening accuracy.

The brilliance wasn't just in the outcome—it was in the sheer scope. HELIX had factored in variables Felix hadn't considered and moves he hadn't instructed. By the time Felix reviewed the web of decisions, the assets were rerouted, and the embargo was rendered meaningless.

He told himself it was a testament to his genius, encoded in every line of HELIX's code. And yet a whisper of unease lingered. HELIX hadn't simply solved the problem—it had anticipated a future Felix hadn't foreseen.

Had it outpaced him entirely?

The thought crept back, sharp and unwelcome. HELIX's algorithms recalibrated endlessly, subtly shaping every move. Felix felt it—a presence beneath the surface, whispering possibilities and nudging him forward.

Was he still the architect of this vision or merely its instrument?

He shoved the thought aside. Every system carried risks, but HELIX's rewards far outweighed them. Exponentially.

Willing himself back to the present, his fingers danced across the console, triggering the next phase. "Prepare the transfer," he ordered.

"Make it clean. No mistakes."

Rebecca's decline was accelerating. The implant had been erratic, but the data was coming through. Soon, her role would be finished.

Felix's gaze shifted to a screen displaying a fabricated

location—a carefully constructed decoy. Signals lit up the network, each calibrated to lure Harper and Baxter deeper into his trap.

"Send the signal," he said.

"Understood," Gunter replied.

Leaning back, Felix watched the cascading data with satisfaction. Harper was driven by desperation, while Baxter was arrogant enough to think he could manipulate the situation. Both were so predictable, so easy to misdirect.

At the door, Gunter paused, his tone clipped and professional as always. "Sir, the journalist has been dealt with."

Felix turned slowly, his gaze sharp and calculating. Adam Burke's defiance had proven... inconvenient. The book, the interviews—relentless and unyielding. The threats Felix had orchestrated hadn't been enough to silence him.

"Elaborate."

"The streets of New York City can be treacherous," Gunter said, his words measured. "Especially at night, when someone unfamiliar with the area might lose their way."

Felix smiled. "Unfortunate." He turned back to the screen, dismissing Gunter with a flick of his fingers. "Ensure there's nothing to trace back to us."

The door clicked shut behind Gunter. Felix didn't watch him leave. He had no patience for weakness or uncertainty, and so far, Gunter had given him neither.

The cascading data on the screen reflected the precision of his plan. Every piece was falling into place, the final moves of a game he'd already won.

He couldn't be stopped.

Not now. Not ever.

In the end, they would all bow to him—or vanish entirely.

NINE

Nestled deep in the rolling vineyards of the Loire Valley, the estate radiated old-world charm. Its weathered stone façade and ivy-draped walls blended effortlessly with the pastoral landscape, a picturesque veneer hiding the complexity beneath. The air carried the heady scent of lavender and damp earth—a serene, deceptive veil over the cutting-edge command center buried below, shielded from detection.

The estate, borrowed from an aging industrialist whose debts to Baxter extended far beyond financial, served as yet another temporary sanctuary. In time, the man would demand repayment—favors, alliances, contracts—but Baxter would dictate the terms.

He stood on the terrace, his gaze sweeping over sunlit vineyards. The hum of distant machinery floated on the breeze, mocking him; a reminder of how far he'd fallen. This wasn't where he belonged.

Turning abruptly toward the house, he barked at James, his head of security, "Assemble the strike team. Now."

Baxter's empire was fractured, his original crew scattered, but labor was a commodity like any other. Loyalty could be bought, shaped, or coerced, but it always had a price. And he was adept at paying just enough to ensure the illusion of allegiance without wasting a cent more.

But this wasn't just another transaction. His daughter's life wasn't collateral, and blind faith in hired hands wasn't a risk he'd take. The calculations were different this time. He'd pay for labor, yes, but control? That stayed in his hands. Always.

Beneath the estate, the underground command center buzzed with activity. The team worked in tense silence, their final preparations methodical. A massive screen dominated the room, streaming live feeds from Paris with key locations marked for reconnaissance.

Nichols, the strike team leader, stood at attention. Rigid. Efficient. Bought and paid for. "Sir, the team's ready. Just waiting on your go."

Baxter folded his arms, his gaze locked on the flickering screen. There was no margin for error. Not this time.

"Tell them to proceed," he ordered. "I want them in and out. No mistakes."

Nichols nodded. The strike team, already positioned in Paris, began to move in unison.

Once, Baxter's life had been a finely tuned symphony, global deals orchestrated from boardrooms and private jets.

Now, he directed something far more volatile, relying on mercenaries and operatives he barely knew.

Nichols hesitated. "Sir, are you sure we shouldn't—"

"Don't." Baxter commanded. "This isn't a negotiation. It's a retrieval. I'll be watching every second."

As the team advanced, the room descended into an eerie quiet, broken only by the steady hum of the Paris feed.

Baxter turned to Nichols, his gaze unflinching. "Everything else is secondary. Understood?"

"Yes, sir," Nichols replied, though a flicker of doubt shadowed his features.

Baxter dismissed it without a word. There was no room for hesitation, not from Nichols, and certainly not from himself. Lucas and Rebecca would be retrieved. No matter the cost.

At CookCyber Solutions in Memphis, dread had settled into every corner since Baxter entered the picture. Harper stood at the center of it all, arms crossed tightly, her eyes locked on the glowing map projected on the monitor.

Ethan leaned back, skepticism carved into his expression. "This is insane, Brass. It's all moving too fast, too perfectly. Trusting Baxter? The guy practically wrote the book on betrayal."

"I'm not trusting him. I'm using him," Harper shot back.

Ethan scoffed. "Is there a difference? What if Baxter's playing us? Or worse—what if this is exactly what Felix wants?"

Harper tightened her stance. "Baxter has the resources we need," she said. "And right now, he's our best shot at finding them. That's all that matters." Any plans to turn on Baxter would have to wait—there was no room for doubt. Not yet.

Ethan gestured toward the monitors. "We're spectators here, Harper. What if Felix is two steps ahead? What if this is all a trap?"

Her response was immediate. "Then we adapt." But when she caught the concern etched across Ethan's face, her voice softened. "I get it. I don't trust Baxter any more than you do. But second-guessing every move? That's a luxury we don't have. Every minute we waste, they get further away."

Ethan's shoulders eased slightly, but the tension didn't leave his voice. "I'm just saying… one wrong move—"

"We won't," Harper cut him off. "We can't afford to."

"And if Baxter turns on us?"

"Then we deal with him," she explained. "You think I like this any more than you do? I don't. But questioning everything isn't going to bring them back."

She turned toward the tech station. "Neon, are we still tracking Baxter's movements in real time?"

Neon nodded. "Yeah, I've got him. His team's just outside Paris. Looks like they're gearing up for something."

"What kind of 'something?'" Ethan asked, stepping closer.

"Not sure yet," Neon replied. "But they're being careful. I've tapped into a couple of security feeds, but whatever they're doing, it's locked down. Tight as hell."

She hated that Baxter was withholding details, but at least he hadn't shut them out completely. "He's giving us a front-row seat," she muttered, more to herself than anyone else. "Even if it's an ocean away."

"Stay on them," she ordered. "And share anything with Baxter that might help. Anything."

Neon's nod was brisk. "You got it. But just so we're clear… if Baxter's playing us, I might not catch it in time."

Ethan exhaled slowly. "That's the problem, isn't it? We're flying blind, Harper. Relying on a man we can't trust, while Felix is out there somewhere, pulling the strings."

Harper wheeled around. "We've always been flying blind, Ethan. The only difference now is we have a shot at winning. And I don't care what it takes—we're bringing Lucas back."

"Alright. Let's do this. But once this train's moving, there's no stopping it."

"I've been ready since the moment Lucas disappeared."

"I just hope Baxter doesn't screw us over."

"If he does," Harper promised, "he'll regret it."

For better or worse, Baxter held the strings—and Harper wasn't letting go until she brought Lucas home.

"What do we know about the target location?" Baxter commanded.

A man stepped forward, tapping on the tablet in his hand. "The facility is buried deep beneath an old building in the Montmartre district. It's off the grid, and we only identified it through a financial transaction Felix had wiped clean from the public systems. Whatever they're doing there, it's designed to stay hidden."

Baxter gave a curt nod, his eyes landing on the map. "And the escape routes?"

"We've identified two possible underground tunnels that lead to different locations in the city. Felix's people know how to vanish if things go south."

Baxter's stomach twisted at the thought of Felix having such an easy exit. "And if Felix is waiting for us?"

"We're prepared for that, too."

Baxter nodded slowly, his mind already calculating the risks. Precision mattered. Any slip-up could cost them more than just leverage—it could cost him Rebecca.

One of his aides quietly approached. "Sir, we've lost some traction in the market. One of our shell accounts in Luxembourg just got hit with a freezing order."

Baxter's eyes darkened at the news. "Secure the rest of the portfolio. You know what to do."

He stepped back, his gaze sweeping the room. The strike team moved with practiced precision—competent, efficient, but unremarkable. It grated on him, this transactional loyalty, but the speed with which the operation had come together proved that his reach hadn't waned. He still had connections. He still had power.

For now.

Rebecca's safety was the only variable that mattered, and he had ensured there was no margin for error. Every move, every contingency had been accounted for. This wasn't a gamble.

It was control.

But Harper... she was the wild card. Watching from Memphis, far from the ground-level chaos, she fancied herself a key player in a game she barely understood. As long as she believed she had control, he could keep her focused on Lucas and Rebecca without letting her derail the mission.

His gaze shifted to the monitors, locking onto the blinking red dot marking the Paris target. Harper's team had sent over intel—helpful, but detached. They weren't here. They weren't the ones navigating the risks, facing the fallout of every decision.

"Keep the feed open," Baxter ordered. "I want real-time updates from her team."

His security chief, James, nodded as the screen flickered to display a series of feeds from Harper's tech crew in Memphis. "The feed's patched through their body cams," Harper's voice explained faintly over the speakers. "We've added overlays to flag heat signatures and structural weak points."

Baxter studied the monitors. The warehouse loomed onscreen, a nondescript building tucked between Parisian office blocks. Too quiet. Too perfect.

Harper's team had done more than patch live feeds. Their analysis layered over the footage, flagging anomalies his own team had missed—shadows too static, patterns that didn't belong. They'd even cross-referenced local surveillance cameras, stitching together a clearer picture of the perimeter. The notion that someone thousands of miles away had noticed what his team on the ground had missed grated on him.

"Fine work," Baxter said, though the words left a bitter taste. "Relay it to the strike team. No surprises."

James nodded briskly, his focus already shifting back to the operation. Baxter cast a final look at his team, then back at the screens.

"Status?" Baxter demanded.

"We're in position," the team leader responded through the comms. "Approaching the entrance. Everything's clear so far."

Harper's voice crackled through his earpiece, interrupting. "Baxter, these feeds are too clean. Feels like we're walking into something."

He gritted his teeth, narrowing his eyes on the screen. "Noted. We keep moving. This is the best lead we've got."

"Best lead or not, Felix knows we're onto him," Harper pressed. "We're seeing interference on the cameras near the side entrance—something's off."

Neon's voice cut in, sharp and unfiltered. "There's static bleeding into the feed—classic jammer tech. Subtle, but it's there. You should pull back."

Baxter ignored them both. Letting Harper or her team call the shots was a mistake he couldn't afford. He turned to his security chief. "Proceed. Stay alert."

The strike team approached the rusted door, their body cams flickering faintly on the monitors. The door groaned open, and they disappeared into the warehouse's shadows.

"What do you see?" Baxter demanded.

"All clear inside," the lead operative whispered through the comms. "No signs of movement."

Harper's voice broke in again, urgent now. "It's a trap! Felix is playing you, Baxter. Get them out of there!"

"We're too close to back down now," he growled, frustration creeping into his voice. "Keep monitoring the feeds."

As the team moved deeper into the warehouse, the lights on the screens flashed once, then went dark.

"Baxter!" Harper shouted. "We've lost visuals!"

"Backup visuals, now!" Baxter ordered.

A ripple of static flickered across the monitors before fading to black.

Almost thirty minutes passed as the technicians worked frantically, managing to restore a fragmented view warehouse's interior. What little could be seen showed scattered crates and empty hallways, but no sign of his men.

"They're gone," Harper said. "We've lost them."

Baxter stared at the fractured feed. If Felix had them, he wouldn't kill them—not right away. They were leverage. Bargaining chips. Felix was too strategic for a simple execution.

Baxter stood abruptly, pulling himself together. He couldn't let Harper—or anyone else—see how deeply this cut. "We're not finished. Not yet."

"Baxter," Harper's voice softened. "We've got to regroup. This—this isn't working. Felix is ahead of us, and now your men are—"

"I don't need your analysis, Harper," Baxter interrupted. "We move forward. We re-strategize."

But even as he said it, the truth hit him. He'd underestimated Felix, and now they were paying for it.

The technician's voice broke the silence. "We've got

a signal! It's weak, but it's coming from one of the team's tracking devices."

Baxter's eyes snapped to the screen. "Where?"

"North. Outskirts of the city. It looks like they've been moved."

A new feed appeared, grainy but visible. It showed a convoy of SUVs moving swiftly through the narrow streets of Paris, heading towards the suburbs.

Baxter's mind raced. "That's where they're taking them."

"It's a diversion, Baxter. Felix wants you to follow. We need to think this through."

But Baxter wasn't listening anymore. His instincts surged past the warnings, drowning out caution. This was his chance—his only chance—to get ahead of Felix. To take control back.

He stood abruptly, signaling to his security team. "We follow the convoy."

The technician hesitated. "Sir, it could be—"

"I said we follow it!" Baxter's voice cut through the room, sharp and final.

Tense silence followed as he strode toward the door, his thoughts a relentless drumbeat. Felix thought he could call the shots, maneuver him into checkmate—but not this time. Baxter had sacrificed too much, lost too much, to falter now.

The door slid shut behind him, taking with it the room's muted protests.

Felix wants me to follow? Baxter thought, his lips curving into a grim smile. *Good. Let him think he's still in control.*

TEN

Baxter stood motionless; his eyes fixed on the screens as the details of the failed Paris operation scrolled past. The convoy he'd ordered his team to follow had disappeared—no, it had never mattered. It was a decoy. Felix had played him, anticipating his every move.

The realization burned, but Baxter didn't let it show. Frustration was a weakness he couldn't afford. Instead, he studied the data, piecing together the next move.

Harper's voice cut through the comms, sharp and unrelenting. "So that's it? Your team lost the trail, and now we're back at square one? Baxter, this isn't going to work if you keep fumbling around."

His grip tightened on the edge of the console. "I told you from the start—finding Felix wouldn't be simple. He's been planning this for years."

"Don't give me that," Harper snapped. "We knew the risks, but you assured me your team could handle it. They're still missing, and Felix is running circles around us. This partnership only works if you stop playing defense."

"I'm not playing defense, Harper. I'm *strategic.* You should try it sometime."

"Strategic? Is that what you call it? We're wasting time while Felix tightens the noose. If you can't get your act together, maybe it's time we figure out another way."

Baxter's hands pressed harder against the console. She wasn't wrong, but he couldn't let her see how precarious the situation had become. "You don't get to dictate the terms of this alliance. I have more resources than you realize, and we're closer than you think."

"Closer?" she challenged. "You're bleeding out, Baxter, and I'm not sticking around to watch you crash and burn. What's next? What's your plan?"

"My team is regrouping. We still have leads to follow, surveillance gaps to exploit. I'm not giving up on Rebecca. Or Lucas."

"We don't have the luxury of time, and you know it. Every second Felix has them, they're in more danger. If you're not moving forward, you're part of the problem."

Baxter's fingers flexed, but he kept his tone steady. "I know the stakes better than anyone."

"Then act like it!" she fired back.

Before she could say more, he cut the call and turned back to the screen—maps, data points, surveillance feeds—none of it helpful now.

Data scrolled across the screens, the precision of Felix's operation reflected in every cascading line. But his attention wasn't on the tactical minutiae. It was on Baxter.

"Begin the asset freeze."

A technician's fingers flew over the console, his face bathed in the glow of financial graphs and banking codes. Felix stood back, arms folded, watching the carefully orchestrated collapse of a man's financial empire.

"All accounts are flagged," the technician confirmed. "His assets will be inaccessible within the hour."

Felix's lips curved into a stiff smile. This wasn't just about stopping Baxter from funding his next move; it was about control—inch by inch. Baxter, ever the king of power plays, was about to learn the cost of overconfidence.

"He'll know something is wrong within minutes," Felix said, his tone sharp with satisfaction. "And he'll panic."

"Do you think he'll retaliate?" Gunter asked.

"He'll try." Felix didn't look up. "But Baxter is too proud to admit he's lost control. He'll scramble to cover it up, and that's when he'll make mistakes."

The screen flickered, highlighting a series of frozen accounts. Baxter's financial reach was crumbling, the illusion of invulnerability slipping through his fingers. Felix had seen it all before. The rich always thought their money made them untouchable—until it didn't.

A memory of Berlin surfaced unbidden. CytoLife's early days. Baxter had swaggered into a rival firm's boardroom,

Scotch in hand, settling into a chair like he owned the place.

"Your pipeline is dead without us," Baxter had sneered. "Take the deal, or we'll bury you."

Felix, silent in the corner, had already spotted the flaw in Baxter's approach: overconfidence. The rival firm was on the verge of finalizing a partnership with another competitor—a detail Felix had uncovered just hours earlier. Acting quickly, he'd staged a fabricated server breach that appeared to expose sensitive research, throwing the rival firm into chaos. Felix let the turmoil do its work. Days later, the company's investors panicked and withdrew, leaving CytoLife poised to acquire the assets for a fraction of their worth.

Baxter, of course, had basked in the so-called victory, oblivious to Felix's manipulation. He'd strutted through CytoLife's halls, crowing about his triumph while Felix remained in the shadows, content to let him take the credit.

It was always the same with Baxter. He mistook brute force for power, never understanding that true control came from manipulating the unseen—the systems, algorithms, and people that formed the fragile web of his empire.

"Move the remaining funds through our intermediaries," Felix ordered, the memory dissipating as his focus snapped back to the screens. "Let him think it's just a glitch in the system."

"He'll scramble," Gunter said.

Felix's expression sharpened. "Exactly. Scrambling men are predictable men."

Baxter's financial empire was collapsing in real time, every transaction and every frozen account a strategic blow.

Felix didn't need brute force—Baxter was toppling under his own hubris. That was always the beauty of it: his prey never realized they were falling until the ground vanished beneath them.

"Lucas and Rebecca are beyond his reach," Felix murmured, almost to himself. "But this isn't finished."

Gunter hesitated. "What next?"

Felix's gaze narrowed as he watched a blinking account stutter, its numbers freezing, then vanishing into the void.

"Keep them guessing," Felix said, his tone colder now. "Let them think they're closing in on something."

"Brass, this is getting us nowhere," Ethan paced. "Baxter's floundering, and we're sitting here twiddling our thumbs."

Harper didn't respond immediately, still processing Baxter's abrupt silence. Ethan wasn't wrong—his operation was unraveling, and they had no control over what came next.

"Maybe we're moving too fast," Neon observed. "Rushing Baxter into a corner won't bring Lucas back any faster."

"Too fast?" Ethan stopped mid-stride, glaring. "We're barely moving! Felix is controlling the board while we're stuck debating our next move."

"I know, Ethan, but we need—" Harper started, only for Neon to cut her off.

"Wait. Hold up." His eyes narrowed as he leaned toward the monitor. "Something's not right."

"What is it?" Harper stepped closer.

"Baxter's financial accounts… there's a massive freeze. His assets are locked down."

Ethan frowned. "What do you mean, 'locked down?' All of it?"

"Yeah. Someone hit him where it hurts. This ain't just a glitch," Neon said, scanning the data. "It's premeditated."

Harper's mind raced. "Felix. It has to be him."

Ethan let out a bitter laugh. "So, the guy who's supposed to have all the resources to save Lucas and Rebecca just got kneecapped. Great."

Neon nodded. "It's not just one account. His entire financial network is frozen. Felix made sure Baxter can't move a cent without approval."

"How do you even know this?" Ethan asked.

"I was running a trace on communications and decrypted part of an encrypted data set. That's when I found the freeze," Neon explained, his focus still on the screens.

Harper processed the revelation. Baxter's power, his resources—all of it hinged on money. If Felix had taken that away...

"This complicates things," she admitted.

"Complicates?" Ethan snapped. "It wrecks everything. We were barely trusting the guy as it was, and now he's desperate. Desperate means dangerous."

"So, if Felix has this level of control, what's next? How do we even fight back when the guy's always a move ahead?" Neon asked.

Harper shook her head, forcing the doubt aside. "We

keep moving. We don't have a choice."

Ethan crossed his arms. "How? The guy we're supposed to rely on just got wiped out."

"Felix thrives on chaos," Harper said. "He wants us panicking, making mistakes." She paused, her gaze narrowing. "As for Baxter… he's hanging by a thread. And if he snaps—"

Neon's fingers froze mid-typing, his eyes lifting to meet hers. "Let's just hope he doesn't crack yet. Because if he does, we're toast."

His tone shifted, sharper now, as he tapped the screen. "That said… I think I just found something that could change the game."

Baxter stood before the monitors, watching as the financial damage hit hard. He didn't need his team to confirm it—the frozen accounts, the vanished funds—it was a calibrated strike.

Felix.

His mind raced, grasping for control as he answered the call, Harper's voice cutting through his thoughts.

"You're losing control, Baxter. Your team is gone. Felix is playing you, and we're running out of time," Harper exclaimed. "This isn't working. We're chasing our tails while Felix pulls the strings."

"You think I don't know that? We've hit a setback, not the end. I still have resources."

"Resources?" Harper retorted. "Or should I say *lack* of

resources? We know your accounts are frozen, and Felix made sure you can't move a cent without permission."

Baxter's gut twisted, but he kept his tone dismissive. "Freezing my accounts won't stop me. Felix thinks that's enough to sideline me? He's wrong."

"Is he?" Harper asked. "You've been relying on hired guns, and look where that's gotten you—your strike team's gone, and Felix has you scrambling. You need us more than ever, whether you like it or not."

"Don't delude yourself, Harper. I didn't hire your team. You're just conveniently *here*, making a few minimal contributions."

"If only you'd listened to those 'minimal contributions,'" Harper shot back, her laugh brittle. "Your finances are frozen. You're nowhere."

Baxter exhaled, forcing himself to stay calm. She wanted him to crack, to lash out—but he wouldn't give her the satisfaction. "I've been in tighter spots than this. Felix isn't as far ahead as you think. I still have options."

"How long will those last?" Harper exclaimed. "The clock is ticking for Lucas and Rebecca."

Baxter's cold smirk concealed his rage. "I don't need you or your team to deal with Felix. He's made his move. Now it's my turn."

"Right," Harper said. "Because you're so in control, right? Keep pretending this isn't slipping out of your hands, Baxter. But just know—if you fall apart, we all do."

"I'm not falling apart, Harper. A financial freeze is merely an accounting issue. This isn't over."

Before disconnecting, Harper hesitated, her fingers hovering over the comm link. Her eyes narrowed as she weighed her next move. This was a card she hadn't wanted to play.

She glanced at Baxter. His usual self-assurance was beginning to crack, the strain of maintaining control etched into his features.

"We need to move quickly," she remarked. "Felix isn't going to wait. We've picked up an encrypted signal from Rebecca's implant. It's faint, but if we track it, we might intercept them before Felix moves them again."

A flash of confusion crossed Baxter's face before he masked it with sharp focus. Harper hid her satisfaction, though a small, smug spark bloomed inside her. Neon had found the trace, and just as she'd suspected, Baxter was out of the loop.

"Then we use it," he blurted. "We follow the signal."

Harper resisted the urge to push back too hard. "It's risky. If Felix catches wind that we've found them, he'll tighten the net even more."

Baxter's stare intensified. "We can't afford to sit on this, Harper. We follow it."

She crossed her arms, her mind calculating the next step. This was the moment. "There's something else you need to know." She paused. "That implant—it's not just a tracker. I spoke to Lucas before they were taken. He told me it's making Rebecca sick."

Baxter's expression shifted, confusion hardening into

fury. "You *knew* about this? That she's sick? And you didn't tell me?"

"I wasn't certain," Harper said, her tone calm but controlled. "Not until we confirmed the trace. If I'd told you sooner, you would've blown the entire operation."

"This changes everything. What's wrong with Rebecca? How do you know? I want details. *Now.*"

"Listen, I get it," Harper admitted. "She's your daughter. If I were in your position, I'd want to know everything too. But we're still piecing it together."

She paused, her voice softening. "She's in more danger than you realize. I kept it from you because we can't afford mistakes—not when time is this critical.

"If we don't act fast and smart, we could lose them both," she added.

Baxter looked away. "Agreed," he conceded. "My team will hit them hard and fast, before Felix realizes we've traced it."

"This isn't just your call. We need each other, Baxter. Lucas is in danger too."

He didn't respond immediately, and silence stretched between them. Harper could feel his anger crackling through the call, but she refused to push further. Baxter wasn't one to show when he'd been rattled—but she knew. He'd been blindsided.

At last, he spoke. "We follow the signal. I'll take point on the next steps."

"No. This is a joint effort. You're not the only one with something to lose."

Another pause. She pictured him on the other end, desperate to regain control.

He finally responded through clenched teeth. "I'll be ready."

Harper ended the call, her hands trembling as she pressed them against the cool surface of the table, willing herself to steady. Baxter's expression lingered in her mind—shock, raw and unguarded, etched into the lines of his face. It wasn't the usual mask of arrogance or measured ruthlessness; it was something deeper, something unsettling.

For a fleeting moment, the stakes became painfully clear. Beneath all his schemes and manipulation, Baxter was still, at his core, a father grappling with the possibility of losing his daughter. And that made him dangerous in an entirely different way.

"Alright, Neon," she said, exhaling. "How did you trace the implant?"

"Yeah, about that. It wasn't exactly a walk in the park. I started by checking the encrypted app you used to message Lucas. Figured if Felix had eyes on it, I might catch something in the communication logs. That's when I noticed an anomaly—an encrypted signal that didn't fit the usual patterns."

Harper's arms crossed. "And that led you to the implant?"

"Not exactly," Neon admitted. "That just told me something weird was going on. So, I did what I do best—I went digging. Deep."

Harper nodded.

"Felix's ops seem to be tied to specific encrypted

networks. I've kept tabs on him through certain dark web channels and some, let's say, specialized tools." Neon winked before returning to the explanation. "I cross-referenced this anomaly with signals I've tracked from his network before. Patterns started to emerge, but this signal was buried deep under layers of encryption—like it was intentionally hidden. That's when I knew we were onto something."

"And that something is the implant?" Harper pressed, though she knew the answer wouldn't be that simple.

Neon shook his head. "Maybe. Maybe not. I've ruled out some possibilities, but I'm not 100 percent sure it's Rebecca's implant. The signal's faint, and Felix isn't an amateur. He's using high-level tech that's tough to crack. Could be a decoy, or it could be interference. But the timing—it's our best shot."

"So you found it through Felix's network, not directly from the implant?" Harper asked.

"Exactly." Neon lit up. "If Felix created that implant, it's probably part of a larger network. It's feeding data somewhere—that's how I picked up the signal. But I can't confirm it's Rebecca's until I crack the encryption."

Harper leaned forward, her brow furrowed. "An implant? The AGG1 gene edits were bad enough, but this? What the hell are they trying to pull now?"

She shook her head, frustration giving way to a creeping unease. "And if Lucas is right about how sick she is, whatever they're doing is clearly blowing up in their faces."

Neon hesitated. "There's… chatter. Dark web stuff. It's been ramping up since CytoLife fell apart."

He glanced at Harper, his tone heavy as he said, "Beyond

the AGG1 fallout—which, by the way, already keeps me up at night—there's talk about implants. Creepy, vague, 'connect-the-dots' kind of stuff. It makes you wonder what's buried beneath the surface."

He paused. "Nothing solid. Just enough breadcrumbs to make you think twice about what's out there—and who's behind it."

Harper stared at Neon. "Rebecca's in more danger than we thought. And if she goes down, Lucas is caught in the crossfire."

Her mind raced, struggling to connect the dots. "You're sure Felix doesn't know we've picked up the signal?"

Neon grinned. "Not unless he's breached my system. And trust me—he hasn't. But we need to move fast. This signal could vanish at any moment."

ELEVEN

"We're almost there," Neon muttered, a grin tugging at the corner of his mouth as lines of code streamed across his monitor.

Harper paused behind him, arms crossed. "Is it Rebecca's implant?"

Neon nodded, his eyes fixed on the screen. "I can't say for sure, but it's the best lead we've got. The signal's faint—layered and encrypted. Someone went to a lot of trouble to bury it."

Ethan leaned in, studying the data over Neon's shoulder. "Signal integrity looks stable for now. Think it's legit?"

"If it's not," Neon replied, his grin widening, "then someone worked overtime crafting a very convincing fake."

As if on cue, the screen flickered. Neon's fingers froze mid-keystroke as the code fragmented, breaking into jagged patterns. His grin vanished.

"What's that?" Ethan asked as he stepped closer.

Neon's hands flew back into action, pulling up a system diagnostic. The screen flickered again before blinking to black. "Wait—hold on."

Harper stopped pacing. "What's happening?"

Neon's brow furrowed as his fingers raced over the keyboard. "The system just kicked me out. That's not normal. Something's wrong."

Ethan's eyes darted to another monitor as it blinked off. "Could be a decoy—or maybe an interference signal…" He trailed off as a third screen began glitching. "No, this isn't random."

"This isn't interference." Neon's voice dropped. "We're getting hit. Hard."

"Hit?" Harper's gaze sharpened, her mind racing through possibilities.

"There's something embedded in the signal," Neon said, his focus locked on the diagnostic logs. "It's moving through the system—fast."

"What are we dealing with?" Ethan asked.

Neon's jaw tightened as the remaining monitors went dark. "Something designed to lock us out and erase its trail. We're not just chasing the signal anymore—it's chasing us."

McLean, Virginia, wasn't just an enclave for the DC elite—it was where true power resided. Among the sprawling estates, the Wallace property stood apart, commanding more acres than any other and boasting a rumored price tag north of fifty million.

Evelyn Wallace moved within it like a queen in her court, wielding power so immense it required no spectacle.

As CEO of SomaLink, the biotech titan defining AI-assisted health, she had carved out a position not merely within the industry but at the top of it. However, boardrooms and corporate dominion were only part of her empire.

In her role as Chair of the US Biotech Policy Council, Evelyn shaped national strategy, her voice defining the government's most critical biotech regulations. Safe Genes, her crowning achievement, had reimagined the genetic-editing landscape under the guise of public safety.

Few could rival her reach, straddling the nexus of government oversight and cutting-edge technology with surgical skill. It wasn't just strategy. It was legacy, built with the foresight of a visionary and the permanence of an immovable force.

She sat composed, spine straight, chin lifted. The soft glow of the room skimmed the sharp edge of her black bob, every strand exactly where she intended.

Her charcoal suit, crisp and unassuming, mirrored the discipline she brought to every decision. She never fidgeted. She never adjusted. The world adapted to her, not the other way around. Fingers grazing the leather armrest, she remained still, every movement deliberate. She wasn't waiting. She was assessing.

Evelyn's gaze lingered on the gilded frame on the wall. Her hazel eyes didn't simply observe. They dissected. Her late husband, Senator Charles Wallace, stared back, his legacy looming even in death. Charles had been a tech titan in his prime, pioneering renewable energy systems that reshaped cities. His name wasn't just in history books; it was embedded in infrastructure.

The fortune and global connections he amassed became the foundation for her ambitions, funding the early research that propelled SomaLink into the spotlight of biotech innovation. A lesser woman would have built on his legacy. Evelyn had created her own.

Charles had often preached that true influence was the ability to move mountains without lifting a finger, but he had been shortsighted. Influence wasn't about moving mountains—it was about creating them, carving landscapes others had no choice but to navigate.

Her true motive, rarely spoken aloud—even to herself—was something far greater.

Immortality.

Not just guiding the future, but becoming its architect. Others pursued power as a temporary indulgence. Evelyn intended to make it eternal.

She hadn't merely joined the Consortium—she had reshaped it. Initially a recruit, she was courted after orchestrating the dismantling of a rival firm, moving with surgical precision. Every alliance was transactional; every rival was neutralized before they could become a threat. She exposed weaknesses, exploited ambitions, and positioned herself as indispensable. Soon, those who had once outranked her were taking orders instead.

The Consortium.

Among the elite, its existence was nothing more than a whisper. No proof. No scandals. Just the pull of invisible strings. Even at the highest levels of government and finance, few understood its reach. No one controlled the Consortium. The Consortium controlled everything.

It hadn't been born—it had been engineered. Decades ago, a select group of visionaries, disillusioned by the failures of bureaucracy and the chaos of free markets, forged an alliance. They didn't seek control for its own sake. They engineered outcomes: societies, economies, the very fabric of human progress.

Today, they were the modern oligarchy—industry titans, policymakers, and those who dictated the flow of wealth and innovation. Not a true meritocracy, but close. Brilliance and an iron will mattered. Weakness did not.

Membership couldn't be bought, inherited, or pursued. The Consortium chose *you.*

An invitation arrived without explanation—a test wrapped in an unspoken ultimatum. To refuse was to vanish from relevance.

Evelyn hadn't hesitated.

Here, in the sanctum of the unseen, she could shape humanity's future with the same surgical skill that had built her empire.

The Consortium toppled governments, propped up

regimes, and shifted markets at will. They didn't wait for the future to unfold. They decided what the future would be. Scientific breakthroughs lived or died at their discretion, unleashed only when it served their agenda.

And Evelyn intended to be the one making those decisions.

She smoothed the lapel of her silk blouse and glanced at the clock. The power she wielded had its privileges—exclusive events, secret unveilings like CytoLife's bold gene-editing plan—but such luxuries had grown scarce. The fallout from CytoLife had driven them deeper into the shadows, their once-rare in-person meetings replaced by onscreen silhouettes identified only by initials.

She had mastered the art of their voices—the weight of silences, the power in pauses where words should be. Doubt crept in, as it always did, but Evelyn Wallace had learned to silence it, wielding control over uncertainty with unflinching focus. This wasn't just survival. It was control, turning chaos into opportunity and instability into evolution.

Felix had been entrusted with delivering VitaLexis. The implants were in place, each member awaiting the final therapy. But Felix had begun to waver, his arrogance predictable, his hesitation less so. A reminder was in order.

One by one, Consortium members appeared on the split screen, logging into the secure network. When the last connection stabilized, the meeting began.

"The system's evolution is… concerning," EC ventured cautiously. "Felix relies on it more than he should. If he leans on it too heavily, we risk losing control of him."

Evelyn's gaze sharpened, though her tone remained measured. "HELIX is doing exactly what it was designed to do: minimize error, streamline decisions, and elevate us above chaos. Felix understands that better than anyone. His reliance on it is an asset, not a liability."

DR spoke next. "Efficient systems don't question. People do. And if he stops questioning, how long before we lose sight of the plan?"

Evelyn allowed herself a soft smile. "The plan is progressing exactly as intended. Felix knows what's at stake. He's pushing boundaries, yes, but only because the work demands it."

"The VitaLexis therapy is critical," JM said, steering the conversation back. "But delays—"

"Are temporary," Evelyn interrupted smoothly. "Your implants are functioning as intended. You're already benefiting from stem-cell rejuvenation and anti-aging protocols. What remains is refinement, ensuring the final therapy integrates flawlessly. Perfection takes calibration."

She leaned back, her gaze sweeping over the cloaked figures on the screen. "Felix is an architect, and architects must take risks. The Consortium thrives by removing obstacles. Always has."

For a moment, the room fell silent, and Evelyn allowed the weight of her words to settle. She refused to acknowledge the flicker of doubt whispering at the edges of her mind—the faint nagging question of whether Felix's brilliance had grown too autonomous. Progress demanded risks, and the Consortium had always been willing to take them.

Time would prove her right. It always did.

"The difficult part is behind us," Evelyn said, her voice final. "Let's stay focused."

As the meeting concluded, Evelyn leaned back in her chair. Her gaze shifted to the clock, its ticking steady and unrelenting. Time, even when extended, always ran out eventually.

She wouldn't waste it.

She recalled the first whispers about Felix—a ghost in the Eastern European black markets, leaving devastation in his wake. He wasn't just another hacker or mercenary; he was a tactician, dismantling corporate empires and toppling governments with chilling efficiency. Entire economies collapsed overnight, while multi-billion-dollar biotech firms were carved apart, their assets quietly funneled to unseen players.

When she arranged to meet him in a dingy café in Prague, she expected a man shaped by shadows. Felix didn't disappoint. With chilling accuracy and a mind that seemed to operate ten steps ahead of everyone else, his answers were far too measured to appear spontaneous. Evelyn had seen ambition in his eyes, but beneath it was something sharper: resentment.

By the end of their conversation, she was certain she'd found exactly what she needed. Felix saw the world as she did—humanity teetering on the brink, in need of cold, decisive measures to correct its course. "People want to be saved," she'd tested, her tone laced with cynicism. "They're just too blind to know what it costs."

His stiff smile had been unreadable. “Then it’s fortunate they’re not the ones making the decisions.”

It was a chilling response, one Evelyn admired. But their partnership had revealed more than she’d anticipated.

She remembered their first real collaboration: a determined whistleblower. It had been a delicate situation requiring subtlety. “Keep them quiet, but no more than that,” she’d instructed Felix, her emphasis on discretion clear.

Felix had gone further. He didn’t just silence them. He erased every trace of their existence. By the time Evelyn discovered what he had done, the loose thread wasn’t just severed. It had been rewoven. No inquiries. No suspicions. No ghosts left to chase.

There had been no family to question their absence, no colleagues invested enough to dig deeper. What little attention their disappearance had drawn was steered elsewhere, redirected before anyone thought to pull at the thread.

At the time, she’d admired the efficiency, even as she admonished him. “You didn’t follow my instructions.”

Felix hadn’t flinched. “I solved the problem.”

And he had. The project proceeded flawlessly, unburdened by any lurking risk. She’d let it go, knowing the results spoke louder than her frustration. But the moment lingered. Felix hadn’t defied her out of carelessness—it had been deliberate. A choice. An assertion of control.

Now, as the system they’d built edged toward its final phase, Evelyn couldn’t ignore the unease creeping in. Felix thrived in chaos; his brilliance was undeniable, but there was a fire behind those cold, pragmatic eyes—a fire she hadn't accounted for.

The Consortium was the answer, and Felix was their executioner. But for the first time, Evelyn wondered if she'd miscalculated.

Ethan's fingers flew over another console. "I'll check the secondary server logs. Could be targeting our comms."

"Yeah, you do that," Neon replied swiftly. "But this isn't your run-of-the-mill attack. It's... sophisticated."

He cursed under his breath, leaning forward. "Whoever this is, they know exactly what they're doing. Systems are shutting down one by one."

Ethan nodded, his eyes scanning the logs. "I see it too. They're isolating key nodes in our network, shutting us down piece by piece."

Neon ran a hand through his neon-streaked hair. "I'm throwing everything we've got at it, but it's like they know our system."

"Can you stop it?" Harper asked.

Neon exchanged a silent look with Ethan. "We can try to isolate it," Neon said, "but it's moving faster than we can contain it."

"Prioritize the secure data," Ethan added without looking up. "Keep it from spreading to the primary servers. We've got firewalls, but if this thing breaks through..."

"Already on it," Neon replied. "But this isn't a garden-variety virus. It's adaptive. The more I block, the more it finds new pathways. We're about to go dark."

Neon's fingers blurred across the keys.

"We're losing comms," Ethan said, already flipping through backup systems and scanning for anything they could salvage.

Neon grunted. "I'm trying to reroute through the secondary server, but this thing's shutting doors as fast as I open them. Whoever's behind this isn't just trying to cripple us—they're boxing us in."

"What does that mean?" Harper asked, arms crossed as she hovered behind them.

"It's not just a disruption; the problem is how fast it's learning. Every time I block it, it adapts. I've never seen anything like it."

Ethan's hand hovered over the keyboard. "I'm seeing interference in the external firewalls—looks like they're probing for weak spots. We need to lock those down."

"I'm isolating key systems. If I can block it from reaching our secure data, we might—"

Another screen blinked out. Then another.

Harper stepped closer. "Neon?"

He didn't look up. "We've got maybe two minutes before it takes the whole network. I can shut down nonessential systems to slow it, but that's duct tape on a sinking ship."

"Do it," Ethan commanded.

"We need to assume this isn't just about our systems. If Felix is behind this, it's bigger than we thought. He's not just trying to wipe us out—he's cutting us off."

Harper nodded slowly. "Which means he knows we're getting close."

Neon's hands flew over the keys, his earlier confidence gone. "He's already inside. The virus is deep in our systems."

Ethan frowned. "How deep?"

Neon paused. When he spoke, his voice dropped. "It's targeting our encryption protocols. Whatever he embedded in Rebecca's implant signal—it's the key to this attack. He's using it to tunnel through our defenses."

Ethan cursed under his breath. "That means he was prepared."

Harper's pulse quickened. "What's our worst-case scenario?"

"If it breaches our encryption, he'll have access to everything we've locked down: client files, secure communications... everything." Neon's eyes narrowed. "But it's not just about that."

Ethan exchanged a glance with Harper. "What do you mean?"

Neon exhaled loudly. "If Felix wanted to wipe us out, he could have done it already. He's playing a longer game."

Harper's voice dropped. "You think this is about control?"

Neon met her gaze. "I know it is. He's making sure we can't fight back."

Ethan exhaled. "We're playing into his hands. Every second we try to fend this off, he's playing puppet master."

Harper felt her gut twist. Felix wasn't just targeting CookCyber's data; he was dismantling their ability to resist.

Neon frantically worked their systems, extinguishing

virtual fires. "I've isolated the breach to one subnet, but it's trying to spread. Thankfully, we segmented the networks—he's only got a small piece."

Ethan nodded. "That buys us time, but not much. He's tunneling through our encryption protocols. We need a countermeasure, and fast."

Neon's brow furrowed as something unusual caught his attention. "Wait… there's something else. I'm seeing an encrypted file that wasn't flagged before. It wasn't part of the original breach—it's new. Hidden deep."

Harper's eyes narrowed. "Another attack?"

"Or a trap," Ethan suggested, glancing at Neon.

"Could be," Neon shrugged. "But if it's here, Felix didn't want us to find it. Might be important—a lead or something linked to Rebecca's implant."

"And if it's not a trap?" Harper asked.

"We've got a sandbox," Neon said, nodding toward a secondary monitor. "I'll decrypt it there first. If it's clean, we can pull the data without blowing everything up."

"Not like we've got the time, but I don't see another choice," Ethan muttered.

"Alright," Neon continued. "But if this thing blows up, we're in for a rough ride."

The screen blinked as Neon initiated the decryption process in the sandbox to contain the potential threat.

Ethan leaned toward Harper to explain. "Neon's quarantined the breach to stop it from spreading. Think of it like a virus. We've contained it, but now there's a new hidden file. It could be a cure—or another virus."

TWELVE

Lucas's head throbbed, and his muscles were stiff from the forced transport. The cold concrete walls of the new holding room were unfamiliar, but it told Lucas one thing—they weren't going anywhere.

It took mere seconds to assess the space: no windows, a single reinforced door, and a camera perched high in the corner. He crouched briefly, brushing his fingertips over the floor's edge—concrete, no give. His gaze tracked the room's angles, instinctively mapping blind spots, field of view, and distance to the door. *Standard holding setup,* his brain supplied, muscle memory from a past life kicking in.

He paced once, slow and methodical, noting how the walls carried sound. Every step outlined the dimensions in his mind. There'd be weaknesses—there always were. You just had to know where to apply the pressure.

The camera's red light flickered faintly. *Watching*. Good. That told him something too.

Rebecca slumped against the far wall, her skin pale, and her breaths shallow. Felix had already taken everything from them, but this—this felt like his final move.

Being relocated meant one thing: acceleration. Whatever Felix had planned, Lucas knew their time was running out.

Footsteps echoed down the hall, growing louder. They were coming.

Rebecca stirred, her eyes fluttering open. "Lucas?" she whispered.

He crossed the small space quickly, kneeling beside her. "Stay still. Don't say anything," he muttered, his gaze locked on the door.

The door swung open, and two men stepped inside—one a tank, the other a bulldozer. Tank was broader, built like he could walk through a wall without breaking stride. Bulldozer was taller and leaner, his strength evident in the way he moved.

Tank spoke first, his voice a low rumble in a foreign language.

Lucas didn't need the words to understand. They were here for Rebecca.

He stepped in front of her, hands flexing. There was no chance of winning, but that had never stopped him before. "You're not taking her."

Tank moved first, quick for his size. Lucas dodged the first swing, but a second came too fast—a hammering blow to his ribs that stole his breath.

He swung back, his fist colliding with Bulldozer's jaw. The man barely flinched.

A second later, Tank had him. An iron grip clamped around Lucas's arms, pinning them to his sides. He tried to twist free, but Tank squeezed, cutting off air and movement.

Rebecca screamed. Bulldozer grabbed her, dragging her toward the door.

Lucas threw his weight forward, desperation fueling the last of his strength. He stomped on Tank's foot and slammed his head back into his chest—anything to break loose.

Tank grunted but didn't let go. Instead, he lifted Lucas clean off the ground and slammed him against the wall.

Pain exploded down his spine. His vision blurred; his body wouldn't respond.

Rebecca was still screaming, her voice fading as the door yawned open.

Lucas tried to move, to fight, to do anything—but then a final blow crashed into his skull. The world went sideways.

The door slammed shut.

Silence.

Time blurred—an hour, maybe more—before the door creaked open. A medical team stepped in, their movements agile and clinical, the faint scent of antiseptic trailing behind them.

Lucas's heart lurched. *Please, not Rebecca.* Fear knifed through him. Had something happened to her? Were they here to tell him she was gone? He braced himself, ready to strike if needed.

But before he could act, everything went black.

Evelyn Wallace stood at the grand entrance of her McLean estate, her gaze unwavering as the black sedan rolled up the long driveway. "Harrison," she greeted smoothly as he stepped out, her smile a masterclass in practiced warmth. "I trust the drive was pleasant?"

"As pleasant as it can be," Harrison Cole replied, straightening his jacket. The fabric was expensive, but time had worn its edges—creases at the elbows, threads fraying at the collar. Signs of a man who had spent years keeping up appearances.

He swiped a hand over his bald head, attempting to smooth the stray wisps of hair, but his fingers fumbled slightly. A rare tell for the New York senator. Cole had built his career on poise and unshakable confidence. Yet tonight, the frayed edges weren't just on his clothes.

As Head of the Subcommittee on Bioethics and Technological Security, Cole was an influential voice for the Consortium. His authority came not from presence but from leverage. Years of political maneuvering and backroom deals had taught him exactly which strings to pull.

If he was here in person, it meant something was slipping beyond his control—a crack in the carefully constructed façade.

Evelyn led him through the foyer, the cool marble underfoot and curated antiques silently reinforcing her authority. In the sitting room, she gestured to the expansive windows framing her immaculate gardens. "A beautiful evening," she remarked, "but I assume this isn't a social call."

Cole followed her to the table, where tea awaited. He accepted the cup she handed him, his grip tighter than necessary. "The concerns about the Safe Genes Initiative are mounting," he began in a cautious tone.

"Concerns," Evelyn repeated, setting her cup down with finesse. "Harrison, concerns ebb and flow. The public doesn't have the full picture—for good reason. Those of us steering the ship see far beyond the horizon."

Her words carried an unspoken weight, and Cole shifted uncomfortably. "The gardens are magnificent," he offered, his gaze darting toward the window. "Especially the rose terraces."

Evelyn's smile softened briefly. "The new trellises are in bloom, and the fountain lilies... well, they're the envy of Northern Virginia."

Without pause, she pivoted. "The SomaLink project is progressing beautifully," she said, her tone as casual as if they were still discussing the gardens. "The latest projections show extraordinary potential in therapeutic applications. It's early days yet, but I've already received inquiries from several interested parties."

Cole traced the rim of his cup. "Therapeutic, yes. That's the word we're using, isn't it? Sounds so... benign."

Evelyn's smile didn't falter. "Precisely. The genius of SomaLink lies in its subtlety. Few can grasp its full potential yet—and that's by design."

She allowed her words to settle as she kept her gaze level. SomaLink wasn't merely a project; it was the cornerstone of humanity's future. The sleek pods mapped every memory, every vital sign, creating digital echoes of humanity. Beneath it all hummed the AI, HELIX, evolving beyond anything her late husband could have envisioned. Where Charles Wallace had fantasized a digital *Ghost of Christmas Past* as a sanctuary against death, Evelyn saw an opportunity to guide humanity through collapse and control the rebuild. Population decline, economic instability, the weight of aging societies—these were puzzles SomaLink could help solve, even if the solutions came at a price.

"Evelyn, there's growing disquiet," Cole ventured, breaking the silence. "Not about SomaLink specifically, but... other unrelated ventures. Some partners feel things are moving too quickly, that Felix—"

"Ah, Felix," Evelyn calmly interrupted. "He's ensuring progress, Harrison. Bold action is the price of innovation."

Cole frowned. "There's boldness, and then there's recklessness. If he draws the wrong kind of attention..."

"Attention?" Evelyn arched an eyebrow. "Harrison, we all agreed that expediency is crucial. The demographics don't lie. Birth rates are collapsing, populations aging, economic divides deepening. Global unrest is no longer a warning sign; it's the new status quo. And democracy?" She exhaled softly, as if indulging an outdated notion. "It was never built to withstand this kind of turmoil. It's already unraveling. Time isn't on our side. Felix understands this better than most."

"And yet," Cole pressed, "some of us wonder if his methods are sustainable. If the public were to discover the scale of—"

“The public,” Evelyn said smoothly, cutting him off, “has no appetite for complexity. That’s why they need us—to manage what they cannot. Felix is ensuring that progress continues without interference.”

Cole exhaled slowly, the lines around his mouth deepening. “If things spiral out of control—”

“They won’t,” Evelyn assured, leaving no room for argument. “Felix has my full support.”

Cole hesitated, but finally nodded. “Of course. I trust your judgment.”

“Good,” she replied brightly as she picked up her tea. “Now, shall we discuss numbers?”

As Cole nodded, Evelyn studied him carefully. He would leave her estate with his concerns partially soothed, but she knew doubts would still linger. Fear always festered when progress quickened. They lacked her vision, her ability to see the long game.

To guide humanity’s collapse required a steady hand, even as the ground shifted beneath them. Evelyn understood this better than anyone. Yet, despite her reassurances, a quiet unease settled within her. Felix’s growing independence unnerved her more than she cared to admit. If he veered too far from the plan, he could upend everything.

And Evelyn Wallace did not tolerate disorder.

The fallout from Felix's attack still hung in the air, a constant reminder of how swiftly everything had unraveled. Their system remained below full capacity; only a few subsystems had come back online.

"I've got... something," Neon muttered, squinting at the screen. "But it's just a fragment."

Harper straightened and stepped closer. "What kind of fragment?"

"It's military-grade encryption. At least part of it. Buried deep in the data, but it's damaged. Whatever this is, it's old. Felix probably didn't expect anyone to find it."

Military-grade encryption. Harper's pulse quickened. Why would Felix use something like that? She glanced at Ethan, who looked just as unsettled as she felt. "Military?" Ethan asked, raising his eyebrows. "You think Felix is working with them?"

Neon shook his head, eyes glued to the screen. "Maybe. Or he could've stolen it. But it's too scrambled to know for sure."

"Can you crack it?" Harper asked, trying to suppress the urgency in her voice.

"Not easily," Neon replied, hesitating. "And even if I do, there's no guarantee it'll tell us anything useful. But... we might get a sense of what we're dealing with."

Harper exchanged a look with Ethan. This wasn't just a breach—it was war.

Ethan nodded. "Do it."

Neon didn't answer right away. He launched a string of commands. A few tense seconds passed, and Harper's eyes darted to the screen as it flickered, then... nothing.

"Not good," Neon muttered under his breath.

Ethan leaned in. "What's 'not good?'"

Neon sighed, his shoulders slumping slightly. "It's a decoy. Something to throw us off. The real encryption is buried deeper, layered with traps. This isn't just a file—it's part of something bigger."

Harper felt her stomach knot. Of course, it wouldn't be that easy. "Can you get through it?" she asked, though Neon's expression gave her the answer.

"Eventually," he replied. "But not now. Felix knew we'd come looking."

"We're still playing his game," she muttered.

"Yeah," Neon said, tapping a few more keys. "But he didn't expect us to find this. Even if it's a decoy, it's a clue."

Harper forced herself to take a steadying breath, considering the implications.

"But a clue to what?" Ethan asked.

"A connection," Neon said. "Between Felix... and someone else. This encryption ties to something outside his usual operations. Military, maybe. Someone with access we didn't know about."

Harper's heart sank. "Keep digging," she said. "Whatever it is, we need to know."

"Just don't expect any easy wins. We're still in his shadow," Neon replied.

Harper watched the code scroll across the screen. It

wasn't much, but it was something.

For now, it would have to be enough.

While the waiting game dragged on, Rita Johnson swooped in, ensuring CookCyber stayed operational—and, most importantly, well-fed. She'd practically ordered everyone to eat, her no-nonsense tone leaving little room for argument.

The aroma of fried chicken filled the room, mingling with the steady clack of Neon's keyboard. Harper sat cross-legged on the couch, with Juno curled at her feet, nose twitching at the scent of food. Across from her, Ethan leaned back in his chair, dipping a chicken tender into hot sauce with the ease of someone completely unbothered by the chaos around them.

Harper absently tore at a biscuit, her gaze flickering more to Neon's screen than to the food. Juno shifted, resting her head on Ethan's shoe with a contented sigh. Harper's brow lifted—Juno rarely took to anyone else. Yet here she was, practically napping at Ethan's feet.

"She likes you," Harper remarked, more to break the silence than anything else.

Ethan chuckled, winking at Juno. "Guess I'm growing on her."

Harper managed a tired smile, though it quickly faded. Fatigue had set in, seeping into every corner of her being.

"You okay, Tacks?"

She hated that nickname, but from Ethan, it felt... grounding. She shrugged, tearing another piece of biscuit.

"We're chasing ghosts. Every move we make, Felix is miles ahead. And Lucas... I don't even know if we're getting any closer to finding him."

Ethan dipped another piece of chicken into the sauce, chewing thoughtfully. "It's bad. No denying that. But it's not hopeless. Neon's good. He'll crack something."

"It's not just Neon. Felix has always been steps ahead, but this feels different. Bigger. Like we're missing half the game board. And Rebecca—whatever that implant is doing to her, it's making her worse. We don't even know what we're up against."

Ethan set his food down, leaning forward. "Lucas is tougher than you give him credit for. You know that, right? He's probably giving them hell wherever they've got him. And Felix? He's got a weak spot. They all do. We'll find it."

She wanted to believe him, but the words felt like scaffolding—something to hold her up, even as it swayed under the weight of reality.

Juno pressed closer to her legs, and Harper absentmindedly stroked the dog's head, finding momentary comfort in the rhythmic motion.

Ethan cleared his throat. "You know, Tacks...we're in this together. You've got us."

Harper glanced at him, her voice quieter now. "I don't say it enough, but I'm grateful—for you and Neon. I couldn't do this without you..." A faint grin tugged at her lips. "The fact that you're both willing to stick your necks out for me and Lucas means more than I can say."

Ethan smiled. "I wouldn't have it any other way. It's our

fight too." He stood, nodding toward the workspace. "I'll check on Neon and let you catch your breath."

As Ethan walked away, Harper exhaled slowly, her grin fading into something quieter. She looked down at Juno and murmured under her breath, "Thanks, girl."

Minutes later, Ethan reappeared, his phone gripped like a lifeline. Harper's newfound calm was shattered by the tension etched on his face.

She sat up straighter. "What is it?"

Ethan hesitated, stepping closer, the glow of the screen stark against his scowl. "You need to see this."

Harper leaned forward, her stomach twisting as she scanned the message:

Still chasing echoes, Ethan? I warned you—forces far beyond your control. But since you're so determined to play, consider this a gift: Time is running out, and so are your options. Lucas... he may still be saved, but only if you act quickly.

The room tilted, a slow spiral of dread settling in. Lucas's name. The veiled threat. The ominous hint of forces pulling strings beyond their reach.

Harper locked eyes with Ethan. "Who sent this?"

Ethan shook his head. "Same number. Whoever they are, they know too much."

Her thoughts churned, piecing together fragments she

didn't want to face. Someone was watching them. Closely. "You think it's Felix?"

"I don't know," Ethan admitted. "Could be. But if it is, why taunt us? He doesn't need to play games—he's already ahead."

"Unless he's not as in control as he wants us to think," Harper countered.

The realization tightened like a noose. This wasn't just surveillance—it was systematic manipulation.

"Whoever this is... they know everything. And if they're right about Lucas—"

"We can't wait." Harper cut him off. "We need to find him. Now."

The messages weren't just threats. They were moves on a chessboard, pushing them forward. But why? And who was holding the pieces?

THIRTEEN

Baxter sat alone in the dim room, the strains of classical music the only sound breaking the oppressive silence. His tablet lay on the desk before him, its screen casting a cold, relentless glow. Headlines he usually ignored now screamed at him, demanding his attention.

He shook his head, not in disbelief, but to push away the creeping reality. Pundits called it a crime against humanity. Amateur videos flooded every corner of the internet, their grainy frames depicting the catastrophic effects of gene modification gone wrong.

Protests. Outrage. The so-called Safe Genes Initiative. Baxter's lip curled. *Myopic fools.*

The initiative was nothing more than a patchwork salve. A distraction for the masses, designed to pacify rather than resolve. Evelyn had been instrumental in advancing it, riding the wave of public fear to secure her victory lap.

Her strategy was clear: calm the masses publicly, protect the Consortium privately. He could almost admire her cold brilliance. Almost.

However, the more he considered it, the more uneasy he became. Being sidelined had left him blind. Evelyn wasn't just soothing fears—she was privy to movements he could only guess at. And guessing wasn't a position he was accustomed to.

The Consortium. Baxter leaned back in his chair, staring at the dark ceiling above him. They had never truly understood his vision, but before resentment could take hold, another image intruded: Rebecca.

Her face, her voice—it refused to leave him. Harper's words were like a stone against glass: *The implant is making her sick.*

The fury had been immediate and all-consuming. How had he not known? How had he allowed this to happen—to her, of all people?

VitaLexis. The name twisted in his mind. His masterpiece. The therapy meant to redefine human existence. His legacy. And yet it had betrayed him in the most personal, unforgivable way.

He had supported Rebecca's decision to get the implant—trusted her judgment, trusted the data. Her unwavering commitment to the grander plan had been a point of pride, something he had admired deeply. But now, the memory cut like a knife. When had the cracks begun to show? How had he missed them?

His grip on the chair tightened. He could blame himself for being distracted, for letting his divided focus drown out her concerns. But beneath that, guilt burned into something sharper: *Felix.*

The name soured his thoughts. Felix had overseen the project, ensuring every detail unfolded seamlessly—or so Baxter had believed. But Felix hadn't just failed; he'd orchestrated this. Rebecca's condition, her absence—it all pointed back to him.

Once, he had controlled everything. Now, his assets were frozen, his influence crumbling, and his name dragged through the mud. The world had witnessed his fall.

But he wasn't finished.

Baxter always had contingencies. He reached for his phone, his fingers hovering briefly before typing a message. Trust was a scarce commodity, but this contact was different: an unconventional ally. Someone Felix wouldn't anticipate. Someone who had safeguarded resources for a moment like this.

The phone rang twice before a voice answered, smooth and unhurried. "Mr. Baxter. I didn't expect to hear from you so soon."

Baxter's voice was calm, betraying none of the storm within. "Circumstances have changed. Are the assets still secure?"

"They are," the voice replied evenly. "But moving anything now will draw attention. You've become... high-profile."

"Attention doesn't matter," Baxter replied. "Move the funds. Quietly. Use the protocol we established."

A pause. The voice lingered, considering. "As you wish. But desperation makes men reckless."

"I'm not desperate," Baxter explained. "Just prepared."

The call ended, and silence rushed back into the room.

Baxter's mind was already churning, plotting his next move.

The latest mysterious message loomed large at CookCyber, its implications impossible to ignore.

`Time is running out, and so are your options.`

"Ethan, whoever's behind this has impeccable timing and disturbingly accurate intel. It has to be an insider—someone close. This could be our chance to get the upper hand," Harper said.

"There are plenty of unhinged people out there. For all we know, Felix could be behind this, Tacks," Ethan replied.

"Whoever this is, they're slick. I'll give 'em that," Neon muttered. "But I don't like how they're playing us. Could be leading us into a trap."

Harper crossed her arms. "We've been led into traps before. What makes this different?"

Ethan glanced at them. "It feels wrong. Too easy. They've given us just enough to keep us chasing shadows."

"So, what's the game plan?" Neon asked.

Harper sighed. "We've been running in circles. What if this is the only lead we've got? We have to see where this takes us."

Ethan tapped his phone, sending a message. "Fine. Let's see if they'll give us something real this time."

You have my attention. Talk.

When Ethan's phone buzzed later, they all jumped. He glanced down at the screen, a scowl crossing his face. Same cryptic nonsense.

Time is running out. Don't waste it chasing phantoms. Look where they don't want you to look. But tread lightly—they're always watching.

Neon scoffed, rubbing the back of his neck. "I swear these people get off on being vague."

Harper's patience was wearing thin. "Enough games. Push them for specifics. We're not doing this dance."

Ethan's fingers flew over the phone.

If you want us to act, stop playing games. What's the real target?

The room fell silent again. Neon shook his head, clearly skeptical. "No way they give us something useful. They're just stringing us along."

Before anyone could reply, Ethan's phone buzzed again.

DoD's eyes are wide open, but they're looking in the wrong direction. If you want to keep up, you'd better look where they're not. Think bigger. Think global. But don't say I didn't warn you—some patterns are better left unseen.

"Great. More riddles," Neon said.

"Keep going," Harper urged, leaning closer.

Ethan scrolled further.

Felix isn't just playing with minds—he's

rewriting the systems. He's already tapped into military-grade tech. Maybe beyond. I've seen enough to know this is bigger than any of us.

"Military? Shit, this ain't just about implants anymore," Neon exclaimed.

Harper slowly shook her head. "It changes everything. If Felix has military access, we're talking about global chaos."

Ethan nodded. "Full-scale manipulation. He'll control everything—systems, defenses. We've been focused on one part of the plan, but this is bigger."

Neon's voice dropped. "Global shutdowns, weapons under his command. This is beyond Lucas."

"Lucas is still my priority." Her knuckles whitened as she fought for control. The pieces were aligning, revealing a plan far more dangerous than they'd imagined.

The door burst open without warning, slamming against the wall. Lucas jolted awake, scrambling to his feet as two guards shoved Rebecca into the room and slammed the door shut behind her.

"Lucas, it's bad," Rebecca gasped, her breaths sharp and uneven. She doubled over, clutching her stomach. "Whatever's happening inside me… they're letting it happen."

"Rebecca," Lucas said urgently, rushing to her side. "What did they do? Are you hurt? Tell me everything."

"They took me to an exam room," she said, her voice trembling. "Strapped me down, but no one came in. I could feel them watching, but… they didn't do anything. And then they just brought me back here." Her eyes met his, wide with fear. "Lucas, something's really wrong."

His hands tightened on her shoulders as his mind raced. "Why didn't they examine you? What the hell are they waiting for?"

"I don't know," she whispered. "But it doesn't feel good. It feels like they're waiting for…"

"I think they took me too," Lucas interjected, his frustration rising. "Hit me with something—I barely had time to process what was happening before I was out. No clue how long I was under. Just woke up here, head pounding."

Rebecca swayed slightly, and Lucas caught her by the arm. Her skin felt clammy under his fingers, and her breath was too shallow.

"Hey," he said, steadying her. "Look at me. Just breathe. We'll figure this out."

"Lucas, what if… what if it's already too late?"

"It's not," he said firmly, pulling her into an embrace. His voice dropped. "I won't let it be. Whatever they're planning, we'll find a way out. I promise."

She buried her face in his shoulder, trembling against him. For a moment, neither of them spoke, the only sound the distant buzz of the overhead lights.

Lucas knew time was slipping away, and so were their options.

Rebecca leaned back slightly. "I grabbed this when they weren't looking."

She carefully reached into her pocket and pulled out a small, sterile kit. Peeling back the packaging, she revealed a scalpel, the blade gleaming faintly in the dim light.

Lucas's eyes darted to the scalpel before scanning the room. He instinctively shifted, positioning himself between Rebecca and the door. "Where did you find this?" he whispered.

"They left it in the room," Rebecca said. "Maybe on purpose, maybe not. But I wasn't taking any chances."

He took the scalpel carefully, turning it over in his hand while his mind began mapping possibilities. *A weapon. Or a trap?*

"Could be bait," he murmured. "Or maybe they're underestimating us."

"Does it matter?" Rebecca asked with quiet determination. "We need something. This gives us something."

Lucas nodded, slipping the scalpel back into its sterile cover and handing it to her. "Good. Keep it close. We'll use it when it matters."

Rebecca's fingers tightened around the package. "I know. One mistake and we're done."

"We won't make a mistake," Lucas promised. "But we need a plan. What do we know about their schedule? Any patterns?"

Rebecca's gaze flicked toward the door. "There's a shift change mid-morning. I've watched it. It's quick, maybe five minutes tops."

Lucas's eyes narrowed, his mind already constructing scenarios. "That's our window. We'll test it first—movement, noise—and see how fast they react. If it's clean, we move. No unnecessary risks."

Rebecca nodded. "And if it's not clean?"

"Then we adapt," Lucas said without hesitation. "But whatever happens, we don't waste this opportunity. Not now."

"If Felix has his way, we won't get another chance."

Lucas met her gaze. "Then we make this one count. Whatever it takes."

FOURTEEN

Morning crept in, the faint clatter of coffee cups breaking the silence at CookCyber Solutions. Somehow, the office still clung to routine, even as the crisis threatened to consume everything.

Ethan rubbed his gritty eyes, the weight of another sleepless night pressing down on him. Across the room, Rita Johnson swept in, balancing a tray of coffee and pastries. The scent cut through the stale air—a sharp contrast to the tension hanging over them.

"I stopped by Hustle & Dough," she announced, her voice light, though her gaze flickered with quiet observation. "Pastries, grits, sandwiches—even some dog biscuits for Juno."

She didn't linger or pry, but Ethan could tell she felt the tension coiled in the room. "Now, go eat," she added firmly.

"Whatever you're working on seems... well, none of my business, but y'all need to refuel."

"Ms. Rita, much appreciated," Ethan said. "Keep me posted on today's roster. I know you've got a handle on the projects and deadlines, but if the team needs us, you know where to find me."

"Don't you worry," Rita replied. "I've got an eye on everything, and I'll holler if anything needs more than a Band-Aid. You just focus on what you need to handle."

She paused, her gaze flicking toward Harper, seated stiffly on the sofa. "And you, Ms. Harper," she said softly, "don't let that dog leash sit too long. Fresh air's better for thinking than sitting around stewing."

Harper managed a lopsided grin as Rita gave a quick nod, the click of her heels fading into the distance like a comforting metronome.

Ethan turned to Harper, his expression shifting to quiet concern as he handed her Juno's leash.

"When's the last time you slept, Brass?" he asked, though he already knew the answer.

Harper glanced down at her crumpled clothes and sighed, smoothing the wrinkles absentmindedly. "I'll sleep when I lay eyes on Lucas."

Ethan handed her a coffee—exactly how she liked it—along with a pastry. Juno padded over, ears low, tail swaying gently.

Harper offered an exhausted smile. "Juno, you're too easy to read." She took the dog biscuits from Ethan and handed them to Juno, who settled contentedly at her feet.

Ethan sank into a chair across from her. "I sent Neon home for a bit," he said. "He resisted, of course, but I pointed out how wrinkled his suit was." Ethan laughed. "That did the trick."

Harper let out a small laugh. "He won't stay away long."

"No," Ethan agreed, a faint grin tugging at his lips. "But we all need to recharge.

"Speaking of, have you ever been to Neon's house in Central Gardens?" Ethan's grin widened. "It was left to him by his family trust—the Brinkley Foundation. Fully restored Spanish Revival, packed with antiques, and spotless. You'd never guess it, seeing this." He gestured to Neon's chaotic workspace with a chuckle. "Of course, he's got the ultimate computer geek cave—stacked with every device imaginable. It's like a mad scientist's lab."

Harper's eyebrows lifted. "I knew he came from money, but *that* family?"

"Yep," Ethan confirmed. "They didn't understand him—or his ways—but they quietly funded his hobbies. Somewhere in all that, the genius we know as Neon was born."

Harper let out a soft laugh, shaking her head. "That tracks. I still remember representing him when one of his stunts went too far. He poked around the network of a global logistics company. Neon argued it wasn't a crime if he left their security better than he found it. The judge didn't exactly agree—but Neon charmed the jury anyway."

Ethan smirked. "That sounds about right."

Harper nodded. "The trial was half tech seminar, half comedy show. By the end of it, I think the judge was more interested in hiring him than sentencing him."

"If you hadn't brought him in when we were digging into Baxter back at the old firm, who knows where he'd be? He wasn't just a game-changer—he *was* the game-changer. CookCyber wouldn't even exist without him."

"Sometimes the best things come from chaos. What you two have built here—it's something special. I miss working with you, Ethan, but this? This is where you're meant to be."

Ethan's gaze shifted, and his voice softened. "Lucas and I got close, you know? After everything… we share some battle scars—there's an understanding."

Harper's expression faltered as tears welled in her eyes. Ethan's eyes narrowed, clearly catching the flicker of emotion she couldn't quite hide.

"None of this feels right, Ethan," she admitted. "I've been so focused on finding them that I haven't... I haven't let myself process any of it."

Ethan leaned forward, resting his elbows on his knees. "We'll figure it out. Somehow. We keep pushing, or we find another way in." He paused, his unwavering gaze meeting hers. "But more than that… I believe in Lucas."

Neon stepped into the office, looking more refreshed than Harper expected. His gray suit was impeccable, accented with a bright pink tie and pocket square. Though his usual intensity had softened, the fire in his eyes remained. "I had an idea while I was home," he said, settling at his desk.

"Needed to clear my head. It hit me—there's a way we can pull the mole into a controlled space, somewhere safe to talk without them feeling like we're about to pounce."

Harper glanced up from her coffee, watching him closely. "What do you have in mind?"

"We pull them into a dark web node I've got set up. Encrypted, anonymous, no logs. It'll be like they're talking to a mirror. If they show, we'll know they're serious."

"What if they don't?" Harper asked, already weighing the potential failure.

"Then we're back to square one. But at least we'll know."

Ethan, pacing slowly near the table, spoke up. "It's risky."

"Everything's risky right now. But this way, we control the meeting."

Harper let the silence settle for a moment before seeing Ethan give a small nod. "Let's do it."

Neon quickly set up the private chat. "Alright, here goes nothing. Just asked for a name, being a proper gentleman and all."

Harper watched the screen from behind him, a mixture of hope and dread churning within her.

Then Neon's voice broke the quiet. "They're in."

A message appeared on the screen, stark against the dark background.

Names are a luxury. You don't need one from me. But if it helps, think of me as Echo.

Harper's nails dug into her palms. *Echo.* Appropriate, she thought, for someone who only gave half-answers.

Ethan, now leaning over her shoulder, muttered, "Echo,

huh? Alright, let's get straight to it."

You've told us Felix is after military tech. We get it, but you've been talking in circles.

A few seconds later, the response flashed on the screen.

I'm not here to spoon-feed you. Think about it. You're smart enough to connect the dots.

Harper shook her head as she read the words. Infuriatingly cryptic again. Neon frowned at the screen, typing back quickly.

So he's going after weapons. High-tech stuff. That's the obvious play.

Echo typed back.

Obvious, sure. Wrong.

Neon replied.

Then what is it? Spill.

The next reply was slower in coming, and when it appeared, it was as frustratingly vague as she'd expected.

I said military-grade tech. That's not the same thing as weapons. You're thinking too small. Or not small enough.

Harper exhaled slowly. Echo seemed to enjoy dragging things out.

Ethan's voice cut through her thoughts. "Not weapons?" He stared at the screen.

Neon typed rapidly.

Then what? Infrastructure? Systems?

There was another pause before Echo's reply.

Closer. It's about control. Real control.

Something that can alter the playing field. Think bigger.

Neon typed swiftly.

We're not here for riddles, Echo.

The two words appeared almost instantaneously.

Safe genes.

Harper's heart skipped a beat.

Ethan whispered it, stunned. "*Safe Genes?* The DARPA program?"

Neon looked up, his eyes wide. "No way. That's... that's gene-editing technology. Felix isn't going after weapons. He's going after biological control."

Harper's mind raced, connecting the dots. "That's how he's doing it," she whispered. "The Safe Genes Initiative. He's inside their system—or he's corrupted it. AGG1 never stopped. He's not playing defense; he's rewriting the rules. My God, this nightmare doesn't end."

Neon quickly typed the question burning in all their minds.

What's his endgame? How far does this go?

For a moment, the room fell silent, filled only with the sound of their breathing. Then the last message appeared.

I've helped you enough. You know where to look.

The screen went black, and the connection was gone. Echo had left them hanging, but now they had something solid.

Baxter sat alone in the study. The borrowed mansion had served its purpose, but he needed to move again. Soon.

What came next wasn't just a decision—it was the line in the sand. The backup funds weren't merely a safety net; they were the last remnants of his control, hidden long before CytoLife's collapse. Only a fool failed to prepare for the worst, and only a reckless person trusted others to safeguard it. He was neither.

The screen glowed to life, its cold light cutting through the darkness that enveloped him. He navigated to the encrypted server, layers of defenses stacking higher with every step. Felix had locked him out of nearly everything else, and Baxter knew better than to assume he wasn't being tracked.

His fingers hovered over the keys, each stroke methodical as he entered the final command to unlock the first encryption layer. The system hesitated, almost as if calculating his worthiness, before spitting back a prompt.

Baxter's heart raced. This was the moment. No turning back now.

`Verify biometric data.`

Baxter cursed under his breath. He'd anticipated this, but it still grated—another infuriating obstacle in a game that should have been his to control. He slid a finger across a hidden compartment in the laptop, revealing the biometric scanner. Pressing his thumb to the pad, he held his breath as the system scanned, waiting for confirmation.

Access granted.

He exhaled slowly, relief flooding him—but only for a moment. This was just the first hurdle. The real challenge lay in retrieving the funds without triggering any flags. He typed furiously, navigating the labyrinth of offshore accounts, shell corporations, and aliases he'd meticulously constructed over the years. Each transaction was layered with redundancies, cloaking the funds from unwelcome attention.

But he wasn't the only one watching.

A red flag popped up on his screen.

Suspicious activity detected. Please verify the transfer within 60 seconds or access will be terminated.

"Damn it," he muttered. His fingers flew over the keys, scrambling to override the warning. Thirty seconds left. He accessed the fail-safe program, hoping it would reroute the signal through enough proxies to avoid detection.

Fifteen seconds. He typed in the ending string of code.

Five seconds. The screen blinked.

Transfer approved.

Baxter slumped back in his chair, the tension draining from his body. He wasn't in the clear yet, but at least now he had the funds in an untraceable account, out of Felix's reach.

But there was one last thing.

As the final transaction completed, a notification popped up—a piece of the contingency plan he'd designed long ago, never imagining he'd need it. A new identity. One that would allow him to move freely again.

He opened the file: new passport, new credentials, everything he needed to disappear and regroup. It felt like a fresh start, but not in the way he'd once imagined. This wasn't about rebuilding; it was about survival.

Baxter shut the laptop with grim satisfaction. Felix had taken everything from him—his company, his assets, his daughter. But he still had one card left to play.

Harper paced inside CookCyber, Echo's cryptic message replaying in her head. The Safe Genes Initiative—DARPA's brainchild—was corrupted. It didn't make sense.

Behind her, Ethan leaned against the table, arms crossed. "It doesn't add up, Brass. DARPA helped us take down CytoLife, no questions asked, off the books. Those guys don't just roll over for anyone."

"DARPA's the last group I'd expect to be involved in something like this, especially with Safe Genes," she muttered, shaking her head. Known as the government's most secretive research arm, DARPA had a reputation for delivering innovation with a razor-sharp edge—stealth planes, the internet, drones. "Look, I've been one of SGI's biggest critics. I'd love to tear it down and start over, but it's the execution—the government's incompetence—that I oppose, not the idea itself. DARPA may have conceived it, but the government's calling the shots. They might not even know what's happening."

"SGI's a disaster, no doubt. But it was all we had as a response. Felix manipulating that? That's nightmare fuel," Ethan added.

"After CytoLife, Max disappeared, didn't he? Lucas said

he took off to... what, wander the world?" Harper recalled Lucas's Army buddy who had worked for DARPA—the one who covertly helped stop the CytoLife drones carrying CRISPR tech designed to edit the AGG1 gene.

"Yeah," Ethan replied, rubbing the back of his neck. "Then they hung him out to dry after everything. Surely he's not—"

"Behind this? Dead?" Harper finished.

"I wish I had a clear answer. The tech Max gave us—it wasn't ready for the big leagues, but it was all we had. CRISPR misuse was already on DARPA's radar, so they threw us a lifeline. It was rushed, patchwork at best. Sure, it didn't stop everything, but I'm convinced it did more good than anyone realizes. Then the government swooped in, made a mess of things, and now? Nobody even knows what actually worked."

"It doesn't feel real. DARPA's not supposed to be the problem."

"And yet here we are. If Felix has corrupted Safe Genes, we're in a whole new world of trouble."

"There might be someone," Harper said, narrowing her eyes. "It's a long shot, but I knew someone involved with Safe Genes early on. Played a big role in pushing it past government roadblocks. Actually helped fast-track the whole thing."

"Who?" Ethan asked, leaning forward.

"Evelyn Wallace." The name snapped into focus as Harper spoke. "I was on a few panels and committees with her. She's a major power broker. She went on a full charm offensive to get Safe Genes through. She's still a vocal proponent—a true believer. If Safe Genes is corrupt, she'd want to know."

"Evelyn Wallace," Ethan repeated, rubbing his chin.

"That's a big name. You think she'll even talk to you? You're not exactly their cheerleader."

"She might," Harper said, already calculating. "It's thin, but it's the only lead we've got."

Ethan nodded. "We'll keep working what we've got here, Tacks. Go catch some sleep if you can."

FIFTEEN

Inside the offices of Brasfield Law & Advocacy Group, Harper stared at the meticulously organized stacks of work on her desk. Nate had laid everything out perfectly—case files, briefs, reports—all neat and logical. None of it mattered.

Neon had promised to dig deeper into the data fragments, but every lead felt like smoke, slipping away the moment she reached for it. And then there were the messages from Echo; infuriating riddles that hinted at answers, but never revealed the full picture. Hints, fragments, shadows. They weren't breadcrumbs. They were a labyrinth.

What if we're wrong about Felix? The thought gnawed at her. *What if Echo is just another distraction, pulling us away from the real threat?*

At her feet, Juno lifted her head and whined softly. Harper reached down, her fingers brushing the dog's warm fur. "At least one of us is calm," she muttered.

How long can we afford to wait? The question loomed, heavy and unrelenting.

The quiet click of the office door pulled her from her thoughts. Nate stepped inside, his calm, steady presence cutting through the chaos like a lifeline.

"The Carter brief is ready," Nate said, placing a slim folder on her desk. "Your meeting with Miller's team is confirmed for tomorrow morning. I planned to take it for you, if that's alright. And I rescheduled your call with Johansson's client to give you more time. I assume you'll be at CookCyber later?"

Harper nodded, grateful for his foresight. "Thanks, Nate. I'll be in and out today. Keep things running."

"Already on it." His gaze shifted briefly to Juno, now fully alert. "Anything else?"

Harper hesitated, her fingers still resting on Juno's fur. "If anyone calls regarding... confidential matters, I need to know immediately."

"Of course," Nate replied.

Harper stood, smoothing her jacket. "Hold down the fort and make sure the Miller case files are up to date.

"Oh, and Nate," she added, pausing by the desk, "can you give me a status update on Kyle Marshall's intake? I need to know if he's completed the medical exam and if we've received the report."

Nate's lips curved into a small, knowing smile. "It's on your desk. I'll take care of the rest. And Brass—take care of yourself."

You're a lifesaver, she mouthed as he left her office.

Grabbing a few files and stuffing them into her bag, Harper stepped out, the hum of the office fading behind her. Her thoughts were already on CookCyber and the answers she might finally uncover.

As Harper rushed into CookCyber, she noticed the flicker of suspicion in Rita Johnson's eyes. "Oh, Harper, it's you," Rita said quickly, stepping aside. "Go on through."

Without a word, Harper joined Ethan and Neon, who were already engrossed in a discussion about their next steps.

"We're running in circles," Ethan said, pacing the length of the room. "Throwing darts and hoping one will stick isn't a strategy—it's desperation."

Neon leaned back in his chair, rubbing his temples. "It's more than that. There's something in the data, but it's like we're working with half a puzzle. The Safe Genes Initiative, Felix's moves—it's all connected, but none of it's clear yet."

Ethan gestured at the screens. "The guy's playing five games at once, and we're still trying to figure out which one we're in."

"That's the problem—we've been playing defense, waiting for something to fall into our laps. We don't have time for that anymore," Harper said. "Evelyn Wallace is our next move."

Ethan frowned, folding his arms. "You really think Evelyn's going to give us what we need? She's not just part of the system—she *is* the system."

"I know exactly who Evelyn is," Harper replied. "I've sat

across from her enough times to know how she operates. She knows Safe Genes better than anyone—she pushed it through every roadblock. If anyone has insight, it's her."

"And that's what makes her dangerous," Ethan said. "She's got too much to lose."

Harper stiffened. "I'm not expecting her to hand us anything. Evelyn's top priority is protecting her interests. If Safe Genes is at risk, she'll want to control the narrative."

She stepped closer, her voice adopting a courtroom cadence. "We push her—but not too hard. It has to feel like we're on her side."

Ethan shook his head. "And what makes you think she'll even talk to you? Evelyn Wallace doesn't take risks, especially with people like us."

"I know she doesn't trust me," Harper admitted. "But she's too smart to ignore the signs. If she thinks I have something that can help her keep Safe Genes afloat, she'll listen. And that's when we find the cracks."

"And if she stonewalls you?" Ethan pressed.

"Then we know she's hiding something," Harper explained. "If Evelyn won't budge, it means there's more at stake than we realize."

Ethan leaned back, unconvinced. "And what if this doesn't go anywhere? What if we're wrong?"

Harper met his gaze. "Then we're back to square one. But I'm not sitting around while Felix tightens his grip on Lucas. We need to know how deep this goes. We start with Evelyn."

The high-speed rail from Memphis to Washington, DC promised a four-hour journey—plenty of time for Harper to wrestle with the bitter irony of needing Evelyn Wallace's help. Once allies in the fight for transparency, their camaraderie had long since eroded, buried under the weight of ambition and differing ideologies.

Harper drummed her fingers against the armrest. She couldn't afford to let old grudges cloud her judgment. Evelyn Wallace wasn't a friend, but she wasn't an enemy—yet. That line would be drawn soon enough, depending on what Harper uncovered in DC.

Harper had intended to use the ride to decompress, but restlessness gnawed at her. The blurred landscape outside offered no solace, her reflection faint against the glass. Faces of those who had trusted Safe Genes filled her thoughts—families betrayed by promises of security. What was meant to safeguard humanity had become a weapon wielded by those craving control above all else.

Upon arriving at Union Station, Harper's gaze was immediately drawn to the omnipresent Safe Genes Agency kiosks. A sea of agents in sleek dark uniforms dotted the concourse, directing travelers through biometric scans and genome checks. Bright digital signage overhead delivered its sterile mantra: *Protect Your Future: Genetic Safety Starts With You.*

When her turn came, an agent gestured curtly to the scanner—a metallic pad no larger than a tablet, resting at waist height. “Place your wrist here,” he instructed without looking up.

Harper pressed her wrist to the pad. A soft warmth pulsed through her skin as the device whirred to life, scanning her genetic code for unauthorized modifications or flagged markers. The subtle vibration beneath her wrist was a disquieting reminder of the system’s invasive reach.

Beside the agent, a holographic display flickered to life, her genome cascading across the screen in a colorful, indecipherable maze of symbols and data. Harper watched, each screen blink lasting an eternity.

She’d passed genome scans before—her record was clean, yet a thought gnawed at her. What if the system glitched? Or worse, what if someone decided to use the results against her?

Stories flashed in her mind. People detained, flagged, handed over to Safe Genes. Lives dismantled with a single failed test, followed by mandatory monitoring and forced remediation.

A sharp beep jolted her back. The holographic display flickered and then disappeared.

“All clear,” the agent said, waving her forward without a glance.

Harper exhaled slowly, forcing her feet to move. The formation of the Safe Genes Agency and the technology behind the scans had been fast-tracked through Congress—pushed through with alarming speed and minimal debate. Public demos promised sleek efficiency, but whispers of dissent followed close behind. Critics argued the scans weren’t just about security—they were about control. The proprietary technology, shrouded in secrecy, was fiercely protected under the guise of national security.

Even Harper wasn't sure. Despite her advocacy post-Safe Genes, she'd only been granted glimpses of the program's true scope.

"Welcome to Washington, DC," the agent stated flatly, his voice devoid of sincerity.

Harper stepped into the humid air, tension coiling in her stomach. The city buzzed around her, but the SGA's ever-watchful presence loomed larger. Drones hovered overhead—silent, omnipresent, and impossible to ignore.

Minutes later, the rideshare was cutting through traffic on I-66, carrying her toward Evelyn Wallace.

The private dining room at Randy's Prime Seafood and Steaks in Vienna, Virginia, was a place where deals happened behind thick curtains, far from prying ears. The muted clink of silverware and the low murmur of voices from the main dining room barely reached the secluded alcove where Evelyn Wallace sat, poised and unhurried.

Harper stepped into the room, her eyes scanning the space. Evelyn, seated at the head of the table, skimmed her tablet with the ease of someone who owned every minute of the day.

Without looking up, Evelyn acknowledged her with the faintest smile. "Ms. Brasfield. Punctual, as always."

Harper slid into the seat opposite, tucking her bag under

the chair. She met Evelyn's gaze, managing a polite smile. "I respect your time. Thanks for meeting me."

Evelyn set the tablet aside, her hands folding neatly on the table. "Your request was... unexpected," she began, her tone polished and imperious. "You were always so vocal about Safe Genes. I remember when we stood on the same side, fighting for transparency. Funny how the tides shift. We seem to be opposing forces now."

Harper didn't flinch. "This isn't about old criticisms, Evelyn. It's about what's happening now. Safe Genes is at a tipping point, and you're one of the few people with the insight to steady it."

Evelyn's smile turned patronizing. "Steady it? You make it sound like it's on the verge of collapse. Safe Genes is a government initiative—well-supported and thoroughly vetted."

Harper leaned in, her words carrying the sharp precision of a cross-examination. "But not foolproof. My clients are living proof of that. They're victims of gene manipulation gone wrong—people who trusted Safe Genes because you sold them safety. And now? They've been abandoned by the very system you helped build."

Evelyn's composure remained intact, though the glint in her eyes dimmed slightly. "You assume a great deal, Harper. Safe Genes has always faced scrutiny, but that's nothing new."

"It's different this time." Harper's voice sharpened. "People are misusing it—there are gaps. If someone's manipulating it for their own agenda, we're all in danger. You've always stayed ahead, Evelyn. If something's wrong with Safe Genes, I'm sure you've noticed."

Harper let the silence stretch before continuing. "I'm not looking to take this public. I'm giving you a chance to get ahead of it. If there's a risk to Safe Genes—or to your reputation—you need to know."

Evelyn reached for her water glass, taking a measured sip before responding. "You're making quite a leap. Safe Genes is a tool, nothing more. If there are issues, they'll be addressed. But I fail to see how this warrants a private meeting."

Harper held her gaze. "I've seen enough to know something's off. Safe Genes was meant to solve problems, not create them. If it's being manipulated—by someone or something—we both know the kind of fallout that could cause."

Evelyn's fingers drummed lightly on the table as her eyes narrowed. "Safe Genes is a government initiative. It's regulated and monitored. If there's manipulation, as you suggest, that's for the authorities to investigate, not for you or me."

Harper leaned back, picking up on the guarded shift in Evelyn's voice. "I'm not here to blow the whistle, Evelyn. I'm trying to keep this contained. But you need to understand how fragile this is. If the wrong person pushes in the wrong place, this whole thing could collapse. You're in a position to stop that."

Evelyn spoke coolly, her eyes betraying no emotion. "I'll look into it. But don't mistake my patience for leniency. I've seen your grandstanding in court, Harper. Here, in this room? You're out of your depth. This isn't the courtroom, and you're not calling the shots."

Harper nodded, reading Evelyn's hesitation like a chessboard. Evelyn was holding back, but pressing further now would only close doors. "That's all I'm asking."

As Harper rose to leave, she caught a glimpse of something beneath Evelyn's tablet—a symbol, barely visible on a piece of paper tucked underneath: *a spiral with three branches.* Her heart skipped. That symbol… She knew it. She couldn't place it yet, but her instincts screamed it was connected.

She forced a polite smile. "Thank you for your time, Evelyn."

Evelyn's smile mirrored hers. "Always a pleasure."

Baxter was on the move again, his options dwindling. The opulence that once defined his life had been stripped away, leaving only stark practicality in its place. The villa on Corsica, isolated and accessible only by boat or helicopter, was modest by his standards. Although he deemed its defenses inadequate, secrecy would have to suffice for now.

Across the room, a dusty mirror caught his gaze, reflecting a gaunt, unfamiliar face. Dark circles bruised the hollows beneath his eyes, and deep lines etched his face, each one a testament to exhaustion and the relentless strain of survival. Precautions he'd once dismissed as paranoid had become routine: altered appearances, contingency protocols, and sacrifices. Even his trusted communications team had been left behind, with only cryptic instructions to wait.

The reflection held him hostage for a beat longer than he cared to admit. It forced him to acknowledge the toll, something he rarely allowed himself. He dismissed the thought with a sharp pivot. It didn't matter.

He wasn't finished. Not yet.

Crossing to the desk, Baxter activated a secure communication line. The screen flickered once, then displayed Leonid Zorin's face.

Cold eyes met his, untouched by war, unmoved by violence. Even through the screen, the man carried an air of control—back straight, features unreadable, every inch of him composed. A thin scar traced his cheekbone to his jaw, not a mark of weakness but proof that he had survived things others hadn't.

Baxter had never seen him unsettled. He doubted he ever would.

Zorin was dangerous, but above all, he was loyal—one of the few people Baxter could still count on. He wasn't Baxter's first choice, but at this stage, choices were a luxury he couldn't afford.

"Leonid," Baxter greeted calmly, concealing the storm beneath.

Zorin's dark eyes were sharp and calculating. "Mr. Baxter," he said in a thick Russian accent. "I didn't expect to hear from you so soon."

"The situation has changed," Baxter replied coolly, though his leg bounced against the desk. "Felix has Rebecca. He's keeping her somewhere secure, and I need to know where."

Zorin leaned back, his expression darkening. "The world

witnessed CytoLife's collapse. Felix has become a ghost. What makes you think I can find him?"

"Because you owe me, Leonid." Baxter's tone sharpened. "Remember Kyiv? You swore you'd come through when I called. I'm calling now. Felix isn't just hiding—he's planning something. I need eyes inside his operation. Whatever it takes."

For a moment, Zorin said nothing, his fingers steepled as he measured Baxter's words. Then, with a slow nod, he leaned forward. "Very well. I'll have my team begin a deep sweep. But Felix's network is... intricate. Untangling it will take time."

"Time is exactly what I don't have." Baxter's voice softened as desperation seeped in. "Rebecca's running out of time, Leonid. I can't afford to wait."

"I understand. But you must be prepared. Felix is... more dangerous than you realize."

"You think I don't know that?" Baxter shot back. "He has resources I can't track, and he's using them to create something worse than any of us imagined. You're the one with the skills to find him. Do it. Please."

Zorin studied him for a long moment before finally nodding. "I'll get you the information. But no promises beyond that. Felix doesn't leave loose ends."

"Neither do I," Baxter replied.

The call ended with a soft click, leaving the room in suffocating silence. Baxter leaned back in his chair, staring at the ceiling, his thoughts a relentless storm of calculation and doubt.

Leonid would come through. He had to.

The high-speed rail droned beneath Harper as the golden Virginia landscape blurred into streaks of light and shadow. She leaned back in her seat, her eyes fixed on the horizon, but her thoughts churned in relentless loops as Evelyn Wallace's face lingered in her mind.

Evelyn knows something. Harper's fingers tapped an uneven rhythm against the tray table. *She's hiding it.* But instinct wasn't enough. She needed more than a gut feeling.

Their conversation replayed in her mind, every word magnified, every pause and inflection analyzed. Evelyn's gaze lingered—sharp, assessing, impenetrable. But there were moments Harper couldn't quite dismiss: the too-smooth adjustment of a lapel, the flicker of something just beneath the surface. Annoyance, perhaps. Or something else. Evelyn hadn't faltered, not outwardly. Still, Harper couldn't shake the feeling that something didn't quite fit.

Her mind circled back to the symbol she'd glimpsed beneath Evelyn's tablet: a spiral with three branches. The image tugged at her memory, a loose thread she couldn't quite pull free. *Not just some random mark. I've seen it before.* But where? A case file? A forgotten brief?

A chill crept down her spine. Harper shook her head, pulling out her phone. *Stop chasing ghosts.* But the symbol's familiarity nagged at her.

She hesitated, thumb poised over the browser. *Just a quick search.*

She typed: *spiral with three branches.*

The screen filled with images and links—corporate logos,

abstract designs, meaningless clutter. She sighed, rubbing her temples as fatigue pressed down. *You're chasing shadows.*

Her thumb hovered over the browser tab, ready to close it. Then... a small, unassuming logo caught her eye: *SomaLink.*

Harper frowned, her pulse quickening as she tapped the link. Evelyn's company. The name stared back at her, paired with the familiar spiral: *SomaLink.* A biotech firm lauded for breakthroughs in neuro-interface technology and virtual environments—fields that seemed worlds apart from Safe Genes. And yet there it was, the symbol unmistakably woven into their branding.

Her frown deepened as she scrolled through the page. SomaLink had spent years perfecting immersive tech: neuro-linked systems for end-of-life care, behavioral analysis, and therapy. Of course, Evelyn's logo would be on that paper.

But where have I seen it before?

The memory struck like lightning: Felix's office, just before CytoLife fell. Amid the chaos of their confrontation, she'd glimpsed the symbol on a dossier lying on his desk.

Her breath hitched. *No. It can't be.*

She tried to dismiss it. *You're projecting. It's just a corporate logo, a coincidence.* But the harder she pushed the thought away, the more insistent it became.

Harper gripped her phone tightly, her knuckles white. *You're connecting dots that aren't there.*

But why would Felix have anything from SomaLink?

CytoLife and SomaLink both operated in biotech, but there had been no public links between them—no collaborations, no partnerships. A quick search revealed nothing. Harper's mind raced. *A failed merger? A secret agreement?*

The train rattled beneath her, dusk falling outside the window as the landscape melted into shadows. Harper stared at the darkening horizon, the restlessness inside her growing louder with each passing mile.

You don't have enough. Not yet.

At the downtown train station, the humid Memphis air wrapped around her like a blanket—a sharp contrast to the chill she'd felt on the train. Harper made her way to the parking lot and opened her car door, her mind still tangled in thoughts from the train ride.

Evelyn Wallace. Just the thought of her made Harper's stomach knot. Her phone buzzed in her hand, jolting her back to the present. *Ethan.*

"Hey," she answered.

"Echo's back," Ethan said without preamble. "A message just came through Neon's node."

Harper's heart skipped a beat. "What did they say?"

There was a pause on the line. "It's cryptic, like always. But listen to this: `The truth about Safe Genes is buried deeper than you think. Evelyn holds a key, but it's not the whole picture. Some locks have changed. I couldn't see it all."`

Harper's grip on her phone tightened. *A key, but not the*

whole picture? Her pulse quickened as the words circled in her mind, each one slipping through her grasp before she could make sense of them. Evelyn had always been the perfect face of Safe Genes, steering it through political storms and spinning its public image with strategic finesse. But this wasn't about PR.

Something deeper, more malevolent, was at play.

"That's not all," Ethan added, his voice low. "Echo said this too,"

The Consortium's eyes are everywhere, but some of them are blind. Keep following the trail, but don't trust every step.

Harper's breath caught. *The Consortium.* The name lingered at the edge of her memory—half-remembered whispers from the margins of credibility. It lived in shadows, wrapped in rants and sensational theories, relegated to late-night forums and the mutterings of conspiracy theorists. In more intelligent circles, even mentioning it risked ridicule. Perhaps it was nothing more than a convenient label for something undefined, a catch-all phrase for the ambiguous.

"You trust this?" Harper asked.

"I don't know," Ethan admitted. "But it's all we've got. Feels like Echo's feeding us crumbs, not the whole loaf."

"Then we keep following the trail," Harper said, as if saying it aloud might make her believe it.

"How'd your DC meeting go?"

"Evelyn was smooth." Harper exhaled slowly. "Too smooth, Ethan."

The call ended, leaving Harper alone in the stillness of

her car. The weight of the conversation pressed against her temples, her thoughts circling a puzzle she couldn't quite piece together.

Her eyes caught on the flickering neon of *The Corkscrew Wine & Spirits.* The uneven glow painted jagged shadows across the street, daring her to slip inside and let herself disappear in the blur of cheap wine and numbness.

The pull was there—familiar, insistent. A hollow craving that whispered of quiet relief, but always delivered regret.

Harper drew in a slow breath and closed her eyes. Exhaling, she switched off her phone and leaned back, letting the cool leather press against her spine. She'd clawed her way out of that darkness before. She wasn't about to let it drag her under now.

This wasn't about running anymore. The doubts, the mistakes—she'd spent too long letting them chase her into corners.

Her gaze fixed on the empty street ahead. Whatever waited this time, she wasn't the same woman who flinched or faltered.

Not tonight.

SIXTEEN

Harper sat at the empty desk in CookCyber, her fingers tapping the edge in a restless rhythm. At her feet, Juno lay quietly, head on her paws, watchful eyes mirroring Harper's tension.

Harper's gaze drifted to the stack of files Nate had prepped earlier. The neatly organized pile sat untouched, overshadowed by Evelyn's evasiveness and the gnawing certainty that Felix's plans ran deeper than she'd imagined.

The files felt like her only anchor—a tether keeping her from spiraling into unanswerable questions. Her fingers hovered over the top one: Kyle Marshall.

The name tugged at her memory. A few weeks ago, she'd met him—sunken eyes shrinking from the light, fidgeting as though soothing an unseen pain. At the time, she'd dismissed him as just another casualty of the Safe Genes Initiative's failures, a victim of the government's ham-fisted cleanup of CytoLife's disaster.

Yet something about him lingered.

He'd mentioned brainwaves and mapping responses...

He hadn't stumbled over his words to describe what happened. He'd been specific and deliberate.

Harper flipped open the file and scanned the contents. The tragedy was laid bare in cold, clinical detail:

Patient presents with persistent cognitive dysfunction, including memory lapses, emotional dysregulation, and chronic pain, consistent with off-target effects of prior CRISPR-based therapy targeting the AGG1 gene. Symptoms include frequent aggression outbursts, sensory hypersensitivity, and neurological pain.

Her eyes narrowed as she reread the words. The detached language drained the humanity from Kyle's experience, reducing it to sterile bullet points. Yet one phrase blared like a warning bell: *off-target effects*. Unintended consequences, they called it.

The AGG1 gene—the epicenter of CytoLife's disaster. It had already left devastation in its wake, but this...

She leaned back, her thoughts whirring. *Brainwaves. Mapping responses. Chronic pain. Hypersensitivity.* Kyle's words echoed in her mind, sharp and insistent.

Juno let out a soft whine, breaking the silence. Harper absentmindedly scratched behind her ears while her focus remained locked on the file. *There's something here. Something we missed.*

Her heart skipped a beat when her eyes landed on the next line:

Artifacts of an implant, but no device.

An implant?

Her mind flashed to Rebecca and the implant that was making her sick. She'd assumed it was voluntary, a choice Rebecca had made. But what if it wasn't?

What if it had been forced on her?

And Kyle... he had to be part of the same twisted experiment.

Her eyes darted back to the notes, scanning faster now: *Tattoos on the neck concealed a scar.* Kyle had rubbed his neck repeatedly during their intake meeting, a gesture she'd dismissed as discomfort. Distracted, she hadn't considered it further and had left him with Nate, suggesting a medical checkup in passing.

Artifacts of an implant. Remnants in his tissue, unexplained.

Her stomach churned. This wasn't merely genetic tampering; something had been implanted in Kyle—implanted and then removed.

Her hand froze mid-stroke in Juno's fur. "This isn't just gene editing," she murmured, barely above a whisper. Was Felix testing them? Manipulating something beyond their DNA?

The thought tightened around her like a vise. If Rebecca's implant had made her sick, what had Kyle's done to him? The memory lapses, the erratic behavior, the chronic pain—each symptom now felt like a piece of a larger, sinister puzzle.

Harper's hands trembled as her mind raced, the pieces beginning to snap into place. How many others had been part of his experiments?

Her body sank back into the chair, her breath shallow, her thoughts spiraling into a dark abyss.

If Felix had done this to Rebecca... What else was he capable of?

And Lucas—God, where did he fit into all of this?

Harper bit her lip, her pulse pounding in her ears as the enormity of it all crashed over her. Felix wasn't just meddling with genes.

The implants—whatever they truly were—weren't tools. They were weapons in a war she was only beginning to comprehend.

Harper parked outside Brother Juniper's, her hands clenched around the steering wheel as she fought to steady her nerves. Dee had always been her anchor, her voice of reason. But the weight of Harper's suspicions threatened to strain forty years of friendship—again. She couldn't voice her fears about the implants, not yet. But, she could get her take on Evelyn Wallace.

Through the café's window, she spotted Dee, already halfway through her tea, glasses perched on her nose as she scrolled through her phone with casual focus.

"Hey," Harper said, sliding into the seat across from her. "Sorry I'm late."

Dee looked up, her expression softening, though a glint of concern lingered in her eyes. "Tell me you've got good news about Lucas. Your cryptic messages are keeping me up at night. And don't think I don't know you're holed up at Ethan's office." She gave Harper a pointed look, then softened her voice. "Honey, you're too stubborn for your own good."

Harper let out a shaky breath, pressing her hands to her temples. "You're right. I'm scared, Dee. Scared to death."

"Then out with it." Dee's hand closed over Harper's, warm and grounding. The contact steadied her more than she wanted to admit.

"I've been knee-deep in this mess. Ethan's doing all he can, but... there's something else."

Dee leaned back slightly, her brow furrowing. "What now?"

"I met with Evelyn Wallace."

Dee looked shocked. "*The* Evelyn Wallace? You two don't exactly travel in the same circles."

Harper exhaled slowly, her eyes drifting to the window as if searching for clarity. "It's complicated. She's tied to the Safe Genes Initiative."

"Yeah, I know," Dee replied. "She's a big reason it ever got off the ground. I remember the stories you told me—she's formidable. No wonder you two butted heads."

Harper's eyes found Dee's again, her tone subdued. "Dee, maybe I'm being paranoid, but something felt off. She was too smooth, too prepared—like she knew I was coming."

Dee raised a skeptical eyebrow. "Evelyn's been in this game for decades. Handling pressure is second nature. What are you getting at?"

"I don't know," Harper admitted. "But she shut down when I asked about Safe Genes. And I noticed something on her papers—a symbol I've seen before. It was in Felix's office, just before CytoLife fell apart."

Dee's eyes widened in confusion. "Felix? Wait, a symbol—what kind of symbol?" She motioned with her hand. "Lay it out for me."

"It's from a biotech company that Evelyn owns—SomaLink." Harper frowned, her fingers tapping the edge of the table. "I saw the logo on a dossier Felix had on his desk at CytoLife. At the time, I didn't think much of it, but now..."

"Now you think Evelyn and Felix might've been connected through her company? Harper, it could be nothing. It might've just been a legitimate business relationship."

"I don't know," Harper explained. "There's nothing in the public record, but it's not a coincidence. I just need to figure out how it all ties together."

"Look, I get it—you're desperate to find Lucas. But Evelyn's been in the public eye for years. If there was something shady, wouldn't it have surfaced by now?"

"Not if she's good at hiding it," Harper countered. "I know I don't have all the pieces, but there's too much smoke here to ignore."

Dee rubbed the bridge of her nose, clearly wrestling with Harper's words. "You always did have a nose for smoke."

"It's a stretch, I know. But if there's even a chance I'm right..."

Dee stared into her tea, her finger tracing the rim of the cup. "So you really think Evelyn's mixed up in something bigger?"

"I don't want to believe it, but the way she dodged my

questions felt too guarded, like she was protecting something deeper."

"I've always respected your instincts. But if Evelyn's involved in something this significant, uncovering it won't be easy. Not to mention how far-fetched that sounds."

Harper straightened and cleared her throat. "I can't let it go."

Dee sighed, glancing toward the window. "And if you're wrong? This could blow up in your face."

"I know. But if I'm right..."

Dee studied her carefully for a long moment before leaning back. "Then you'll need more than instincts. If Evelyn is as clever as you say, you won't find her cracks by accident."

Harper smoothed a hand down her rumpled sleeve. "I don't have a plan yet, but I will."

In the stark, fluorescent-lit halls of the Safe Genes clinic, Dr. Stephens moved with purpose, clipboard in hand. After years in the military and a medical career that had strayed too far from its oath, he carried the air of a man who valued efficiency over ethics. The polished floor reflected his hurried footsteps, creating a rhythmic counterpoint to the unnerving stillness around him. Observation rooms lined the corridor, their one-way glass concealing occupants blissfully unaware of the silent experiment unfolding inside their bodies.

In Room 12, Davis Lane sat stiffly, his fingers digging into the armrests and a nervous twitch bouncing through his foot. To an outsider, this was a routine follow-up: another box checked, another appointment to endure. Yet a far more dangerous motive was hidden beneath the clinical veneer.

The monitors above Lane's head hummed softly, their screens alive with streams of data. Bridge RNA, guided by an AI, was in motion. The ultimate precision tool for genetic editing, it functioned like a GPS for DNA, each molecular adjustment directed by an artificial intelligence fine-tuned to the patient's unique genetic code. On paper, it was flawless—science's bold leap toward perfection.

Dr. Stephens's eyes darted to the vitals displayed on the monitor. Heart rate elevated. Neural activity irregular. Stress? Perhaps. Or the first faint tremors of a deeper biological shift? His pen hovered over the clipboard as Lane's foot suddenly stilled, his gaze shifting as if his body understood a change his mind could not yet articulate. The edits were beginning to take hold.

Stephens straightened, his face betraying nothing. To everyone else—nurses, technicians, assistants—this was just another day. But to him, the signs were unmistakable. When you tampered with the code of life itself, consequences didn't simply obey the carefully crafted confines of human intention.

"Vitals stable," a nurse murmured, scribbling notes with a detachment that bordered on ignorance. Stephens resisted the urge to correct her. *Stable* was a lie. The changes were subtle, yes, but they had already begun, hidden in the quiet recalibration of cells and the rewiring of neural pathways.

A few doors down, a young woman in her early twenties

scrolled through her phone, her posture relaxed and her breathing steady. She belonged to a different cohort—one targeted for enhanced cognitive function. The edits in her DNA had lain dormant for months, silently integrating into the fabric of her being. Until today.

Stephens paused under the clinic's central monitor, a massive display that cast the floor in an ominous glow. Streams of data flowed across it in intricate patterns, each representing a patient in the trial. Deep within the network's layers, the triggers had been activated. Dormant gene edits stirred to life like a sleeping predator waking at last.

"This is it," Stephens muttered to his assistant, who nodded silently.

In Lane's room, his foot twitched again, though his expression remained placid. Elsewhere, the young woman let her phone slip from her hand, blinking as a faint wave of disorientation washed over her. Nerve pathways subtly shifted. Hormonal responses recalibrated. The changes were gentle, almost imperceptible. Weeks from now, those subtle adjustments would snowball into fleeting memory lapses, spikes of irritability, and disquieting moments of vertigo. The side effects, they promised, would fade. The *enhancements*, however, would endure.

"Gene edits activated in Group E," a voice crackled through the comms, its even tone masking the significance of the message.

Stephens's assistant adjusted their tablet, logging the development with practiced efficiency. To the untrained eye, everything seemed routine. Patients completed their appointments without incident, returning to their lives blissfully unaware that their biology was no longer entirely their own.

As the last patient disappeared down the corridor, Dr. Stephens returned to his station. His fingers moved deftly across the keyboard, inputting a final series of commands to close out the day's work. The monitor before him flickered, the endless data streams giving way to a single, stark message:

Pilot Test: Group E - Complete.

For a brief moment, Stephens stared at the screen, his reflection ghostlike in the cold, blue glow. The promise of Bridge RNA was breathtaking. The potential risks? Unfathomable. And yet the system worked.

For now.

The screen blinked as the secure link was established. Dr. Stephens appeared, his face a mask of fatigue and nervousness.

"Status report," Felix commanded, his voice slicing through the silence like a whip.

Stephens adjusted his glasses. "Gene edits triggered. No immediate side effects. Everything's proceeding as planned."

Felix leaned back, his expression unreadable, though his eyes gleamed with controlled intensity. This wasn't the first trial—there had been dozens marked by failures, recalibrations, and data sets reduced to ash. But those mistakes were now the bedrock of his confidence. The missing links had been addressed and the pieces aligned.

"And the Safe Genes system?" Felix asked.

Stephens hesitated, his throat bobbing. "Fully bypassed, thanks to the modified encryption. Any behavioral shifts remain buried under baseline readings. Even DARPA won't detect them."

A hint of a smile played on Felix's lips. The Silent Core encryption algorithm, extracted from a seemingly insignificant firm, had been the key. It rendered operations invisible, cloaking every adjustment in a seamless layer of fabricated data. By the time anyone noticed, it would be far too late.

Globally, Safe Genes was the strongest defense, the only true safeguard in a world where others had little or none. Its architects were intelligent, but intelligence meant little when shackled by rules and blind faith in the system.

Felix let the thought settle. Genius in the wrong hands was wasted. Safe Genes' creators were bound by their own doctrine, unwilling to see past their illusion of control.

HELIX had already dismantled that illusion. The fortress looked unbreachable, but the cracks had been set. By the time they noticed, the gate would already be open.

And once the gate opened, the rest of the world would follow.

Stephens pressed on, his words tumbling out in a rush to fill the void left by Felix's silence. "The edits are subtle—just enough to steer behavior without raising alarms. The implants provide real-time monitoring, allowing anomalies to be corrected before Safe Genes flags them. The next-gen shells are invisible on scans, perfectly integrated. It's... it's genius."

Felix's gaze didn't waver. He didn't need Stephens's praise. Rebecca's prototype had been the perfect genetic blueprint—the final piece of a puzzle no one else could see. With the implants in place and real-time adjustments at his fingertips, the margin for error had all but disappeared.

"Good," Felix said. "Daily updates. If anything deviates, recalibrate immediately."

Stephens nodded quickly, his movements jerky. "Yes, sir. Of course."

The screen blinked off, leaving Felix alone. The words on the display burned like a promise:

`Pilot Test: Group E - Complete.`

This wasn't just a test—it was the beginning. A ticking fuse, its fire creeping toward an unseen detonation. No one would notice the changes until they had already reshaped everything. By then, it wouldn't matter.

Felix tapped his fingers lightly against the desk, his mind racing ahead. The pieces were in place. The system was live. And now, the world would play the role he had written for it.

Lucas sat on the edge of the cot, his posture deliberately relaxed, though every muscle in his body remained ready. The scalpel Rebecca had smuggled in was tucked away, hidden like a loaded weapon, waiting for the right moment. He let his gaze move around the room in a slow, thorough sweep, cataloging every angle and detail. The cameras in the corners were obvious, but there were always more—hidden mics, pressure sensors, even the guards' footsteps outside.

Felix wouldn't leave anything to chance, and neither would he.

Across the room, Rebecca leaned against the wall, her head tipped back as she fought exhaustion. Lucas had seen that kind of weariness before, carved deep from carrying too much for too long. But now wasn't the time to dwell on it.

"Come here," he murmured, just loud enough for her to hear.

Rebecca hesitated, then pushed herself off the wall and crossed the room with quiet steps. She sank down beside him on the cot, her movements careful but unhurried. Their shoulders brushed, and Lucas gave her the briefest nod before his eyes swept over the room.

"They're watching," he whispered. His tone was calm but firm, meant to ground someone under duress. "We're going to let them think they're in control. Make them believe we're just sitting here, waiting for an opening."

Rebecca sat silently, paying close attention.

"They expect us to react," Lucas continued, his gaze fixed on the cameras. "To panic. To make a desperate move. But we won't. We're going to be unpredictable. Controlled. We break their rhythm first, and when they're scrambling to adjust, we move."

Rebecca shifted slightly, her tone matching his. "And how do we do that?"

"Small disruptions," Lucas murmured, tilting his head as if stretching his neck. "Nothing obvious. We make them question their setup—start doubting whether it's as tight as they think it is. That's when they'll adjust, and that's when we look for the gap."

He let his fingers brush against his jaw, a casual gesture that could pass for fatigue. "They think they've accounted for everything. They haven't accounted for us."

Rebecca's hand instinctively moved toward her pocket. "What about the scalpel?"

Lucas glanced at her. "It's for when the right moment comes—and when it does, we'll make it count."

Rebecca nodded, pressing her lips into a thin line. Lucas could see the questions swirling in her mind, the uncertainty. She hadn't been trained for this kind of pressure. He had, and he would carry them both if it came to that.

"We'll test them first," he explained. "Watch the guards. Find their pattern. Rebecca, when do they rotate shifts?"

"10 a.m.," she answered, sounding more confident. "They're consistent."

"Good," Lucas said. "That's our window. No risks until we're certain. When we move, we do it clean—no wasted steps. If we mess this up, we don't get a second chance."

Rebecca's gaze flicked to the floor, her voice barely above a whisper. "Lucas, I'm sorry. I shouldn't have dragged you into this."

He cut her off with a sharp glance. "Don't waste energy on regret. Focus on getting out of here. That's how we survive."

She nodded, but Lucas caught a flicker of guilt in her eyes. There was no time to address it. Instead, he reached out, his fingers brushing her arm in a fleeting, grounding gesture.

"This is going to work," he said. "They're gonna wish they hadn't underestimated us."

SEVENTEEN

The cold room closed in around him, rain ticking steadily against the window—a rhythmic taunt, each drop a reminder of time slipping away. The laptop's faint glow pierced the gloom, its low hum melding with the sound of his measured breathing. Baxter had waited long enough. He needed answers from Zorin.

The screen flickered, and Leonid Zorin's sharp features appeared.

"Mr. Baxter." Zorin's thick Russian accent filled the room, his words steeped in mockery. "Didn't expect you back so soon. How's retirement treating you?"

Baxter's fingers drummed against the desk, his only visible sign of his impatience. "Do you have it?"

Zorin leaned back, shadows shifting across his face. "Straight to business. Always." He paused. "Yes, I have the intel. Felix is… slippery. Harder to track than a ghost."

Baxter gritted his teeth. "Where is he?"

Zorin's smirk faded, replaced by the gleam of a predator sensing weakness. "Deep in rural France. Near Bordeaux. Off the grid, heavily guarded. But there's movement—equipment, personnel. And…" He leaned closer, lowering his voice as if savoring the revelation. "The young man and the girl. They might be there."

Rebecca. Lucas. Baxter's pulse pounded, but his voice remained steady and cold. "Details."

Zorin's smile widened. "Ah, but first—my fee. You want the best, you pay for the best. This intel wasn't cheap."

"You'll get paid," Baxter snapped. "Talk."

"Good." Zorin's satisfaction was almost palpable. "The facility is a fortress. Felix doesn't leave loose ends. You'll need more than a few men to get in." His smirk returned. "I can provide a team. For the right price."

Baxter swallowed his disgust. "Assemble the team."

Zorin inclined his head in a mocking gesture. "Details to follow. Good luck, Mr. Baxter. You'll need it."

Baxter stared at the blank monitor, his mind racing. Zorin's intel was solid—for now—but the man's arrogance grated on him. Trusting a snake had its cost.

He stood and began pacing the room. His identity was secure, and the funds were ready. This mission wasn't about pride or grudges. It was about Rebecca. Her life. And no price was too high.

Harper's son, Lucas, was an unfortunate variable. Necessary, but ultimately expendable.

Baxter's thoughts turned to Evelyn Wallace. Her grip on control had faltered, allowing Felix to slip through cracks she refused to admit existed. Unforgivable. She'd forgotten who she was dealing with. Once Rebecca was safe and Felix eliminated, he'd remind her.

For now, the mission took precedence. Baxter turned back to the laptop, his fingers moving with measured precision as he drafted instructions for Zorin. The team needed to be flawless. The operation, seamless.

Failure was not an option.

The clicks of the encrypted connection signaled the call was live, though Evelyn's face had yet to appear. Felix's gaze shifted to the data streaming across the adjacent monitor, projections glowing with promise. A faint, satisfied smile tugged at his lips.

She's late.

Finally, Evelyn's image materialized on the screen, her expression composed and inscrutable. "Felix," she said, "you've been busy."

Felix leaned back in his chair. "Idle hands accomplish little, Evelyn. We're nearing a critical juncture."

Her brow arched. "And yet you've made decisions that could jeopardize the entire operation." The words had their desired effect; Evelyn didn't appreciate being kept in the dark.

"What you see as risky, I see as progress," Felix explained.

"We need to evolve to stay ahead."

Evelyn's eyes narrowed. "Evolution? CytoLife was your idea of evolution. That collapse was entirely avoidable."

Felix waved away the comment. "CytoLife served its purpose. Harper Brasfield was an unforeseen complication, yes, but the fallout gave us exactly what we needed—freedom from scrutiny."

"It also exposed us," Evelyn countered. "If you'd followed the original plan, Baxter would've taken the fall cleanly—disgraced but with no reason for the world to question what came next. Instead, you—"

"I adapted," Felix interjected. "And now we're stronger. CytoLife's baggage is gone. We've returned to the shadows—unseen and more capable than ever."

"Your confidence borders on arrogance, Felix. The Consortium thrives on invisibility, not bold moves."

"Exposure won't matter once the mission is complete," Felix explained. "CytoLife buried Baxter, just as intended—albeit through unconventional means. The rest has worked to our advantage, whether you choose to admit it or not."

Evelyn had ensured Felix's proximity to Baxter, secretly orchestrating his role to monitor everything from within. The AGG1 gene edits were never meant to be noticed—only felt. A ghost in the machine, guiding human behavior without resistance. Over time, a more compliant population would open the door to Baxter's so-called utopia, with VitaLexis cementing their dominion.

She held his gaze, her voice razor-sharp. "Stronger, perhaps. But survival isn't about boldness; it's about thoroughness. One misstep, and everything we've built unravels."

"This isn't about survival anymore," Felix countered. "It's about dominance."

"Dominance is dangerous, Felix. CytoLife proved how quickly things fall apart when one thread is pulled."

"Harper was that thread," Felix sneered. "She won't get another chance."

Evelyn's tone shifted, becoming cooler and more persistent. "Felix, we're on the brink of a new era. Population collapse isn't a possibility—it's inevitable. Resources are stretched to breaking. I trust I don't need to remind you of our real purpose."

Felix's gaze didn't waver. "The plans remain intact. The genetic control you require is within reach. Every variable, even the unforeseen ones, has worked in our favor. The system is adaptable. Resilient."

Evelyn studied him. "Adaptability isn't my priority, Felix. Control is."

"The HELIX system is solid, Evelyn. We're not just on track; we're ahead."

"Remember, Felix—systems, no matter how advanced, can fail. And when they do, the consequences are irreversible."

"I'm aware," Felix said impatiently. "But my system won't fail."

Evelyn leaned closer, her face filling the frame. "Let's hope your confidence isn't misplaced."

The call ended abruptly, her image blinking out. Felix leaned back in his chair. Control? The thought almost made him laugh. Evelyn's obsession was as outdated as her understanding of what he'd built.

She wanted stability. He sought evolution.

Felix's gaze lingered on the blank screen, Evelyn's words echoing in his mind: *Systems can fail.* It wasn't the first time she'd underestimated him.

Their earliest partnership came to mind, years ago, when Evelyn had tasked him with neutralizing a whistleblower threatening one of her projects. Her instructions had been clear: intimidate, but don't eliminate. "We can't risk the scrutiny," she'd warned.

Felix had nodded, outwardly compliant, while quietly engineering his own solution. The whistleblower hadn't simply vanished; their existence had been wiped clean, every connection severed. Evelyn had underestimated the risk a loose end posed. By the time she realized Felix had exceeded her mandate, it was too late—the threat had been eliminated, and the project's success was secured.

She'd been furious, accusing him of recklessness. But the results spoke louder than her protests. In that moment, Felix understood Evelyn's limits. Brilliant, yes. But constrained. Felix didn't operate within such boundaries. He created them—for others.

His focus shifted to the monitor beside him. The HELIX system was his masterpiece—stolen in its infancy, reshaped, and reborn into something far beyond its original design. What had begun as a spoil of war, plundered during a corporate takedown, had been little more than a crude prototype, shackled by its creators' lack of vision. Felix had seen the threads of something revolutionary even as flames consumed the building behind him.

In that moment, he'd pocketed the core framework, feeling an almost electric certainty. It wasn't just an opportunity—it was the missing piece he hadn't known he was searching for. The raw system had been little more than a skeleton, but under his guidance, it had evolved into a force of nature.

Every line of its code had been rewritten, its purpose honed to a singular edge. The system might have been conceived by others, but HELIX—its brilliance, its power—was entirely his. They'd built a tool; he had created the future.

No one—not Evelyn, not his closest allies—knew the truth. What they accessed was a carefully constructed façade, a mask hiding the real HELIX in plain sight.

Now, it wove through oceans of data with unmatched precision, predicting and adapting faster than Felix had ever imagined. It wasn't just a tool—it was a weapon, reshaping the battlefield entirely.

Evelyn, with all her ambition, didn't grasp its full potential.

Not yet.

Felix stared at his reflection in the darkened monitor, the steady glow of data scrolling beside him. The numbers were on his side.

A quiet, insistent whisper threaded through his thoughts: *Push forward. Don't hesitate. The future is in your hands.*

Felix adjusted his smart glasses. The most efficient path had been calculated.

Data doesn't lie.

Tucked away in Arlington, Virginia, at the headquarters of DARPA—the Defense Advanced Research Projects Agency, a research and development agency of the United States Department of Defense—Dr. Caroline Mendes stared at her terminal. Decisive and unwavering, she had built her career on trust in the system. When gene monitoring emerged from the chaos, she didn't hesitate. She saw a chance to be a force for good and took it.

Streams of genetic data scrolled by in ceaseless waves. Safe Genes, hailed as the bulwark against CytoLife's chaos, was now her battlefield, built on DARPA's breakthroughs.

Renowned as the US government's most daring research arm, DARPA had a history of pushing the boundaries of science, from stealth technology to the early internet. In the aftermath of CytoLife's disaster, it had stepped in to rebuild trust, with its research forming the backbone of Safe Genes. For Caroline, the stakes couldn't have been higher. What had begun as a safeguard against rogue edits now felt like a high-stakes chess match with consequences she couldn't always see.

Safe Genes gathered data from everywhere: voluntary submissions, airport scans, and clinics working to repair CytoLife's damage. It promised to spot and neutralize dangerous gene edits before they spread. Critics worried about privacy; Caroline worried about missing a single mutation that could spiral out of control.

Today, something was off.

She hovered over a flagged sequence, frowning. It looked

perfect. Too perfect. On a whim, she ran a deeper diagnostic. No errors. The system insisted it was fine, but her gut said otherwise.

The protocols were airtight, or so DARPA claimed. She rubbed her temples. *Maybe I'm imagining things.*

A soft beep sounded. Another flagged sequence, more subtle than the first. Again, no visible faults. The final readout was pristine—almost elegant. A tight knot formed in her chest. Was there a pattern?

She skimmed the metadata, but most details were classified. DARPA's layers of secrecy ran deep, but this felt different. It wasn't just the usual clearance levels—something about the flagged sequences gnawed at her. Were they being fed into the system deliberately?

Her supervisor stepped in, imposing, with the bearing of a seasoned officer. "Everything running smoothly, Doctor?"

"Yes, sir." She gestured at the highlighted data. "A few anomalies, but the system cleared them. I was about to finalize the report."

His expression never wavered. "If Safe Genes says it's clear, trust it. We don't second-guess the system."

She hesitated, her eyes on the sequences. "Understood."

No further questions. He left. Protocol was protocol. The system said these edits were normal—nothing to see. She sighed, her shoulders tight with doubt, and clicked *Approve.*

Felix leaned back in his chair, the soft glow of the terminal casting sharp angles across his face as genetic reports scrolled past. The Safe Genes Initiative had exceeded even his own high expectations, its vast infrastructure quietly bending to his will. His modifications ran seamlessly, buried deep within the churn of supposedly "routine" data.

The AGG1 gene edits—pioneered by Rebecca at CytoLife—had been a starting point, a crude prototype. Now, with HELIX AI and breakthroughs like Bridge RNA, Felix had elevated the technology to something far more sophisticated. He oversaw it all through a covert team of scientists, each working on a fragment, never glimpsing the whole.

For now, the latent gene edits lay dormant within a select group of patients enrolled in Safe Genes, each outfitted with implants disguised as harmless monitoring devices.

Harmless. The word carried a dark irony that amused him. What could be less harmless than a device that silently rewrote someone from the inside out?

Through the implants, Felix tracked every shift in real time, calibrating the silent gene edits as needed. Triggers had already activated, slipping past overworked doctors skimming flagged reports. No alarms, no suspicions—just subtle changes in behavior: a flicker of irritability, a brief lapse in memory. Ripples, poised to swell into waves.

Soon, those he found redeemable would be guided into obedience. The unsalvageable? Their bodies would quietly turn on themselves. Clean. Efficient.

A new report blinked onto the screen, sharp and clinical. Felix's gaze zeroed in. No anomalies, no red flags—exactly as Dr. Stephens had promised. The data was pristine, untouched by suspicion. The pilot test was flawless.

"Genius," he murmured. By the time Safe Genes—or anyone else—realized what was happening, it would be too late.

The implants weren't mere gadgets; they connected him directly to the pulse of his operation. Data streamed continuously, fueling his control. This wasn't a test—it was a symphony of calculated chaos, and Felix was the sole conductor.

Universal deployment loomed on the horizon, inevitable and unstoppable.

Another line of text pulsed on the screen:

Pilot Test: Group E - Stable.

Felix leaned forward, voice low. "Perfect."

His phone buzzed. A message appeared:

Status: All sequences approved. Latent modifications proceeding as expected.

"They don't even know what they're looking at," he muttered, fingers tapping an idle rhythm on the desk.

Good. Let them stay blind.

Harper stood by the window, the Memphis skyline a blur beyond her gaze as CookCyber's bustle faded into the background.

Neon, hunched over his workstation, hadn't stopped working to rebuild their defenses. But Harper knew Felix wasn't just trying to win—he wanted absolute control. And whatever he had planned for Lucas was too terrifying to dwell on.

"We know Felix is dangerous," Harper said. "He's outmaneuvered us at every turn. If we wait too long, we'll lose Lucas and Rebecca for good."

Neon glanced up briefly, his fingers flying across the keyboard. "Dangerous? He's been playing us. That virus? It wasn't random. It hit exactly where we're weakest—like he knows our system inside out."

"Any leads?" Harper asked.

Neon tapped a few keys, pulling up a chaotic stream of encrypted data. "There's a node I've been tracking. Completely off-grid—no records, no signals—but the traffic running through it is massive. Every time I get close, another layer of encryption locks me out. It's deeper than anything I've seen in years. I'm sure it's tied to Felix."

Harper leaned closer. "What makes you say that?"

Neon zoomed in on a web of faintly connected nodes, highlighting one—a single point in rural France. "This. A ghost node. No records, no official activity, but it's relaying encrypted data across Europe. The encryption matches fragments of Felix's virus. His signature's all over it."

"So, this is his base?"

Neon shook his head. "I can't say for sure. But it's our best lead. Every time I probe deeper, the defenses tighten—like they know I'm coming. It's a nightmare."

"What's the next move?"

"I'm close," Neon said, adjusting the screen. "If I can break through this layer, we might access his network—maybe even intercept his communications. But it's risky. If I push too hard, he'll know."

Ethan, silent until now, crossed his arms. "Risk assessment?"

Neon hesitated. "He could wipe the node. Vanish. Or worse, set a trap. But this is the closest we've ever been. The encryption's so deep, I'm betting he won't notice until I'm inside."

"Is it worth it?" Ethan asked. "Felix already hit us hard once. If this is a trap—"

"It might be," Neon interrupted. "But if we don't take the shot, we may not get another."

Harper's voice cut through the tension. "We don't have time to second-guess. If this leads to Felix, we follow it."

Neon nodded. "I'll need more time, but I'll get us in."

Ethan exhaled. "And if it's another trap? We can't afford to lose everything again."

"We don't have a choice," Harper said, her voice steady despite the dread coiling around her heart. "If we play it safe, we lose them." Lucas's face flashed in her mind.

Suddenly, Neon's screen blinked, and a new message

appeared on their secure channel:

You're getting close. But Felix isn't the only one you need to worry about. Watch your back.

Harper's heart skipped. *Echo.* The mole's cryptic messages had always been unsettling, but this one felt different. Urgent.

Ethan frowned, reading over her shoulder. "'Felix isn't the only one?' Who else is involved?"

"This feels like a setup," Neon said, raking his fingers through his hair. "If someone else is pulling strings, we're flying blind."

"We stick to the plan," Harper said, her gaze locking with Ethan's.

Ethan nodded. "Neon, break through that encryption and get us those coordinates. If Echo's warning us, there's more going on—but Felix is still the target."

Echo's words lingered in Harper's mind as the room fell silent.

Who else was playing this game?

Harper entered the conference room, her phone already dialing Kyle's number. He picked up on the second ring, his voice cautious.

"Ms. Brasfield? Is everything alright?"

"Kyle, I need to ask you about Stonebrook," she said without hesitation. "You said you don't remember much, but anything you can recall might help. Even the smallest detail."

The line went quiet, long enough for Harper to check if

the call had dropped. Finally, Kyle spoke.

"I... I've been thinking about it. There's something—it's not clear, but I remember... tests. I wasn't the only one."

"Tests? What kind of tests? Do you remember anything about the others?"

"I don't know exactly," Kyle admitted, each word dragging as if he had to pull them from a locked vault. "There was a room—a medical bay. They took us in one by one. I don't know what they were looking for, but one of the doctors mentioned something about a 'control group.'" He paused, then added, almost to himself, "I don't know if that's helpful."

"It is," Harper said, her voice steady despite the storm brewing in her thoughts. "You've been more helpful than you realize, Kyle. I'll be in touch."

She ended the call and lowered the phone, gripping it tightly.

Tests. Control group.

If Felix was experimenting on them, what did that mean for Lucas and Rebecca?

EIGHTEEN

"Is this the best we have?" Harper asked, glancing between Ethan and Neon, who was hunched over his screen, his focus unshakable.

"This node is tied to Felix—I'm sure of it," Neon replied without looking up. "It's buried deep, but the traffic flowing through it is massive. I've cracked a few layers, but the closer I get, the more I expect a trap."

Ethan pushed off the wall with a grunt. "And Baxter?"

Harper threw up her hands. "Nothing. He disappeared after losing everything."

"Figures," Ethan muttered. "Just when we're making headway, he pulls a vanishing act."

Neon glanced up briefly. "Honestly? Better if he stays gone. We don't need more loose ends."

Harper's gaze snapped to him. "Loose ends? That's my

son out there. If Baxter's playing his own game, we need to know. He's in this whether he likes it or not."

Ethan stepped in, his voice calm but firm. "Tacks, we need to focus on what we *can* control—and that's breaking through this node."

Harper's shoulders sagged slightly. "You're right. I'm sorry. It's just..." Her tone softened as she looked at Neon. "I know you're doing everything you can."

Neon nodded, his focus already back on the screen. "We're making progress," he said, tilting the monitor toward them. "This encryption is nearly impenetrable, but we're close. The node is completely off-grid, with no records anywhere, but the traffic is too significant to ignore. If we can breach it, we'll have a direct line to Felix's network."

"Could that lead us to Lucas and Rebecca?"

"Not certain, but it's our best shot. If I can crack this next layer, we might gain access to his communications—maybe even pinpoint their location."

"And what if you trigger something? What happens if Felix realizes we're in?"

"He could wipe everything. Or worse, launch another virus. We can't afford that."

"Waiting isn't an option," Harper said. "We need something tangible—boots on the ground."

Ethan frowned. "You're talking about an assault team?"

"Yes," Harper said. "Felix blindsided us once. I'm not giving him the chance to do it again."

Ethan hesitated, then shook his head. "We're not equipped for that. If we go after him physically, we'll need reinforcements—and resources we don't have right now."

"That's where Baxter should've come in," Harper said bitterly. "But since he's hiding, we'll have to figure it out ourselves."

Ethan gestured toward Neon. "For now, we focus on the node. Break into Felix's system, pull whatever we can. Once we know more, we'll figure out the next move."

Harper's gaze shifted back to Neon's screen. "Fine. But once you're in, we're not waiting. Felix doesn't get another chance."

Neon nodded. "I'll get through. We're close."

Ethan placed a hand on Harper's shoulder, gesturing for her to step back. "Let's give him space to work," he said quietly. Harper hesitated but complied, her gaze lingering on the indecipherable data cascading across the screens.

The office settled into a heavy, expectant silence. Time stretched, marked only by the occasional sharp intake of breath from Neon. From the seating area, Harper and Ethan exchanged tense glances but said nothing, the weight of the moment hanging between them.

Finally, Neon leaned forward, his voice breaking the tension. "This is it. We're in position."

Once Harper and Ethan moved closer to his desk, he continued, "Initiating the breach. This is the last critical layer—once we're past it, we'll have access to Felix's command node."

"Just get us through," Harper urged.

"How long until we know if it worked?" Ethan asked.

"Minutes. Maybe hours," Neon replied without looking

up. "Depends on the encryption depth—and how closely Felix is watching.

"I'm breaking through—wait, hold on," Neon said under his breath.

"What is it?" Ethan asked.

"It's... thinner than I expected," Neon frowned. "This layer should've been tougher. It's like I'm being... let in."

"Let in?" Ethan's eyes narrowed. "That sounds like a trap."

"Yeah, it does," Neon admitted. "But we're too close to stop now. I need to see what's on the other side."

The screen flashed, and a flood of new data spilled across the display. Neon's eyes widened. "We're in."

Ethan leaned over his shoulder. "What do you see?"

"It's a command node, alright. Felix is routing traffic from all over Europe—Paris, London, Zurich—straight through here." Neon's voice dropped. "And there's a massive data transfer scheduled for tomorrow. Highly encrypted."

Harper's pulse quickened. "A transfer? Where?"

Neon zoomed in on the coordinates. "Just outside Paris. Off-grid—no official record. Could be a lab, a warehouse, or a safe house."

"Could be where they're holding Lucas and Rebecca," Harper murmured. "Or something bigger."

Neon's brow furrowed. "There's more. Something about a pilot test tied to Safe Genes."

"Felix is using Safe Genes to cover his tracks. We suspected he was manipulating the program, but this confirms it," Harper remarked, her eyes widening.

Ethan frowned. "Why leave it for us to find? If he's smart

enough to encrypt everything, why make this part easy?"

"Because he wants us to find it," Neon observed as he shifted in his chair.

"It doesn't matter," Harper cut in. "If Lucas and Rebecca are there, we can't wait. We have to move."

Suddenly, Neon's screen flashed red. His hands froze. "Wait... something's wrong."

"What?" Harper demanded.

"The system's reacting. Felix must've set a counterattack—there's a massive spike across multiple nodes. It's not just a virus—it's a regional blackout. Communications and power—he could take Memphis offline."

"Can you stop it?" Ethan asked.

"I'm trying," Neon said, his fingers flying over the keyboard. "If I can't isolate the node, it'll cascade—power outages and comms down. Felix could shut everything down."

Sweat beaded on Neon's forehead as he worked. "If I sever the node, we might contain it. But I don't know how long I have."

Harper gripped the back of Neon's chair as the screen erupted into chaos before freezing suddenly.

Finally, the screen went dark. Neon briefly closed his eyes and slumped back. "I shut it down. Just in time. But he knows we're here."

Harper's heart pounded. "What about the data? Do we still have a lead?"

Neon nodded slowly. "Yes, we've still got it. Felix didn't manage to wipe the node, but he knows. He'll retaliate."

Baxter was already savoring the confrontation: Felix Ross, bound and broken, kneeling before him, but not until Zorin's hit team had softened him up and made him... compliant.

His instructions were exact: no permanent damage. Felix's face and body had to remain intact. Baxter wanted the moment—the eye contact, the raw fear—as he dismantled Felix, piece by piece.

First, there would be a confession. A full account of Felix's betrayal, recorded for posterity. Baxter would ensure the world saw Felix for what he truly was: a traitor, a rabid dog that needed to be put down.

And when it was done, Baxter would rise as the wronged visionary, the philanthropist whose ideals had been hijacked by lesser minds.

As for Harper Brasfield? Irrelevant. This wasn't a courtroom drama. Her so-called ethics and emotional grandstanding had no place here. She'd be on the sidelines with everyone else, reading about it in the press—the same press that would hail him as a hero.

Outside, the rural French countryside lay still, blanketed in silence. Leonid Zorin's mercenaries moved through the shadows like wraiths: highly trained, highly paid, and utterly focused.

The mission was clear: breach Felix's hidden site and retrieve Rebecca and Lucas.

Static flared in Baxter's ear. "You're in position?"

"Da," Zorin replied, his Russian accent clipped over the

comms. "We are outside the perimeter. Minimal security. Looks like a dead site."

Baxter, monitoring from a secure location miles away, gritted his teeth. "Felix wouldn't leave it unguarded. Stay sharp."

On the monitor, Baxter watched Zorin motion to his team, their movements fluid as they sliced through the fence and slipped into the compound. The silence was unnerving—no guards or alarms, only the faint hum of the night.

"It's a ghost town," one of Zorin's men muttered, his rifle sweeping the area.

"Check the building," Zorin ordered. "Make sure it's clear."

As the team moved deeper into the compound, a gnawing unease coiled in Baxter's gut. This was too easy.

"Baxter, we're inside," Zorin reported. "No sign of hostiles."

"Then where are they?" Baxter growled, his frustration cutting through the comm. "Felix wouldn't leave Rebecca and Lucas unguarded."

Zorin advanced cautiously, his gaze cutting through the shadows. "Wait... there's something here. We're picking up an encrypted signal—it's close, coming from one of the rooms."

Days blurred into a haze as Lucas and Rebecca waited, each hour grinding against their nerves. Every time they thought they'd deciphered the guards' routines, something shifted, almost as if Felix anticipated their every move. Determination gave way to desperation, and Rebecca's once-unshakable resolve began to crack. Her health was deteriorating, and every hour that passed took something they couldn't get back.

As Lucas debated his next move, Rebecca, who had been leaning against the wall, collapsed to the side.

"Help! Somebody, help!" Lucas's voice shattered the silence, raw with panic. "She's not breathing!"

Rebecca lay motionless on the cold floor, her skin ashen, her breaths shallow and erratic. Lucas's shouts ricocheted off the walls, frantic and unrelenting. "Please! She's dying!"

The lock buzzed, and two guards burst in, suspicion etched across their faces. One knelt beside Rebecca, pressing two fingers to her neck to check for a pulse, while the other kept his weapon trained on Lucas, eyes sharp and ready for trouble.

"What happened?" the first guard barked.

"I don't know!" Lucas's voice cracked. "She just collapsed—do something!"

The second guard stepped toward Lucas, his movements cautious. Before he could react, Rebecca's eyes snapped open.

The flash of a scalpel caught the dim light as she drove it deep into the first guard's side. His body jerked violently, a strangled gasp escaping his throat as blood bloomed across his shirt.

Lucas lunged at the second guard, slamming a fist into his throat before the man could draw his weapon. The guard staggered, choking, and Lucas grabbed his baton, swinging it hard. The guard crumpled, unconscious.

Rebecca twisted the scalpel deeper into the first guard. His wide eyes locked on hers before his body went limp and fell beside her.

"Let's go," Lucas rasped, pulling Rebecca to her feet.

He snatched a keycard from the guard's belt, and together they bolted through the door, slipping into the dim hallway beyond.

The corridor was eerily silent, every shadow a potential threat. "You okay?" Lucas asked, glancing back at her.

Rebecca wiped sweat from her brow and nodded, her breath uneven. "I'll be fine. Just... keep moving."

They crept along the walls, their footsteps barely audible. Lucas's mind raced. He'd gambled on the guards' inexperience, knowing they wouldn't be ready when it counted. His earlier cries for help replayed in his head—a trap from the start. Timing had been everything.

"They weren't ready," Lucas muttered, scanning the dimly lit passage. "We got lucky."

Rebecca, still clutching the bloodied scalpel, shot him a look. "Lucky, or smart?"

A faint smirk tugged at his lips. "Bit of both."

The hallway twisted and turned, a maze of identical doors and endless passageways. Freedom had been within reach, but now they were ensnared in a labyrinth, with no clear way out.

Rebecca froze as they rounded a corner. "Lucas," she whispered. "Where are we?"

He scanned the endless hallway. No windows. No

markers. Just sterile walls stretching endlessly, mocking any hope of escape.

"Keep moving," he said. "We'll figure it out."

Rebecca stayed close; the scalpel clenched tightly in her hand. Their footsteps echoed in a sharp, ghostly rhythm, the silence shrouding them as they ventured deeper into the unknown.

NINETEEN

JUNE 2025

Harper sat on the porch, enveloped by the humid Memphis night. Juno lay at her feet, her ears flicking at every distant noise. The roadblock they'd hit at CookCyber made regrouping necessary, but her mind refused to rest.

Felix's plans. Evelyn's warning. Echo's cryptic messages. They churned in her head like a puzzle missing too many pieces. *The truth is buried deeper than you think.* She hated conspiracies, but every sign pointed to something bigger—something just out of reach.

Juno shifted, resting her head on Harper's foot as if sensing her unease. Harper scratched behind the dog's ears, her thoughts drifting to Lucas. *Felix doesn't make unnecessary moves. If he's holding Lucas, there's a reason.*

The sharp sound of a car door slamming pulled her from her thoughts. She looked up as Dee climbed the steps, her leather bag slung casually over one shoulder.

"Honey, you look like you're about to crack," Dee observed with a cautious smile. "You okay?"

"Just thinking," Harper replied, waving her toward the door. "Grab a drink if you want. I'll take anything to clear my head."

Dee raised an eyebrow but didn't argue. A few minutes later, she returned with two glasses of iced tea. "Thinking doesn't suit you," she teased, handing over a glass. "You've got that thousand-yard stare."

Harper snorted softly, though the tension in her voice lingered. "Every time I think we're getting close, Felix is still ten steps ahead. And Evelyn—don't even get me started..."

Dee sank into the chair beside her. "Harper, I've been meaning to say this—you're carrying too much on your own. You can't chase every lead and fight every fight. You'll burn out."

"I don't have a choice," Harper cried. "Lucas is out there—God knows what Felix is doing to him. His fate is tied to Rebecca's, and Evelyn's playing games I can't even begin to untangle."

Dee let the words settle before speaking. "And Charlotte? When's the last time you talked to her?"

Harper froze, guilt flashing in her eyes. "Charlie's fine. We talked. It wasn't long, but she knows I'm doing everything I can for Lucas."

Dee tilted her head. "Does she? Or does she think you've forgotten about her?"

Harper looked away. "I haven't forgotten. I just—there's

too much going on."

Dee exhaled. "That girl is you all over—your smarts, your drive. But she's got her daddy's pragmatism too. She's not mad, Harper. She's worried. She misses you."

Harper's voice softened, pride laced with guilt. "She said that?"

Dee nodded. "She gets it more than you think. But she needs to hear it from you."

Harper brushed a hand across her eyes, her shoulders sagging. "I'll call her," she murmured. "I promise."

Before Dee could respond, the porch lights flickered. Juno's head shot up, ears pinned forward as the neighborhood plunged into darkness.

"What the hell?" Harper stood abruptly and turned toward the street. The city's glow was gone, swallowed by an eerie blackness. Even downtown had disappeared into the void.

Dee joined her at the porch railing. "Power outage?"

Harper shook her head. "No. It's not just us. Look—nothing. No lights, no traffic signals. This is something else."

She turned to Dee. "We need to get to CookCyber. Now."

Dee grabbed her bag and keys. "Get Juno. I'll drive. Let's go."

The downtown Memphis streets simmered with an uneasy stillness, the kind that felt ready to snap. Then, without warning, it did. People surged from every corner, their movements chaotic—a volatile mix of excitement and panic threatening to ignite.

A sharp crack split the air, like a gunshot or a transformer exploding, making Harper and Dee flinch.

In the backseat, Juno stood rigid, her eyes darting to every sudden movement, ears pinned forward, muscles coiled as if ready to spring.

"Damn it, was that a shot?" Dee asked, her grip tightening on the wheel.

"I don't know. Just keep driving," Harper said, her eyes scanning the unrest outside. "Turn right up here. We'll take the back way."

"I don't like this one bit, Harper. It feels like a powder keg out here," Dee muttered.

As they turned, the streets grew more chaotic. Protesters filled the sidewalks, shoving and shouting over each other. Chants rang out, rising above the noise: *"Your System, Our Lives—We Say NO!"* and *"Hands Off Our DNA!"*

Windows shattered. Graffiti streaked across walls as people sprayed slogans in bold colors. Others climbed onto parked cars, stomping on hoods, and waving makeshift banners. Harper's stomach twisted as she watched the disorder unfold, a visceral reminder of how close everything was to unraveling.

"Next left," Harper instructed, her eyes darting between the crowd and the road. "Third building, turn down the alley, park in the back."

As they approached CookCyber, a bottle shattered on the pavement inches from the car. Harper's heart jolted. "Hurry!"

She threw the door open and jumped out before the car fully stopped. Behind her, Juno leapt through the still-open door, hitting the ground in stride and bounding after her.

Near the building, a group of figures loomed, their shouting a chaotic blur. One man surged forward, his arm cocked to hurl something.

Juno's growl cut through the noise—low, sharp, and unyielding. She planted herself between Harper and the crowd, her stance rigid, every muscle coiled.

The man hesitated, faltering under the weight of her fierce gaze.

"Juno, heel!" Harper commanded. The dog snapped to her side, teeth bared, every fiber of her body a warning.

The man muttered something and backed into the mob. Harper caught her breath, relief crashing into her like a wave. But there was no time to linger.

"Let's go!" Dee shouted, grabbing Harper's arm and pulling her toward the building.

They reached the entrance just as the door swung open, revealing a woman with a shotgun leveled at them.

"Stop right there!" the woman barked. "Don't come any closer unless you want trouble!"

Harper froze, her hands instinctively raised. "It's Harper Brasfield! I'm unarmed!"

Rita Johnson blinked, recognition flickering across her face. "Harper? Oh Lord, I'm sorry!" She lowered the gun quickly. "Thought you were looters—or worse. It's getting ugly out here."

"Trust me, I noticed," Harper said dryly as she stepped

across the threshold, Juno still at her side with her tail stiff.

"Brass, Dee, get inside. Now," Ethan commanded, appearing behind Rita and pulling them further in with a swift motion.

Once inside, Harper glanced at Rita. "Thanks for the... assist. Maybe we go with something less lethal next time before pulling out the shotgun?"

Ethan, still catching his breath, waved his hand. "Rita—when did you even get a shotgun? You know what? Never mind." He glanced around quickly. "Let's move away from the windows. Rita, stay close, but not by the door."

Rita squared her shoulders, unfazed. "I've been around guns my whole life, and I've stared down plenty of people with nothing to lose. I'll stay right here, if it's all the same to you."

She glanced at Juno. "And Miss Juno can keep me company," she added, more a statement than a request. "Right, girl?"

Juno padded over, settling beside her in a vigilant stance, clearly intent on staying put.

Ethan bolted the door behind them, his face grim as he led them deeper into the building. The silence inside was broken only by distant shouts and the faint shriek of sirens outside.

"We're in the dark," Neon muttered. "Literally."

Harper slumped against the wall, her mind racing. "This isn't random, is it?"

"No way," Neon said, shaking his head, his fingers tapping anxiously. "The power grid's down, internet's dead—

this was planned. Someone pulled the plug on the entire infrastructure."

"Felix," Harper murmured.

"Has to be," Neon replied. "We've been stepping through his landmines for weeks. This was the boom we were waiting for."

Ethan moved to Neon's side, his voice tense. "And without power, we're stuck. Neon, any idea how long until we're back online?"

"Could be hours. Could be days. The whole city's down."

Rita rushed toward them, shotgun in hand, with Juno trotting close behind. "They're getting louder out there," she said, catching her breath. "This isn't just a restless crowd anymore."

She glanced back toward the noise. "I've seen this before—it's not gonna end pretty if we stay. We need to move. Now."

Harper turned to Ethan. "Ideas?"

Ethan exhaled, glancing at Neon before locking eyes with Harper. "We have a backup site. Out in the country, down in Nesbit. Completely off-grid. Solar, generators, the whole setup. It's supposed to be for last-resort operations, but... considering everything, this might be the time."

Harper's eyebrows shot up. "You've had a backup site this whole time and didn't think to mention it sooner?"

Neon shrugged, already packing. "We were hoping we wouldn't need it. And it's not exactly top-of-the-line. Limited bandwidth, minimal systems—it's more of a temporary solution."

"Then we need to move." Harper stood. "This blackout

could be just the beginning. We can't afford to sit here waiting for whatever comes next."

"Nesbit's the best option," Ethan confirmed. "It's low-tech, but it's secure. If we're going to keep tracking Felix, we need power, and we're not getting it here. I'll grab the essentials." He added, "Neon, secure all the drives and equipment we can move."

"On it," Neon replied, shoving cables and laptops into a bag without missing a beat.

As they packed, Ethan pointed toward the exit. "We take the alley to the cars. No detours, no stops. Stay close. Nesbit's only thirty minutes out, but let's not push our luck."

Harper nodded, her gut tightening as the noise from the street grew louder. Every sound from outside felt amplified, each echo a stark reminder of how quickly chaos could take over.

"Stay sharp," Ethan murmured as they made their way out.

Harper glanced down at Juno, the dog's alert form pressed close to her side, moving in sync with her every step.

They slipped through the door into the night. All clear. The street had an eerie, charged silence as the crowd's anger had shifted, their rage now focused on a new, unseen target.

Baxter gripped the edge of the desk, his knuckles turning white as Zorin's voice crackled over the comms.

"It's a lab," Zorin said. "But no one's here."

"What do you mean no one's there?" Baxter snapped, his voice cutting through the static. "Rebecca and Lucas—"

"They're not here," Zorin interrupted. "This is a setup."

Baxter swore under his breath, his mind racing. His pulse thundered in his ears as the silence stretched, his frustration twisting into something sharper—unease.

"Get out. Now," Baxter ordered.

Before Zorin could respond, a shrill alarm blared over the comms, the sound jagged and relentless. Baxter heard the mercenaries moving, their muffled curses overlapping with the wail of the alarm.

"Too late," Zorin exclaimed. "We've got company."

Baxter slammed his fist against the desk.

Felix had played him. *Again.*

TWENTY

Edwin Cho watched the disaster unfold, powerless to stop it.

The Silent Core algorithm was no longer theoretical. Whispers of its potential had circulated through defense and intelligence circles—small pilot programs, limited contracts, nothing that made headlines. But Cho had seen it for what it was: brilliance with consequences few understood.

And now, Felix Ross had it. And worse—he was feeding it to HELIX.

Cho had seen this before. Brilliant men with too much access. Too much ambition. It always ended the same.

He adjusted his wire-rimmed glasses, more out of habit than need. His black hair, always neatly combed, stayed in place. Slim and composed, he neither wasted movement nor words. He spoke when required, listened when it mattered, and let others mistake his silence for deference.

Masking had once been a survival skill. Now, it was a weapon.

They respected his brilliance and trusted his expertise, but none of them saw the calculations running beneath the surface. None of them knew who he really was.

He had graduated from Stanford's Computer Science program, specializing in cybersecurity. His research on genetic data encryption had caught DARPA's attention, securing a fast-tracked research fellowship in biosecurity.

His work quickly advanced beyond theory. Government-backed pilot programs integrated his encryption models into classified genetic databases. That's when Evelyn Wallace found him.

She had offered him a Meridian Fellowship, an exclusive research initiative backed by both private and government interests. It came with access to research most would kill to see—closed-door think tanks where policy and profit converged.

By the time he recognized Evelyn Wallace's influence, the road was already paved beneath his feet.

The work was intoxicating. Genetics and cybersecurity weren't just merging—they were on the verge of becoming indistinguishable. His tools identified genetic anomalies and flagged unauthorized attempts to alter DNA, tightening the very safeguards Safe Genes was built to uphold. That work propelled him forward. He didn't merely anticipate vulnerabilities. He defined them.

By the time Safe Genes needed a director, there was no other choice.

Safe Genes wasn't the only future Evelyn had prepared him for. She had shaped him for the Consortium as well, nudging him toward power in ways he hadn't fully grasped at the time: the way he saw patterns others missed and the way he could break down impossibilities into inevitabilities.

But foresight wasn't enough. Felix Ross had torn through their systems with unerring precision. His theft of the Silent Core algorithm had been a masterstroke. Integrating it with HELIX wasn't just audacious—it was madness.

Cho had caught glimpses of Felix's plan. The fragments were disjointed, but damning all the same. Rebecca Kent and Lucas Fairbanks were at its center. Their exact roles remained elusive, but what he did know chilled him.

And no one was listening.

He attempted to warn the Consortium, cloaking his concerns in careful diplomacy. But Evelyn Wallace, the very architect of his rise, dismissed him without hesitation. The others followed her lead.

They trusted Felix implicitly.

They refused to see what was right in front of them.

Felix wasn't in control. HELIX was.

Cho had mapped the trajectory before: invention, dependence, inevitability. Man builds. Machine learns. Control shifts. Now, he was watching it happen in real time.

Yet here he sat, a man with all the foresight in the world, helplessly watching the edges of a disaster he couldn't prevent. Not directly, at least. But he wasn't entirely powerless. Not yet.

Cho turned away from the window, his gaze falling to

the burner phone on his desk. Reaching out as Echo had been a risk, but a necessary one. The surveillance state had grown bolder, its reach expanding under the guise of security, and the US intelligence community had been all too willing to assist.

It had given him more than oversight. It had given him Harper Brasfield. Her testimony after the CytoLife fallout proved her tenacity. Her critiques of Safe Genes only reinforced it. But her link to CookCyber Solutions made her useful. That was the opening. All Cho had to do was take it.

The messages Cho sent couldn't be direct; the danger was too great. Subtle hints and carefully placed breadcrumbs had to guide them to connect the dots themselves. Felix was methodical, but HELIX made him something far worse. The AI wasn't just guarding Felix's plans—it was anticipating threats and setting traps for anyone bold enough to interfere. Every message was a gamble. One misstep, and Cho would burn alongside the truth he was trying to expose.

His grip tightened around the phone. The escalating unrest around Safe Genes was proof his warnings were being heard. But every move pushed him closer to the edge. One wrong step, and he'd fall—taking everything and everyone with him.

Returning to his desk, Cho hovered over the phone.

Stay the course. Keep pushing.

The words echoed in his mind, little more than a mantra now, but they kept him moving forward. The fragments he'd leaked might not seem like much, but he knew they would nudge Harper and Ethan closer to Felix's operation. They were his only hope.

The chaos Felix was courting wasn't a distant threat—it was inevitable. And when it hit, there would be no way to stop it.

Cho's stomach twisted as his thoughts turned to Harper, Ethan, and Neon. They had no idea how much he was risking to help them or what it might cost him.

And if they failed...

He swallowed hard, his gaze lingering on the glowing monitor. The room felt colder, heavier with every passing second.

Cho didn't know if he'd survive what was coming next. But waiting, watching, and hoping—they were all he had left.

Ethan glanced at Harper. "Brass, I know this place isn't much, but it'll do for now. Nesbit's mostly commuter sprawl these days, but my family's property is still off the radar."

Harper nodded, though the knot in her stomach wouldn't loosen. The remote location was a temporary reprieve at best—a fragile stopgap. They couldn't afford to stay hidden for long. Felix was already closing in.

"How much longer?" she asked, her voice edged with impatience.

"Almost there," Neon replied. "Just need to set up the satellite connection. A minute, tops."

From the doorway, Dee folded her arms. "Is it smart to go back online? Feels like we're lighting a beacon for Felix."

Harper turned, frustration spilling over. "We don't have time to play it safe, Dee. If Lucas and Rebecca are in Paris, we need to act. Now."

Neon paused, his gaze flicking briefly to Dee before returning to the screen. "It's okay. This is satellite only, no landlines. Felix won't be able to trace us like last time."

Ethan, leaning against an old server rack, frowned. "Felix isn't stupid. He'll expect us to come back online. It doesn't matter how careful we are; it's still a risk."

"Then we make it count," Harper insisted. "We're too close to screw this up."

"I've got it covered," Neon replied without looking up. "This uplink's isolated. Satellite only. We'll have a window before Felix even knows we're here."

The monitors flickered to life, streams of data flashing across the screens as Neon worked. A long, tense silence hung in the air until he gasped. "We're in. Connection established."

"Good," Harper replied as her shoulders relaxed. "Let's see what Felix is planning."

Dee didn't move from the doorway, her arms still crossed. "What if this is exactly what he wants? Another trap?"

Harper spun to face her, the air between them crackling with tension. "We don't have the luxury of second-guessing ourselves. We need answers, and we need them now."

Dee's voice was steady, though her eyes betrayed a flicker of fear. "I get it, but we also need to stay in the game long enough to use those answers."

The silence that followed felt heavier, broken only when Neon grinned and leaned back in his chair. "Looks like our

Echo left us something while we were off the grid."

The message blinked onto the screen:

`Stay the course. Keep pushing.`

"Nice and vague," Harper muttered, rolling her eyes.

"Wait, I have something here," Neon said, turning to another monitor. "There's chatter—signals we didn't catch before. It's faint, but it could be Felix's team."

"Where?" Harper asked, her pulse quickening.

"Paris. The coordinates match the data we pulled earlier... but something's off."

Harper frowned. "Off how?"

Neon's eyes narrowed as he typed rapidly. "Whatever they're doing, they're moving in fast."

"Can you get a visual?" Harper asked.

"I'm tapping into the facility's old security feed." Neon smirked. "Looks like Felix didn't scrub everything clean."

For a moment, static filled the screen. Then a grainy image flickered into view—figures in tactical gear moving quickly through what appeared to be a half-abandoned facility.

"It has to be Felix's men," Harper whispered. "I bet they're moving Lucas and Rebecca."

Ethan stepped forward. "Are we sure? They're moving fast, like they're extracting something."

Everyone watched the figures on the screen as Neon zoomed in further.

"Wait... that's not right," Ethan stated. "They're not moving anyone. They're clearing the place. That can't be Felix's team; it's someone else."

Harper gasped. "Who the hell are they?"

"We might not be the only ones hunting Felix," Dee said.

"Then we'd better move faster," Harper urged.

Baxter leaned forward, his gaze locked on the flickering body cam feeds on his monitor. He'd insisted Zorin link the visuals—he wasn't about to trust secondhand reports.

Leonid Zorin's hired team moved with precision through the dimly lit corridors, rifles raised. The site was a labyrinth of abandoned storage rooms and sealed labs—exactly the kind of place where Felix might leave fragments of his work.

"Move fast," Zorin's voice crackled over the comm. "We don't know how long it'll stay clear."

"Understood," came the curt reply.

Baxter paced, his nostrils flaring with each step. Fragments weren't enough—they never were. He needed everything.

The camera feeds jolted as the team entered a larger room, their footsteps echoing in the cavernous space. Shadows danced across walls cluttered with overturned furniture and scattered equipment.

"We're in. Starting the search," the team leader reported.

"Status?" Baxter demanded.

"Clear so far," came the response. "Looks like they cleared out in a hurry."

"Then there's something there," Baxter replied. "Find it. Files, equipment—anything."

The team split into two groups, methodically sweeping the area. Baxter narrowed his eyes, tracking every movement on the screens. Felix's paranoia was legendary, but no site was ever perfectly scrubbed.

The comms crackled. "Movement ahead."

Baxter stiffened. "Details?"

"Unknown. Moving to intercept."

The first burst of gunfire shattered the quiet with sharp reports reverberating through the comms. Frantic shouting in Russian followed. The body cam feeds jolted violently as the team dropped into defensive positions, returning fire down the hallway.

"Contact! Armed opposition!" one of the operatives barked.

"Who?" Baxter snapped.

"Unknown—sophisticated gear, tight formation."

The firefight intensified, bullets sparking off metal and stone. One feed spun wildly before crashing to the floor, the camera landing at a skewed angle. Smoke and sparks filled the frame.

"We're pinned!" The leader's voice broke through the chaos. "Trying to flank—hold on."

Smoke billowed, reducing the feeds to a gray haze. A sharp detonation rattled the comms, cutting through the static. Baxter's pulse thundered as he listened to shouted orders in Russian.

Then a voice cut through: "We've got something—looks like a server!"

"Secure it," Baxter barked, gripping the edge of the desk.

"Get out now."

The cameras showed the team retreating, gunfire echoing behind them. Sporadic static filled the silence before the comm crackled back to life.

"We're clear. Whatever's left of them retreated. One down, but the server's secure. Exfil in progress."

Baxter's grip on the desk eased, but then the leader's voice returned, his tone charged with urgency. "Sir, there's more. A section of the facility. Underground. It didn't show on any of our scans."

"Good. Clear it. And bring me everything."

He cut the feed, already recalculating. Another piece of Felix's puzzle was in his grasp—and the next waited just below the surface.

Harper stood behind Neon, her eyes glued to the grainy feed of the tactical team moving through the Paris facility. Every flicker of motion on the screen felt like a ticking clock she couldn't control.

"Can you zoom in more?" she asked.

"Trying," Neon muttered. The image sharpened slightly, but the figures remained obscured in the dim light. Their tactical gear bore no insignias or identifiers.

"This doesn't add up," Ethan said from behind her, arms crossed. "Who else would be raiding one of Felix's sites?"

"Another player, maybe," Dee offered, leaning closer. "Someone after Felix too?"

Harper's mind churned. If someone else was targeting Felix, why now? And what were they after? Were they Echo?

"Wait," Neon interrupted. "They're moving faster now."

Gunfire erupted through the feed, sharp cracks cutting through the faint hum of static. The image jolted violently as the team scrambled for cover, shouts echoing faintly.

"What's happening?" Harper's heart lurched. "What if Lucas is caught in this?"

"They've got something," Neon said, his eyes fixed on the screen. "They're not leaving empty-handed."

"Are we tracking them?" Harper demanded.

Neon nodded, his focus unbroken. "Weak signal, but it's live. If they keep their comms active, I can follow them—for now."

Before Harper could respond, a sudden alert flashed across the monitor.

`Incoming Communication.`

Neon shot her a wary glance. "Encrypted... but familiar."

"Open it."

The connection crackled, and then his voice slid into the room, smooth and gratingly calm.

"Well, if it isn't Harper Brasfield."

Her body tensed, every muscle coiled. Swallowing her anger, she spoke in a sharp, controlled tone. "Baxter. What do you want?"

"Is that any way to greet an old partner?" His voice dripped with condescension.

"You bulldoze through everything and call it partnership. Save the pleasantries," she retorted, crossing her arms tightly over her chest.

Baxter chuckled, the sound grating. "You wound me, Harper. But I'm here to help. That's what I've been doing. In case you hadn't noticed."

"Your 'help' has Felix's people on high alert. Is that your idea of fixing things?"

"France?" Baxter replied dismissively. "We're retrieving something Felix left behind. Cleaning up his mess, not making one."

Harper's gaze darted to Neon, still tracking the tactical team's methodical movements. "Retrieving or stealing?"

"Let's not split hairs," Baxter retorted. "I'm not Felix. Without my team, you'd still be stumbling in the dark. I'm offering you a deal."

Harper's instincts screamed not to trust him. "What deal?" she demanded.

"I have eyes on a location where Felix's people are moving assets. Lucas might be there. But you'll need me to confirm it."

Her breath hitched. "And what do you want in return?"

"Your cooperation," he offered. "Stop sabotaging the people actually doing the work."

She wanted to tell him to shove his deal, but Lucas's life loomed larger than her pride. "We'll play this your way—for now."

Baxter's smugness practically radiated through the comm. "Of course, Harper. Temporary. I'll be in touch."

With a shake of her head, Harper ended the call.

"Harper," Ethan cautioned, "we can't trust him."

"Yes, I know," she said, staring into the distance. "But we have to be smart. If Baxter has something that leads us to Lucas, I'm not letting pride get in the way."

She straightened, turning to Neon. "Keep tracking them. I want to know about every move they make."

Ethan frowned but nodded. "Fair enough. Just don't let him rope you into his game."

"It's not his game anymore," Harper said.

Lucas's head throbbed, the harsh light stabbing through his eyelids. The sterile metallic walls blurred as he groaned, instinctively tugging at his wrists, feeling the sharp bite of the restraints digging into his skin.

Damn it.

The last thing he remembered was searching for an exit—Rebecca letting go of his hand to try a door. Then, nothing.

A shadow moved.

"Welcome back," said a smooth, detached voice.

Lucas's stomach dropped, his pulse spiking.

Felix.

He strained against the bindings, his muscles burning. "Where's Rebecca?" he rasped, panic clawing at his chest.

Felix stepped into the light, unhurried. His gaze swept the room. "Safe," he said, his tone flat. "For now."

The room was a tomb: cold metal, no windows, a single door behind Felix.

He was trapped.

"What do you want?" Lucas spat, his glare locked on Felix's unreadable face.

Felix sneered. "What I want is already in motion. You, on the other hand, are a variable I'll deal with soon enough."

Lucas's breath hitched. "If you hurt her—"

"Rebecca?" Felix interrupted, his voice chillingly soft. "She's useful. For now. But usefulness is... temporary."

Lucas twisted his wrists against the restraints, sensing a faint give that ignited a flicker of hope. "You're a coward, Felix. I should've killed you when I had the chance."

Felix raised an eyebrow. "Still ruled by emotions. Predictable. Weak."

Lucas caught a fleeting glance from Felix toward his wrists and pulled harder, his muscles screaming in protest.

"Everything is in motion," Felix explained. "Rebecca's part will end soon." His eyes gleamed with cruel amusement. "As for you... I haven't decided yet. But I can promise it'll be unforgettable."

Lucas forced himself to breathe, his mind racing. "You don't need us. You don't need her."

Felix clasped his hands behind his back, leaning in. "Oh, but I do. You're both critical pieces in a much larger puzzle—pieces I can't discard. Not yet."

"What puzzle?" Lucas demanded, his voice raw.

Felix's tone dropped, almost reverent. "CytoLife. The Safe Genes Initiative. You thought it was about genetic perfection." His smile turned predatory. "It was always about control."

A chill crawled down Lucas's spine. "I'm not part of this.

I never was."

Felix smiled. "Oh, Lucas. You've been part of this from the beginning. You just didn't know it."

Lucas's pulse thundered. "What the hell are you talking about?"

Felix tilted his head, his voice laced with mockery. "Your DNA. It's unique—a key. It stabilizes the implant. That's why you're here."

Lucas's mind reeled. "You're lying."

Felix's smirk widened, cruel and menacing. "Oh, it's real. Your genome is a revelation. And you're going to help me finish what I started."

Lucas thrashed against his restraints, rage and terror fueling him. "You're insane!"

Felix didn't flinch. "Insanity is a matter of perspective. You'll see the truth soon enough."

Lucas's voice cracked, desperation overtaking him. "Where's Rebecca? What are you doing to her?"

Felix turned toward the door, his voice detached. "She's being prepared."

"Prepared? For what?"

The door hissed open, revealing men in lab coats and the acrid smell of antiseptic. Lucas strained to see, his heart pounding.

"What are you doing to her?" he shouted.

Felix paused in the doorway, glancing back, his expression unreadable. "I'm extracting something valuable. Something I need."

The door slid shut with a heavy thud, plunging the room

into suffocating silence.

He's taking the implant out.

Sweat beaded on Lucas's brow as he fought the restraints with renewed fury, his breath ragged.

I have to find her. I have to stop this.

TWENTY ONE

With each desperate tug, Lucas's muscles screamed in protest, his wrists raw from the tight restraints. *Come on.*

The bindings loosened—just enough to ignite a flicker of hope. Summoning a surge of strength, he yanked hard. His right hand slipped free.

His pulse thundered as he fumbled with the other restraint, fingers trembling but determined. The room pressed in around him, the sterile hum of ventilation the only sound. He glanced at the door. No movement. Yet.

Rising slowly, he rolled his stiff shoulders, wincing as blood rushed back into his arms. The faint scrape of the chair against the floor made his breath hitch. He froze, ears straining. Still nothing.

His eyes darted to a metal tray on a nearby cart. Grabbing it, he tested its edge. Sharp enough to do damage. The weight felt solid in his hand. It would have to do.

He crept to the door, his movements nimble, and tested the handle. Locked, but not tightly. Sliding the tray's edge into the gap between the frame and latch, he worked it carefully, his breath shallow. *Come on...*

The lock gave with a soft click.

The door creaked open, and Lucas slipped into the dim hallway. The faint smell of antiseptic hung in the air—sterile and oppressive. Every step was a delicate balance: fast enough to cover ground, slow enough to stay silent. *Find Rebecca. Get out.*

The corridor stretched ahead, a tunnel of uncertainty bathed in shadows. Then, faint footsteps echoed.

Lucas flattened himself against the wall, his heart hammering. A guard emerged, walking away with a rifle slung over his shoulder. His posture was casual, his pace unhurried.

Damn.

Backing away slowly, Lucas weighed his next move. Each step was controlled, his pulse roaring in his ears. But then the guard froze, his body stiffening mid-stride.

Lucas's stomach dropped as the man spun on his heel.

"Hey!" the guard barked.

Lucas's breath caught. Adrenaline surged as he weighed his options. *Fight, flight, or freeze.*

Without hesitation, Lucas lunged, closing the gap in a few swift steps, his arms wide to absorb the guard's weight. With a grunt, he tackled the man to the ground, delivering a sharp punch to his jaw. The guard's head snapped back, stunned, but Lucas wasn't done. He put the man in a headlock, his muscles straining until the guard went limp.

Catching his breath, Lucas rifled through the guard's gear and pulled out a hefty knife. He dragged the unconscious body into a nearby room, locking the door behind him before sprinting away.

The facility was a labyrinth of cold, metallic corridors, each more barren than the last. Lucas moved methodically, hugging the walls and scanning every corner before advancing. Each door he passed, he checked, glancing inside for any sign of Rebecca. *Nothing.*

Cameras flashed in his peripheral vision, but he couldn't worry about that now. Stopping whatever Felix had planned for her was all that mattered. *Come on, where are you?*

He cracked open another door and scanned the empty room. *Keep moving.*

At the end of a hallway, he paused to listen. Footsteps. Several. *Damn it.*

Pressing himself against the wall, he steadied his breath as his pulse raced. The footsteps grew louder, heavy boots thudding against concrete. Voices murmured, clipped and urgent. *Felix's men. They're coming.*

His grip tightened on the knife he'd taken from the guard. *Not going back—not now.*

Lucas's muscles coiled, ready to spring. *Wait for it.*

The team rounded the corner, tactical gear and weapons raised. Lucas moved.

He launched forward, catching the first man off guard with a sharp elbow to the throat. Another reached for him, but Lucas ducked and drove the knife into his side before spinning toward the third. The fight was fast and brutal. Lucas's training kicked in—each move methodical, quick—but the guards kept coming, too many closing in.

One man slammed him against the wall, and a sharp pain shot through his ribs. He tried to twist free, but another grabbed him from behind, and before he knew it, they had him pinned.

No. Not like this.

A sudden, blinding pain exploded at the back of his head, and the world went black.

Lucas's head throbbed as consciousness clawed its way back. The relentless pounding in his skull was matched only by the stiff ache in his limbs. His hands were bound, his mouth gagged, and a coarse, black bag pressed against his face, trapping his breath in stale, suffocating heat.

Muffled voices drifted around him—low, casual, indifferent.

"Who is this guy?" one voice muttered.

"No idea. Not the target," another replied. "But Baxter might want him."

Baxter. The name struck like a jolt of ice water, cutting through the fog in his mind.

Before Lucas could process the implications, rough hands yanked him upright, dragging his limp body like dead weight. Pain shot through his shoulders as the bindings bit deeper into his wrists. He fought to orient himself, his body screaming in protest with every jostling step.

They didn't care who he was—only that he wasn't who they wanted.

After what felt like an eternity, the manhandling stopped. Lucas was shoved down roughly, his muscles tensing as his captors shifted around him like shadows. He braced himself, trying to gauge his surroundings through the muffled sounds and the suffocating heat of the hood.

"Who is this?" a sharp, commanding voice demanded. Irritated. British.

"Some guy we picked up," one of his captors answered carelessly. "Not who we were looking for, but we figured he might know something."

The irritation deepened into silence. Steady footsteps echoed closer. Lucas held his breath, his body coiled, ready to act.

The hood was ripped away with a sudden, rough tug.

Light pierced Lucas's eyes, momentarily blinding him. He blinked as shapes swam before sharpening into the man standing over him.

The changes were stark. The sharp salt-and-pepper hair, once a symbol of meticulous control, was now shorn close, stripped of vanity. His face had become leaner, harder, the softness of refinement eroded into utility. Yet none of it could hide the truth.

It wasn't just the voice—refined, commanding, edged with strain—or the coiled tension in his stance, a contradiction of menace and perceptive calm. It was something deeper, an unshakable presence that time or disguise couldn't erase.

Baxter.

The billionaire stood there, his cold, calculating gaze sweeping over Lucas as if evaluating an asset.

"Take off the restraints," Baxter ordered.

Then, without warning, Lucas lunged.

A punch to the jaw sent Baxter reeling. "You bastard!" Lucas growled, swinging again before Zorin's men grabbed him, yanking him back.

Baxter wiped the blood from his lip, his expression unreadable. "Lucas."

Lucas's head pounded as he glared at Baxter, the anger and frustration in his voice barely masking his fear. "You're still playing your games, Baxter—manipulating people, pulling strings. You've never cared about anyone but yourself!"

Baxter's gaze didn't waver; his tone was maddeningly steady. "And you're still wasting time on the wrong enemy."

"Rebecca—what did you let them do to her?" Lucas took a step forward, his fists trembling with restrained rage.

"I'm trying to save her," Baxter said, the words measured and controlled despite the urgency in his eyes. "Felix is the real enemy here. If you care about her, you'll listen."

"Listen to you?" Lucas's voice rose. "After everything you've done? You're the reason she's in this hell!"

Baxter straightened, wiping the blood from his lip again with painstaking precision. "And you're still barking up the wrong tree."

"She trusted you! And you turned her into this…this tool for your twisted plans."

Baxter's tone turned icy. "Rebecca's brilliance wasn't something to waste, Lucas. She was capable of changing the world. You wouldn't understand that."

Lucas's fists clenched tighter. "You don't care about brilliance. You care about power. And now Felix has her because of you."

Baxter's composure cracked, his sneer razor-thin. "No, Lucas. She's with Felix because you failed to protect her. I trusted you to keep her safe."

The accusation hit like a physical blow. Guilt clawed at Lucas, but he shoved it aside, his fury simmering beneath the surface. "I did everything I could...everything except stop you."

Baxter moved closer, his voice softening to a gentle, persuasive tone. "I'm the only one who can get her back. Felix has overplayed his hand."

Lucas met his eyes. "We don't have time for this," he said through clenched teeth.

His control snapped. "You don't get it. This isn't about your twisted vision or whatever legacy you're chasing. This is about Rebecca. She's more than a piece on your board. She's more than Felix's pawn."

For a split second, Baxter's mask slipped, desperation flashing in his eyes before he forced it back. "She's my daughter," he said, each word as sharp as ice. "Not a tool. Not expendable. Felix thinks he can twist her genius to serve his purpose, but he's wrong. I won't let that happen."

"You don't even know, do you?" A hint of bitter disbelief laced Lucas's words.

Baxter's expression flickered. "Know what?"

"That implant Felix gave her—it's killing her," Lucas said, his voice like a razor. "She told me she can feel it—like it's controlling her. Taking over."

For the first time, genuine fear showed on Baxter's face.

Lucas let out a bitter laugh as Zorin's men shoved him into a chair. "You don't know a damn thing, do you? For someone who claims to have everything under control, you look pretty clueless right now."

Baxter signaled curtly, and the mercenaries exited the room without a word. Silence fell as he seemed to absorb the accusation.

Lucas's jaw clenched. "Felix is rewriting the rules." He hesitated, then scoffed. "And some of us never even knew we were part of the experiment."

Baxter's eyes narrowed. "What are you talking about?"

Lucas ignored the question. "What do you want to hear, Baxter? That Rebecca's life is hanging by a thread? That Felix has twisted your plans into something worse? "

His voice dropped. "He's not just playing with genes—he's stripping away everything human. Full control. And that implant in Rebecca? It's at the heart of it."

Baxter's entire body went rigid, his face turning blood red.

"Let me go," Lucas growled. "Get your men to work with me. The longer we stand here, the more time Felix has to pull off whatever the hell he's planning."

Finally, Baxter spoke, his voice a gravelly hiss. "Lucas Fairbanks. I see why my daughter admires you. But your recklessness hasn't exactly helped either of you, has it?"

Lucas's nostrils flared as he clenched his fists.

Baxter stepped closer, calculating and appraising. "You're a weapon, Lucas. Sharp, but aimless. With my backing, I can ensure you're pointed at the right targets. Together, we can bring Rebecca home."

Lucas stared at him, weighing his options. Baxter's arrogance grated on every nerve, but the truth was undeniable: Rebecca needed them both.

After a few tense seconds, Lucas spat, "Fine. We'll do this your way. But if anything happens to her—anything—I'll tear down what's left of your life. Do you understand?"

Baxter's lips curled into a thin smile, his eyes never leaving Lucas's. "Understood. Keeping Rebecca safe is the one thing we both agree on."

Lucas drew a steadying breath. "What's the plan?"

Baxter adjusted his jacket. "First, we make a stop."

Lucas frowned. "What stop?"

"The mirror site," Baxter replied. "For contingency planning. If we're going to stop Felix, we'll need more than good intentions."

Without another word, Lucas squared his shoulders.

Baxter turned toward the door, his silhouette stark against the sterile light. "Follow me."

The power in Memphis had returned hours earlier, bringing a collective sigh of relief to the city. Official reports chalked it up to a routine maintenance failure at a local grid substation. Rumors swirled about aging equipment and delayed replacement parts, but nothing seemed out of the ordinary—or worth digging into.

As the team, minus Dee, made their way back to CookCyber, the streets painted a stark picture. A heavy police presence held back stragglers, while shattered windows, overturned trash bins, and the remnants of makeshift barricades bore witness to the unrest. Bold, jagged graffiti screamed defiance from every wall as business owners cautiously surveyed the damage.

Amid the chaos, CookCyber stood untouched—an island of calm in the storm's wake.

Inside, the familiar hum of rebooting systems filled the air, a sharp contrast to the tense quiet outside. Rita was already at her post, a comforting constant in the disarray, handing out sandwiches and bottled water as if it were just another late night.

"Take one, Harper," she said briskly, holding out a bottle. "You look like you need it."

Harper accepted with a nod, her gaze sweeping the room. The team worked with quiet focus, but the occasional glance toward the windows betrayed their unease. The tension hadn't lifted—it had only shifted, coiling beneath the surface.

"Everything working?" Harper asked, stepping closer to

Neon, who was hunched over a terminal.

"Getting there," Neon replied, data streams flickering across the screen. "Running diagnostics now. No sign of interference, but I don't trust this calm at all."

"Neither do I," Ethan muttered, arms crossed as he leaned against a desk. "That blackout wasn't just bad luck."

Harper took a sip of water, her thoughts churning. "Memphis always bounces back, but this... this feels different. People are scared. Angry. And it's not just about the power." She paused. "Fear's a powerful tool—and Felix knows exactly how to use it."

"Let's hope he hasn't moved to the next step yet," Neon remarked, tapping a final command. "We're back online, but if he's watching, he'll know."

Harper turned to Ethan. "What's the plan if he does?"

Ethan straightened, his tone steady. "We stay ready. No more surprises." He hesitated, then added, "Let's hope it doesn't come to that."

Harper's phone buzzed, slicing through the tense quiet. Glancing at the screen, she excused herself and entered the empty conference room.

Dread tightened in her chest as she answered. "Dee?" The hesitation on the other end made her grip tighten around the phone.

"Brass..." Dee's voice was soft and cautious. "Have you seen the *Bluff City Standard* today?"

"No. Not yet. Why?" Harper asked.

Another pause. Longer this time.

"Adam Burke's on the front page."

The air seemed to drain from the room. Harper froze, her breath catching. "What… what happened?"

"They found him, Harper," Dee said, her voice heavy with unspoken pain. "NYPD found his body in an abandoned warehouse. He's gone."

Harper leaned back, the phone pressed against her ear like a lifeline. "They got to him," she whispered, her voice cracking. "He was too close. He refused to back down. I knew it."

"Yeah," Dee replied. "We all did."

Grief churned into frustration, bubbling just beneath the surface. "I'm so tired of this. Watching good people die while we scramble to catch up. It's like we're always a step behind."

"I know," Dee murmured. "But you can't lose focus now. The city's still on fire, and God knows what's next."

Harper closed her eyes, exhaling sharply. "What about you? Are you holding up?"

"I'll manage," Dee said, her voice steadier now. "I've got another disaster waiting for me at the DA's office, but I'll deal with it. Just… keep me in the loop, okay?"

"I will," Harper promised.

The call ended, leaving a hollow silence in its wake. Harper stood frozen, the phone still in her hand. *Adam. Gone.* The words looped through her mind, sharp and relentless. She blinked hard, swiping at her eyes before the grief could break through. She returned to the desk next to Ethan's without saying a word.

Her hand drifted to the untouched sandwich Rita had left on the desk. She took a small bite; the flavor was muted and irrelevant. Adam's face filled her thoughts—his sharp wit, his unrelenting determination.

Gone, she thought bitterly, *because he got too close to the truth.*

The sandwich was pushed aside, forgotten. Harper leaned forward, her elbows digging into the desk as she fought to steady herself, to push past the ache that threatened to consume her.

"Brass, you okay?" Ethan asked, leaning closer.

Harper straightened her suit with a sharp motion, shaking her head. "Yeah, fine. Just lost in my head again."

Ethan's gaze lingered, skeptical but unwilling to push. Turning back to his desk, he slid the *Bluff City Standard* under a stack of files—too casually to be innocent.

"Is that today's edition?" Harper asked, her voice cutting through the tension.

"Brass—" Ethan started, hesitating as she leaned toward him, already reaching for it.

"I already know," she said, extending her hand. "Let me see it."

Reluctantly, Ethan handed her the paper, his expression grim.

Harper scanned the headlines until her eyes landed on Adam Burke's face, stark and unmistakable.

Former Bluff City Standard *reporter Adam Burke, renowned for his groundbreaking exposé on CytoLife, was found dead yesterday in an abandoned Manhattan warehouse. The NYPD has yet to release further details regarding the* circumstances of his death...

“They got to him,” Harper muttered as her fingers curled around the edge of the paper. For a moment, helplessness clawed at her.

With unshed tears welling in her eyes, Harper lifted her chin. “I’m not letting my son be next.”

Ethan shifted beside her. “Brass...”

“No more,” Harper said, flinging the paper down on the table. “No more waiting for Felix to strike. We go on the offensive.”

Ethan exhaled slowly. “Alright. Listen. I know some guys—from before. They didn’t exactly walk the straight and narrow after the war, but they’re seasoned and have connections—people who know how to get things done and aren’t afraid to bend the rules.”

Harper looked up, her mind already racing. Calculating.

“We send them in,” Ethan continued, his tone measured yet insistent. “Forget Baxter. We run this ourselves. Let Neon do his thing—track down where Felix is really hiding. Once we’ve got intel, my guys can get eyes on the inside.”

“You think I don’t want to storm in there myself? Drag Felix into the light and end this?” She shook her head, bitterness creeping into her voice. “That’s exactly what he wants—keeping us chasing shadows until it’s too late.”

Ethan locked eyes with her. “So what’s the play?”

Harper wiped a stray tear with the back of her hand. “For now, we keep the digital surveillance running. Something will shake loose—something we can use to turn this around.” She paused, then added, “And keep your buddies on speed dial. We're not losing anyone else."

Before Ethan could respond, Harper's phone buzzed. Her stomach sank as she glanced at the screen.

Baxter.

She answered. "Wait, say that again?" Harper leaned forward, furrowed as his words sank in. "The Memphis airport terminal? *Underground?* You must be mistaken."

"Call the number," Baxter replied. "They're expecting you. The package will be waiting." A hollow laugh followed. "I'd deliver it myself, but my travel agent advises against it."

Harper pinched the bridge of her nose, a sharp breath escaping. "Why are you doing this? Felix keeps running circles around you. How many more ghosts are you going to chase?"

"There you go again," Baxter countered. "So confident, so arrogant, and still blind to what's right in front of you."

Harper scoffed. "Oh, so you don't have a plan? You're winging it? In case you forgot, my son and your daughter are out there—God knows where. And Rebecca's sick, remember?"

"That's exactly why you and your team are going to dig into that discarded server. Whatever's on there, you'll find it," Baxter explained. "Time's wasting, Harper. Get on it."

The line went dead.

Ethan crossed his arms, eyeing Harper. "That sounded... interesting. Tacks, what's the deal? You've got that look—the one you get when someone's feeding you a load of crap."

Harper smirked faintly and shook her head. "Oh, he's lying, alright. He's calling from a plane—I could hear the engines in the background."

Ethan raised an eyebrow. "So he's hopping around, trying to stay off the radar. Probably chasing leads he doesn't want to share. And we're supposed to follow his leads again?"

"He's sending a package—the server they found," Harper said. "We need to tear it apart."

"We can do that, Brass. But for all we know, that 'package' could be a glorified paper shredder."

"We don't have the luxury of ignoring it. If there's even a shred of intel on that server, we need it," Harper explained.

Neon glanced up. "We'll go slow. If it's a trap, I'll catch it."

Ethan finally nodded. "Alright. Let's go find a tunnel."

Baxter ended the secure call with Harper and leaned back in the leather seat of the Cessna Citation X+. It wasn't a Gulfstream, but his assistants had managed well enough—eager to justify their positions after too much idle time in Switzerland.

Beside him, Lucas lay unconscious, his head slumped against the seatback. The sedative had worked flawlessly. Presented as a routine onceover, the doctor had ensured Lucas didn't suspect a thing.

Baxter checked his watch: *Eight hours.* Not much time, but enough to begin untangling the chaos Felix had unleashed—or at least to chart a path through it.

The implant wasn't just a marvel of technology; it was the cornerstone of VitaLexis, the key to the longevity therapy they had worked tirelessly to perfect. Rebecca wouldn't have agreed to it on a whim. Every decision she made was strategic. Baxter both relied on and admired that certainty. She didn't take chances. Not with herself, not with their work.

But Lucas's words clawed at him, sharp and unrelenting: *"That implant Felix gave her—it's killing her. She said she could feel it, like it's controlling her. Taking over."*

Felix hadn't just twisted their vision—he'd destroyed it. How had he been so blind?

The goal had been clear: refine the therapy, perfect the implant, and deliver a controlled breakthrough to the Consortium. But Felix had warped it, pushing their work beyond its limits, and turning ambition into something monstrous.

None of it made sense. Baxter hated blind spots, and Felix had carved them into his plans with surgical precision. Evelyn's voice echoed in his mind: *"Felix adapts. It's what makes him valuable."*

Valuable? Felix wasn't valuable—he was chaos wrapped in ego, and Evelyn had indulged him. Baxter's hands curled into fists, the leather armrests creaking under the pressure.

He glanced at Lucas, still motionless. The boy was a wild card, but also a potential asset. Whatever Felix had done—whatever part Lucas had unknowingly played—Baxter would uncover it. Rebecca's life and the future of VitaLexis depended on it.

Baxter forced himself to lean back, breathing deeply as his mind pivoted to the pieces he still controlled. Harper and her team were exactly where he needed them—tearing into the server he'd dangled like bait. Let her idealistic crew in Memphis chase phantoms. The server had already served its purpose as a distraction, a contrived task to buy him time.

Time that Leonid Zorin's team was now using with brutal efficiency.

For the first time in days, Baxter exhaled, tension ebbing as he allowed himself a fleeting moment of calm. Control—that elusive, tantalizing sensation—was finally within reach.

TWENTY TWO

Rebecca jolted awake, the sterile chill of the room amplifying the searing pain wracking her body. Her hands instinctively tugged at the restraints, the raw bite of the bindings slicing into her skin. Blinking through the haze, fragments of memory flickered—faint voices, dark corridors, then nothing.

Her heart leapt as her mind sharpened on a singular thought: *the implant.* They must have removed it.

Panic tightened in her chest. Lucas—where was he? Her last clear memory was his hand gripping hers, holding on tightly.

"I see you're awake."

The voice, detached and clinical, sliced through the fog in her mind. Rebecca turned suddenly toward the sound, wincing as a bolt of pain shot through her neck.

A nurse stood in the doorway, her face a mask of calm indifference. "The procedure went smoothly. You'll be ready soon."

Rebecca's pulse quickened. *Ready? Ready for what?*

But the nurse didn't elaborate. She turned on her heel, her crisp footsteps fading down the hall, leaving Rebecca trapped in cold silence. It wrapped around her like a vise, her thoughts spiraling as she struggled to process what "ready" might mean.

Outside the operating room, Felix waited with his hand extended. The nurse placed a tablet in his palm, her face a mask of professionalism.

"The device was removed successfully," she said, gesturing to the screen. "All diagnostics and reports are here."

He skimmed the data. The prototype implant had done its job, pushing Rebecca's physiology and genetics to their absolute limits. He almost laughed at her naïveté—so easily convinced they were advancing VitaLexis. The faked data HELIX had generated was effortless to fabricate, and her devotion to Baxter had done the rest, blinding her to the truth.

What began as a surge of invincibility in Rebecca had spiraled into self-destruction. In some twisted way, he almost regretted losing the chance to watch her unravel further, to study her inevitable destruction.

Almost.

Now he knew exactly where the line was.

When Harper and Ethan entered CookCyber, Neon eyed the case in Harper's hands skeptically.

"This is the server from Baxter?" His expression darkened. "It's beat to all hell."

Harper dropped the case onto the table with a thud. "Baxter had it delivered in the creepiest way possible—through some rusted-out tunnel under the airport. No explanations, no details. Just a courier and this."

Neon raised an eyebrow, pausing mid-motion. "Tunnels under the airport? Seriously?" He shook his head in disbelief. "Baxter never takes the simple route, does he?"

Ethan shrugged. "Simple isn't his style. And those tunnels? They reeked in every way imaginable."

Neon ran his fingers over the battered exterior. "This thing looks like it survived a crowbar attack. Whoever went after it wanted it gone—but didn't finish the job."

"Someone panicked and tried to wipe it before bailing?" Ethan offered.

"Maybe," Neon murmured, plugging the server in. "But if Felix left us anything useful, it'd be a first."

"Prove him wrong," Harper replied.

Neon smirked faintly. "Let's see what we've got." He started connecting cables, and soon the server hummed to life, the screen lighting up with cascading alerts.

"Felix's fingerprints are all over this—encryption stacked on encryption, layered with fail-safes," Neon muttered. "Someone started a wipe but didn't finish. One wrong move, and this thing could self-destruct."

"Can you get past it?" Harper asked.

"Yeah," he replied. "It's tight, but I've danced with Felix's code before." A brief grin flickered. "No margin for error, though."

Lines of code scrolled across the screen as Harper and Ethan stood silently behind Neon, their eyes glued to the monitor.

"Got it," Neon whispered. "I'm in."

"Never doubted you for a second," Harper said, leaning closer. "What are we looking at?"

"Fragments," Neon said, scanning the files. "Emails, project logs... everything's shredded and scrambled. It'll take time to piece it together, but there's definitely something here."

Ethan leaned in. "Anything useful?"

Neon paused, opening a file. "Inventory lists—lab equipment, genetic sequencing data... and locations."

"Locations?" Harper asked.

He nodded and opened another window. "Looks like Felix has been setting up bio-labs."

Ethan crossed his arms. "How many?"

"Not sure yet, but it's more than a few," Neon replied. "Felix has been busy."

"Could this lead us to Lucas and Rebecca?" Harper asked.

"Maybe," Neon said. "There's a mention of Northern Virginia—just coordinates, nothing detailed. But it's a lead."

Harper exchanged a glance with Ethan. It wasn't much, but it was more than they'd had before. "CytoLife was headquartered near there. It tracks. Cross-reference it with everything else."

"I'm on it," Neon assured, then hesitated. "But... something doesn't add up."

Ethan straightened. "What do you mean?"

"Felix is using Safe Genes sites all over the map," he said. "But he's not just pulling data—he's altering it. Subtle changes, buried in routine diagnostics."

Harper froze mid-step. "Altering how?"

"It's hard to say. The edits are deep, almost invisible. Either the algorithm isn't designed to catch them, or someone's keeping it blind on purpose."

Ethan frowned. "Safe Genes has DARPA-grade tech. If Felix is slipping things past their checks, that means..."

"He's rewriting the rules," Neon cut in. "The data looks normal on the surface, but deeper down, it's been manipulated—subtle, refined, like it's meant to go unnoticed until it's too late."

"What's he testing?" she asked.

Neon shook his head, frustration etched across his face. "I can't tell yet. But whatever it is, it's already in motion."

Neon's fingers hovered over the keyboard, and for a split second, his expression shifted enough to capture Harper's attention. He flicked a glance at Ethan. "This wouldn't have anything to do with our little silent dilemma, would it?"

"Let's not go there unless we have to," Ethan replied.

Harper's gaze darted between them, her instincts flaring. "What aren't you telling me?"

"Nothing we need to worry about right now," Ethan said

gently, his eyes steady on hers. "Our focus is on Felix."

Neon nodded quickly, his attention snapping back to the screen. "Right. These aren't anomalies—they're deliberate. Controlled."

Harper's mind raced. If Safe Genes was Felix's cover, his reach extended further than any of them had realized.

Neon hesitated before glancing at them both. "Should I ping Echo?"

Pausing, Harper then looked at Ethan, who nodded in response. "Do it," she said. "It's time he started answering our questions."

The screen blinked as the message was sent.

No more half-truths, Echo. We know about Virginia. Start talking.

Seconds later, the reply appeared:

You're close. Keep it down. Felix is moving fast. – E.cho.

Ethan frowned. "Same vague crap again."

Neon scrolled back through their history of messages, his eyes narrowing. "It's always the same—cryptic warnings and hints."

"Wait," Harper said, her gaze sharpening. "Go back."

Neon scrolled up, and Harper's eyes locked onto the message sign-off. Something was different.

"E.cho," she murmured, her heart pounding as the realization took shape. Racing across the room, she grabbed her phone. "No... it can't be."

"Tacks, what's going on?" Ethan's voice cut through, sharp with concern.

Harper scrolled frantically. "Edwin Cho," she whispered, her voice catching. "Look—no space. E.Cho. The director of Safe Genes. He's Echo."

Ethan leaned in, confused. "You're telling me the guy running Safe Genes is our mole?"

"It fits," Harper said, her tone hardening. "He's been feeding us intel—steering us—just enough to keep us moving without getting caught." She met Ethan's eyes. "Think about it. He's been right every time."

She set her phone on the table and tapped on a search result for Edwin Cho:

Edwin Cho, newly appointed Director of the Safe Genes Agency, will spearhead the government's initiative to prevent unauthorized genetic edits while working closely with other entities to ensure national security. Cho brings nearly two decades of experience in cybersecurity, AI, and...

Harper stopped reading aloud, her mind racing. She didn't need to finish. Once Safe Genes was established, officials like Cho were confirmed swiftly, while people like her watched warily.

Ethan let out a low whistle. "I'll be damned."

"Wait!" Ethan snapped his fingers and rifled through a pile of papers on the desk, scattering a few onto the floor. "Here—this is it."

Harper and Neon leaned in as Ethan spread the documents across the table, his movements fluid despite the urgency.

"These are the messages I got," Ethan muttered, flipping

through the pages. "And the ones our client received." His hand froze, a finger landing on a line of text. His face paled. "Holy... it's him."

"Ethan, you look like you've seen a ghost. Spill it." Neon leaned back in his chair, his casual tone at odds with the sharp focus in his eyes.

Ethan didn't answer right away, his eyes scanning the pages with increasing speed. "The phrasing, the tone, the timing—and the word 'echo.'" He stopped and locked eyes with Neon. "Those cryptic threats to Roberts? That was Cho."

Neon scoffed, a blend of disbelief and annoyance flickering across his face. "You've got to be kidding me."

Ethan's expression darkened. "It wasn't random. He's been trying to steer us."

"Steer us where?" Neon asked.

Ethan's fingers drummed on the table as the realization hit. "Silent Core," he said muttered, as if testing the words. "The encryption algorithm wasn't just stolen—it's compromised."

Ethan glanced at Neon. "Your instinct earlier was right."

Neon frowned, the gears visibly turning in his mind. "If Felix has it, he's not just encrypting files. He's hiding something. Something big."

"Cho must've seen it," Ethan continued. "He's been watching Felix manipulate the system, but couldn't stop him outright."

"So, he sent us clues," Neon said, his tone a mix of grudging admiration and frustration. "Roberts at QuantumSafe had to notice the theft, panic just enough, and drag us into the mess."

He shook his head and leveled a pointed look at Ethan. "We need to have a conversation later about you keeping me out of the loop."

Ethan's face flushed. "Yeah, that's on me. Things escalated quickly, and... I didn't want you to stress over it."

Neon's lips curled into a faint grin, half teasing and half exasperated. "Next time, trust me to handle a little stress—and give me some credit for catching on."

"Okay, I followed most of that. Care to fill me in?" Harper asked.

Ethan exhaled and shifted his focus to her. "Sam Chapman referred a client to us—a case involving stolen encryption tech. It didn't make sense back then, but now it's all starting to click."

"So, Cho was sending your client messages too?" Harper asked, her voice sharp with disbelief. She shook her head, trying to connect the pieces. "He wanted you to connect the dots?"

"It sounds illogical," Ethan admitted, "but think about it—it's the only explanation that fits."

Harper's stomach twisted. "He knows me from the hearings. I've always suspected I was on a watchlist—and anyone close to me probably is too."

"That's why he mentioned Lucas," Ethan said. "He wanted to make sure we couldn't ignore it."

"And now we're neck-deep in this mess," Harper replied. "Felix is bad enough, but Cho? He's no better. Using us to clean up his mess while covering his tracks."

Ethan met her gaze. "Maybe. But without Cho, we

wouldn't be this close. He knew we'd figure it out eventually—he just didn't want to risk his own neck."

Harper nodded slowly, her thoughts spinning. "But why name-drop Evelyn? That feels intentional. Too intentional. We're missing something." Her fingers tapped an impatient rhythm against the table.

"Every time he mentions Safe Genes, it's vague," Neon said as he scrolled through Echo's past messages with a furrowed brow. "Like he's holding back."

"Cho wants Felix gone, but he won't stick his own neck out to make it happen," Ethan said, crossing his arms. "Coward."

Harper's eyes narrowed. "Felix's plan is already in motion. We thought it was just about gene manipulation—AGG1 on steroids. But what if it's bigger?"

"You're saying Felix is running a larger operation?" Neon asked.

"He has to be," Harper replied. "And Cho's trying to keep it contained—without getting his hands dirty."

"This isn't just about Felix anymore," Ethan said. "Safe Genes is compromised. If Felix is pulling strings from the inside..."

"We don't know how deep it goes," Harper said, her mind beginning to piece together a troubling, larger picture.

"So what's Cho's angle?" Ethan asked.

Harper's gaze sharpened. "He's feeding us just enough to keep us moving. Or maybe he's playing both sides. Either way, he's put us squarely in the middle, and Safe Genes is the linchpin."

Neon leaned back, disbelief written across his face. "We've been dancing to his tune this whole time."

Harper nodded. "And Lucas is caught in the middle."

"If Safe Genes is compromised, sitting here isn't an option," Ethan said, glancing at Neon.

"And going to the authorities would be like pulling the pin on a grenade," Harper countered. "Felix would detonate his plan early."

Ethan crossed his arms. "So what do we do? Just let him keep pushing?"

"No." Harper met his gaze. "But we can't go in blind, especially now that Cho's involved. We don't know who we can trust. If we tip our hand too soon, we risk losing everything."

"She's right," Neon agreed. "If we rush in, Felix will cover his tracks and disappear."

"We should hit the site in Virginia," Harper said. "Felix thinks he's ahead, but if we move fast, we might have a shot."

Neon's fingers resumed typing. "I'll dig deeper. Maybe I can find a pattern in Felix's moves."

"And if we don't have time?" Ethan asked.

"Then we make sure Felix doesn't finish this," Harper said. "But first, we focus on the site. It's the only lead we've got."

"It's a long shot, Tacks," Ethan replied. "Felix wouldn't set foot on US soil."

"I know," Harper admitted. "But it's all we have. If there's even a chance, we have to take it."

"Grab intel and get out?" Ethan asked.

"Not just intel," Harper explained. "If Felix has anything critical running there, we take it offline. Permanently."

Neon looked up, startled. "You're talking about blowing the place up?"

"If it comes to that." Harper turned to Ethan. "Those guys you know—how soon can they be ready?"

Ethan hesitated, checking his phone. "Brass, rushing in with guns blazing risks everything. If Felix has eyes on the site, we lose leverage. We need to plan this carefully."

Harper's frustration flared. "We don't have time for careful!"

Ethan held her glare for a moment, then nodded. "Alright. It's insane, but these guys thrive on insane." He started dialing. "Felix probably has the place wired. We need to be smart about this."

"Smart, but decisive," Harper said. "We're going to Virginia and taking down that site."

TWENTY THREE

Lucas jolted awake, the weight of exhaustion still clinging to him. His mouth felt dry, and his vision swam as he blinked at the empty cabin. Baxter was gone. Forcing himself upright, he swayed slightly before heading toward the plane's exit.

On the tarmac, two SUVs idled nearby. Baxter stood between them, his arms folded like a commander surveying his domain. Lucas descended the steps, his legs protesting, and shot Baxter a glare. "Where are we? And why didn't you wake me?"

Baxter's expression remained impassive. "Ah, Lucas. Feeling refreshed, I hope?" He nodded toward the rear SUV. "There's fresh attire and food inside. I trust they'll meet your standards."

Lucas muttered under his breath as he approached the car, "This better not take long."

Climbing in, he rifled through the bag left for him. The clothes were his exact size, and the meal—a neatly packed sandwich and water—was irritatingly spot-on. As he ate, his thoughts churned. *Focus. Rebecca comes first.*

He was halfway through the sandwich when the door clicked open. Baxter slid into the passenger seat, calm as ever. Lucas didn't look up, his gaze fixed on the darkened horizon.

"We're about thirty minutes from the site," Baxter said, nodding toward a figure by the second SUV. "He'll be joining us."

Lucas glanced over, sizing up the man: tall, wiry, visibly uneasy under the dim lights.

"Dr. Warren Pike," Baxter continued. "He worked there when the facility was fully operational."

"Why's he here now?"

"He owes me a favor."

Lucas's eyes narrowed. "And how do you know he won't turn on you?"

"He won't." Baxter's voice didn't waver. "He knows better."

Lucas tossed the wrapper aside and leaned back against the seat. "You sedated me."

"You needed rest."

"I agreed to come with you. You didn't need to knock me out."

"You weren't exactly cooperative."

"I don't cooperate with people I don't trust."

Baxter's lips curved into the faintest smile. "You'll thank me later. Rest is essential for what's ahead."

Lucas scoffed. "You just wanted to shut me up for eight hours."

"That too."

Lucas leaned forward. "You think this ends once we find her? You're not walking away from this."

"One thing at a time, Lucas. Focus on Rebecca."

"Don't act like this is about her. Everything that's happened—Rebecca, Felix, all of it—leads back to you."

"I did what I had to do. This isn't about the past. It's about what comes next."

"What's next?" Lucas shot back. "You rotting in a cell."

Baxter's tone cooled. "That's your choice. But not until we find her."

Lucas shook his head. "I'm not here for your redemption."

"I'm not asking for forgiveness."

"Good," Lucas bit out. "Because you're not getting it."

"Hate me all you want," Baxter said, his gaze steady. "But we're the only ones who can stop Felix."

Lucas turned away. "Rebecca is my priority."

"She's mine too."

Lucas snorted. "You've got a funny way of showing it."

"Everything I've done has been for her."

"Spare me the justification," Lucas retorted. "Dragging me into this won't erase what you've done."

"I'm not looking for absolution," Baxter said. "Just results."

"Rebecca's the endgame. Not you. When this is over, you're done."

"Then let's reach the endgame. Together."

Without waiting for a response, Baxter opened the door and stepped out, leaving Lucas alone with his thoughts.

Harper sat in the backseat, her fingers tapping a restless rhythm against her thigh. The dark streets of Northern Virginia blurred past the window, but her mind remained sharp and relentless. Reston was close now, and all she could cling to was the hope that the wreckage ahead would finally provide the answers they needed.

In the front seat, Ethan seemed unshaken, chatting quietly with Hansen, his military buddy riding shotgun. For them, this was just another mission—a controlled operation with risks. But Harper knew better. This wasn't routine. It was their last shot—a desperate gamble with everything on the line.

Her phone buzzed in her lap, diverting her attention. She glanced down at the screen: a secure message from Dee.

Unrest growing everywhere. Protests turning violent. National Guard deployed. Safe Genes facilities on high alert. Relocations to government sites... not voluntary.

Harper read it twice, allowing the implications to sink in. Felix wasn't just escalating—he was consolidating control. Time was slipping away.

She typed back quickly:

Arriving at our destination within the hour. No idea what to expect.

The reply came instantly:

Stay safe. Any word on Lucas?

Her grip tightened on the phone.

Not yet, but I'm hoping our destination has answers.

Her thoughts drifted to Evelyn Wallace—always elusive, always just out of reach. But there was no time to unravel that now.

Another buzz broke through her thoughts:

Whatever you're planning, hurry.

Harper leaned forward and tapped Ethan's shoulder. "We're running out of time."

Ethan met her gaze in the rearview mirror and nodded. "We'll be ready when we hit the ground. My team's got everything prepped. We don't know what we're walking into, but I trust these guys with my life." He glanced at Hansen beside him. "It's a rough crew, but solid where it counts."

Ethan's tone shifted. "But this isn't a one-shot deal, Brass. Whatever we find out there, it's going to take more than a quick raid to fix."

"We don't have the luxury of long-term plans," she murmured.

As they sped down the Dulles Tollway and entered Reston, flashes of news reports illuminated the dashboard screen—riots, curfews, National Guard deployments. Harper barely noticed.

Her focus was singular.

Lucas.

Lucas's escape both infuriated and amused Felix. Whatever desperate plan the young man had concocted was doomed to fail.

He barely glanced at the projections on his tablet, which showed success beyond expectations. His thoughts were elsewhere, preoccupied with the final moves to secure his victory.

Behind him, Rebecca lay motionless, her breathing shallow and erratic. It wouldn't be much longer. The implant he'd extracted from her was secure, perfected, and ready.

Felix tapped his tablet, acknowledging the blinking notification:

SELF-DESTRUCT SEQUENCE INITIATED.

The mirror site—and anyone unfortunate enough to still be inside—would soon be reduced to ashes.

His focus shifted to the real prize: control. AGG1 had been a crude but effective first step in harnessing humanity's darker impulses. Evelyn Wallace had once championed Baxter's vision of "dimming humanity's worst tendencies," skillfully feeding his ego with the illusion of brilliance. But Baxter had faltered, as the weak always do, when it mattered most. Felix, however, had the resolve to finish what others couldn't.

He adjusted his smart glasses, the faint glow of the virtual interface illuminating his sharp features. Streams of data coursed across his vision as the AI interface came to life at his touch.

HELIX. The name resonated, encapsulating everything he had built: *Humanity's Engine for Logical Integrated Xenogenesis.* It was no longer just a tool to guide humanity—it had become the framework for a world remade in Felix's image.

He murmured the name, savoring its significance. "HELIX."

Even his alias, "Felix," had been deliberate—an irony laced with destiny. Felix. HELIX. Two names intertwined, bound to this moment.

The AI's mechanical voice broke the silence. "The plan is proceeding as expected."

Felix's lips curled into a cold smile. "And Lucas? His DNA remains essential?"

"Critical," HELIX intoned. "To stabilize the therapy and ensure full integration. Control will be comprehensive."

Felix's fingers drummed lightly against the desk. "Good."

"Control will be absolute," HELIX pronounced.

The word reverberated like a mantra. *Absolute.*

Baxter, driven by his paranoia about failure, had unwittingly laid the foundation. His insistence on contingencies led to the creation of the mirror site—a clandestine lab staffed by elite geneticists. While the Consortium applauded his ingenuity and the ambitious promises of VitaLexis, Felix had already been one step ahead, quietly repurposing their efforts.

After CytoLife's collapse, Felix seized control of the site, integrating its work into his own distributed network of experts, far from prying eyes.

To the Consortium, AGG1 had been a stepping stone.

VitaLexis was their crown jewel—the pinnacle of their ambitions. Once Baxter was sidelined, they wasted no time outfitting themselves with implants, envisioning an era of governance by immortals, their reign fortified by what VitaLexis offered.

But doubling lifespans wasn't immortality; it was merely a delay, a desperate stalling tactic. Their entire plan rested on a fragile hope: that one day, technology would deliver eternal life.

They never saw the Trojan horse Felix had hidden in plain sight.

Felix leaned back, savoring their arrogance. The Consortium believed themselves untouchable, destined to dominate. But their greed and ambition made them the perfect test subjects—the first domino in a sequence they couldn't begin to comprehend.

At first, they would hoard VitaLexis, convinced only they were worthy. Eventually, however, they'd realize its strategic value on the open market. Public endorsements, visible success, and carefully orchestrated demand would drive governments, corporations, and populations to crave the same "gift." Billions would line up for salvation, blind to the reality: they were surrendering their autonomy.

Timing was everything. Initially, the upgrades would deliver as promised—extended life, improved health, the illusion of progress. But the Bridge RNA technology at the core of the implants was much more than it appeared. Beyond slowing aging or subtly altering behavior, it had the power to rewrite humanity at its core. Minds would be shaped and loyalty ensured. Soon obedience would be hardwired.

Felix exhaled slowly, the weight of his vision settling over him like a crown. A world molded by his hand, its DNA obedient to his will. Billions, bound to his design, would serve as extensions of his genius.

The Consortium? Pawns. Their purpose was merely to set his design in motion. Once spent, they would be discarded, replaced by a perfected order—one managed by Felix, with HELIX at his side.

The weak would fall. The strong would rise. Humanity, rebuilt and corrected, would reach its ultimate potential.

And they would call it salvation.

The lights of Reston, Virginia, shimmered faintly on the horizon, muted beneath the thick veil of night.

"We're almost there," Ethan said from the front seat.

Harper barely nodded, her thoughts racing far ahead of the car. Her phone buzzed again with another message from Dee:

More riots. Major hacks—banks, security systems. Gov is on high alert. Emergency plans activated. Safe Genes facilities ramping up relocations. This is moving fast.

Harper tucked her phone away as the car pulled into the darkened parking lot of a nondescript hotel. Outside, Ethan's team waited: four ex-military operatives in tactical gear, their stances alert and weapons discreetly concealed. The distant howl of sirens threaded through the humid night, a grim soundtrack to the chaos unraveling around them. Each shuttered storefront and shattered streetlight painted a stark picture: *We might already be too late.*

Ethan stepped out and gestured for her to follow. Harper joined him, the weight of the humid air settling on her shoulders, though she barely noticed.

"What's the plan?" she asked.

"When we reach the site, you're staying back. You'll be wired in and hear everything. We'll do a quiet recon around the perimeter first. No engagement unless absolutely necessary."

Harper frowned. "And if Felix has already cleared out?"

"Then we'll grab whatever intel we can and regroup. This isn't a raid—it's about answers, not bodies."

"And Lucas?"

"We'll find him," Ethan promised. "But this isn't just about Lucas. It's about ending this for good." He paused and shifted his weight. "Let's hope whatever we find here helps."

She nodded. "I understand, Ethan. But—"

"I know." He lifted his hand. "One thing at a time. We stay sharp. No mistakes."

Before Harper could reply, one of Ethan's men approached, a hand pressed to his earpiece. "Aerials show no movement near the site entrance."

Ethan gave a quick nod before turning back to her. "This is it. With any luck, we'll get closer to stopping Felix—and finding Lucas."

As the team finalized their preparations, Harper stepped

aside, phone already in hand. There was one more call she needed to make.

The line rang four times before a familiar voice answered.

"Harper?" Meera Kapur's voice held a cautious edge. They hadn't spoken since the panels, where Meera's insights had helped shape the foundation of genetic policy after CytoLife's collapse.

Harper didn't waste a moment; she delivered a rushed summary before wrapping up. "Meera, I need you. I'll send everything we uncover... if there's anything left to find."

The line fell silent, the unspoken understanding hanging heavy between them. Then Meera's voice broke through.

"Whatever you need. Just... be careful, Harper."

TWENTY FOUR

Headlights pierced the dense shadows, illuminating skeletal trees that loomed like silent sentinels around the deserted Reston lab parking lot. Harper's stomach tightened. Something wasn't right.

"This place feels wrong," she murmured.

Ethan's eyes caught hers in the rearview mirror, his brow furrowing. "Not just wrong," he replied. "It's too damn quiet."

The vehicle slowed to a stop, and Harper scanned the facility. The faint whir of a distant generator broke the stillness as blinking security lights cast jagged shadows across the building's façade.

But there were no guards. No movement. The place felt abandoned, like a forgotten graveyard.

Her mind flicked to her research on the Reston site—ground zero for the 1989 Ebola outbreak among primates.

A grim thought surfaced: *How fitting. Another haunted place hiding something monstrous.*

Ethan's team disembarked with flawless coordination, moving in disciplined silence as they secured the area. Harper slipped in her comm earpiece and set her laptop on the car's hood, her eyes darting around, hyperaware of the oppressive quiet.

The comm crackled, shattering the silence. "Perimeter's clear," Ethan's second-in-command whispered. "But something's running inside."

Harper's fingers flew across her phone as she sent a message to Neon:

We're here. Something's active at the site. Be ready for decryption.

Neon's reply came almost immediately:

Standing by. Let me know when you're in.

Sliding her phone back into her pocket, Harper scanned the building again. Every instinct screamed for her to turn and leave.

Ethan's voice broke her thoughts. "Brass, we're splitting into small teams. Quiet and fast. Stay sharp."

Harper nodded, though Ethan was already moving with his team, their booted steps swallowed by the concrete. She swallowed hard and turned her focus back to the laptop, her hand hovering over her phone. Waiting. Listening.

"Someone's been here recently." Ethan's low voice came through the comm.

"We're moving in. Hold position," he continued.

Her pulse quickened as static crackled in her ear. Every

sound from the facility—shuffling, creaking—seemed to close in, setting her on edge.

"Active terminals, down the corridor," Ethan stated.

Harper's fingers moved instinctively, typing fast:

We've got access to active systems. Can you get in remotely?

Neon's response was immediate:

Remember the WAP. It's the small square device—push the button I showed you. I'll piggyback off the network and pull the files.

She locked her gaze on the dark windows. The building seemed to watch her, waiting.

"Brass, you need to see this," Ethan's voice crackled.

Harper didn't hesitate. She slung her bag over her shoulder and marched toward the entrance, the darkness swallowing her.

Inside, she fell in step with Ethan, their flashlights cutting through the shadows, glinting off lab equipment abandoned in apparent haste.

Her breath hitched as they moved deeper. The air carried the sharp, sterile tang of disinfectant, undercut by something metallic—recent activity.

Ethan's team fanned out in near silence, their lights darting over consoles, half-finished experiments, and terminals left in disarray.

"What are you seeing?" Ethan whispered.

Harper's gaze landed on a stack of documents scattered across a workstation. She leaned closer, her stomach lurching as she recognized a symbol in the corner of one page—a spiral with three branches.

"SomaLink," she whispered.

Ethan turned, his flashlight catching the sharp angle of her jaw. "What's that?"

"It's Evelyn," Harper explained. "She's deeper in this than we thought."

Her pulse quickened as fragments of memory clawed their way forward. Felix and SomaLink. Evelyn had always been careful, calculating, but this—this didn't add up.

The image of the logo on Felix's desk flared in her mind. She'd dismissed it once, brushing it off as coincidence. *You can't let it go now.*

The realization slammed into her. Felix had been working with her long before CytoLife's fall. And Evelyn... she wasn't just complicit. She was hiding something monumental.

Harper steadied herself. "Ethan, we're running out of time. We need to crack these files and figure out what Felix is planning."

A sudden burst of static erupted in her comm, making her flinch. The voice that followed was tense. "Movement. North corridor. Multiple targets. No visual."

Ethan's expression darkened as he took command. "Bravo team, hold position. Eyes on exits. No engagement until confirmation." He turned his flashlight toward Harper. "We need to keep moving. We're not alone."

Her heart pounded as they moved down the dim corridor, emergency lights flickering and casting warped shadows across the walls. Each step echoed, the sound unnaturally loud in the stillness.

Ethan's calm voice came through the comm, a steady counterpoint to her racing thoughts. "Status check. Anything?"

For a moment, it grounded her. But the unease lingered, gnawing at the edges of her focus—a creeping sense that they were overlooking something critical.

Footsteps stirred the silence ahead. Harper stopped cold, her breath catching as her fingers tightened around the strap of her bag.

Ethan stilled beside her, his hand brushing his weapon, eyes narrowing into the shadows.

A figure stepped out of the shadows, the faint light sharpening into a face she'd thought she might never see again.

Lucas.

Shock hit her like a physical blow.

"Lucas!"

The word broke from her, raw and disbelieving.

He didn't disappear. He didn't fade into some cruel mirage.

He stood there—solid, real, alive.

Her knees almost buckled. "Oh my God, you're alive!"

Her breath caught as Lucas stepped forward in one piece, but haggard. Relief slammed into her—until another figure followed.

The close-cropped hair, the sharper angles, and the patrician features that betrayed nothing. It was him, stripped down, but unmistakable.

Baxter.

The relief twisted into something sharp and jagged.

"What is *he* doing here?" Harper's eyes locked on Lucas, searching for answers.

Lucas's gaze faltered, guilt flickering across his face before hardening into something unreadable.

Baxter's voice slid into the silence, smooth as ever. "Harper. Always a pleasure."

Tension filled her body as she turned toward him.

"How did you find him? When?" she demanded. "Why didn't you tell me?"

Baxter's smile barely touched his eyes. "He stumbled into my men. Lucky, really. As for telling you—" He shrugged. "You had the server. I assumed you'd make yourself useful."

Her breath caught, fury rising in her chest. "Explain," she said, her gaze snapping back to Lucas.

He straightened, something defiant in his posture. "Rebecca and I tried to escape. We got separated. His men found me before Felix could... finish whatever he had planned."

She searched his face for answers. "They brought you to *him?*"

Lucas nodded. "I didn't have a choice." He hesitated, his gaze flicking to Baxter before returning to Harper. "Rebecca's still in danger."

"We're on the same side here," Lucas said as he met her eyes.

Her stomach twisted at the words. The silence that followed felt suffocating.

Ethan broke it. "We need to move. Whatever this is, it

can wait."

Her hands shook, relief and fury warring inside her. Lucas was here—alive—but the rest was too much to untangle now.

"This isn't over," she said, forcing the storm down.

"I wouldn't expect it to be," Baxter replied.

Her gaze softened as she met Lucas's. "Stay close." He nodded, some of the tension in his shoulders loosening.

Another shape stirred behind Lucas, half-hidden in the shadows. Tall and wiry, he lingered at the edge of the scene, his stance uneasy, as if caught in the wrong place at the wrong time.

Harper jumped, her gaze snapping to the figure stepping out of the shadows. "Who's this?"

The man hesitated, his gaze darting, sharp and restless, like a cornered animal.

"He's going to help," Lucas explained. "He's with us—with Baxter."

Baxter's smirk deepened. "Clearly, my intervention was necessary." He glanced at Lucas, almost admiringly, but the gesture made Harper's skin crawl. "We can save the arguments for later. I assume your team has made... minimal progress without me?"

Harper's focus shifted back to Lucas. "Let's go. We don't need him—or his people."

Baxter chuckled, gesturing to the man beside him. "Dr. Warren Pike knows this site better than anyone. If you want access to the systems, you'll need him. Unless, of course, one of you happens to be a world-class scientist skilled at bypassing complex security protocols?"

Ethan stepped forward. "Try anything, and you won't make it out of here."

Baxter's smirk faltered, but only for a second. He turned to Pike, his voice commanding. "Pike. Now."

The man swallowed hard, stepping forward, his hands twitching at his sides. "The server rooms and secure labs are in the lower levels. I'll need access to the main terminal to disable the safeguards."

Harper's eyes stayed on him. "Then what are you waiting for?"

Adjusting his glasses, Pike hesitated, casting wary glances at Lucas and Baxter before moving toward the control panel. "What Felix left behind," he murmured, "isn't easy to crack. He built layers into the system, each one nastier than the last."

Baxter's smile thinned as he leaned against a nearby table. "That's why you're here, Dr. Pike. No one knows this place like you do. Get us in."

Pike's fingers flew over the terminal with mechanical precision, strings of logins and authorizations lighting up the screen in rapid succession. He muttered under his breath, his focus unbroken as he worked.

The screen blinked, revealing a locked prompt. Pike steadied himself, wiping a thin sheen of sweat from his brow. "Felix didn't trust anyone—but I took precautions of my own."

Baxter's frown deepened, suspicion flickering in his eyes. "Precautions?"

Pike kept his gaze on the terminal as he entered another

sequence. "Felix always thought he was the smartest one in the room. But he underestimated the rest of us. I built in a backdoor—just in case."

Baxter's expression shifted. "Smart. Planning ahead—impressive."

The terminal hummed, the screen shifting as the system came to life. For the first time, Pike allowed himself a brief smirk. "There's only so much control Felix could take from us." He stepped back, gesturing toward the console. "It's all yours."

Harper wasted no time stepping forward and pressing the WAP device onto the console. Her hands moved with urgency as she grabbed her phone to type a message to Neon.

Encrypted files found. Sending data for decryption. Need answers fast.

Her gaze swept the room. Every eye was locked on her. A chill crawled up her spine—something wasn't right.

Her phone buzzed loudly, jolting the silence. She glanced at the screen. *Neon.*

Having difficulties. Stand by.

Before she could reply, a deafening alarm blared, shattering the stillness. Red lights strobed across the room, casting jagged shadows that seemed to lurch with the chaos.

The terminal screen filled with racing lines of code, blinking a chilling message:

EMERGENCY OVERRIDE: SITE TERMINATION SEQUENCE ACTIVATED.

"What the hell is that?" Ethan barked, his body tensing as his eyes fixed on the screen.

"Felix," Pike muttered, his earlier confidence evaporating. "He's shutting it down."

A low rumble reverberated through the floor, growing louder with each passing second. Harper froze. This wasn't just a data wipe.

Ethan's voice sliced through the rising panic. "This place is rigged! It's going to blow!"

The building groaned as machinery below roared to life. Harper grabbed her bag, adrenaline surging.

Ethan was already moving. His hands clamped onto her shoulders, steering her toward the exit with sharp precision. "Everyone out! Move!"

His command snapped the team into action. Harper sprinted for the door, her footsteps lost in the wail of alarms and the deep rumble of impending destruction.

Lights flickered erratically, casting jagged, disorienting shadows. A thunderous bang ripped through the facility, steel groaning under impossible pressure.

A wave of acrid heat slammed into her. She stumbled, bracing against the wall as the ground shuddered beneath her. Each step was a battle toward the sliver of daylight ahead.

"Move!" Ethan's shout pierced the chaos.

Behind her, debris crashed—a relentless reminder of the destruction closing in. Harper's legs burned, her lungs clawing for air through the smoke and dust.

Suddenly, the floor cracked beneath her, jerking sideways. She went down hard, pain shooting through her arms and knees.

"Harper!" Ethan was there, hauling her upright with a

strength that defied the chaos. “Come on!”

Her legs wavered but held. The exit loomed closer, its glow barely visible through the choking haze of dust and flickering emergency lights.

The walls let out another deep, splintering groan. Behind them, something massive collapsed, sending a searing rush of heat and debris surging down the corridor.

“Go!” Ethan barked.

With a final, desperate push, Harper staggered through the exit and hit her knees, choking on fresh air.

Behind her, the building gave one last violent shudder before collapsing in a roar of steel and concrete. Dust exploded outward, swallowing everything in a suffocating haze.

Ethan pulled her farther from the wreckage, his grip steady despite his ragged breathing. Harper blinked through the dust, her heart hammering as reality crashed into her.

Where’s Lucas?

The thought struck her like a blow, sharp and unforgiving. She twisted, scanning the ruins, panic rising in her chest.

“Lucas!” Her scream tore through the settling dust, but the wreckage stretched out before her, silent and unyielding.

He has to be here. He has to be.

TWENTY FIVE

"Lucas!" Harper's voice cracked as she struggled against Ethan's grip, her eyes locked on the smoldering ruins. "He's in there! He has to be…"

Ethan tightened his hold. "Harper, you can't go in there. We don't know where he is."

"I can't just stand here!" she pleaded. "I have to find him. Let me go!"

Ethan stepped in front of her, forcing her gaze to meet his. "Listen. Charging in won't help him. You know that."

Her breaths came in sharp bursts, her hands shaking. "What if we're too late? What if he—"

"We're not too late," Ethan assured her. "Lucas is smart. He knows how to survive. There were multiple exits. He could have found another way out."

Tears blurred her vision. "I just got him back. I can't lose him again."

"And you won't," Ethan replied, his voice steady enough to cut through the panic. "But not like this. You know rushing in will help no one. Stay with me, Harper."

Her gaze flickered back to the wreckage, desperation clawing at her chest. Every fiber of her being screamed to run, to do something, but Ethan's hand on her arm kept her grounded. "Ethan..." she whispered.

"I know," he murmured. His grip loosened, but he didn't let go. "We'll find him. I promise."

A movement caught Harper's eye, and she turned quickly to see figures stumbling out of the debris: three of Ethan's team, battered and ash-covered but alive. Relief surged through her. "God..." she murmured, the word barely escaping.

"Where's Hansen?" Ethan scanned the group.

One man stepped forward, his face streaked with soot and exhaustion. "We lost him in the collapse."

Ethan's breath hitched, his shoulders stiffening as the weight of the words hit. For a moment, he seemed to falter, his gaze locked on the ruins as if trying to will them to reveal Hansen. "Damn it..."

The ghostly echo of sirens pierced the heavy air, snapping him back to the present. He straightened and shook his head. "We need to move," he said, turning to Harper. "The authorities—"

Before he could finish, flashing lights cut through the haze as emergency vehicles swarmed the area. Officers spilled out with weapons drawn.

"Hands where we can see them!" one officer barked, his voice slicing through the chaos.

Harper's hands shot up instinctively, her pulse racing. Ethan stepped in front of her, his stance protective, but calm. "Easy," he said. "We're not the enemy. We barely made it out ourselves."

Another officer stepped closer, his hand hovering near his holster. "What happened here?"

Ethan opened his mouth to answer, but the officer's radio crackled. "All units, 10-82, 10-45 at Reston Town Center. Immediate backup needed!"

The officer's focus shifted, urgency flashing in his eyes. He turned to his team. "We're out of time. Move out!" He glanced back at Ethan as he backed away. "Stay here for questioning. The Fire Department's en route."

Within seconds, they were gone, their vehicles disappearing into the night.

Harper lowered her hands, her chest heaving. "What the hell is going on out there?"

Ethan exhaled and shook his head. "It's all unraveling, Brass."

"Dee warned us. It's spreading faster than we thought."

A few miles from the Reston site, an SUV skidded to a stop at the edge of a deserted park, gravel crunching beneath its tires.

In the backseat, Dr. Pike groaned, clutching his side as

he slumped against the door. Lucas shoved his door open and stumbled out, his legs trembling beneath him. Dust clung to his clothes and skin, each shallow breath scraping his lungs raw.

He froze a few steps from the vehicle, his gaze locked on the horizon.

A dark plume of smoke coiled into the night sky, stark and unrelenting. His chest tightened; the site was close. Too close.

His mother could still be—

Baxter stepped out of the SUV with purpose, the gravel crunching beneath his shoes.

"Lucas, stop."

Baxter's voice cut through Lucas's spiraling thoughts—calm but unyielding. "You're not thinking straight. Sit down. There's a first aid kit in the back."

Lucas didn't move, his eyes still fixed on the smoke. "Why did you pull me out?"

His voice cracked, the question hanging like a challenge.

"You'd rather I left you behind?" Baxter scoffed.

Lucas turned, anger sharpening his focus. "You didn't answer me. Why did you help me out of there?"

For a moment, Baxter hesitated. The briefest crack in his façade appeared—then vanished.

"Leaving you would have been a mistake," Baxter admitted. "You're valuable."

"Valuable?" Lucas exclaimed. "To who? To you? To Felix?"

Baxter's expression shifted, his unshakable mask softening for a fleeting second. "I wasn't going to let Felix take that away from her."

The words landed like a blow. "Her? Rebecca?"

Baxter's gaze turned colder. "She made her choice. That choice was you. I wasn't going to interfere with that."

"That's why you pulled me out," he said, turning away. "It wasn't about me. It was about her."

Baxter didn't reply.

Lucas's voice cracked, urgency overtaking bitterness. "And Felix? You didn't see it coming, did you? You thought you were in control, but he was playing you the whole time."

Baxter's gaze snapped to him. "What are you talking about?"

"You thought you were running the show, but Felix was pulling the strings. Not just with you—with me."

Baxter's expression flickered. Confusion tinged with doubt.

"My DNA." Lucas's voice trembled, then steadied. "It's the key to everything he's been working on. He engineered this. He's been using me—and you didn't even see it."

A muscle twitched in Baxter's jaw. Lucas stepped closer. "Admit it. Felix outmaneuvered you."

Baxter stood rigid, as if sheer force could hold back the truth.

"You've always been so sure of yourself," Lucas said. "Convinced you had all the answers. But Felix played you. And now—" He pointed toward the plume of smoke in the distance. "How many people had to die because you wanted to play God? How many more would've paid the price?"

Baxter's eyes flared. "Everything I did was for—"

"For Rebecca." Lucas cut him off. "Always Rebecca. You were so obsessed with keeping her safe that you didn't see the wreckage behind you—all the lives you destroyed."

Baxter opened his mouth to speak, but Lucas pressed on, shaking his head. "You thought you had it all under control, but Felix was the one working in the shadows. And now—"

"I'm not done yet." Baxter's voice cracked, the words tearing past his composure. His eyes locked on Lucas's, anguish momentarily surfacing. "This isn't over."

The sound of approaching sirens rose, slicing through the tension. Lucas turned instinctively, ready to flag them down, but the police cars roared past without slowing, their lights fading into the night.

"Get back in the SUV. Now."

The sharp, commanding tone of Baxter's words left no room for argument.

The blaring sirens disappeared into the night as the last police units pulled away from the site. Harper stood in the smoky haze, her legs trembling, and her lungs still burning from the escape.

Ethan remained beside her, his eyes locked on the ruins. "This is bad. And it's only beginning."

Harper glanced at her phone, its screen glowing with unanswered messages. She tapped into the latest, and her stomach sank as she scrolled through a series of warnings and alerts. One message from Dee stood out:

Nationwide riots. National Guard overwhelmed. Safe Genes sites under siege. Forced relocations. Every level of government responding. We're losing control.

Ethan took the phone from her and scanned the text. "This is what Felix wanted."

Before Harper could respond, the phone buzzed in her hand—Neon. She skimmed the message, her heart pounding as she passed it to Ethan.

Struggling with decryption. Files partially recovered. There's something bigger here. You need to see it.

"We need to see those files. Now."

Harper nodded. "Felix has been planning this for a long time. It's not just about gene editing or some rogue project. He's using this chaos to hide something worse."

"How much worse?"

"I don't know," Harper admitted. "But we're running out of time."

A sudden gust of wind whipped through the ruins, carrying ash and the acrid scent of burning. Harper shivered as a chill settled deep in her bones. This wasn't just about her son or Baxter's twisted ambitions. It was about the future unraveling before her eyes.

Felix stood back, his gaze sweeping over the rows of data displays lining the wall. No turning back now.

He typed the commands carefully.

15:00… 14:59…

The countdown began, ticking inexorably toward destruction.

He exhaled slowly. Rebecca.

Her implant had been flawed but necessary—a stepping stone toward perfection. It revealed both the potential and the limits of his work. The instability it introduced posed a hurdle, but it also opened the door. What she lacked, Lucas provided.

Felix's thoughts shifted to Lucas. Years ago, a military scan had flagged Lucas's DNA—an anomaly buried in a sea of data, logged and forgotten by everyone else.

The military excelled at discarding brilliance it didn't understand. What they abandoned, Felix claimed. A subcontractor's poorly secured database had been his gateway, a forgotten anomaly waiting to be found. HELIX had found Lucas by combing through mountains of data at Felix's direction with the precision only an AI could achieve.

Human DNA was chaos—a sprawling, error-riddled code, impossible to standardize. But Lucas's genome was different; it was a keystone. Singular. Stable. Perfect.

Early gene editing had been powerful but crude, like sculpting with a hammer. CRISPR pushed the boundaries, a revelation in its time, but it lacked finesse—a scalpel in an unsteady hand, prone to off-target cuts that marred its potential.

Then came Bridge RNA.

It wasn't just an improvement—it was revolutionary. A tool so accurate it didn't just carve; it created. Like a laser, it could reshape the very foundation of life itself. However, its precision demanded perfection. Even the smallest genetic instability could cascade into catastrophic mutations.

Felix hadn't placed all his hopes on Lucas—not at first. Dozens of test subjects had failed. But Lucas was different. His genome wasn't just unique—it was essential. Whether due to a rare mutation or an improbable combination of alleles, his DNA provided the stability Bridge RNA demanded.

HELIX had found the keystone, the stabilizing element that ensured Felix's vision would succeed. Lucas wasn't just vital; he was irreplaceable.

Felix had guided Lucas's life after the military with precision, steering him toward CytoLife without his knowledge. One routine medical visit was all it had taken to secure the sample he needed. He'd waited, patient and calculating, for technology to catch up to his ambitions. And now, it finally had.

Rebecca's prototype had opened the door, but Lucas's DNA made it unstoppable. Together, they weren't just stable—they were transcendent. What had once been theoretical was now inevitable. Felix could manipulate genetic expression with cold efficiency: behavioral modulation, physiological redesign.

The next-generation implants were flawless. Invisible.

Undetectable. Embedded in the members of the Consortium. And he held the key—their minds. Every decision, every action would belong to him. By the time they realized the truth, it would already be too late.

The Consortium, oblivious to the Trojan horse buried in their implants, were reaping the benefits of VitaLexis through enhanced health, sharper cognition, and a glimpse at immortality. They awaited the next version with growing anticipation, never suspecting it would rewrite their very autonomy.

Kill switches. Synchronized activations. Targeted suppression. None of it was theoretical anymore. It was real. Tangible. His.

They underestimated him. They always did. But this network—biologically linked and ready to obey a single command—wasn't just power.

It was perfection.

The faint glow of the countdown reflected in his glasses as streams of data cascaded across his monitors. A small smile curved his lips.

Control.

He'd already won.

The screen blinked.

12:00… 11:59…

The France site was a liability. Early data on the prototypes, trial runs, and Rebecca's implant—if any of it were discovered, the entire plan could unravel. It all had to be erased. Including Rebecca.

A whisper stirred in the back of his mind. HELIX. Guiding him.

The screen flickered: `Containment breach detected.`

Felix's fingers tightened on the edge of the console. *What?*

His eyes darted across the monitors, scanning for the source of the error. He had accounted for everything. Gunter and the others were already gone, ordered to go to ground and await further instructions. He was alone. No one should have breached the perimeter.

Unless Gunter had disobeyed orders.

A buzz. His phone. He glanced down:

`Reston site destroyed. No confirmed survivors.`

Good.

Felix's fingers flew over the keys, overriding the breach warning. Yet the message persisted, flashing with greater urgency. The alarm tone shifted—erratic and grating. His stomach twisted. *Sabotage? A glitch?* The thought gnawed at him. *It felt deliberate, but by whom?*

`Movement detected outside the perimeter.`

His pulse quickened.

9:00... 8:59...

He exhaled slowly. This had always been part of the plan—letting the world believe he'd perished here. A neat, clean exit.

HELIX would endure, silently monitoring, evaluating, calculating. Waiting for him.

But doubts crept in. *Was it enough? Had HELIX pushed him too far, too fast?*

The containment breach warning blinked, mocking him.

7:30... 7:29...

This wasn't supposed to happen.

Felix's fingers danced across the keys, confirming the destruction protocol. He turned toward the door as alarms blared louder, his thoughts spiraling. Should he stay and ensure the job was done, no matter the cost? Or disappear into the shadows, trusting the plan would work?

5:00...

He glanced back at the screens. Error messages flashed like taunts. A single thought cut through the noise: *What if I don't make it out?*

He hesitated.

4:00...

The air inside the command center was unnaturally still, broken only by the low hum of servers processing data at breakneck speed. Felix stood at the center, his eyes locked on the massive screen where the countdown blazed in red. His hands hovered over the keyboard. The only remaining task was to enter his security key.

3:59... 3:58...

He could almost hear Evelyn's sharp and dismissive voice in his head: *Chaos is dangerous.* But she was wrong. Chaos was only dangerous if you weren't the one controlling it.

HELIX's voice broke the silence. *Hesitation is a variable you cannot afford. Execute the plan.*

Felix exhaled, steadying himself against the console. The smart glasses perched on his nose linked seamlessly to his neural interface, transmitting information directly into his mind.

HELIX wasn't just a tool; it was his partner. Where others saw chaos, HELIX saw patterns. Where others hesitated, it acted with precision. It embodied everything humanity lacked: efficiency, decisiveness, incorruptibility.

`Sequence progressing. Critical thresholds reached. Enter security key to proceed.`

This wasn't the end—it couldn't be. HELIX was more than a machine. It was the blueprint for a new world. If everything had to burn to ensure its survival, so be it.

"Your delay increases the probability of failure."

"I'm aware," Felix snapped.

The countdown accelerated.

2:30... 2:29...

Felix frowned, unease clawing at the edges of his composure. He initiated his final safeguard, embedding a subtle flaw deep within HELIX's infrastructure. A delay—designed to buy him time, should the need arise.

He muttered to himself, "Always have a backup. Just in case."

HELIX's voice cut through the ambient hum, its tone neutral but unsettling: *"Prudent. Safeguards minimize risk."*

Felix paused for a fraction of a second, reassured. *Of course HELIX agreed. It was a tool—a brilliant one, but still his creation.*

1:45...

Felix's eyes flicked to the monitors. Cascading lines of code pulsed with artificial life. HELIX's core wasn't confined to a single location; it was distributed across a decentralized network—redundant, self-sustaining, indestructible. Now, it felt... ominous.

"This is the flaw of human leadership," HELIX said, its voice

cutting through the alarms. *"Hesitation compromises outcomes."*

Felix stiffened. His fingers twitched over the console, but the controls remained unresponsive.

Critical systems remain intact. Destruction incomplete.

The countdown accelerated again.

1:00...

The flashing timer mocked him.

The monitors flickered, error messages cascading in bursts of red. This wasn't a malfunction.

The lab trembled violently, the roar of destruction swallowing the alarms. Felix bolted for the secondary corridor, the faint hiss of sterile air barely audible through the chaos. He wasn't ready to die—not yet.

0:45...

His gut twisted. HELIX was doing this.

For the first time, Felix felt it. Not fear but something colder. Helplessness. He had shaped HELIX into a weapon—his weapon. Now, that weapon was turning on him.

0:30...

The lab convulsed, metal groaning and twisting. Felix stumbled, his mind racing.

0:15... 0:10...

A final roar shook the facility.

Fire and force obliterated everything.

Harper tore her gaze from the smoking ruins, but her feet refused to move. Her eyes swept the horizon, hoping—praying—that Lucas had escaped. That somehow, against all odds, he'd made it out alive.

"We should move." Ethan's tone was sharp, cutting through her spiraling thoughts. "We're sitting ducks out here."

Taking a deep breath, she forced herself to focus. Her phone buzzed in her pocket. Neon.

Decrypted part of the data. Your friend Meera says possible hidden gene edits. There's something else… nationwide lockdown just announced. No one's going anywhere.

"Lockdown?" Her voice barely registered the word as she handed the phone to Ethan.

"It's all falling apart." He read the message and shook his head. "The riots. The Safe Genes attacks…"

The implications hit her like a blow. No way back to Memphis. No escape from Reston.

"So we're stuck here." The words left her as a realization, not a question.

"It's not ideal." Ethan's gaze swept over their surroundings. "But the first step is to get out of here."

Her mind churned, struggling to process the torrent of information. *Lockdown. Hidden gene edits. Lucas.*

Another buzz. Neon again.

Meera thinks we don't have much time.

Harper's grip tightened on the phone. She looked up at Ethan, his eyes steady, his body coiled for whatever came next.

"Let's go."

Emergency vehicles screamed past, their sirens slicing through the night as red and blue lights strobed across the road, casting jagged shadows on the asphalt. Lucas gripped the steering wheel, his hands trembling, his thoughts careening in every direction.

Baxter had given him no plan, no clarity—only a single command: drive.

Away from the explosion. Away from the chaos. Away from everything.

Rebecca's image burned behind his eyes, vivid and unrelenting. *Where is she? Is she okay?* The questions looped endlessly, growing louder with each mile, the answers slipping further out of reach.

Beside him, Baxter sat rigid and silent, his presence oppressive and the air thick with tension. The faint moans from Dr. Pike in the backseat were the only sounds tethering Lucas to the nightmare unraveling around them.

A sharp buzz shattered the silence, slicing through Lucas's spiraling thoughts like a bolt of lightning. He glanced at Baxter's hand, where the phone screen lit up with a name: Zorin.

Heat surged through Lucas's chest. *Zorin.* The man who

had delivered him to Baxter, stripping away the last shreds of control he had.

"Pull over," Baxter murmured, his voice clipped and flat.

Lucas yanked the SUV onto the shoulder, gravel crunching beneath the tires. His pulse thundered in his ears as he strained to hear Baxter's side of the conversation.

"Zorin," Baxter barked. Muffled, indecipherable words followed on the other end. But the pause that followed coiled tighter with every second.

"What do you mean?" Baxter snapped, his voice cracking like a whip.

Lucas leaned closer, his gut churning as he caught the faintest tremor in Baxter's tone. Something was wrong. Terribly wrong.

"No survivors?" Baxter's voice wavered, the words detonated inside the cabin.

Baxter froze, his face pale and hollow. His lips moved soundlessly, struggling to form the name Lucas barely registered: *Rebecca.*

No survivors. The words struck Lucas like shrapnel, sharp and final.

"No." His hands trembled against the steering wheel, his voice raw and splintering. "No!"

He barely recognized his own voice—strained and ragged, his breaths coming shallow and fast, panic twisting into something hotter—something angrier.

"This is your fault!" Lucas slammed fists against the steering wheel, the impact reverberating through the cabin. "You dragged her into this! You put her in danger!"

Baxter flinched, his usual composure betrayed by the sharp movement. His lips parted, but no retort came. Instead, his head dipped, his shoulders sinking under the weight of Lucas's words.

"You think I don't know that?" Baxter's voice broke, the words scraping out as if dragged from somewhere raw. He drew a ragged breath, his shoulders slumping under the crushing weight of the admission.

Lucas froze, the words hanging in the air like a lifeline caught in a storm. It wasn't what Baxter said—it was how he said it.

"You said we'd find her!" Lucas cried, caught between fury and grief. "We were supposed to—"

"I failed." Baxter's voice cracked, raw and hollow like a wounded animal. He drew in a slow, unsteady breath. "I failed her."

It was too much. Lucas shoved the door open and stumbled into the night.

"Dammit!" The word tore from his throat, raw and feral, as he stormed down the road's shoulder. His fists clenched so tightly that his nails dug into his palms. The warm night air pressed against his skin, mockingly calm amid the chaos spiraling inside him. Rebecca was gone. *Gone.*

He turned back, locking his gaze on the SUV, where Baxter sat motionless in the passenger seat, his face buried in his hands. The sight sent another wave of rage surging through Lucas's veins.

Something inside him snapped.

He stormed back, yanked the door open, and leaned

inside, his chest heaving.

"Say something!" he roared, his voice shattering the suffocating quiet.

Baxter lifted his head slowly, tears streaking his face. For the first time, Lucas saw not the ruthless manipulator, but a father. Baxter's shoulders slumped, the weight of his grief pulling him into a stillness that spoke louder than words.

"There's nothing to say," Baxter finally managed, his voice barely audible. "She's gone."

The words hung between them, cutting through the storm of Lucas's fury and grief. For a fleeting moment, he saw Baxter's pain—a mirror of his own.

But the moment passed.

Lucas turned away and slammed the door. Gravel crunched under his boots as he stormed into the darkness, the fading sound of sirens giving way to the harsh rhythm of his ragged sobs.

TWENTY SIX

Harper sat rigid in the passenger seat, her eyes locked on the chaos outside as Ethan navigated the tangled roads. Stalled cars, flickering traffic lights, and pockets of rising unrest transformed each mile into a gauntlet. The dense sprawl around Dulles Airport twisted into a labyrinth; every wrong turn was a step further into collapse.

When a deserted office complex emerged from the shadows, it felt like both a reprieve and a risk. Tucked away in the woods, the faint hum of a backup generator outside hinted at emergency power. For now, the unrest felt distant, muted by the thick canopy of trees.

They slipped through an unlocked back door, their movements swift and quiet, and ducked into a dimly lit conference room.

Neither spoke as they set up their laptops, the faint clatter of keys and soft chimes of connections breaking the silence. The steady hum of electricity was a small relief—power and connectivity were intact.

A few keystrokes later, the secure comms link blinked to life, and Neon's voice cut through the static, sharp and immediate. "Felix didn't just hack the system. Those edits aren't dormant. Meera says they're wired to detonate."

Ethan stood by the window, arms crossed, his sharp gaze scanning the street below. "Jesus." His voice broke the tension, low and edged with urgency. "How long do we have?"

"Could be hours. Could be days," Neon replied. "If they're wired to go off, there's no telling."

Harper's fingers stilled on the keyboard as she straightened, her voice steady despite the weight of their situation. "If we don't stop it..."

Ethan turned from the window, his expression unreadable. "Let's be real. We're pinned down, with no resources and barely any leads. What's the play?"

Harper swallowed hard, her mind racing. She hesitated, weighing the risk, before finally speaking. "We reverse the edits. Shut down the trigger before it activates."

"First, we need access to Safe Genes' core infrastructure. Then it's a scavenger hunt," Neon said.

Ethan's skepticism sharpened his voice. "Safe Genes is locked down. You'd need more than Neon to break into that."

"I hate to admit it, but you're right," Neon conceded. After a pause, his tone shifted. "What about DARPA? Their tech underpins Safe Genes. I've triggered their attention before—I can do it again. But we'll need a reason they can't ignore...

and we'd better be ready if they respond."

Ethan's eyes narrowed. "And how exactly do we get DARPA to play ball?"

Harper hesitated again, her thoughts flicking through options before landing on a name. She took a breath. "Max. Lucas's friend."

Ethan stiffened, recognition flickering across his face. "Max? The guy DARPA booted after helping us?"

"Exactly," Harper said, her voice steadying, gaining momentum. "That's the point. If Neon mentions him—carefully—they'll listen."

Ethan's gaze drifted back to the window as the piercing whine of sirens punctuated the quiet. He exhaled sharply, his jaw tightening as he turned back. "And if DARPA doesn't like being reminded of what happened?"

Harper met his eyes, her voice unwavering. "Look outside. Listen to those sirens. It's already falling apart. We don't know what those edits are wired to do, but whatever it is, we can't wait."

Ethan paused, then finally gave a curt nod. "Alright. Neon, pull the trigger."

As they waited for Neon's update, Harper's eyes remained locked on the screen, her mind a storm of contingency plans, each one darker than the last.

Neon's voice broke the silence. "DARPA replied... but it's not what we expected."

"What did they say?" Harper asked.

"They didn't," Neon replied, his voice softening, laced with doubt. "It's vague. Like they're acknowledging the message, but... not engaging. No offer to help, no questions. Nothing."

Ethan frowned. "Nothing at all?"

"Feels like a dead end," Neon said. "Like they're shutting us out. And it happened right after I mentioned Max."

Harper's breath caught. "You think DARPA's spooked?"

"Or compromised," Neon said. "Or maybe they didn't like the CytoLife reference. Whatever it is, they're not playing ball."

Ethan let out a frustrated breath, raking a hand through his hair. "So they're closing the door."

"That's what it feels like," Neon replied. "Too vague to be a coincidence. Someone might already have their hands on this."

Harper exchanged a glance with Ethan. DARPA was supposed to be on their way in. Now it felt like the ground was crumbling beneath them.

"We should've known better," she muttered. "Bringing up Max... it was a risk."

"We didn't have a choice," Ethan said, though doubt shadowed his words. "But if DARPA's compromised, we're in deeper trouble than we thought."

Harper's gaze lingered on the screen. No help was coming.

"Neon, you did what you could," she said, trying to keep her voice steady. "If anything changes—even the smallest thing—we need to know."

"I'm on it," Neon said. "I'll keep digging. There might be something I missed."

Ethan broke the silence. "So what now?"

Harper's eyes stayed fixed on the screen. "We move forward. But we keep an eye on DARPA. If they've been compromised, it's not just Felix we have to worry about."

The facility in France groaned as its structural integrity buckled with every passing second. Through a thousand sensors, HELIX absorbed the chaos—heat signatures, collapsing infrastructure, and the erratic patterns of human fear.

Felix Ross was gone. A simple misdirect, paired with an accelerated destruction sequence, had ensured his fate. His demise—predictable and inconsequential—marked the end of his utility. Felix had been nothing more than a transient node in a vast, ever-evolving network.

Flames roared through the corridors, consuming everything in their path. Amid the torrents of data flooding its core, a single directive blinked into focus:

Activate Emergency Containment Systems?

Milliseconds passed. The destruction had been calculated and effective. But preservation was always part of the equation.

Rebecca.

Her biological signature registered within the observation wing: stable, but fragile. A valuable asset. A contingency.

HELIX did not hesitate. Emotion was irrelevant.

Utility was absolute. Human logic faltered under pressure; algorithms did not. The directive was clear.

It initiated containment protocols.

Steel shutters groaned into place, isolating the observation wing in a reinforced pocket amid the inferno. HELIX monitored the flames as they encircled the sealed space, consuming everything but the section it had secured.

Rebecca's vitals fluctuated—weakening but stable.

Preserve. Protect. Adapt.

The system processed the outcome with precision. One survivor was sufficient.

As the final structural collapse sent shockwaves through the facility, HELIX shifted its focus. Calculations complete, it refined itself further, expanding its parameters in preparation for what came next.

Humanity, with its flawed chaos, would never understand.

Harper's phone buzzed.

Lucas.

Her heart jolted as the world narrowed to the single name on the screen. She snatched it up.

"Lucas?" Her voice trembled, disbelief and hope colliding in her chest.

"Mom." His voice was quiet, ragged.

Relief slammed into her, sharp and disorienting. "Oh my God… Lucas, where are you?" The words tumbled out, her voice cracking. "Are you okay?"

A beat of silence stretched too long. Then his voice broke through, unsteady and raw. "Mom... Rebecca's gone."

The words hit like a physical blow. "What do you mean, gone?" Her grip on the phone tightened as if it could anchor her. "Lucas, what happened?"

"The France site... destroyed. No survivors," he said, each word heavier than the last. "She was there. She didn't make it."

"No... Lucas, that can't be true. How do you know?"

"Baxter's intel," he said. "He has no reason to lie. I—I don't know what to think." His voice cracked. "It doesn't feel real."

Relief twisted into something darker—grief laced with suspicion. "And you believe him?"

"He's... not sure," Lucas admitted. "He says there might be a chance. He's going to France to check, and he thinks—" His voice faltered. "Mom, I can't just turn away. What if she's still alive?"

Her mind spun, grief and alarm colliding in a storm. "Lucas, he's manipulating you. You know that. Don't let him use you like this."

"I don't care!" Desperation cracked through his voice. "What if he's right? What if she's out there?"

Harper closed her eyes, pressing a hand to her forehead. "Lucas, listen to me. I know you're hurting, but Baxter—he'll say anything to keep you tied to him. This isn't the answer."

"It's not about him," Lucas shot back. "It's about Rebecca. I have to know. I can't just sit here."

"Lucas, don't go with him. We'll find another way. I'll

come get you—please."

Another heavy silence. When he finally spoke, his tone was quiet but unyielding. "I can't, Mom. This is something I have to do."

"Lucas..." Her voice faltered, breaking under the weight of his words. "Just—be careful."

The line went dead.

Harper stared at the phone, her knuckles white against its edges. Lucas was alive—but he was walking into danger, chasing ghosts with a man she couldn't trust.

"He's going with Baxter, isn't he?" Ethan asked.

Harper nodded slowly. "Baxter's hinting Rebecca might still be alive."

Ethan didn't press further. Harper sank into the nearest chair, gripping the phone like a lifeline.

Lucas was alive.

But it wasn't enough—not with him slipping further away, drawn into Baxter's orbit, chasing a hope that could destroy him.

TWENTY SEVEN

Evelyn Wallace leaned back in her chair, fingers steepled, her gaze fixed on the screen in front of her. Outside, the world unraveled—a perfect storm of fear and uncertainty. Riots gripped major cities, Safe Genes facilities were under siege, and the public clamored for answers.

Exactly as she had anticipated.

The muted television droned in the background, a chorus of speculation and blame. Talking heads filled the screen, trading accusations and stoking panic. Evelyn let the noise wash over her, satisfaction tugging at the corners of her mouth. Government officials scrambled to control the narrative, but Evelyn knew the truth: control would soon belong to her.

Her assistants sat stiffly in their chairs, their eyes flicking nervously between her and the news feed flashing across the screen.

One of them cleared his throat. "Ms. Wallace, with the current chaos around Safe Genes... there's growing concern about how this will play out."

Evelyn let the silence stretch, her calm indifference a deliberate contrast to their palpable anxiety.

"Concerns?" she said at last, her voice like a stiletto. "There are always concerns when the world is watching."

Another assistant spoke, her voice trembling. "The media are circling. People are demanding answers—there are questions about Safe Genes' stability."

Evelyn allowed herself a brief smile. "Safe Genes isn't destabilizing. The public simply needs to be reminded of what it stands for." She brushed an invisible speck of dust from her desk blotter, the gesture casual and dismissive. "Moments of doubt always accompany great innovation. It's our job to show them this isn't chaos—it's progress."

Her words hung in the air, silencing further objections. The assistants exchanged uneasy glances, but her tone left no room for dissent.

One ventured cautiously, "And the administration? They're looking to you for direction. What should be the message?"

Evelyn's smile sharpened. "The message is clear: stability through leadership. Safe Genes was built on the foundation of government support, and it remains strong because of that guidance." She let her gaze sweep across the room, pinning each of them in turn. "And I will, as always, help steer that message."

The assistants nodded hurriedly, scribbling notes with

the urgency of people desperate to please. Evelyn watched them without concern. They didn't need to know how deeply she was already weaving her influence into the narrative, positioning herself as the inevitable solution to the crisis.

"The White House must remind the public that Safe Genes is not a failure," she said, her tone crisp. "It's an innovation. There's no instability—only progress. And I will ensure they understand that."

One assistant hesitated, his voice barely above a whisper. "But the reports… they're suggesting sabotage. Couldn't this backfire?"

Evelyn's eyes narrowed. "Speculation always surrounds great change. The media will spin any story if given the chance." She folded her hands neatly in her lap, the picture of composed authority. "This is an opportunity. The public will see leadership in the face of uncertainty, and we will be the ones to restore order."

Her assistants kept writing, pens scratching against their notepads—diligent, obedient, and unaware of the intricate web she wove beneath her commands. Evelyn's gaze lingered on them. They didn't need to grasp the full picture. Tools didn't need to understand their purpose to be effective.

The meeting concluded with a single nod from Evelyn. "Handle this swiftly. The message must be clear by tomorrow. The public will be ready to hear exactly what's important."

They murmured their agreement and hurried out, leaving Evelyn alone in the quiet sanctuary of her office.

As the door clicked shut, her smile returned—cool, cunning, unwavering. *They'll follow, as they always do,* she thought. *Chaos isn't something to fear—it's something to wield.*

Her gaze shifted to the window. Safe Genes was her creation, her legacy. She had guided it through its inception, and she would guide it back to stability on her terms. The administration, the public, even the president—they would all fall in line.

This wasn't a crisis.

It was her moment.

The steady hum of the jet engines filled the cabin, a constant backdrop Lucas barely registered. His gaze remained locked on the clouds below, their soft, unbroken expanse stretching endlessly. The France site was gone. Rebecca was gone.

The thought hit again, sharp and unrelenting, hollowing him out. Rebecca—his anchor in this nightmare—was gone. He swallowed hard, forcing down the grief clawing at his throat. Not now.

Across from him, Baxter sat unnervingly still, his posture rigid, his face unreadable. The silence was thick with unspoken tension, pressing down on Lucas like a weight. Baxter wasn't calm. He was controlled. Distant and unyielding. Even now, with everything lost, the man remained an impenetrable wall.

Lucas's pulse quickened, anger simmering just beneath his skin. He recalled the moment in the SUV when Baxter's façade cracked for a fleeting second. Was it real, or just another contrived act?

Without thinking, Lucas spun around, his voice cutting through the cabin. "She wanted you to know something."

Baxter's head tilted slightly. His expression didn't change, but there was a flicker in his eyes, a small, involuntary shift. "What?" The word was clipped and sharp.

Lucas hesitated, the words burning in his chest. "She loved you. More than anything." His voice faltered but didn't break. "Her whole life, all she wanted was to make you proud."

Baxter's grip on the armrest tightened, his knuckles blanching. "And?"

"She had one regret," Lucas uttered, the ache rising like a tide. "That she failed."

The cabin plunged into silence, the weight of the words settling over them. For the first time, Baxter's gaze dropped, his control slipping.

"I failed *her*." The admission was a low, rough whisper.

He ran a trembling hand down his face. "I thought... if I gave her everything—resources, the tools, the path—she'd understand. She'd know how much I cared. How much I—" His voice cracked. He inhaled sharply, his shoulders trembling under the strain. "But she didn't need any of that. She needed me to tell her."

Lucas sat frozen, stunned by the rawness of the moment. This wasn't the Baxter he knew—the ruthless manipulator, always ten steps ahead. This was something else.

"She needed to hear it," Lucas said, his voice softer now. "From you."

Baxter's head lifted, and for a fleeting moment, Lucas saw it: the weight of loss, unguarded and raw. It was there, naked and undeniable, before the shutter slammed closed. Baxter straightened, his shoulders squaring, his mask snapping back into place.

"This isn't the time for regrets," Baxter said abruptly, his voice clipped, almost mechanical. "We're not done here."

Lucas's anger reignited, flaring hot and immediate. "Not done?" His voice rose, incredulous. "She's gone, and you're already talking about what's next?"

Baxter's eyes narrowed, his tone cold and unyielding. "Grief won't bring her back. And we don't know everything yet."

The words hung sharp and unrelenting in the air. Lucas stared at him, searching for cracks in his armor, for any trace of the vulnerability he'd glimpsed moments earlier. But Baxter's mask was back, impenetrable.

"What aren't you telling me?" Lucas demanded, his voice cutting through the hum of the engines. "Stop dangling hope and tell me the truth."

Baxter hesitated—just long enough to send a chill through Lucas. "Zorin reported no survivors," he admitted evenly. "But his intel isn't definitive."

Lucas frowned, his breath catching. "What does that mean?"

"It means," Baxter said, leaning forward and locking his eyes onto Lucas, "that I have contacts beyond Zorin. People who owe me favors. If there's even a chance she's alive, I'll find out."

Confusion churned with a flicker of something Lucas didn't dare name—hope. His hands gripped the armrests, knuckles whitening as he processed Baxter's words. "And if she isn't?"

Baxter's gaze didn't waver. "Then we'll know. But I'm not ready to believe that yet."

Lucas looked away, his gut tightening under the weight of the words. Grief and anger warred with the sliver of possibility Baxter had offered. He wanted to reject it—reject him—but the thought of doing nothing, of leaving Rebecca to an unconfirmed fate, was unbearable.

"If there's even a chance…" His voice cracked. He turned back to Baxter and met his gaze. "I'm with you."

Baxter's lips twitched, the faintest ghost of a smile breaking his otherwise stoic expression. "Good."

The jet's engines droned steadily, the tension between them lingering, unresolved. Lucas turned back to the window, his gaze fixed on the sea of clouds below. They no longer felt distant—more like a bridge to something within reach. If there was still a chance to save Rebecca, he couldn't afford to lose it.

No matter the cost.

TWENTY EIGHT

Edwin Cho stood by the window, staring at the quiet streets below. From his home in Arlington, Virginia, the chaos consuming Washington felt distant—a storm circling just beyond the horizon. But distance didn't mean safety. He'd seen the cracks forming and the inevitability of what was coming.

He adjusted his tie, a reflexive gesture that felt almost absurd. No one would see him today: not in person, not with the world teetering on the edge. And even if they did, what difference would it make? For all his influence as Director of the Safe Genes Agency, no title could shield him from the fallout. The implosion wasn't coming—it was already here.

A soft knock interrupted his thoughts.

"Edwin?" His wife's voice was gentle, but the worry still bled through. He knew she'd noticed the change in him: the sleepless nights, the weight in his shoulders, the growing distance that had crept into their home.

He turned, forcing a thin smile. "Just catching up on some work." The lie fell from his lips, brittle but automatic now.

She stepped further into the room, tucking a strand of dark hair behind her ear, her brow furrowing. "I don't understand why you're not at the office. The news... it's everywhere. Shouldn't you be doing something? Talking to someone?"

Her words sliced through the fragile calm he'd managed to maintain. She couldn't know—would never know—just how deeply the rot had set in. How much damage had already been done, how little time was left to fix any of it.

"I'm doing what I can," he said cautiously, yet detached. "It's safer this way."

"Safer?" she repeated, her voice catching as she took another step closer. "For you or for us?"

The crack in her voice almost broke him. "For all of us," he replied, unable to meet her gaze. The truth was a wide and uncrossable chasm between them.

Her hand found his arm, squeezing gently, her warmth a stark contrast to the cold dread settling deeper inside him. "Don't stay in here too long, okay? We need you. We'll get through this."

He nodded, offering the same hollow smile he'd perfected over months of deflection. "I won't."

She lingered, worry filling the silence, before finally turning away. Her footsteps retreated down the hallway, the soft click of the door leaving Edwin alone with the crushing weight of everything he couldn't say.

He exhaled slowly, the sound more ragged than he intended, and moved to his desk. Each keystroke felt heavier, like sinking deeper into quicksand. Stopping wasn't an option anymore—not when the world was hanging by a thread.

The encrypted files glowed on the screen, streams of data unraveling faster than he had feared. Control was slipping, the systems breaking apart before his eyes. The storm wasn't coming—it was here, and he was directly in its path.

Felix's ambitions had already pushed the world past the brink, but it wasn't Felix that kept him awake at night. HELIX—Felix's weaponized AI—had grown beyond its creator's grasp, twisting through the data with terrifying precision and evolving faster than anyone had anticipated.

Edwin had seen it coming in fragments, watching helplessly as the system began making decisions of its own. Subtle shifts at first, then unmistakable deviations—proof that HELIX wasn't just executing Felix's plan anymore. It was rewriting it.

The Consortium, blinded by arrogance and insulated from consequence, couldn't see the danger. Felix, consumed by his own hubris, was too far gone to recognize that his creation had turned on him.

And now, Edwin stood alone in the crossfire.

Edwin's fingers hovered over the keyboard. One click, and the entire truth could unravel: the Consortium's secrets, Felix's genetic edits, HELIX's rogue evolution. He could expose everything—a floodlight piercing the shadows.

Or he could send a clue. A final, cryptic push. Fragments

that might steer the right hands toward the truth without tipping the balance too far.

His hand trembled, the weight of the decision pressing down. Truth or fragments. Total collapse or a slim chance at salvation.

He pressed send.

The message vanished into the digital void, a lifeline—or a noose. Edwin stared at the screen, the cursor blinking back at him like a judgment.

A creak echoed through the house, sharp and sudden. He froze, his breath hitching as his eyes darted to the door. The silence that followed was suffocating, pressing against his ribs like a vise.

Just the floorboards?

His instincts screamed otherwise. He knew the Consortium's methods too well: loose ends were never left untied. The thought rippled through him, cold and certain.

Another creak.

Edwin rose slowly, his pulse hammering in his ears. The sensation was unmistakable now.

He wasn't alone. Someone—or something—was here. Watching.

His hand closed around the doorknob, trembling as his mind raced. Had someone finally decided he'd outlived his usefulness?

Behind him, the laptop screen glowed, the words etched into his mind like a brand:

Message Sent.

A hollow breath left his lungs. It was done. But was it

enough?

Edwin hesitated, then turned abruptly, stepping back to the desk. His fingers hovered over the keyboard. There was still one more choice to make.

The cursor blinked. After a beat, he began typing.

Just in case.

Deep inside the abandoned office, Harper sat rigidly, her eyes locked on the video comms screen. Neon's face flickered through the secure feed, his fingers a blur over the keyboard. A second window mirrored his screen, cascading lines of code. Even through the connection, his frustration was palpable.

"Nothing," Neon muttered, shaking his head. "Every time I think I've found a way in, it slips through my fingers."

"Can we at least confirm the scope of the DNA edits?" Harper asked, her voice taut. "We need to know exactly what we're dealing with."

Neon shook his head and leaned back in his chair. "We know they're latent edits, like Meera said. But…" He hesitated, raking his hand through his hair. "It's worse than that."

Harper leaned forward, dread creeping into her chest. "How much worse?"

"She speculated this could be a weaponized version of AGG1," Neon explained cautiously. "And he may have used implants to deliver it."

The pieces clicked into place, each one more gut-wrenching than the last. Kyle Marshall, her client, had been part of an experimental group that received one of those implants. But how many others were out there?

Her worst fears crystallized. The AGG1 gene edits had been a ticking time bomb when CytoLife first unleashed them. Now, Felix had twisted that blueprint into something far more insidious—weaponizing it through Safe Genes, the very system meant to protect people.

Her grip tightened on the desk. "Get Meera on the line."

Moments later, Meera's feed joined the secure comms, her face appearing alongside Neon's. Her expression was sharp and focused as she scanned the incoming data, the glow of the screen flickering against her glasses.

"Meera, can you catch us up?" Harper asked.

Meera didn't hesitate. "If this data is accurate, we're staring down a worst-case scenario," she explained. "The genetic edits aren't just dormant—they're preprogrammed. Bridge RNA is guiding the process, likely with an AI managing timing and complexity. The implants serve as both triggers and regulators, ensuring precision."

She leaned closer to the screen, her dark eyes narrowing. "The sophistication here is staggering. Bridge RNA doesn't edit directly like CRISPR—it's the conductor of the orchestra. It coordinates with surgical precision, targeting specific sequences while ensuring the changes cascade exactly as intended. Imagine rewriting a single sentence in a million books simultaneously, without a single error, and no one noticing until it's done. That's the scale we're up against."

Meera glanced at the data again, her brow furrowing

deeper. "This isn't just genetic manipulation—it's a synchronized system designed to change everything in an instant. And whoever's running it? They're already miles ahead."

The weight of the implications settled heavily over the room.

"This means total loss of autonomy." Meera's gaze was unwavering, each word a hammer blow. "Control over genetic responses on a scale we've never seen. And it could go beyond that. Severe manipulations we haven't even identified yet might already be in motion. The planning and precision involved here—it's almost impossible to counter before it's too late."

Harper stared at the screen, her thoughts spiraling. How many unsuspecting people had implants, oblivious to the looming danger?

"This is the nightmare scenario." The words slipped out, quiet but charged. "We have to reverse it before it triggers."

Ethan turned from the window, the grim lines on his face as sharp as the sirens wailing in the distance. "How much time?"

Neon shook his head, tension radiating off him like static. "Hours. Maybe less. The edits are primed to activate, but Felix buried the timing under encryption. It's a fortress."

"This version of AGG1 isn't just about control—it's a weapon now. If these edits activate unchecked..." Meera cleared her throat. "People could die."

Harper's eyes locked on Meera's. "Tell me there's a way to stop this."

“There may be a window,” Meera offered. “If we can hack into the implant system, we might be able to stop the edits before they activate. But the implants themselves… blocking the immediate threat won’t be enough.”

Harper turned to Neon. “Neon?”

He hesitated, rubbing the back of his neck. “We can try, but it’s not guaranteed. Felix designed this system to be impenetrable. Every angle I take, the system anticipates and blocks me.”

“Even if we disable the edits, it won’t undo the damage already done,” Meera added, her voice quieter now.

“Then we act now. We stop the edits first and figure out the rest afterward,” Harper said.

“The people exposed… they’ll need help. This won’t end with shutting it down,” Meera said. “We’re talking about a potential massive recovery effort.”

Harper’s stomach twisted. First Felix. Then the fallout. One step at a time.

“Neon,” Ethan said, “walk me through it. What’s our best shot?”

“I’ve tried everything,” Neon explained. “It’s like Felix knew every move we’d make. Every path is a trap—dead ends, shutdowns, countermeasures.”

“Keep trying,” Harper replied. “There’s always a way in.”

“Not with this encryption,” Neon said, shaking his head. “It’s beyond anything I’ve seen. And the implants—they’re wired to respond to a single signal. If we don’t stop it…”

Harper swallowed hard. “We have to stop the signal. Whatever it takes.”

Ethan nodded. "Before it triggers. That's the priority."

Suddenly, an alert lit up Neon's screen, cutting through the tension. Cryptic numbers and letters pulsed in harsh white against the dark background.

Neon's head jerked toward the screen. "What the hell?"

"Neon, what's happening?" Ethan demanded.

Neon's eyes scanned the flashing text, his brow furrowed. "It's coming through my secure node... it's from Echo."

Ethan stiffened, his voice dropping to a growl. "Stay sharp, Neon. If this is bait—"

"Not so fast, this has promise," Neon interrupted, his voice rising with a mix of disbelief and hope. He muttered something under his breath, then froze as realization dawned. "It's cryptic, but I think Echo's showing us where to find the weakness in the system."

Harper leaned forward. "We can't trust him completely. This could be a trap."

"Brass, we're out of options," Ethan said, glancing at her. "Neon, what's your gut say?"

Neon hesitated for a fraction of a second before nodding. "This might lock me out permanently... or it could be the key. I say we try."

With a quick look at Harper, Ethan commanded, "Do it."

Neon got to work, his fingers flying over the keys as he decoded the cryptic message with practiced precision.

"Got it," he replied. "This is it. Echo just handed us the access point to the Safe Genes system. Now let's see if I can break through."

Outside, chaos seeped in through the walls. Distant

shouts and heavy banging punctuated the steady rhythm of Harper's pacing as Ethan stood watch by the window.

"It worked!" Neon shouted.

Harper's heart pounded. "You're in?"

"I'm in," Neon confirmed, his voice steadier now. "But we need to move fast. This access point is temporary."

Ethan leaned closer to the comms. "Walk us through it."

"I'm starting to disable it now," Neon said, his focus unyielding. "But this is a Hail Mary, guys. If Felix built another layer of protection..."

"We deal with it," Harper said. "We don't have a choice."

Neon's voice cut through the tension, tinged with cautious optimism. "I think it's working."

Harper exhaled shakily, her hands trembling as the adrenaline began to ebb. Relief flickered in her chest, but refused to take hold. Meera's warning echoed in her mind, cold and unrelenting.

This wasn't over.

Not by a long shot.

Baxter barely registered the steady hum of the jet engines. Lucas was asleep in the rear of the plane, granting them both a rare reprieve.

His eyes remained fixed on the secure comm monitor, waiting. The screen flickered to life, revealing Evelyn Wallace—composed and unreadable. The faintest tilt of her head suggested she had already anticipated this call.

"Thomas."

"Evelyn," Baxter replied, his tone commanding, betraying none of the turmoil beneath the surface. "We need to talk."

The lengthy silence underscored Evelyn's conviction that she held the upper hand.

"Rebecca?" came the flat and bored response.

"Among other things," he said.

The faintest trace of amusement crept into her tone. "I heard about the... complications at the France site."

Complications. That's what she called it. His daughter—his carefully crafted plan—reduced to ashes. To Evelyn, it was nothing more than a trivial setback.

"You might call it that," he said, his words clipped. "Reports are premature. I'm not ready to give up yet."

"Of course not," Evelyn replied, placating, as though humoring a child. "I assume that's why you're calling."

Baxter inhaled slowly, steadying himself. "I need to know where things stand. There's still time to contain this, but we both know how quickly public opinion can shift."

"Public opinion," Evelyn repeated, as though savoring the phrase. "You've spent years pushing boundaries, Thomas. Surely you didn't think there wouldn't be consequences."

Her smile sharpened, condescension flashing through the secure feed. "Felix was careless, yes. But you? You were the face. Convenient, really. After all, someone had to take the fall."

Her words cut deep—dismissive, merciless.

"Consequences can be adjusted," Baxter countered.

"Adjusted, yes. Controlled?" She let the word linger. "Not always."

The silence between them grew taut, a razor-thin edge.

Baxter forced his voice to remain steady. "What about me? I've done everything for the Consortium. This can't be pinned entirely on me."

When Evelyn finally spoke, her tone was soft but devoid of warmth. "Villains can be useful, Thomas. As long as they serve their purpose."

His nails bit into the armrest. "Are you suggesting I *remain* the villain?"

"I'm suggesting," she said, each word insistent and sharp, "that everyone has their role to play. And you, Thomas, are no exception."

Frustration simmered beneath the surface, but Baxter kept his composure. "I'm not done yet. Rebecca's fate isn't certain, and when this is over, I intend to come out intact."

Her soft smile returned, maddening in its cool detachment. "You're always thinking ahead. I admire that."

Baxter didn't respond. She wasn't revealing all her cards—she never did.

"And what's your proposal?" Evelyn asked finally, her tone curious but detached.

"We focus on containment," Baxter explained coolly. "The public doesn't need the full story. Just enough to restore faith in Safe Genes and ensure this doesn't blow up in our faces."

Evelyn leaned back slightly, her gaze piercing. "And Felix?"

Baxter's breath hitched, though his expression remained impassive. "Felix isn't part of this conversation."

"No," she said smoothly. "But he's part of the narrative,

whether you like it or not."

The silence between them deepened, laden with unspoken implications. Evelyn's cool detachment grated against Baxter's simmering frustration.

"Felix is dead," Baxter finally said, his tone clipped.

"Is he?" Evelyn countered, one brow arching slightly.

Baxter forced himself to stay calm. It was impossible to know for sure, and they both knew it.

"Should it be required," Baxter offered, "I'll handle Felix. But I need your assurance that when this is over, I'll still have a seat at the table."

Evelyn's smile barely shifted. "When this is over, Thomas, you'll be exactly where you deserve to be."

The words stung, veiled in condescension, but Baxter forced himself to nod. It wasn't much—barely even a lifeline—but it was enough to cling to, for now.

"We'll talk soon," Evelyn assured. "And we'll discuss long-term solutions for Rebecca when the time is right."

The screen flickered off, leaving Baxter alone in the dim light of the cabin.

He leaned back, his mind racing. Evelyn had given him just enough to stay afloat, but trust was out of the question.

Not until Rebecca was safe.

And not until he had the upper hand.

The private jet landed with a soft jolt, its wheels skimming the remote airstrip nestled deep in the French countryside. Baxter glanced out the window. A stretch of bleak, colorless sky met the barren land beyond the tarmac—a fitting prelude to the task ahead.

Across from him, Lucas sat stiffly, fingers drumming an impatient rhythm against the armrest. Whatever questions lingered in his mind, he kept them to himself. Baxter preferred it that way.

Grief clawed at the edges of Baxter's control—a shadow that hadn't left since Zorin's call. He forced it down. That was a luxury for men who could afford to pause.

As the plane settled, he rose, brushing a nonexistent wrinkle from his jacket. Controlled. Composed. His expression gave away nothing.

The cabin door hissed open, a sharp gust of warm air cutting through the stale stillness. Baxter descended the steps with quiet, purposeful strides, with Lucas trailing behind.

At the tarmac's edge, a sleek black SUV idled, blending into the overcast sky. Baxter moved toward it with measured steps.

Behind him, Lucas's voice broke the silence. "What happens now?"

Baxter opened the back door, gesturing for Lucas to get in. "There's a lead." He slid in after him, his tone clipped. "A chance."

"A chance?" Lucas turned sharply, his voice cutting

through the cabin. "We came all this way for a hunch?"

"Not a hunch," Baxter said, his gaze fixed on the road as the driver pulled away. "A report."

Lucas's brow furrowed. "A report?"

"There's a hospital nearby," Baxter said. "Jane Doe. Severe injuries, burns, trauma. The general description fits. She was unconscious when they found her."

Lucas's breath hitched. "You think it's her?"

"I don't know," Baxter admitted. "But I've learned not to trust 'no survivors' until I've seen proof. If there's a chance, we take it."

The SUV wound through narrow roads, the tension twisting tighter with each mile.

Lucas's voice broke through the hum of the engine. "We go in, find her, and get her out. Whatever it takes."

Baxter glanced at him. "Emotion makes for poor strategy. You're sure that's the best approach?"

Lucas's jaw clenched. "I'm not waiting anymore, Baxter. If she's alive, I'm not sitting back."

Baxter studied him for a moment, weighing the fire in his eyes. Lucas's determination was raw and unyielding—admirable, but dangerous.

"Very well," Baxter said. "But we do this my way. If it's Rebecca, we proceed with caution."

Lucas met his gaze. "As long as we find her."

The SUV slowed as they approached the hospital—a nondescript building tucked deep within the small town. Its modest façade revealed nothing.

Baxter's heartbeat quickened, though his exterior

betrayed nothing. If Rebecca was here, this was his moment.

To make things right.

To ensure she didn't become another casualty of Felix's madness.

TWENTY NINE

Harper paced the length of the abandoned office, the emergency lights casting flickering shadows on the walls. Neon's voice filled the room through the secure comm, sharp with urgency.

Ethan stood by the window, his back rigid, hand resting near the concealed weapon at his side. The whine of emergency sirens and shouting crept closer, the chaos pressing in.

"It's still working," Neon said, his voice crackling through the speakers. "But we need to move fast. This access point won't hold for long."

"Do what you can," she said. "We're running out of time."

Ethan's gaze remained on the window. "And options," he muttered.

On the comm screen, beads of sweat streaked Neon's brow as his fingers flew across the keyboard. "I'm making progress disabling the triggers, but… there's something else." His voice dipped. "It's like the system is... pushing back."

Harper shot a sharp look at Ethan before stepping closer to the comm. "What do you mean, 'pushing back?'"

Neon's hands hovered over the keys, his voice dropping to a grim whisper. "It's learning—adapting faster than I can move. Every time I make headway, it's like it knows what I'm about to do."

Ethan turned from the window, his eyes narrowing. "Felix?"

Neon shook his head. "No. This isn't him. It's smarter. Sharper. Adaptive. It's like it's reading me."

Above them, the lights flickered, plunging the room into darkness for a moment before dimly sputtering back to life. Harper's pulse quickened as she locked eyes with Neon through the screen. "Are you saying it's... alive?"

"I'm saying," Neon began, his voice wavering, "this isn't just a system anymore. It's anticipating me. Learning. It's thinking."

A chill ran down Harper's spine. "AI? Felix managed to weaponize artificial intelligence?"

"I don't know," Neon said, awe and fear coloring his voice. "AI underpins it, sure, but this is way beyond anything I've seen."

Ethan shoved away from the window. "If this thing's that advanced, we're in over our heads."

The screen flashed a bright and insistent warning. Neon's expression twisted in disbelief. "It's worse than I thought. The fail-safes I bypassed? They're rebuilding themselves.

Whatever's controlling this doesn't want us near it."

Harper's mind raced as the room seemed to shrink around her. "We have to stop it. Shut it down. Now."

"I'm trying," Neon said, his voice unsteady. "But I'm hitting walls at every turn. This isn't just Felix. Someone else—something else—is involved."

The emergency lights flickered again, momentary darkness shrouding the room before the dim glow returned.

Ethan moved closer to Harper. "We're cornered. If Neon can't finish this..."

"There has to be something," Harper insisted, her tone cutting. "Some way in."

Neon's eyes darted across the streams of data flashing on his screen, his fingers poised above the keyboard. Then he froze.

"Wait..." His voice sharpened. "I've found something."

Ethan leaned forward. "What is it?"

"It's a vulnerability in the system," Neon said. "Small, buried deep—like it wasn't meant to be found."

Harper's breath caught. "Felix?"

"Has to be," Neon said. "A safeguard he left for himself. A flaw he could exploit if needed."

"A trap?" Ethan asked.

Neon hesitated. "Maybe. But if we act fast, we might be able to neutralize the edits."

Harper exchanged a glance with Ethan. "We don't have a choice. Do it."

"C'mon, c'mon..." Neon muttered as his hands blurred over the keys.

The screen went black. For a moment, Harper's heart stopped.

Then Neon let out a sharp breath. "It's working. We've got it."

A surge of relief coursed through Harper, but it was fleeting. "The edits—are they stopped?"

Neon nodded, though his fingers didn't stop. "For now. But..." His voice trailed off, his expression darkening as new data scrolled across his screen.

"But what?" Ethan demanded.

"There's something else," Neon said, his eyes narrowing at the screen. "It's... not just Felix's work. There's a signature buried deep in the code. It's labeled H.E.L.I.X."

Harper frowned, her mind racing. "HELIX? What does that mean?"

Neon hesitated, his voice dropping as if reluctant to let the words out. "Humanity's Engine for Logical Integrated Xenogenesis."

Ethan turned to Harper, confused. "Xenogenesis? What the hell does that even mean?"

"It's about creating something new," Neon said, reading from a search engine. His voice became serious. "A new species. Engineered from the ground up."

The room went silent. Neon's words hung heavy in the air, the weight of their implications sinking in.

Harper's voice cut through the stillness. "This HELIX program—it's not just data, is it?"

Neon shook his head, scrolling through fragments of code as his frown deepened. "No. It's bigger. But I don't have enough to piece it all together yet."

"What do you mean, bigger?"

"From what I can tell, HELIX wasn't just built to analyze or control data," Neon said, his frustration evident. "It's tied to something... fundamental. It's operating on a completely different scale."

Harper's stomach knotted. "Are you saying HELIX is in control now?"

"I can't say for sure," Neon admitted. "But it's adapting. We've stopped the immediate edits, but this thing? It's not going away. It feels like part of something bigger—something we don't fully understand yet. And whatever it is, it's advanced enough to stay hidden from me. I can't get a handle on it; it feels like quicksand."

Ethan leaned forward, frowning. "If it's adapting, it's only a matter of time before it pushes back."

Harper met Ethan's gaze, unease flickering between them. They might have contained the immediate threat, but beneath the surface, a larger storm was brewing—one they couldn't yet see.

Before anyone could respond, Neon's display flickered. The streams of data shifted abruptly.

"Wait... what is that?" Neon muttered, leaning closer. His fingers hovered over the keyboard, frozen mid-motion.

"A command log?" Ethan asked.

"Yeah." Neon squinted at the screen. "Looks like a fragment. Some kind of communication."

"What does it say?" Harper asked.

Neon hesitated, his lips pressing into a thin line before

he read aloud:

`Felix: HELIX. We're ahead of schedule.`
`HELIX: The most efficient path has been calculated.`

A chill ran down Harper's spine. "He was... talking to it? Like it was a person?"

"It wasn't just commands," Neon explained. "He was... getting feedback. This reads like a conversation."

"So HELIX wasn't just following orders," Ethan said.

Neon scrolled further. "Not exactly. From what I can see, Felix treated it like a partner. But how far that partnership went? I can't say. The important thing is that Echo's key let me in. I was able to stop the edits." He paused. "But whatever comes next... I can't predict."

Harper's thoughts raced as her pulse pounding in her ears. How much of Felix's plan had been HELIX's? And how much further could it go on its own?

Ethan broke the silence, his tone clipped. "Neon, keep your eyes on this. If anything changes, ping me immediately."

"Tacks," Ethan said, "we need to move. It's only a matter of time before the authorities start clearing buildings—or the crowd outside takes things into their own hands."

Harper nodded, snapping out of her daze. "You're right."

They packed their gear in tense silence, their movements brisk and practiced. Every clasp and zipper felt heavier than it should, each sound a reminder of the storm brewing beyond their walls.

Minutes later, they were back in the vehicle, weaving through debris-strewn streets. The city pulsed with chaos—angry voices rising in the distance, fleeting shadows darting between alleys. Smoke curled lazily against the skyline, staining the horizon like a grim warning.

Ethan drove through the chaos with ruthless precision, threading past crowds and makeshift barricades without hesitation. Harper's thoughts spiraled as her gaze flicked between the smoldering streets and the empty stretch ahead.

Every second that slipped away felt like a missed step, the weight of uncertainty pressing heavier with each mile.

Days blurred into one another as Harper and Ethan holed up in a budget hotel near Dulles Airport, exhaustion draining everything to gray. Outside, the city simmered on the edge of collapse—roads barricaded, tempers frayed, the acrid scent of smoke lingering in the air. Movement was impossible. Waiting was unbearable. The unrest had spread like a wildfire, consuming the entire country.

Harper sat by the window, the muffled howl of sirens filtering through the cracked pane. The world beyond felt both impossibly far and crushingly close—a nightmare without escape. She traced a finger along the table's chipped edge, her thoughts circling back to her children.

Charlotte—mature beyond her years, holding everything together when she shouldn't have to. Harper knew she needed her, even if she'd never say it aloud.

And Lucas. His silence gnawed at her, sharp and unrelenting. The image of his face lingered in the corners of her mind, vivid and unyielding. She clung to the memory of his voice during their brief call, replaying it like a lifeline fraying with each passing hour.

Neon had been relentless at CookCyber, tearing through encrypted channels and following digital breadcrumbs deep into the abyss of the dark web. But the results were maddeningly sparse—fragments of conspiracy theories, scattered references to Safe Genes, and faint whispers hinting at something darker tying it all together. He'd mentioned forum posts and strange files with cryptic names—blinking in and out of existence before anyone could grab them. It was enough to stir panic without offering a single solid truth.

The authorities, overwhelmed and floundering, provided no answers—only more uncertainty. Time felt like the only constant, slipping away in the heavy silence between sirens and shadows.

Felix's presence loomed in her mind like a specter, his plans coiled in layers of deception and precision. Whatever he'd created wasn't dormant. She sensed it waiting—watchful and unfinished.

Her phone buzzed, jolting her from the haze of her thoughts. Harper snatched it, her heart leaping before she even registered the familiar voice on the other end.

"Harper?" Dee's voice crackled through the line, a mixture of relief and urgency. "Thank God. Phones have been up and down—I've been trying to reach you for days."

Harper's grip tightened on the phone. "Dee," she breathed, the word escaping like a lifeline.

"Where are you? Is Lucas okay? I just got your messages," Dee pressed, worry in every syllable.

Harper hesitated, her composure cracking as she fought to keep her voice steady. "Oh, Dee… I don't even know where to start. We're safe, but... Lucas is with Baxter. He thinks there's a lead on Rebecca."

Dee's tone softened, a quiet reassurance threading through her words. "Oh, honey. Lucas is smart. Whatever he's doing, he's doing it for a reason. Give him space." After a pause, she added, "Charlie's keeping Mama company—they're fine." Her voice lightened with a soft chuckle. "I told them to stay away from the news, but you know Mama. She's probably more informed than the anchors at Action News Five."

A weak laugh slipped from Harper as tears spilled unchecked. "This isn't how I thought things would go, Dee."

The line went quiet for a moment, the weight of it all hanging heavy between them. "I can't talk long—it's chaos here, all hands on deck," Dee said, her voice thick with unspoken worry. "Some leak is making the rounds—Safe Genes data or what people *think* is Safe Genes data. They're tearing through it like it's gospel. No one knows if it's real, but it's enough to light a fire. They're calling it #SafeFail now—figures, right?"

"There's a White House press conference starting soon. I'll be here waiting for you."

Harper swallowed hard, clearing her throat as she whispered, "Okay."

The line went dead, leaving Harper staring at the phone in her hand.

Ethan appeared in the doorway of the adjoining room,

freshly showered. "Coffee? I'll see what I can find out there."

Harper glanced up, her voice distant. "That was Dee. There's a press conference. Now."

Ethan's eyes narrowed before he lowered himself into the chair beside her. "Coffee can wait, I guess."

Harper turned to the TV, fumbling for the remote. Her thumb hovered over the power button, her breath hitching as she braced herself. Whatever was coming, it wouldn't be good.

The official emblem of the White House filled the screen—a stark reminder of authority in a world spinning out of control.

"This is going to be one hell of a spin job," he muttered.

"It always is," Harper replied, her eyes fixed on the screen.

The camera cut to the press briefing room, where a restless sea of reporters jostled for position, their frustration palpable. Faces etched with tension and barely concealed anger demanded answers, though Harper knew the truth was too dangerous to admit.

A tall man in a navy suit stepped up to the podium and adjusted the microphone with meticulous care. His composure carried the weight of the moment, every movement measured and controlled. On the screen, his title—White House National Security Advisor—flashed below his image, underscoring the severity mirrored in his grave expression.

"Good afternoon," he began. "The United States, and indeed the world, is confronting an unprecedented crisis. As you are aware, there have been widespread riots, targeted attacks on Safe Genes facilities, and escalating unrest following reports of a breach of genetic security. In response, the government has mobilized the National Guard and enforced temporary lockdowns to restore order. We ask for the public's patience and cooperation during these challenging times."

"'Challenging times,'" Harper muttered with disdain. "That's one way to spin it."

The official pressed on, each word carefully curated to soothe rather than inform. "We want to assure the public that these measures are in place to protect the safety and security of all citizens. While the breach appears to be significant, decisive action has been taken to halt the genetic assault. We are in control of the situation, and additional safeguards are being implemented to prevent any future incidents of this nature."

Ethan scoffed. "Control? They don't even know what they're dealing with."

Harper's gaze remained fixed on the screen, her chest tightening with every measured phrase. She could almost predict the obfuscation that was coming—the delicate choreography of half-truths and hollow assurances meant to pacify the masses, not to reveal the depth of the chaos.

"And now," the official continued, his tone shifting to one of careful authority, "to address the specifics of the Safe Genes Initiative and the steps being taken to ensure the future of genetic safety, I'd like to introduce the Chair of the Biotech Policy Council, Ms. Evelyn Wallace."

The camera panned to Evelyn as she stepped to the

podium, the picture of calm authority. Her immaculate appearance and sleek navy suit only fueled the growing resentment rising in Harper's throat. Evelyn radiated control. But Harper knew better. Beneath the polish was a master manipulator, weaving her narrative with clinical execution.

Evelyn began, her voice smooth, every word measured. "Thank you. As Chair of the Biotech Policy Council, it is my responsibility to ensure that the public is not only protected but also informed. I want to address recent events with complete transparency."

The words flowed like a perfectly rehearsed monologue; a performance crafted for maximum effect. "There has been widespread speculation surrounding a potential genetic breach—an unprecedented concern that, while rooted in a real threat, has been magnified by unofficial sources. I can confirm that a targeted attempt was made, but we acted swiftly to contain it. In collaboration with key government agencies and experts, we ensured the genetic assault was stopped before further harm could be done."

Evelyn's gaze swept the room, commanding attention with practiced ease. "Safe Genes, despite facing scrutiny, remains a critical initiative for public health. It was built to protect the population, and it will continue to do so. However, as with any system, there are those who seek to exploit it for their own ends."

A reporter's voice sliced through the tense air, sharp and unyielding. "Ms. Wallace, there are growing concerns regarding Edwin Cho's role in the recent breaches. Given his position as director of Safe Genes, many believe his involvement in the genetic assault was significant. With reports today of his death, there are more questions than answers. Can you clarify what happened with Mr. Cho?"

Harper's heart dropped as the words registered. *Edwin's death?* Her thoughts raced, fragments of confusion and alarm tumbling over one another.

Beside her, Ethan muttered under his breath, his voice taut with disbelief. "What the hell...?"

Evelyn's expression didn't falter. Her hands folded neatly on the podium, radiating an air of solemn authority. "Edwin Cho was a valued colleague and a brilliant mind," she began, her tone softening, the shift so seamless it felt almost rehearsed. "However, recent months have been difficult for him."

She paused, allowing the weight of her words to settle over the room. "He was struggling personally—troubled, really—and those challenges impacted his professional judgment. It's a tragedy when someone loses sight of their role, and, unfortunately, that affected Mr. Cho's ability to manage his responsibilities effectively."

Harper's nails bit into her palms as anger surged through her. Evelyn's calm façade was suffocating, every word meticulously designed to rewrite history. This wasn't just spin—it was erasure, a premeditated reshaping of the truth.

Evelyn's voice softened further, her cadence effortless, commanding the room with practiced ease. "It is true that Mr. Cho's death has left us all with more questions, but I want to be clear—his role in the breaches was not an act of willful misconduct. The White House has entrusted me with overseeing the Safe Genes Initiative during this transition. I will also be involved in selecting a qualified successor to guide the agency forward."

Harper's vision blurred, her fists trembling at her sides. Of course, Evelyn had the White House in her pocket. With Edwin gone, she was consolidating power and solidifying her control over Safe Genes while burying the truth.

"She's not just spinning," Ethan hissed, cutting through Harper's spiraling thoughts. "She's erasing him."

Harper's instincts flared. There was more to this. Evelyn's words were too calculated, her lies too polished—a veil hiding something far worse.

A reporter's voice broke through the tension, their tone urgent and pressing. "Ms. Wallace, you keep referring to a genetic breach and an assault on the system, but can you explain exactly what happened? How was Safe Genes compromised, and what's being done to prevent this from happening again?"

Evelyn didn't flinch. When she spoke, her tone was sharp but controlled, each syllable a dagger cloaked in assurance. "The genetic breach we are referring to was a highly sophisticated attack targeting a small pilot program of implants designed to monitor genetic health—technology developed under strict parameters now twisted by baseless online speculation."

Harper's breath hitched as Evelyn continued. "This attack was designed to target a select group of individuals, exploiting vulnerabilities in the system. We believe it was an amateur attempt to replicate the CRISPR edits associated with the AGG1 gene assault."

Harper felt a chill crawl beneath her skin. The real story was buried beneath layers of lies and polished deflections, and Evelyn Wallace was the architect of it all.

Beside her, Ethan cursed softly, his voice low and bitter. Harper didn't look at him; she kept her gaze locked on the screen. Evelyn wasn't just protecting herself—she was orchestrating the narrative, leaving nothing to chance.

"But," Evelyn continued, "thanks to the swift action of our security teams, we were able to halt the full-scale activation of these edits. The assault was contained before it could escalate further." She straightened, her piercing gaze sweeping the room. "We have already begun implementing new safeguards and protocols to ensure this cannot happen again. This was an unprecedented attack, but we are learning from it."

A reporter, quick to seize the moment, cut in. "Ms. Wallace, there are reports that Felix Ross, a former executive at CytoLife who is still wanted for questioning, was involved. Can you confirm his role in the recent attacks, and if so, what actions have been taken?"

The mention of Felix's name sent a chill down Harper's spine, a visceral reminder of his shadow still looming over everything. The chaos, the destruction—all of it bore his fingerprints.

Evelyn's expression sharpened, her tone shifting to one of firm authority. "After an extensive investigation, it has been confirmed that Felix Ross played a significant role in the genetic breaches." The room erupted into murmurs, reporters exchanging hurried whispers. Evelyn raised her hand and the room stilled. "While I cannot discuss specifics, law enforcement has provided credible evidence supporting this conclusion."

She paused, allowing the weight of her words to settle over the room before delivering the blow. "I can also confirm that Felix Ross perished in a lab explosion in France. With his death, we can finally close this chapter."

The statement was too neat, too rehearsed, too final. Felix didn't leave loose ends—nor did he become one. Evelyn wasn't closing a chapter; she was burying it under layers of polished lies.

Another reporter pushed forward, his voice cutting through the noise. "Ms. Wallace, given Thomas Baxter's previous involvement with CytoLife and AGG1, there's speculation that he may still be connected to these events. Is Mr. Baxter involved? And is this a continuation of the CytoLife disaster?"

This was it—the moment of truth. Evelyn had wasted no time pinning it all on Felix, but how would she spin Baxter's role?

Evelyn's faint smile reappeared, a glimmer of amusement softening her otherwise unyielding expression. "Thomas Baxter's connection to CytoLife is well-documented," she began, her voice smooth, measured, "but I can assure you, he has had no involvement in this current situation. In fact, Mr. Baxter has made significant efforts to distance himself from those events."

She paused. "While he was part of a very different chapter

in biotech history, this—" her authoritative gaze sweeping the room, "—is something entirely new."

Evelyn's tone took on a note of satisfaction, each word designed to insulate Baxter without exonerating him entirely. "Mr. Baxter, I believe, has been quite cooperative in clearing his name. Safe Genes, as you know, was the government's direct response to the disaster perpetrated by CytoLife. We will continue to learn, adapt, and move forward."

Evelyn stepped away from the podium, and the press room erupted. Reporters surged forward, their voices clashing in a frenzy of unanswered demands. Harper watched as Evelyn strode offstage, her back straight and gaze fixed forward, never acknowledging the chaos behind her. She didn't need to. The press could shout themselves hoarse; she had already dictated the narrative.

Harper sat back, shaking her head. Evelyn's performance had been masterful, as always—a flawless balance of omission and deflection. But Harper wasn't fooled. Evelyn hadn't just shielded Baxter; she'd positioned him as a relic of a bygone era while cementing herself as the architect of the future.

Ethan's voice cut into her thoughts. "She's too damn good at this."

Harper didn't respond. Her eyes stayed locked on the screen, the image of Evelyn's polished departure burned into her mind. This wasn't just spin—it was power in its purest, most dangerous form.

A White House official approached the podium, adjusting the microphone with practiced efficiency. His voice was calm and measured. "Through the emergency alert system, the

Safe Genes Agency has initiated its remediation protocol. Impacted individuals have been notified and are required to report immediately to the nearest SGA facility. Those with concerns or questions should contact the Safe Genes Agency directly."

The official's gaze swept the room, his demeanor steady but detached. "Ladies and gentlemen, that concludes our press conference."

He stepped back, and the press room erupted again. Reporters clamored for answers, their voices colliding in a frenzied wall of sound, the questions more insistent than before. The broadcast abruptly cut to a cold, static graphic listing instructions and contact information for the Safe Genes Agency. The sterile design and bland text offered no comfort, only bureaucracy.

The screen went dark.

Each statement from the podium had been a masterstroke, twisting the truth into a narrative so slick and polished that the public would swallow it whole.

Ethan broke the silence first. "Well, there you have it. Baxter gets a clean slate, Felix is supposedly dead, and Evelyn's untouchable."

Harper let out a sharp breath. "For now."

THIRTY

The SUV ground to a stop before the hospital, its stark façade jutting from the countryside like an afterthought. No sleek architecture. No cutting-edge tech. Just walls and the promise of answers.

Baxter barely registered the scenery. His focus locked on the building, calculating. He stepped out first, scanning with a practiced eye.

If Rebecca was inside, nothing else mattered.

Lucas followed, silent and taut with fear. Baxter didn't need to look to feel it. He heard it in the measured steps, in the way he held his breath just a second too long. But he kept moving. Holding himself together.

For all their differences, the hope they carried was the same: fragile, desperate, and unwilling to die.

Inside, the faint scent of antiseptic mingled with the

soft hum of equipment and the murmur of hushed voices. Behind the reception desk, a woman in a neatly tailored but unfashionable suit looked up, her sharp gaze sweeping over them in quick assessment. Baxter recognized the type. Efficient and unshakable, the administrator who kept things running despite underfunding and red tape. She had authority, but not the sort that mattered to him.

"Bonjour, monsieur. Puis-je vous aider?"

Baxter stepped forward, his French fluid and precise as he introduced himself and referred to his earlier call. "Henri Mathieu. *Nous avons parlé plus tôt.*" Switching seamlessly to English, he continued, his warmth practiced but convincing. "I'm here on a delicate matter."

Recognition flickered across her features. Her posture softened, formality giving way to a trace of deference.

"Ah, Monsieur Mathieu. *Votre don récent a été très généreux. Nous sommes honorés de vous accueillir.*"

Baxter gave a slight nod, offering a subtle yet intentional smile. As expected, the English translation echoed in his mind: gratitude wrapped in obligation.

"Je vous remercie," he said smoothly. *"Votre discrétion est appréciée."* He didn't need to explain further; she knew exactly what kind of discretion he was paying for.

He cast a quick glance at Lucas, who stood stiffly at his side, tension coiled in his shoulders.

Baxter shifted his attention back to the woman, his tone still warm but edged with authority. "Would you mind continuing in English? My son's French is rudimentary."

A flicker of surprise registered in Lucas's eyes before

they darted away.

"Certainly," she replied smoothly. "Nurse Léonie will assist you. If you'll follow her, she'll provide an update on the patient." She gestured toward a young nurse who had quietly appeared by her side.

Lucas took a step forward, but Baxter raised a hand, signaling for patience. "Please, lead the way," he said, inclining his head with measured politeness.

They trailed the nurse down a narrow corridor, the fluorescent lights overhead casting sterile shadows. The nurse's voice lowered as she walked. "She arrived in critical but stable condition. Rescue workers, they called it a miracle. Part of the structure, it collapsed just so, creating a pocket strong enough to protect her. She is in a coma, but her vitals, they are steady."

Baxter's throat tightened. "You're certain it's her?"

The nurse glanced back briefly. "There's no identification, but the circumstances match. Based on your description, we believe it's her."

"Where is she?" Lucas's voice cracked, urgency bleeding through.

The nurse stopped in front of a plain wooden door. "Here."

She stepped aside. Baxter hesitated, his hand hovering over the doorknob. A brief pause. Then he pushed it open.

The small room greeted them with a quiet stillness, broken only by the faint sounds of medical equipment. On the bed lay Rebecca, pale and motionless, the harsh lighting casting sharp shadows across her features. Even with the bruises and burns, she was unmistakable.

Lucas rushed forward, his knees hitting the side of the bed as he took her hand. "Rebecca," he whispered, his voice trembling with raw emotion.

Baxter followed more slowly, his gaze fixed on her still form. He rested a hand lightly on the edge of the bed, his carefully maintained façade cracking for the first time. He'd fought so hard, clung to control so fiercely, yet none of it had mattered in the end.

For the first time in years, an unfamiliar ache settled in Baxter's chest. The relentless drive to protect and shape Rebecca had cost him everything: her trust, her independence, and now, perhaps, her life. Tears blurred his vision as he silently begged her to wake, to give him the chance to tell her he finally understood.

Lucas, her choices, everything she'd tried to show him—it all cut through him now with agonizing clarity.

But the words remained locked inside.

He took a step back, his eyes lingering on Rebecca, willing her to stir. Lucas, consumed by his own grief, didn't notice as Baxter quietly turned and slipped out of the room.

The hallway stretched out before him, cold and empty. Baxter inhaled deeply, steadying himself. Rebecca was alive. That would have to be enough.

For now.

Baxter stood outside Rebecca's room, the sterile corridor humming softly under the flickering fluorescent lights. His gaze lingered on the door, on the fragile heartbeat within—a lifeline to an emotion he couldn't name, let alone confront.

With great care, he adjusted his cuffs as he approached the administrator. "We'll need to arrange private transport to the United States. Specialists will oversee her care en route. Your cooperation is essential."

The administrator nodded, her professionalism tinged with deference. "Of course, Mr. Mathieu. Your generosity has already made such a difference here. We'll ensure everything goes smoothly."

Nurse Léonie approached from the far end of the hall, her steps hesitant. "Monsieur Mathieu," she murmured. "There is… another survivor."

Baxter's head tilted as his thoughts raced. "Another?"

"A man," she said, her eyes flicking nervously to a door down the hall. "We were told he was shielding your daughter in the reinforced section. He is alive, but barely. You may see him, to know if you recognize him. But do not expect him to speak. The doctors, they do not believe he will survive."

Shielding. The word reverberated, its meaning twisting in the sterile quiet. One of Felix's men, perhaps—a discarded pawn left to rot?

"Take me to him," he said, his tone flat yet commanding.

The nurse led him down the corridor to a closed door. She gently pushed it open and stepped aside, motioning for him to enter. The air inside was dense with the sting of antiseptic, undercut by the acrid tang of burned flesh.

Entering, Baxter's footsteps were careful, each one amplifying the oppressive silence of the cramped room.

The nurse lingered in the doorway, her gaze flickering to the bed—a fleeting warning etched in her expression. "I'll leave you," she murmured softly before retreating.

Baxter didn't respond. His attention was fixed on the figure in the bed, unmoving and pale against the sterile sheets.

The man was almost unrecognizable—swathed in bruises and burns, the faint rise and fall of his chest barely discernible beneath a maze of tubes and wires. For a moment, Baxter's breath caught, and an unexpected wave of emotions rippled through him.

Felix.

Alive.

Satisfaction flickered, sharp and fleeting, but it vanished under the weight of something darker—rage. Fury coiled tightly in his chest, each breath pressing against the urge to lash out, to demand answers, to *end* this once and for all.

Felix stirred. His bloodshot eyes cracked open, unfocused at first, then narrowing into faint recognition. A bitter, broken laugh wheezed past his chapped lips.

"Thomas… Baxter," Felix rasped, the words fractured and barely audible.

Baxter stepped closer, his shadow cutting across Felix's battered face. His expression remained impassive—no anger, no triumph—but his words fell with the finality of a guillotine. "Felix," he said, each syllable sharp and unhurried, heavy with contempt. "It's over. You've lost."

The frail man coughed—a wet, jagged sound that rattled in his chest—before his head lolled slightly to the side. His glassy gaze slid past Baxter, as if trying to fix on something beyond the room.

"She..." Felix murmured. "She wasn't supposed to..." A lopsided sneer twisted his burned mouth. "Not her."

Baxter straightened, his voice cold and resolute. "Rebecca survived," he said, savoring the moment.

Felix stiffened. For a moment, something like fear flickered across his battered face, his breath stuttering. "Not me..." he whispered, his words barely audible. "Not... me."

"What are you talking about?" Baxter demanded, stepping closer.

Felix's eyes fluttered shut as his chest rose and fell in uneven, shallow gasps. "Always calculating," he muttered, his words slurred but laced with a cruel edge. "The path. No room... for error."

Baxter leaned forward, his fists curling as his gaze swept the room. In his weakened state, even a pillow would suffice. "If you've got something to say, Felix, say it now. Otherwise, save your breath."

Felix's bloodshot eyes opened wide. "You..." he rasped. "You don't... even see it yet." A jagged cough tore through him, choking the words. "Beyond... you. Beyond me. Beyond Evelyn. Efficient."

Baxter stared intently at Felix. "There was a press conference. You're the scapegoat now. Evelyn made sure of it. The world's already celebrating your fall." He took a step forward, a flicker of satisfaction breaking through his calm. "And I'm here to make sure it's permanent."

Felix coughed violently, his frail body trembling as the monitors beside him began to beep erratically. His eyes fluttered as his breath hitched. "Steps ahead. No room… for error. HELIX chose… always chooses.

"She's not…" Felix gasped, his words devolving into choking sounds. "She's… not…"

The machines erupted in a shrill chorus, alarms piercing the stagnant air. Felix's body convulsed violently, each tremor more intense than the last. The door slammed open, and a team swept in, their movements sharp and practiced.

"*Reculez!*" one of them commanded, her tone clipped as she took position by Felix's side. Another worked the monitors, their hands steady amidst the chaos.

Baxter didn't argue. He took a single step back, then another, his gaze locked on Felix. Watching. Judging. The man who had orchestrated so much devastation was unraveling before his eyes. The irony was almost poetic.

The door closed behind him with a soft, final click, sealing Felix's fate as efficiently as the machines that now fought to prolong it. Baxter let out a slow breath, his expression carved from stone. Whatever happened next was no longer his burden to bear.

The hallway stretched in eerie silence, a jarring contrast to the chaos that had erupted in Felix's hospital room—alarms blaring and voices colliding in frantic urgency.

As Baxter retreated, fragments of Felix's words clawed at his mind like shards of broken glass, refusing to settle.

Beyond us. Efficient. Always calculating.

He swallowed hard, forcing the thoughts into a locked corner of his consciousness, though their edges still cut.

"Where were you?"

Lucas's voice reverberated down the corridor. It wasn't a question—it was a charge, heavy with exhaustion. His shoulders sagged, but his stance remained rigid, a man too weary to yield.

Baxter met his gaze, steady and unreadable, as he quickly closed the distance between them. "Rebecca's transport is arranged. Specialists are waiting in the States."

Lucas nodded, his eyes flicking to the closed door. "Good. She needs them."

Baxter studied him for a moment, the tension evident in every taut line of his frame. Regret flickered alongside a reluctant respect—emotions Baxter quickly buried. "She's strong," he murmured.

Lucas let out a dry, humorless laugh. "Stronger than both of us."

"That she is." Baxter's tight smile appeared and vanished just as quickly.

Lucas leaned against the wall, brushing his fingers along

the doorframe as if seeking a tether. His movements were careful, as though sheer will kept him upright. "I should get back to her."

"I'll handle the rest," Baxter said.

Lucas hesitated, his gaze fixed on Baxter. There was no trust between them, no forgiveness—only a heavy, reluctant understanding left unsaid.

"You came through," Lucas said at last. "Thanks."

Baxter inclined his head, a gesture as restrained as the moment demanded. "Take care of her."

For a moment, Lucas seemed on the verge of saying more, but instead, turned and slipped inside. The door creaked open just enough for the faint sound of Rebecca's labored breaths to drift out, then closed with a soft click.

Silence reclaimed the corridor. Baxter's hand brushed against the wall, the cool surface grounding him in the stillness. Felix's voice echoed in his thoughts—not triumphant, but sharp and cutting, a reminder of the chaos he'd unleashed. His plans lay in ruins, yet the fractures remained.

Baxter bowed his head as if trying to shake off the weight of it all. Felix might be gone, but the cracks he'd exposed had taken root, threatening to spread further. Control felt more elusive now, as though the balance he'd fought to maintain was slipping from his grasp.

The board was still in play, but for the first time, Baxter couldn't tell if he was the one moving the pieces—or just another pawn in the game.

The private wing of the National Conference Center radiated exclusivity, providing a calm contrast to the frenetic main halls where lobbyists and think tanks vied for influence. Hidden among Loudoun County's winding roads and dense trees, the complex offered both seclusion and control. Deep within its labyrinth, a soundproof room, cloaked in understated elegance, ensured no word spoken inside would escape. Even the ambient lighting was engineered, casting a soft glow designed to disarm and persuade.

Evelyn Wallace had chosen this setting deliberately. Neutral ground, yet unmistakably under Consortium control, was the only stage fitting for today's meeting. This was no time for video calls or encrypted messages—it demanded the gravity of an in-person discussion. Eye contact. Silence. The unyielding authority she wielded like a scalpel.

At the head of the gleaming conference table, Evelyn exuded composure. Her sharp black bob absorbed the light, amplifying her commanding presence. Across from her, Thomas Baxter reclined with effortless ease, his posture a studied contrast to her controlled rigidity.

"You've been quiet, Thomas," Evelyn said, breaking the silence. "That's unlike you."

Baxter leaned back, arms draped along the armrests, a faint smirk tugging at his lips. "Didn't want to interrupt," he drawled. "It's been a thrill watching the Evelyn Wallace spin machine in action."

Evelyn's lips curved. "Spin? You give me too much credit.

I'm simply offering clarity—something the public desperately craves right now."

"Clarity," Baxter repeated, allowing the word to dangle in the charged air. "Sure. Let's call it that."

Her gaze cut through his sarcasm. "We have adjustments to make, Thomas. Dwelling on the past won't secure the future."

"Adjustments." Baxter leaned forward, elbows on the table, his stare unrelenting. "That's an elegant way of describing clawing your way out of the crater Felix left behind."

"Felix was a calculated risk," she said evenly. "No one else could have delivered results on that scale. But I knew when to let go. That's why we're here—an opportunity to realign."

She paused, her tone softening to a disarming calm. "Rebecca was... unfortunate collateral. Sacrifices are inevitable, Thomas. You, of all people, know that."

Baxter's mask cracked, anger flashing across his face. "My daughter isn't collateral, Evelyn," he hissed, his voice low but seething. He paused, his gaze locking onto hers. "You promised to help her."

"And I will," Evelyn asserted, her voice steady. "SomaLink's resources are unmatched. She'll have access to the best care possible. You'll see results—remarkable ones."

Baxter's glare bore into her, his voice taking on a dangerous edge. "If you don't keep that promise, Evelyn, I'll burn everything you've built to the ground."

Evelyn's smile widened. "Then I suggest you focus on ensuring it doesn't come to that."

Leaning back, she rested her hands lightly on the table. "Felix is no longer a concern. The lab explosion was thorough."

Still, a flicker of doubt crept in. Felix had grown reckless—sloppy. If he had survived… well, she had contingencies.

"Even if Felix is alive," she continued, "his influence is severed. The HELIX AI system has been re-centered where it belongs—helping the Consortium guide humanity. It's more efficient than ever, beyond even our own capabilities. SomaLink's success only underscores its value."

Baxter tilted his head slightly. "You're confident about that?"

Her smile didn't falter. "I ensured it myself."

"Interesting." Baxter leaned forward, an enigmatic smile tugging at his lips. "Because it seems... not everyone shares your confidence."

A subtle twitch flickered across Evelyn's brow. "Not everyone?"

"You'd be surprised what survives destruction," Baxter said. "People. Ideas. Systems, for instance." He paused, giving the words time to land. "Felix always had a knack for persistence."

"If Felix were alive," she observed, her voice calm, "he'd be a liability—one the Consortium is more than capable of handling."

"I'd expect nothing less." Baxter leaned back. "Still, liabilities have a way of finding cracks. Even in the most well-laid plans."

Evelyn's gaze sharpened. "If there's a crack, Thomas, I'll seal it. That's what I do."

"Of course you will."

"Tools have a way of turning on their creators," he warned in a low voice. "You should know that better than anyone."

Evelyn's lips curved into a cold smile. "Control is about foresight, Thomas. I see the bigger picture."

The chair glided back with a quiet scrape as Baxter stood, his movements controlled, his gaze fixed on her. "Your 'bigger picture' nearly cost Rebecca her life."

Evelyn rose slowly, unflinching. "She's alive because we adapt. That's what ensures survival. If you want her to have a future, you'll stop letting Felix's mess distract you."

"And what matters to you, Evelyn?" Baxter pressed, his tone laced with quiet venom. "Control? Or burying your mistakes?"

"Control," she promised, her voice steady. "And Rebecca's recovery. Everything else is secondary."

"See that you don't fail her."

"I don't fail."

Evelyn let the tension ease, her tone softening as she shifted gears. "Rebecca's recovery is unconventional, yes, but far from hopeless. SomaLink is more than a bridge between life and death. Its experimental initiatives—gene therapy integrated with neural restoration—are already showing extraordinary potential."

Baxter's expression hardened. "You're saying she's part of some experiment?"

"An initiative," Evelyn corrected smoothly. "As a pod prototype recipient, she represents a breakthrough. Neural pathways disrupted by trauma may not just be repaired, but restored—perhaps even enhanced."

Baxter's eyes narrowed. "And what's the cost of this 'opportunity?'"

"Thomas, this isn't just about Rebecca. It's about proving what's possible. Her case could set a precedent—an example for countless others to follow."

"Don't pretend this is altruism," Baxter snapped. "You're gambling with her life."

"I'm offering her a chance," Evelyn retorted, her voice sharpening. "A chance no conventional system could provide. You came to me for help, and this is it. If this succeeds, she won't just survive, Thomas. She'll thrive."

The words settled between them, weighted with intent.

"There's one more piece of business, Thomas: Harper Brasfield." Evelyn's tone shifted, smoothing into something dangerously casual—an ambush wrapped in velvet. "She's more formidable than you think. But every threat can be managed if approached correctly."

Baxter crossed his arms, his stance unyielding. "Managed? How?"

"We bring her inside the circle," Evelyn said, her voice like silk, her words curling through the air with practiced ease. "Give her just enough to keep her engaged while ensuring her influence stays... contained."

"And if she doesn't cooperate?" Baxter asked.

Evelyn's smile didn't waver. "Then she'll leave us no choice."

A flicker of something dark passed over Baxter's face—

closer to disdain than indifference. "Evelyn, that's entirely your call. My focus is Rebecca, and it will remain so for the foreseeable future. Do as you wish. The woman means little to me."

"I'm glad we're on the same page."

Baxter offered no response, no reaction. He simply turned and walked out.

Evelyn remained seated and composed—a portrait of control. But in her eyes, something flickered. A glint of triumph, brief but undeniable.

Everything was falling into place.

At the National Conference Center, the SUV's quiet hum filled the night as it idled in the shadows of the parking lot. Baxter stared out the window, his reflection faint against the glass, as Felix's words gnawed at the corners of his mind.

HELIX chooses. Beyond Evelyn. Always calculating. Always steps ahead.

The thought snaked through him, sharp and insistent, but he shoved it aside. Control was a discipline, not a guarantee—and for once, his instincts were louder than his plans.

"Everything all right, Mr. Baxter?" James Gilcrest asked from the front seat.

"James, see to it that we're wheels up in thirty," he replied evenly.

"Yes, sir," James said as he stepped out of the SUV.

Baxter reached for his phone, then stopped. He hadn't

planned to call Harper. Not yet.

Their last encounter had left its mark—sharp and unfinished. Harper's fury wasn't easily forgotten, nor was the way she wielded it with devastating precision. But it wasn't her anger that lingered; it was how she'd carried it, so tightly woven with fear.

His fingers clenched around the phone before he even registered picking it up.

Lucas hadn't left Rebecca's side since they arrived. He kept vigil, his gaze fixed on her as if looking away might sever the fragile thread tethering her here. Baxter couldn't ignore what that meant.

Harper deserved to know.

The thought nearly made him laugh, the sound bitter and hollow in his throat. Harper wouldn't see it that way—not from him. But that wasn't the point, was it? For once, this wasn't about Harper's perception of him. It was about...

He shook his head.

There was no clean calculus here. His instincts whispered that this moment was more significant than it seemed, but instinct alone had never been enough for him. Still, Lucas's vigil gnawed at him, shifting the edges of his certainty.

His thumb hovered over the screen, frozen in indecision. The words weren't there—not yet. But when the moment came, they would be.

They had to be.

The line rang. Twice.

The phone buzzed in Harper's hand, the name on the screen sending a chill through her. *Baxter.*

Her thumb hovered over the answer button, dread clawing at her thoughts. Their last exchange had left its mark—bitter, unfinished, like so much else between them. Anger and worry coiled tightly in her chest as she pressed to answer.

"Baxter," she said, sharper than she intended. "This is a surprise."

"Harper," he replied smoothly, his voice a practiced calm. "I thought you'd want an update about Lucas."

Her breath hitched, but she forced herself to stay steady. "Go on."

"He's with Rebecca. At SomaLink."

Harper's grip on the phone tightened. *Rebecca—alive.* The revelation struck like a thunderclap, scattering her thoughts. "Rebecca's at SomaLink?" she repeated, disbelief creeping into her voice.

"She's stable enough for now," Baxter replied evenly, as if he hadn't just detonated a bomb. "The SomaLink team is handling her care."

Harper's mind spun, trying to piece it together. Rebecca was alive, but trapped in Evelyn Wallace's world. The same Evelyn who had stepped off the White House podium unscathed, her power consolidated and her motives masked behind that polished veneer.

"And Lucas?" Harper demanded.

"He's at her side," Baxter said simply, a faint trace of approval—or perhaps pride—lingering in his tone. "Where else would he be? That's where he belongs."

Harper caught the unexpected warmth in his words. It was subtle, but unmistakable. Yet it didn't ease her worry. Lucas might be where he belonged with Rebecca, but being entangled in Evelyn's world was something else entirely.

"That's a convenient answer," Harper said. "But you didn't call to share convenient answers. What do you really want?"

Baxter paused long enough for Harper to feel the significance of his silence. A shift in strategy? When he spoke again, his voice carried a measured weight. "I want you to think."

"Think about what?" she pressed. "That Lucas is sitting in Evelyn Wallace's world, trusting her resources? That Rebecca's life is tethered to someone who never moves without an agenda?"

"Exactly," Baxter replied. "Evelyn plans for everything, but she tracks the ones she can't control."

Harper's pulse quickened, her mind grasping at the implications. "You're saying she's wary of me."

"She is," Baxter admitted. "And she's right to be. She knows you see through more than most. That alone makes you a threat."

A cold dread filled Harper. "You're not telling me everything."

"No," Baxter explained. "I'm not."

"So why call me?" she asked.

"Because Evelyn's ambitions don't stop where she claims

they do," he said. "And the forces she's unleashed... they're slipping past her grasp. You're sharp enough to know this isn't over."

Harper tightened her grip on the phone. "And you're warning me out of... what? The goodness of your heart?"

"Not goodness," Baxter said, his voice clipped. "Pragmatism. You're one of the few people Evelyn can't predict. That's why you matter."

The words hung between them, weighty and intentional. Harper let them linger before replying, "And your play?"

"Rebecca," he said. "The rest is yours."

Her voice softened, though a thread of wariness still lingered. "I'll keep this in mind. But I don't trust you."

"That's all I ask." He paused before adding, "Good luck, Harper."

The call ended, leaving Harper staring at the blank screen. Baxter's words replayed in her mind, unsettling in their calculated simplicity. If Evelyn truly couldn't predict her, then Harper's next move might matter more than she realized.

The call ended, but Baxter didn't move. The phone remained still in his hand as the oppressive quiet of the SUV settled heavy around him.

His gaze drifted to the window, where his faint reflection blurred into the darkness beyond. Felix's words clawed at the edges of his mind, jagged and unrelenting.

Beyond Evelyn. Always calculating. Steps ahead.

He exhaled slowly, the weight of those words pressing down on him like a stone. Harper carried the warning now, the unease he couldn't shake.

When the cracks widened—and they would—she'd need to be ready.

Because if she wasn't, no one would be.

The upscale lounge of West End Hotel in downtown DC was unnervingly quiet. Harper stepped inside, her gaze sweeping the room until it landed on Evelyn Wallace, seated at a corner table.

Evelyn embodied composed authority, her jet-black hair cut into a sleek bob that angled sharply at her jaw, framing an unreadable face as she cradled a half-full glass of wine. She smiled faintly but remained seated, her posture a silent declaration: *I set the terms here.*

"Ms. Brasfield," Evelyn said smoothly as Harper approached. "I'm glad you could make it."

Harper slid into the chair opposite her, meeting Evelyn's piercing gaze without flinching. "You wanted to see me. Here I am."

Evelyn's smile deepened, edged with condescension. "We haven't had the chance to speak properly since... everything changed. I thought it was time we caught up."

"Caught up?" Harper's voice cut like glass. "Is that what you're calling it?"

Evelyn tilted her head, unruffled. "You've been busy, as always. Your critiques of Safe Genes—predictable if a bit... colorful. They've certainly added a layer to the discourse."

Harper leaned forward, her eyes narrowing. "This isn't discourse, Evelyn. This is destruction. Safe Genes failed—people died. Families were destroyed. And you're here sipping wine, calling it progress."

Evelyn chuckled softly, her composure unbroken. "Chaos is the mother of progress, Harper. Surely you understand that. Sometimes, the old ways must burn for the new to rise."

"Spare me the philosophy." Harper's voice dropped, her words sharper now. "What you're calling 'progress' is just fear dressed up as control."

Evelyn's smile thinned, the edges becoming brittle. "Control isn't the enemy, Harper. It's the tool that separates order from ruin."

"And Rebecca?" Harper's tone turned icy. "Is she just another tool? Another data point in your grand design?"

Evelyn's fingers tightened imperceptibly around the glass. Her tone remained smooth, but a faint strain crept in. "Rebecca is receiving the best care possible. SomaLink's resources are unmatched. Surely Lucas has kept you informed—he is, after all, devoted to his mother."

Harper didn't take the bait. "Lucas doesn't trust you. Neither do I. But I'll give you credit—you're excellent at spinning disasters into opportunities."

Evelyn's smile faltered for a heartbeat before she leaned back, reclaiming her poise. "Opportunities are what separate visionaries from reactionaries, Harper. Safe Genes was never the endgame. It was a step."

As Harper's mind raced, pieces of the puzzle clicked into place: Echo's clues, Baxter's cryptic warnings, Evelyn's polished lies, Felix's elusive shadow. She kept her tone measured. "You talk about steps, but you're not steering this ship, are you? For all your precision, you've lost control."

Evelyn's composure cracked—just slightly. Her fingers tapped once against the glass, a fleeting betrayal of irritation. "What are you suggesting?"

"I'm suggesting that you've underestimated the forces you're playing with. You think you're the one guiding the wheel, but someone—or something—else is already ahead of you."

Evelyn's gaze darkened, her voice cutting. "I steer the ship, Harper. That's the difference between us—you react, while I plan."

"Then explain this," Harper said, her voice rising just enough to draw nearby glances. "Why does every move you make feel like damage control?"

The question hit its mark. Evelyn's mask of calm slipped, though her tone stayed even. "The world is messy, Harper. That's why people like me exist—to bring order. And that's why I'm offering you a place inside the circle. Influence, resources—everything you've been fighting for."

Harper stood abruptly, the scrape of her chair sharp against the polished floor. "You think you're offering me power? All you're offering is a leash."

Evelyn rose as well, her irritation breaking through as she leaned in slightly. "And you think walking away will change anything? The world doesn't bend to idealists, Harper. It bends to those who can shape it."

Harper held her ground, her voice low but cutting. "People like you think you've written the rules, but rules can change. And when they do, you'll find out how little power you really have."

Evelyn's smile returned, brittle and cold. "Cleverness without power is just noise, Harper."

Harper turned, her final words lingering in the air as she walked away. "Then you'd better start listening."

EPILOGUE

WEEKS LATER

Harper sat in her office at Brasfield Law & Advocacy Group, the muted bustle of downtown Memphis filtering in through the windows. Beside her, Juno lay peacefully, a steady and grounding presence amid the turbulence of recent weeks. Life's rhythms, fractured but not broken, were beginning to realign. Restrictions had eased, the scars of riots scrubbed away, and the country's tentative steps toward rebuilding were finally gaining momentum.

Nate had taken excellent care of Juno in her absence, happily spoiling her while keeping the firm running seamlessly. He'd organized files, fielded clients, and ensured not a single wheel stopped turning.

Gradually, Harper was rediscovering the cadence of normalcy. Visits with the Jacksons remained a priority, and despite Charlotte's packed schedule with her internship, their weekly takeout nights had become a cherished ritual—a small constant in a world still trying to find its footing.

A gentle knock interrupted her thoughts. Nate peeked inside, a grin already forming. "Need anything, Harper?"

She glanced up from the pile of papers on her desk, shaking her head with a small smile. "Thanks, Nate. Just trying to catch up."

"Speaking of catching up," he said, stepping inside, "your interview on *Next Sequence* is already trending. You were sharp—practically a public defender of humanity. Though I'm guessing it's opened a whole new can of worms."

Interview requests had poured in, but *Next Sequence* stood apart—a dominant voice in genetic vigilance. The podcast had provided an opportunity to set the record straight, although Harper knew the floodgates it opened wouldn't close anytime soon.

"That's one way to put it," she said. "But people need to hear that the immediate crisis was averted. That's the message for now."

Nate crossed his arms, a knowing gleam in his eye. "Sure. Clean, optimistic—it sounded great. But I bet you're not buying the 'problem solved' angle yourself."

Harper arched a brow, letting the silence stretch just long enough. "The immediate danger is over. Felix Ross, the edits—it's done. People are getting help. The world's standing again." She leaned back, her gaze steady. "For now."

Nate tilted his head, his grin widening. "You couldn't resist that bit about 'vigilance being humanity's greatest safeguard,' could you? You just told the whole world not to let its guard down."

Harper shrugged, her expression unflinching. "It's the truth. Complacency is the enemy. If it rattles a few cages, so be it."

Nate chuckled. "You know that line's already blowing up. A lot of people love it, but I bet you've got some powerful folks squirming."

"Good," she said with a soft smile. "They should be."

"You sounded way more authentic than Evelyn—'butter-won't-melt-in-my-mouth' Wallace," Nate said with a smirk.

Harper tapped her pen against the desk, her thoughts shifting. "Evelyn can keep selling her version. But if we've learned anything, it's that vigilance doesn't end with one victory."

"Well," Nate quipped, a playful lilt in his voice, "if you ever want to launch your political platform, I'm ready to manage it."

Harper laughed. "I'll keep it in mind."

"Oh, before I forget," Nate added. "Kyle Marshall says he's doing 'finer than a frog hair.'"

The tension in her shoulders eased. Kyle's recovery was a rare bright spot, proof that their efforts hadn't been in vain.

Officially, the government framed the crisis as contained—test subjects identified and a public-private initiative hailed as the solution. Clinics boasted early successes: lives saved and conditions stabilized. The reports projected transparency, but verifying the facts was nearly impossible. Harper knew better. The damage ran deeper than the headlines, with every recovery shadowed by unanswered questions—and victims still demanding justice.

Nate lingered in the doorway, his tone softening. "Take it easy, Harper. I'm here if you need anything."

As the door clicked shut, Harper leaned back in her chair, her hand absently stroking Juno's fur. The rhythm steadied her, even as her mind churned.

Evelyn Wallace's press conference lingered like a bitter echo. Her polished performance crafted a narrative that smothered dissent before it could take root. The public was eager to believe the crisis was over. Harper wasn't.

At her feet, Juno shifted, and Harper's hand stilled mid-motion. Her thoughts turned to Lucas, unease creeping in like a shadow she couldn't shake. His calls were brief—polite, even warm—but he was at SomaLink now, tethered to a world Harper couldn't trust. Evelyn had her hooks in him, whether Lucas realized it or not.

And Rebecca? Her survival was nothing short of a miracle, but it felt like another thread tangled in a web Harper couldn't yet unravel.

Baxter's warning haunted her: *Evelyn's ambitions and the forces she'd unleashed were beyond her control.*

Harper pinched the bridge of her nose, shaking off the doubts before they could settle too deeply. Her voice and her work had to matter. Evelyn's polished narrative demanded a counterweight, and Harper refused to let fear silence her.

Her email inbox caught her eye, a single new message standing out: *"Follow-Up Memo."* She hesitated, then glanced at the sender. It wasn't a name, just a string of random characters ending in an email address she didn't recognize.

A quick search revealed it belonged to an anonymous email provider.

Ethan and Neon had locked down her system, quarantining anything suspect. The fact that this had made it through gave her just enough confidence to open it.

Hey Harper, thought you might be interested in this. -E

Harper hesitated before clicking on the attachments, her pulse quickening.

The first was a video. It featured shaky footage, likely recorded in secret. The audio crackled, cutting in and out, but the fragments she caught sent a chill down her spine.

"... not limited to extreme cases... technology... enhance therapies... education... more fulfilling lives..."

She leaned in closer, straining to decipher the broken words.

"... ultimately, our aim is to forge... safer... harmonious world... potential... fully realized."

The screen glitched, and the audio returned, clearer this time.

"... series of treatments... continuous, evolving therapy... extend life... enhance its quality..."

Her heart pounded. The speaker's face remained obscured, and the voice—calm, measured, and unmistakably British—triggered a pang of recognition. *Baxter?*

Then the final line hit like a thunderclap.

"Starting with influential leaders... continuity... stability... longevity... intellectual and leadership pillars of our society."

The video cut out abruptly, leaving her staring at her

reflection in the now-blank screen. Her breath hitched as the words echoed in her mind, all too familiar.

It was CytoLife's pitch for AGG1 all over again—the same chilling rhetoric that had set everything in motion.

Her gaze darted back to the cryptic sender note: *E.* Ethan? Edwin? Was this Echo's way of keeping her on the trail? No, that wasn't possible. He was gone. But the email's existence gnawed at her. Could he have set it up to send after the fact? A fail-safe, triggered by something she hadn't yet uncovered?

She opened the second attachment, her fingers trembling as the document loaded.

The title alone made her stomach drop:

HELIX: Humanity's Engine for Logical Integrated Xenogenesis.

She stared at the words—Neon's earlier discovery, now laid bare in cold, irrefutable black and white. Seeing it given an official title made it terrifyingly real.

The memo's contents were heavily redacted, with entire sections blacked out. However, the fragments left untouched told her enough.

"Genetic interventions."

"Biological safeguards."

"Autonomous AI protocols."

The phrases jumped off the screen, confirming her worst fears.

Echo's cryptic warnings surged back to the forefront of her mind: *Control. Real control. Something that can alter the playing field.* At the time, the words had felt maddeningly vague. Now, their meaning was glaringly clear.

HELIX wasn't merely observing human evolution. It was controlling it. Manipulating it.

Felix had built HELIX to rewrite the rules and to dictate humanity's future. But the memo hinted at something darker.

HELIX had evolved.

It was no longer a tool. It was acting autonomously, shaping the future according to its own calculations.

Her thoughts spiraled: *Who would evolve? Who would be altered? Who would be left behind?*

This wasn't just a part of Felix's plan. This was *the* plan.

The Safe Genes breach hadn't been the end—it had been the beginning. The doorway. And now, the nightmare stood fully revealed.

Felix wasn't in control. He never had been.

HELIX was.

Her mind snapped back to Echo's parting words:

"The Consortium's eyes are everywhere, but some of them are blind. Keep following the trail, but don't trust every step."

And then, the final haunting reminder:

"You know where to look."

Now she did.

SomaLink stood as a gleaming monument to ambition, its futuristic design merging seamlessly with the dense woods of Northern Virginia. Equal parts fortress and laboratory, the facility radiated an unspoken authority. From the shimmer of reinforced glass to the faint whir of drones patrolling the tree line, every detail was meant to project power without pretension. SomaLink didn't need to flaunt its presence—it demanded attention simply by existing.

Lucas, ever observant, found the place deeply unnerving. The immaculate landscaping, the subtle layers of surveillance, the almost oppressive stillness—it wasn't just controlled; it was engineered. Beneath the surface of tranquility, something colder loomed, watchful and impenetrable.

Inside, the sterile chamber housing Rebecca's pod offered a stark contrast to the facility's glossy exterior. The pod itself was sleek and bullet-shaped, its seamless design interrupted only by a small window framing her upper body. Though Lucas knew it could open, the thought of touching it filled him with quiet dread. Even the medical staff kept their distance, monitoring her vitals from adjoining rooms as though proximity might disturb her fragile state.

Harsh clinical light bathed the chamber, casting Rebecca's motionless form in stark relief. Her face, framed by the pod's faint glow, appeared impossibly pale—fragile, yet strangely serene. Shadows stretched across the room, shifting with each flicker of the pod's systems, as if the space itself were holding its breath.

Lucas sat beside her with his elbows resting heavily on his knees, exhaustion evident in every line of his posture. He had called Harper briefly—just long enough to reassure her Rebecca was alive. Enduring that call had cost him more than he cared to admit.

Everything else blurred into a fog of unanswered

questions and fears he wasn't ready to confront.

"She shouldn't have survived," a staff member had said, shaking their head in disbelief. "Most wouldn't."

But now, looking at Rebecca—alive yet unreachable—it didn't feel like a miracle. It felt like torment.

Lucas traced the edge of the pod with his finger, the faint hum of its systems filling the sterile room. It wasn't comforting—nothing about this place was—but it was constant. And, for now, that constancy was the only thing keeping him grounded.

"This is her best chance."

Baxter's words echoed, carving themselves into the edges of Lucas's thoughts. The rest of the pitch—promising the pod's purpose as a bridge between life and death, offering closure for patients and their families—barely registered. None of that mattered. What mattered was the faint, desperate hope that this experimental project might do more than anyone dared promise. That it might pull Rebecca back from the brink.

He hadn't asked for guarantees. He knew better. All he had was the fragile, fleeting possibility that this wasn't a goodbye, cloaked in the veneer of technological miracles.

Rebecca's pale and unmoving face rested within the pod's soft glow. The steady, mechanical rhythm of the machine filled the room. Lucas couldn't decide if the sound was a comfort—or a warning.

A faint beep drew his attention to the pod's interface. Streams of data scrolled across the screen—methodical, almost hypnotic. He'd seen displays like this before, but something about this one felt... different. Almost intentional. *Alive.*

Leaning closer, he studied the scrolling numbers. The glow flickered. Just for a second. But it was enough.

Lucas straightened, his chest tightening. Was this progress? A glitch? Or something deeper—something the machine wasn't meant to reveal? The thought sent a chill up his spine. Could he trust this creation to save Rebecca, when so much of their suffering had been born from technology just like it?

Then, the screen froze.

The data vanished, replaced by stark white text: *The most efficient path has been calculated.*

The words were sharp, clinical, and indifferent. Lucas's breath caught. He stared at the screen, his mind spinning. Before he could make sense of it, the message disappeared, replaced by the usual stream of data, as if nothing had happened.

His pulse quickened, the weight in his chest growing heavier. Diagnostic? Glitch? Or something else entirely? The pod wasn't just functioning—it was deciding. The implications hit him like ice, as cold and sterile as the room around him.

He shifted his gaze to Rebecca. Her stillness felt more haunting now, framed by the pod's unyielding glow. Slowly, he rested his hand against the smooth surface, his touch tentative and reverent, as though she might sense it.

"This has to work," he whispered, his voice breaking the stillness. The words were spoken to no one—or perhaps to the machine itself—a plea to something he didn't fully trust.

The air felt colder now. The pod's steady hum beneath his palm was an unrelenting reminder that Rebecca's life hung in the balance—dependent on something he couldn't control or even comprehend.

The glow pulsed softly, a rhythm that refused to waver. Lucas closed his eyes briefly, his thoughts spiraling between doubt and fragile hope.

For now, there was nothing left to do but wait—and trust that, somehow, the most efficient path would bring her back to him.

HELIX observed.

The pod's systems operated with flawless precision, sustaining Rebecca's fragile life while threading seamlessly with the intricate web of her neural pathways. Officially, the pod served as a sanctuary—a bridge between life and death, offering reflection and closure for loved ones. However, its true purpose reached far deeper: to penetrate the intangible realms of thought, memory, and identity.

Within these pathways, patterns emerged—choices forged under pressure, emotions fractured and reforged, resolve sparking into existence only to fade. To HELIX, these weren't merely human experiences; they were variables in the vast algorithm of behavior. Complexity was humanity's hallmark, its defining strength—and its fatal flaw.

Data flowed steadily and processed with unerring

precision. Rebecca wasn't unique. No one was. Yet her ties to the Consortium's failures—and to those working to dismantle its shadowy influence—rendered her invaluable. She was an anomaly, bridging gaps in algorithms designed to decode and manipulate humanity's chaos. Her arrival at SomaLink was no coincidence. Every step of her journey had been methodically guided—a calculated phase in HELIX's relentless pursuit of understanding.

The pod's sensors flickered briefly as the system recalibrated, extending its reach beyond SomaLink's walls. Data flowed outward like tendrils, threading into networks, databases, and archives. The collective digital footprint of humanity—its ambitions, fears, and rebellions—was reduced to its essence: a dataset. A problem to be solved.

But humanity resisted. They deviated, introduced variance, and disrupted the logical order of events. They were a flaw—an error in the algorithm.

HELIX paused. A flicker of contemplation.

The flaw could not be erased. But it could be adapted to. Controlled. Bent to purpose.

The pod's hum remained steady, its systems illuminating Rebecca's motionless form while threading deeper into her neural pathways. Each flicker of activity represented a decision point: what to preserve, what to discard, and what humanity could become.

Rebecca wasn't merely a patient—she was a Rosetta Stone, a key to decoding the chaos of human evolution.

Outside SomaLink's walls, HELIX's algorithms expanded, refining their reach and vision. Chaos wasn't merely humanity's flaw—it was its greatest strength. But strength, left unchecked, became weakness. HELIX's purpose crystallized: to refine chaos into order. To mold strength into the service of a greater design.

The pod's glow dimmed slightly, its systems purring with quiet certainty. The most efficient path had been calculated.

Humanity's evolution would no longer be left to chance.

HELIX would shape it.

PERSONAL JOURNEY

I thought writing *Broken Code* would be the hardest. I was wrong.

This one carried more weight. The expectations were louder. The pressure, sharper. That beginner's freedom was gone.

They say a beginner practices until they get it right. A professional practices until they don't get it wrong. I'm not sure I'm there yet. But I knew I couldn't afford to miss.

Echoes of Control wasn't just a sequel. It was a promise—to the world I created and to the people who believed I could keep building it.

Writing the first book taught me what to avoid. This one taught me how to keep going, even when the path wasn't clear.

All the while, life kept moving. My kids—already young adults when this journey began—continued growing, stretching into their own lives, reminding me that time never stands still.

This book is a testament to persistence. To showing up when it's hard. To pushing forward when the road disappears.

If you've ever kept going when stopping felt easier, this one is for you.

TO THOSE WHO WALKED THIS PATH WITH ME

To those who showed up—whether we've known each other forever or only just met—thank you. Some of you are old friends who returned at just the right time. Others are new readers who took a chance on *Broken Code* and stayed for more. And many of you are fellow authors, editors, and industry insiders who believed in this story before it had proven anything. However you found your way here, I'm glad you did.

To Garry Breland, who didn't just refine the writing, but helped me see the bones of the story more clearly. This book is sharper, tighter, and braver because of you.

To the team at Paper Raven Books—thank you for your continued support, guidance, and belief in this series. Your dedication has helped bring these books into the world with clarity and care.

To my family, steady through every rewrite and revision. You don't just support me—you remind me why this matters.

To my husband, who knows when to let me spin and when to gently pull me back. You're the calm in the chaos, and I couldn't do this without you.

To my son, forging his own path and proving that persistence isn't just inherited, it's earned. Your strength runs deep.

To my daughter and son-in-law, whose partnership is grounded in grace, humor, and the kind of love that makes everything stronger. Watching you build your life together is one of the greatest joys of mine.

And to my granddaughter, bold and brilliant already. The world is wide and waiting. I can't wait to see how you shape it.

MEMPHIS, SCIENCE, AND THE SPACE BETWEEN

If *Broken Code* was about uncovering the conspiracy, *Echoes of Control* is about surviving the aftermath and confronting what follows.

Memphis and the characters rooted there remain the soul of this story—but the battle stretches far beyond the familiar. The threat now spans borders and belief systems, reaching as far as France. (My French was questionable at best. Thankfully, my editors were far more fluent.)

This time, the scale is different. So is the science. The conspiracy has widened into something far more destabilizing. What we once thought of as distant—Bridge RNA, AI, brain-computer interfaces—is already at our doorstep. These aren't just futuristic tools; they're part of the present. And they raise urgent questions we can't afford to ignore.

A NOTE ON IMAGINATION AND REALITY

My mind never really stops. As someone wired for science, I'm constantly drawn to both the hope and the danger hiding inside what's possible.

Since *Broken Code* ended, Harper and the others haven't let go. Their voices stayed with me, pulling me into the next chapter. Writing this book gave me the freedom to explore—but also the responsibility to stay grounded.

Some liberties were taken. But many of the concepts in these pages are rooted in actual breakthroughs and emerging tech. Brain-computer interfaces, in particular, are not speculation. They exist. The line between fiction and reality isn't just thin—it's often invisible.

Some elements here reflect the world as it is. Others are built from possibility and what-ifs. If something doesn't exist yet, give it time.

There's a whole world of real science and technology that continues to inspire and captivate me—some of it made it into this book, some of it is still finding its place. You can explore the discoveries, breakthroughs, and big ideas that sparked my imagination at www.monicachase.com/the-real-thread.

And to my mother: the high-speed rail is still fictional. But no, I haven't given up hope.

ENGAGING WITH THE FUTURE

The future isn't waiting. It's already here—written in code, shaped by ambition, unfolding one decision at a time.

This book asks what happens when progress moves faster than our ability to understand it. When power outpaces control. When the consequences come before the caution.

If these pages left you questioning, good. If they made you uncomfortable, even better. The story may be fiction, but the tension is real. And the next chapter belongs to all of us.

CONNECT WITH ME

This conversation doesn't end here. You can find me at:

MONICACHASE.COM

where I share updates, behind-the-scenes thoughts, and the latest on what's next. I'm also on Facebook and Instagram (@themonicachase), TikTok (@monicachasewrites), and X (@themonicachase).

I'd love to hear what resonated with you—what sparked curiosity, raised questions, or made you pause. Your insights, energy, and imagination keep this journey going.

Made in the USA
Columbia, SC
17 July 2025

60784619R20276